JOSEPH
RULER OF ALL EGYPT

A NOVELIZATION OF THE SCRIPTURAL
STORY ADAPTED FROM THE KING JAMES
VERSION OF THE BIBLE

BY

William Lyons

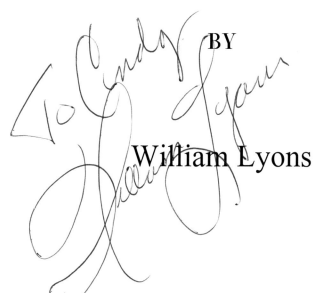

Third Millennium Publishing
A Cooperative of Writers and Resources
On the INTERNET at 3mpub.com
http://3mpub.com

ISBN 1-934805-27-0
978-1-934805-27-5

© 2009 by William Lyons

285 pages

All rights reserved under International and Pan-American Copyright Conventions. Published in the United States of America by Third Millennium Publishing, located on the INTERNET at http://3mpub.com. This book is pure fiction.

Any resemblance to actual persons, places or events is coincidental. The entire story is a creation of the author's imagination.

Third Millennium Publishing
PO Box 14026
Tempe, AZ 85284-0068
mccollum@3mpub.com

Preface

Many novels have been written about Joseph the son of Jacob; who was sold into slavery and ultimately became the ruler of all Egypt. Most Egyptologists place Joseph in the reign of the Hyksos Pharaohs. Unfortunately, there currently is no solid archeological evidence from this period that Joseph actually existed. The Hyksos left little behind to study. They were either poor record keepers or (due to the wet climate of the Delta where they lived) the records they did keep were destroyed. However, there is a dispatch (according to Dr. James Breasted) where Joseph is mentioned. It was sent from the commander of the Pithom fortress to the court of Pharaoh at Tanis, during the reign of Pharaoh Merneptah. The dispatch reads as follows:

"I have passed a group of Edomites into the land of Egypt to feed and water their flocks by the pools of Pithom, as the Hebrews did in the days of Joseph."

This dispatch is an anomaly. It comes from the reign of a Pharaoh whose father, Ramses II, supposedly suffered a very ignominious defeat at the hands of the very Hebrews slaves mentioned in the dispatch. To this author's mind, such a dispatch to such a Pharaoh would be tantamount to a suicide note. It is a true mystery. Anomalies such as this may drive archeologists to drink, but they are the bread and butter of the fiction author!

So, keeping the fiction aspect in mind, if H.G. Wells could have the Earth invaded by Martians that were ultimately destroyed by our evil little germs, Edgar Rice Burrows could get a man to Mars by way of a gas filled cave in Arizona, and Jules Verne could shoot men to the moon in a cannon, then this author has no problem at all placing Joseph in the reign of his favorite Pharaoh, Amenemhet III!

This decision was quite fortuitous. The Middle Kingdom is an excellently documented period of Egyptian history. This wealth of information provided a rich tapestry background upon which place the age-old story of Joseph. Many actual events from this period of Egyptian history are used in the book. These events include a terrible famine known as "The Year of the Hyena," a short story about a cowherd called, "The Tale of Two Brothers", and "The song of Amenemhet," to name a few. Even the names of the supporting characters used herein (but not mentioned in the Bible) were drawn from the Middle Egyptian language. Also, the archaeological treasures of that period, and the rather detailed knowledge of what an Egyptian estate of that period would have looked like, (none of which were readily available for the Hyksos period) were of inestimable value to the author.

Whatever period of Egyptian history the story of Joseph is placed in, it is timeless. It is hoped that the accurate details and the historically accurate background (for the historical period chosen) used herein add to the realism of the story and the reader's enjoyment.

The Author

Acknowledgments

I would like to thank all those that helped or encouraged me during the writing of this book. Special thanks go to my daughter, Kris who encouraged me to write the book in the first place. Her, "You *can* write a book," got me started. Without her insistence the book would never have been written at all . And to my wonderful wife, Karen whose loving encouragement and support kept me going. My brother, Chuck who acted as one of the proofreaders and was my major cheerleader. His, "Okay, it's great - so where is the next Chapter?," was a great motivator! A truly huge vote of thanks goes to Mike Mc Irvin, my editor. His insights and assistance were invaluable and made the manuscript more readable. Last, but definitely not the least, an extremely huge thanks to those who even gave their lives that we might have the wonderful story of Joseph as it is found in the Scriptures; which, are now available to any who desire them because of their tireless efforts and sacrifices.

The Author

Table of Contents

PREFACE III
ACKNOWLEDGMENTS V
CHAPTER ONE 1
   The Tale Begins 1
CHAPTER TWO 17
   The Dreamer 17
CHAPTER THREE 29
   The Fateful Errand 29
CHAPTER FOUR 43
   Valor and Deception 43
CHAPTER FIVE 53
   The House of Potiphar 53
CHAPTER SIX 75
   Joseph and Potiphar 75
CHAPTER SEVEN 91
   The Wife of Potiphar 91
CHAPTER EIGHT 109
   The Baker and the Butler 109
CHAPTER NINE 127
   Pharaoh's Dreams 127
CHAPTER TEN 143
   The Ruler of all Egypt 143
   Chapter Note: 161
CHAPTER ELEVEN 163
   The Dearth Begins 163
CHAPTER TWELVE 179
   Memories and Decisions 179
CHAPTER THIRTEEN 191
   The Brothers Come to Egypt 191
CHAPTER FOURTEEN 209
   The Brothers are Tested 209
CHAPTER FIFTEEN 225
   Decisions and Dilemmas 225
CHAPTER SIXTEEN 239
   The Brothers Return 239
CHAPTER SEVENTEEN 253
   The Final Test and Joseph is Revealed 253
CHAPTER EIGHTEEN 267

The Story Ends 267
AUTHOR'S BIOGRAPHY 285

Chapter One
THE TALE BEGINS

A lone chariot, almost invisible in the dense dust cloud it created, the horses covered with a fine coat of grey-white powder, carried its single passenger, Salith, and his driver on the road to Tanis. The commander of the Fortress of Pithom had dispatched him to Tanis to deliver a message to the Pharaoh. Salith only hoped that there was somewhere that he would be able to clean up before he had to present himself before the Great One.

The dust settled around them as they entered the populated portion of the city, but he knew they must have been a sight, for everyone they passed stared at them as if they were an apparition. This was no city chariot in which he rode, no rich man's toy, but a war machine. Unlike the daintier and more colorful chariots that they passed in the city's streets, this one was dust colored and had an odd, high wicker fringe around its upper half to protect the charioteer from the enemy's arrows and stones. While light, this fringe was very effective, and in one border skirmish, this addition to his war chariot had saved Salith's life. It was no wonder the people stared, however, he thought. This machine represented the might of the Egyptian army.

After a time, their destination, the palace of the Pharaoh, came into sight. It was a beautiful structure with gleaming white pylons adorned with colorful images of the Pharaoh's victories in battle. Soldiers could be seen on the ramparts of those huge pylons in their bright dress tunics, their highly polished weapons shining brilliantly in the sun. The highest flagpoles Salith had ever seen stood before the building, and bright linen pennants of every hue flew bravely from them. It was a sight never to be forgotten.

Chariots were parked everywhere in front of the palace, and people milled about as a small, steady stream of citizens entered the gate. Salith looked at the confused scene for a few moments and then pointed to an open spot. "Why don't you park the chariot over there," he said to his driver. I'll find out how I go about delivering this message and will meet you here when I'm done." His driver, a naturally silent man, simply nodded. Salith then dismounted the chariot through the hole at the back of the armored fringe and walked toward the palace.

This was not like entering the Fortress of Pithom, he thought. For one thing, he was not known here. At the fortress, a simple nod to the gate guard was sufficient to gain entry, but here he had to present papers. As he approached the guard on duty, he reached into the message pouch at his side and extracted the necessary letter of introduction to gain admittance. As he did so, the guard took notice of him.

"Stop and identify yourself!" the guard snapped.

"I am Salith, Messenger for the Commander of the Fortress of Pithom, and I come with a message for the Pharaoh." He returned with all the formality he could muster. He found remaining civil difficult as the guard had come to the ready with his weapon and Salith's sword was still in its sheath.

"Very well. Where is your letter of introduction?" the guard asked, but he did not lower his weapon even an inch.

Looking the guard squarely in the eye, Salith answered crisply, "Here it is." He extended his hand containing the small scroll of papyrus that was his letter of introduction to the court. The guard took the document but did not so much as glance at it or lower his guard. Instead, without turning, he handed it to a scribe at his side whose small table was set up in the shadow of the great pylons.

The scribe slowly unrolled the papyrus and scanned the contents. After a time, the scribe rolled the document and handed it back to the guard, saying in a rather bored voice, "All appears to be in order. This man may pass."

Returning the scroll, the sentry marginally lowered his guard, his weapon dropping only slightly, and repeated stoically, "You may pass."

Not wanting to appear before the Pharaoh looking like a filthy vagabond, Salith asked quietly, "Is there somewhere I can remove the filth of the road before I enter the Pharaoh's presence?"

The guard looked at him in silence for a moment and then said gruffly, "Once you are inside the gate, the guardhouse is to your left and there is a bath in there. As an officer in the army, you are allowed to use it."

"Thank you," Salith replied stiffly, then hurried through the gates and into the guardhouse where he was greeted far more cordially. As he bathed, some of the serving women dusted and cleaned his uniform for him, and in a very short time, he was sufficiently presentable to stand before Pharaoh.

Salith quickly learned that the pylons and the surrounding walls were just the beginning of the place. Inside the walls were many trees, formal gardens with flowers of every hue, huge grape arbors, flagstone paths, and beautiful lily ponds. Near the center of this magnificent enclosure stood the residence itself, which was at least three stories tall with a porch and lotus fluted columns holding up the roof. In the center of the porch was a magnificent double door made of dark wood and inlaid with gold figures representing the Gods.

Salith mounted the porch and slowly passed through the doors and into the building itself. He was trying to see everything, but unfortunately, the study of the building was short lived. Just inside the doors was another scribe sitting at a low table. The scribe looked up from his writing as Salith approached.

"May I help you?" he asked politely.

"Yes, I am a messenger from the Fortress of Pithom, and I carry a message for the Pharaoh from the Commander," Salith replied in like tone.

The man's countenance lighted at the mention of the message. "Ah! The Pharaoh is always interested in such messages. You will be gladly received! What is your name, officer?"

Bowing formally, Salith responded, "My name is Salith, messenger to the Commander of the Pithom Fortress."

The Scribe smiled, nodded, and bent to his writing, apparently entering Salith's name to the list of those that would speak in the court this day. He then looked up at Salith pleasantly and continued speaking. "Enter the chamber and wait in the back row along the right side. When it is your turn to speak to the Great One, the Chamberlain will call you forth. Please, proceed." The scribe nodded in the direction of the second set of doors just beyond his table.

"I thank you!" responded Salith with warmth equal to that given him by the scribe. He then made his way into the grand audience chamber of the Pharaoh Merneptah. The Pharaoh's name was boldly displayed in a golden cartouche on each of the double doors.

The chamber itself was cool and well lighted by windows set high up, next to the roof. The walls were decorated with scenes from both the reign of Merneptah himself and that of his famous father, Ramses II; and, even the ceiling was decorated with a bright painting of the Goddess Nut holding up the sky. Down the center of the room were two lines of brightly decorated columns with lotus blossom capitals, and at the far end of the huge room was a raised platform with three steps leading up to it. In the center of this platform stood Merneptah's wood and gold throne, which rested not upon the floor but upon a huge lion pelt. It was the most beautiful room Salith had ever entered, and he was delighted at this vision of opulence.

The room was not crowded, but there were still a large number of people milling about in the grand chamber. Salith was still taking it all in when an elderly man in spotless white climbed the stair to the top of the platform. He turned to face the room and used his heavy staff of office to pound on the floor. The sound echoed about the chamber and all the people hurried to what were obviously their assigned places in the chamber's main corridor. As soon as the noise of the movement of people stopped, he intoned in a loud voice, "Kneel! Bow! All pay homage to the he who is the brother of the Sun God Ra who illuminates the heavens above. As Ra illuminates the heavens, so does our living Pharaoh provide spiritual illumination for those of us here below! Kneel! Pay homage!"

Unsure what to do in response to this grand demand, Salith simply dropped to one knee and bowed his head. Above the sounds of the entering party he heard a chorus in the chamber chant in unison, "All hail the Great Pharaoh!"

Taking a risk, Salith raised his head slightly to watch the grand entrance. He saw the Chamberlain bow low toward the great double doors to the chamber and then scurry to his place among the courtiers. No sooner had he taken his place than the Pharaoh Merneptah, rigidly erect and wearing a very serious expression, entered through the double doors with his entourage. He was dressed in the resplendent white robes of his station, and in his hands were the crossed crook and flail, the symbols of his office. The double crown of the two kingdoms was on his head. As he made his way to the throne at the top of the magnificent chamber, various people added quiet greetings.

"Hail to you, Great Pharaoh!"

"Live long, Great Pharaoh!"

"May your reign last a thousand years, Great Pharaoh!"

The Pharaoh walked quietly and with great dignity, and upon reaching the platform, he seated himself upon his throne. Then he extended his scepter toward a lad of perhaps ten years of age who was among those who had entered with the Pharaoh. The boy wore a prince's lock and carried the traditional feather scepter of the crown prince. The Pharaoh then spoke. "My Son, join me upon the dais. Stand here, at my right side."

"Yes, my father. I thank you." The lad bowed and then quickly ran to his father's side.

Salith could hear plainly when the young Prince leaned toward his father and whispered, "Why are there so many people here, my father?"

Whispering quietly in his own turn, the Pharaoh responded, "This is where the business of all Egypt is discussed, my son." Then, turning to the stately Chamberlain, Pharaoh asked in a mild tone, "Chamberlain! Who are the petitioners today and what are their numbers?"

"They are legion, Oh Great One!" the man replied, bowing to the Pharaoh. He then quietly commanded, "Scribe. Give the great Pharaoh the exact count of those who wish to seek his divine counsel this day."

The scribe, Salith was surprised to see, was the same one that he had talked to outside the door to this chamber. He had apparently come in with the Pharaoh and his party and was already seated cross legged on the lion skin at Pharaoh's feet. He bowed and then quietly addressed the Great One. "Great Pharaoh, there are one hundred and twenty who seek your wisdom this beautiful day."

"I thank you for your report, and as you say scribe, it is a most pleasant day!" Pharaoh responded, smiling very slightly. He then quietly asked, "Are there any reports from the frontiers?"

"Indeed, my Pharaoh!" The scribe looked at his writing and quickly responded. "There is a messenger from the fortress of Pithom, Great One."

The Pharaoh turned again to the Chamberlain. "Chamberlain, please call forth the messenger from Pithom."

The Chamberlain pounded his staff on the floor three times to get attention of those present and intoned, "Messenger from the fortress of Pithom, step forward. Pharaoh would hear your report!"

Salith was shocked that he was to be the first to report to Pharaoh this day. He stumbled in his haste to come forward and stand before the Great One, but he managed not to fall and came forth to the step next to the top of the platform and knelt before his Pharaoh. After taking a deep breath to calm himself, he said.

"Greetings from the Commander of the Fortress of Pithom, my Pharaoh!"

"Your greetings are pleasant to the Pharaoh's ear, messenger. What is your report?" Pharaoh asked quietly.

Salith plunged his hand into his pouch and pulled out the scroll with the message to be delivered. Taking another calming breath before he spoke, he began reading the message aloud. "The commander of the fortress sends word that he has passed a group of Edomites into the land of Egypt to feed and water their flocks by the pools of Pithom as the Hebrews did in the days of Joseph, my Pharaoh!"

"He has done well! Inform him of his Pharaoh's pleasure in this matter."

"I will do so, my Pharaoh!" Salith then bowed once more and retreated from the dais. However, instead of leaving immediately, he lingered. He had never been to the court before, and since it was permitted, he had decided to witness what went on here. Besides, he knew that the Commander would be as curious as he. It was not often that their remote outpost had something to report to the court, and he would want a full report of all the news Salith heard in this chamber.

"Tell me, scribe, is Potiphihapi among those who seek audience today?"

Looking quickly at the writing before him, the scribe again responded, "He is, my Pharaoh! He has come all the way from the cataracts to speak with you."

"Excellent! Chamberlain, please call forth the priest Potiphihapi."

"At once, my Pharaoh!" the old man replied swiftly. Once again, the Chamberlain pounded his staff of office on the floor and called, "Potiphihapi, priest of the cataracts, he who is dedicated to the divine river god Hapi, step forth! Your Pharaoh would speak with you!"

From the front row, a stately elderly gentleman, wearing a long white robe surmounted by the cheetah pelt of the priestly class, stepped forward. He moved in a courtly fashion, his staff of office tapping loudly on the stone floor as he went. Once he was on the steps, he bowed low to his Pharaoh and said, "Oh Great Pharaoh, your servant is here to do your bidding."

"I am pleased at your coming. Tell me, what is the status of the river at the cataracts?"

The Priest stood erect, as only those of the priestly classes could do in the presence of Pharaoh, and reported, "The River still runs three cubits higher than normal for this time of the year, my Pharaoh."

With deep concern in his voice, Merneptah responded, "Why is that? Is there danger of a second flood?"

"Have no fear, my Pharaoh. The river is running high due to the late rains on the great south lake beyond the cataracts. These rains are reported as light and pose no threat to the safety of Egypt and her life-giving crops, but rather, the rains that keep the water level this high is a blessing from the gods."

The relief was evident in the Pharaoh's manner. "That is good. What is the status of the Great Lake of the Fayum?"

With a very pleased tone, the Priest responded, "The Lake is filled yet to the high water mark for this spring's flood, my Pharaoh."

"I thank you. Your report is most comforting." The Pharaoh nodded toward the Priest with a very pleased expression on his face.

Unlike the father, the young Prince had a very quizzical expression, however; and before the Priest could retire, the lad leaned toward his father and asked, "Father, may I ask you a question?"

"Certainly, my son!"

"Why do you ask these questions about the river? The flood came and there will be crops, is that not true?"

"You have asked a good question, my son!" He turned from the boy and extended his scepter toward the Priest. "Would you care to answer him, Potiphihapi, as you are the Priest of the god of the river and the expert on the ever changing Nile?"

Bowing low in response to the request, the Priest responded, "I would be honored, my Pharaoh!" He then bowed to the Crown Prince. "Son of Pharaoh, as you have said, the river flooded on schedule this spring, and indeed, the yearly flood brings with it far more than just water. It brings rich soil that grows much food, but if the river drops too soon, the crops that are planted in this excellent loam die for lack of water. The water in the lake, along with the great flood this year, means a goodly crop this season. Knowing the water levels along the Nile helps us to predict this."

With the voice of one truly interested, the lad asked, "You mentioned the Great Lake of the Fayum. Why is it important?"

Bowing once more in obvious respect for the adult nature of the question, Potiphihapi answered, "Son of Pharaoh, you again ask a good question! The lake was conceived by Pharaoh Amenemhet II, who noticed that at times of great flooding some of the flood waters spilled over a gap in the western wall and created a fairly large temporary lake in the desert beyond. He was inspired by the Gods to take advantage of this overflow and had a canal dug to allow a huge lake to form in the western desert at the time of the great seasonal flood."

"What good does that do?" asked the Prince, his brow wrinkled in concentration.

"Ah! It does a great deal of good — now."

The Prince asked, "Now?"

With a smile, the old Priest continued, "The son of Pharaoh is shrewd to notice this! At the time it was built, the lake really did little good, but the Pharaoh's grandson, Amenemhet III, a very wise and astute young man like you, was inspired by the Gods to add control gates to the canals. He had a Vizier, Joseph by name, and together they discovered how to do this. The water trapped in the great lake was then controlled, allowing enough water to flow down the Nile during the dry times to permit not one but *two* growing seasons in the lower Nile Valley!"

The boy looked confused for a moment, so the Pharaoh added a further explanation. "That is why, to this day, the workers in the fields sing the song of praise to Amenemhet III for turning the Nile Valley green!"

"I have heard that song, my father! But I have never heard of this Joseph of whom both Potiphihapi and the messenger spoke."

"I have not told you of the Great Vizier, Joseph, my son?"

"No, my father."

With the air of one who has forgotten something important, Merneptah said, "Ah! My son, I must correct the oversight. Joseph, beloved by Amenemhet III, was a favored son who became a slave, then a freed man, a prisoner, a seer, and finally, Vizier of all Egypt and a special friend of Pharaoh!"

"He did all those things?" The youth asked in great surprise. "He must have been a great Egyptian!"

Merneptah responded with a sense of wonder in his voice, "He was no Egyptian, my son. He was a Semite, a Hebrew to be exact."

"My Father, forgive me, but a Hebrew, the people mentioned in the report from Pithom that the messenger just gave to you?"

"Indeed! You pay close attention, my son! In fact, the Edomites mentioned in that report are the descendants of Edom, or Esau, who was the brother of Jacob and the father of the Joseph, of whom we speak."

"My father, you know much of this family! Why is this?"

Much to Salith's surprise, the Pharaoh actually chuckled as he responded to his son's question. "My father, Ramses II, revered Amenemhet III and Joseph, and I heard their stories many times when I was your age! It is time that you too knew their history, my son." Turning to the Chamberlain, Pharaoh said quietly, "Have all present sit and be comfortable."

This command obviously startled the Chamberlain. "Great One, only the scribes may sit in the presence of the Pharaoh!"

"And none should *stand* in the presence of a storyteller!" quipped Pharaoh.

The Chamberlain chuckled at this comment, and with a great smile upon his face, he bowed low and said, "It shall be so, Great One." Then turning to the assembled crowd, he said loudly, "All sit and make yourselves comfortable. The Great One will share a story with you!"

This command was followed by startled murmurs, but all sat, including Salith, who was more than a little surprised. Pharaoh was going to tell a story? He had never heard of such a thing. He determined to listen intently, for if Pharaoh thought this story was of such importance that it could be related to the people gathered here, he vowed not to miss a single word.

On the dais, Pharaoh looked at his son and said quietly, "Sit before me, my son, and I shall tell you the tale." The delighted child literally scampered in front of his august father and sat as Pharaoh removed the crown from his head and handed it to his valet. At the shocked expressions he noted in the chamber, Pharaoh said in an amused voice, "Crowns are for kings, not storytellers." This comment brought nervous chuckles from all present as he sat forward in his throne and stroked his beard thoughtfully. Then he said loud enough for all to hear, "Where to begin? Why not at the beginning, eh? I already told you that Jacob was Joseph's father, did I not?"

"Yes, my father," the child quickly responded.

"Well, Jacob dwelt in a land in which *his* father was a stranger, the land of Canaan. I will begin the tale when Joseph was seventeen years old and feeding his father's flock with his brethren, the sons of Bilhah and the sons of Zilpah, two of his father's wives. As they made their way to the high pastures of Canaan, they talked and teased one another. Like Egypt in the summer, the roads there were dry and dusty. Asher, one of Joseph's brothers, was the whiner in the group."

Pharaoh's voice grew deep and rhythmic with the telling of this tale, and Salith noted that it was as if he watched the story unfold before him as he spoke: "How much further do we have to go, Dan?" complained Asher.

Having heard this question at least twenty times in the last two hours, Dan, who was the leader of their little band, responded in an exasperated tone, "As you know full well Asher, the pasture is just over this next hill!"

Gad, another of the brothers, was also tired of Asher's whining, and asked, "How many times are you going to ask that question, Asher?"

"I'm hungry! Dan said that we cannot eat until we get to the pasture, Gad!"

Joseph, the youngest of the brothers, was the only member of the group who was amused at Asher's comments. "Really?" He began chuckling and asked, "Is that why you have been sneaking food out of the pack ever since we left Father's camp?"

Naphtali, as always, was angry and took offense at Joseph's good humor. "An interesting observation, Joseph! It's easy for you! You're the favorite son! We're little more than slaves! If we starve, nobody would care!"

Dan had heard enough and his response was sharp. "Naphtali! That's enough of that kind of talk. Father cares about us! It isn't Joseph sneaking food — it's Asher!"

Asher was indignant. "Naphtali's right! We are always the last to get anything! Who are you to judge, anyway? You've been known to eat more than your share as well!"

"Perhaps, but I've not been so foolish as to be seen doing it!" Dan replied loftily.

As they went about their tasks in the high pastures, the brothers' bickering, wasteful use of food, water, and even slothful care of the animals under their charge made Joseph uneasy, and when they returned home, Joseph brought his father report of their evil ways.

It was not as though he ran to his father crying aloud, "Father, come see what these, my brothers, have done!" No, Joseph was very sensitive about his position in the camp. His was not an enviable situation. It was true that he was the favored son, but it was that very favor that was the cause of most of his problems with his brothers. They were all considerably older, and in fact, he was next to the youngest and still a teenager.

According to Canaanite law, one of them was to lead the family after their father's death, and tradition held that this leader was to be the eldest son. The eldest son was Ruben, but Joseph's mother was the favored wife, and Jacob considered Joseph to be the eldest because of this. Thus it was that, as they returned to their father's camp, it was Joseph that Jacob hailed rather than the group's leader, Dan.

"Joseph, my son! Dan, Asher, Gad, Naphtali! Welcome back! Joseph, come, come into my tent! It is a hot day and I would hear your report."

"Greetings, my father! I will, but I must help my brothers settle the sheep in the pens," Joseph said respectfully.

"There are four of them, enough for the task. Are you not capable of settling the sheep, my sons?" The old man appeared to ignore the hard stares of Joseph's older brothers, and even to ignore the audible murmur caused by his statement. "Joseph, come in and speak with a lonely old man!"

Naphtali could not contain himself. He glared at both Jacob and Joseph. Then he mumbled loudly, "Nothing but slaves. . .again!"

Dan turned angrily to his younger brother and admonished him sharply. "Silence, Naphtali!"

Jacob appeared to not notice these outbursts, but Joseph knew his father better than that. He heard a distinct "Hmm. . ." before his Father spoke to him again. "Come, come into the tent Joseph. Let us speak." The old man led the boy into his tent where it was cool and quiet. Gesturing to a pile of cushions, Jacob said, "Ah, here we are. Sit, Joseph, sit! How cool and peaceful it is in this tent, is it not, Joseph?"

"It is, my father."

Before either of them could say more they were joined by a handsome middle-aged woman and Jacob greeted her. "Ah, Bilhah! Please, bring us food and drink. Joseph and his brothers are returned! See that your sons and those of Zilpah down by the pens are fed and have enough to drink. It has been a long journey for all of them."

With a smile on her face, Bilhah answered quickly, "At once, my husband!" Then she hurried out of the tent.

Once she had departed, the old man looked at Joseph for a long moment before saying, "I gather that all did not go well. Your brothers do not seem pleased."

Reluctantly, Joseph responded. "They do seem upset, my father."

"You leave much unsaid, my son," the old man said knowingly.

Joseph sighed heavily. "If I leave things unsaid, it is in the interest of peace, my father."

"Peace, my son? Why should their actions and your report cause a lack of peace?"

"I would say no more, my father."

"Your reluctance to speak says much more than your silence, my son. What have your brothers done?"

There was honest reluctance and resignation in Joseph's voice. "There is much discontent among my brothers. Naphtali says that they are nothing but slaves, and Asher agrees, and so they wasted the food and even neglected the sheep from time to time in the field."

"Even Dan?" Jacob asked quietly.

"He was the most diligent and fair, but even he admitted to taking more than his share of the food from time to time."

"Your reluctance to speak of this and your fairness toward Dan in your report, even though it contains evil news, says much for you, my son. Your report gives honor to the one who gave it, as befits the son of a sheik!" Before he could say more, they were again interrupted, this time by another very attractive middle-aged woman carrying a tray laden with dishes and a large jug of wine.

"Ah, Zilpah! You have brought the food and wine! Excellent! Have your sons and those of Bilhah been fed as well?"

"They are eating as we speak, my husband. Bilhah saw to it herself."

"My thanks, Zilpah! Go. Spend time with your sons. They will want to see you."

"I thank you, my husband," she said, and bowing, hurried from the tent.

"Enough talk, Joseph! Now it is time to eat!"

Joseph's problems with his brethren were soon to get worse, Jacob loved Joseph more than all his other children combined because he was the son of his old age. To honor him, he had a coat of many colors made for Joseph. This was no ordinary coat but the traditional coat worn by the eldest son, the son that was to be the camp's leader after the death of the father. The gift of the coat was a singular honor for Joseph, but such homage paid to one of the youngest sons worried Leah, Jacob's wife. As soon as she heard that the gift had been ordered to be made, she came to Jacob to discuss the problems such a move would cause Joseph. She found him in his tent.

He saluted her as she entered. "Peace be unto you, Leah!" He paused, and with a knowing look upon his face, continued. "Your countenance speaks of trouble, my wife."

"I *am* troubled, my husband. I have heard that you have commissioned a coat of many colors to be made in the city."

"That is quite true. Why should this trouble you?"

"I have heard that it is being made for Joseph?"

"That is also true, my wife."

"Forgive me, my husband, but why Joseph? Why is this great gift not for one of your elder sons?"

"Which of your sons do you recommend?"

"What of Ruben?"

Jacob's countenance darkened, and when he spoke there was anger in his voice. "Ruben? He who defiled one of my wives and disgraced me before the entire camp?"

Leah cowered before her husband's anger for a few moments before she timidly suggested, "Well, perhaps not he, but what of Simeon or Levi?"

Jacob's anger intensified. "They who destroyed an entire city? They who in their anger murderously deceived others? They made my name to stink before the smoldering ruin of the city of Shechem!"

Leah's tone was now desperate and she pleaded, "Surely Judah?"

"Judah? Judah is honorable enough, but he, like my brother Esau, married a pagan! He has defiled his heritage and cannot lead the family. He most especially cannot hold the priesthood birthright! All your sons and those of the servants are unworthy! Only Joseph has earned the right to the birthright and the honor of receiving the coat that is being made in the village!"

Word of this "coat of many colors" spread through the camp like a wildfire. When Leah told Bilhah of it, she ran to tell her sons the news. When she found Naphtali, she blurted out her message. "Your father has commissioned a coat of many colors in the village!"

Not understanding, Naphtali was elated. "Finally! Ruben is going to be honored as the eldest!"

"No, he is not." With her head hung and with the shame of a long past incident evident upon her face, she continued very quietly. "Do you not remember, my son? Reuben and I shamed your father before the entire camp."

Deeply embarrassed that he had forgotten such a thing, Naphtali cleared his throat. "Ahem. Well, if not Ruben, then Simeon or Levi?"

"They dishonored the whole family at Shechem."

Naphtali struck himself in the forehead and said, "Oh, I feel the fool not remembering that! Father raged for weeks after Shechem!" He looked thoughtful for a moment. "That leaves only Judah, a natural leader! I am pleased he will wear the coat!"

Unnoticed, Gad had joined his mother and his brother. "What is this all about?" he asked.

"Father has commissioned a coat of many colors for Judah, Gad!" said a delighted Naphtali.

Placing her hand on her son's arm, Bilhah said quietly, "My Son. The coat is not for Judah either."

Naphtali's face turned a distinct shade of purple and he shouted, "NO! This cannot be! You cannot stand there, Mother, and seriously expect me to believe that Father commissioned a *coat of many colors* for that treacherous brat Joseph!" His poor mother could only nod a shamed and silent affirmative.

The commotion attracted Asher, who had also come upon the group unawares. "What is all the shouting about?" he asked.

Naphtali was now almost unable to speak. "Asher! That. . .That. . ."

Dan too had been attracted to his brother's shouting. "Naphtali, what is going on?"

Naphtali was still inarticulate. "Asher, Dan, our. . ."

Dan had never seen Naphtali so angry. "Calm down, Naphtali! Calm down! Now, try again."

Before Naphtali could regain sufficient composure to tell them the news, Gad angrily shouted, "I'll tell them, Naphtali! It's Father! He has commissioned a coat of many colors for the traitorous Joseph!"

"What? Joseph? How can he lead the family? He's just a child!" Dan asked, astounded.

Naphtali had recovered and said loudly and indignantly, "I know that you have always liked the boy, Dan, but our leader should be Judah! He has always been second to Reuben, and since Reuben, Levi, and Simeon cannot lead us, it should be Judah!"

Asher shouted, "I agree!"

"So do I!" Gad added.

Dan was still trying to take all of this in. "There must be some mistake! Mother, did you bring this news?"

"I did, my son. There is no mistake. Leah told me herself just after Jacob informed her that it is Joseph who will lead us."

Dan's response was firm. "I will *not* be governed by a child! I like Joseph, but he is not fit to lead us!"

Even from across the camp, it was obvious that something was very wrong among the sons of Bilhah. Simeon and Levi had noticed the disturbance, and finally their curiosity got the best of them and they joined the group. "What's going on?" Simeon asked.

"Father has commissioned a coat of many colors for Joseph," Dan said angrily.

Levi could scarcely believe what he was hearing. "Surely not!"

"That brat in charge of the family? I'll see him dead before I'll serve him!" Simeon said angrily.

Bilhah had been a second mother to Joseph and Benjamin after the death of their mother, Rachael, and aghast, she blurted, "Simeon! What a horrible thing for you to say!"

Simeon was beyond reason or shame. He shouted at the poor woman. "It is not for you to correct *me*, woman! I'm going to see *my* mother about this! Then, I'm going to see Judah. *If* this news is true, he'll know what to do and can talk some sense into father!"

Naphtali was looking beyond the group and spotted Joseph, who had also been attracted to all the shouting and was walking toward them to investigate. In a voice seething with hatred, he cautioned the rest of the group. "Simeon, quiet! Behold, the *chosen one* approaches!"

Joseph saw that the group was angry and almost turned away, but something would not let him do so. Instead, he gave them a warm and friendly greeting. "Good morning, my brothers!"

His apparent joy was too much for Naphtali, whose own greeting was filled with hatred. "Good morning yourself!"

Joseph was shocked. He was even more surprised when Dan said, "Indeed! Go cause trouble somewhere else!"

Confused and frightened, Joseph sought to make peace. "Forgive me, my brethren! What have I done?"

Simeon was now yet further beyond reason, his anger palpable, and there was a definite threat in his tone. "You exist, that is what you have done! Leave us! Your stench is making the goats sick!"

Chapter Two
THE DREAMER

Joseph's problems with his brethren over the coat of many colors were just beginning. Simeon and Levi were especially livid over the situation that their father had created by commissioning such a coat for Joseph. When the boys had first learned about the coat, Judah was on a spice buying trip, sent by their father; but now Judah, unsuspecting, was returning from the journey and was spotted by Simeon, who was sitting by the fire with some of his brothers. He hailed him. "Judah! Come over to the fire and join us."

Judah waved and shouted, "Just a moment!" He seemed occupied with one of the camels.

While he tarried, Dan quietly spoke to Simeon. "Simeon, did you speak with your mother about that accursed coat?"

Simeon's response was a growl. "I did!"

"Well?"

"Wait until Judah is here and I'll explain to all, Dan," was the curt response.

Judah finished with the camel and was now walking toward them. He continued to speak to the lead camel driver over his shoulder. "That's fine, Abdul. Keep doing that. We'll check on that camel again in the morning!" He then turned and spoke to his brothers. "Peace be unto you, my brothers!"

Almost as one, the brothers responded, "Peace be unto you."

Judah joined them at the fire. Evenings in the desert are cold, and Judah was anxious to reach the warmth. He sat on the rugs they had set next to the fire and began to warm himself, holding his hands to the fire. "It has been many days since I have seen you. It was a long trip! That blasted camel of Abdul's went lame yesterday and we had a bad time getting the beast home in one piece! At least we'll have spi . . . ces . . . and . . ." Judah stammered to a halt. The faces of his brethren indicated that something was definitely wrong. "My brothers, why so grim? What is the problem?"

Before anyone could answer, another happy voice was heard in the distance, Ruben shouting. "Abdul! It is good to see you!"

Looking about, he spotted the group by the fire and shouted, "Judah! Is that you over there at the fire?"

"Ruben, come join us!"

A very jovial Ruben hastened to the fire. He cordially greeted his brothers. "Peace unto you, my brothers!"

The brothers, except for Judah, only mumbled the traditional greeting, "Peace be unto you!" Judah's greeting was hearty.

Ruben, surprised at the unusual ill manners of his brothers, said, "What sort of greeting is this? Judah, you are the only one who does not have a sour look!"

Judah looked at his brothers and then back at Ruben. "I was just asking the same question when you hailed us." He then turned to the rest of his brothers and asked, "Well, brethren, what is the cause of your foul humors?"

"Father!" Simeon growled.

Knowing his brother's volatile nature, Judah paused for a moment before he quietly repeated, "Father?" With a patient sigh, he continued, "What is it Father is supposed to have done *this* time?"

This was too much for Dan. "Don't take that tone of voice, Judah! He has done something. . ." His voice dropped to a near whisper as though what he was about to say was mutinous. "Well. . .stupid!"

"What?" Judah's tone was incredulous that his brother would speak this way of their father.

"He has commissioned a coat of many colors for Joseph!" Dan said in an angry rush.

"Are you sure about this?" Judah asked, surprised.

"Yes! We're sure!" growled Simeon. "Our mother heard it directly from Father, and she told us!"

Judah looked at his irate brothers in silence for a few moments. Then, with tremendous patience, he said, "All right, calm down the lot of you! Ruben and I will speak to Father about this. We'll get this straightened out!"

Ruben, who was their natural leader, used his best conciliatory voice when he said, "Indeed. You all know that Father has a soft spot for the boy." There were angry murmurs at his statement.

Judah and Ruben made their way to their father's tent and spoke with Jacob, who was adamant that Joseph was to have the coat, but he finally agreed that it should be given to the boy in private. Joseph was also to be warned to wear the coat only on special occasions. The entire episode might have ended then and there had it not been for something that was completely out of Joseph's control — a dream.

Thus it was that little Benjamin was awakened in the middle of the night by Joseph's tossing and turning, his loud moaning as the dream unfolded. Benjamin, trying to be quiet so as not to wake the others in his family, attempted to awaken his brother from whatever terror it was that held him in its grip. Benjamin whispered urgently while he shook his brother to wake him, "Joseph! Joseph!"

A very sleepy Joseph responded groggily, "Humph! What? Stop shaking me!"

Benjamin urgently whispered. "Shhh! You'll wake everybody up!"

Joseph responded testily, "Why are you waking me in the middle of the night?"

"Because you were having a nightmare, or so it seemed!"

"What? Oh! Benjamin! I'm sorry. I was indeed having a dream." He paused for a moment and then continued. "A very vivid dream it was, but it was no nightmare, just confusing!"

Excitedly Benjamin asked, "Do you know what your dream means, Joseph?"

"Now who is going to wake the whole tent!" Joseph replied, chuckling at his little brother's obvious excitement. "Yes, Benjamin, now that you mention it, I do think I know what the dream means."

"What does it mean, Joseph?"

There was a tone of warning in Joseph's voice when he answered. "I cannot tell you my dream or its meaning this time, Benjamin. There is too much discord in the camp over my new coat as it is! Ruben and Judah worked too hard to keep the peace the other night. I think I'll keep this dream to myself."

"But Joseph," Benjamin pleaded, "Father says that dreams are important! You have to tell me!"

"Not if it means trouble in the camp. Now back to sleep with you!"

"It's not fair! Everybody leaves me out of everything!"

"That's enough, Benjamin! Now, you get back to sleep. It's harvest time and we have a lot of work to do in the morning."

In a very sulky voice, Benjamin reluctantly conceded, "Oh, all right! Good night, Joseph."

Despite himself, Joseph chuckled. "Good night, Benjamin."

Throughout the following day the work in the fields went smoothly. Simeon was still nasty, but Joseph thought nothing of that for he and Simeon never got along anyway! During their noonday meal, however, Asher and Zebulun innocently pushed the meaning of Joseph's dream to the forefront of his thoughts. Asher decided to have some fun with his brother. "Zebulun! What on earth were you dreaming about last night? Whatever it was, you were smiling and moaning in your sleep! 'She!' you said over and over. I think you must have been with a woman in your dreams!"

"Oh, oh, Zebulun has a woman!" said one of the others.

These comments were accompanied by gales of laughter from the brothers, but Asher wasn't done with the bashful Zebulun. "Would you look at him turn red! Come on Zebulun. What's her name and what's she look like?"

Zebulun's only response was to mumble indistinctly for a few seconds.

Asher was like a bulldog. "Come again? We didn't hear that!"

Zebulun, his face as red as a ripe pomegranate and wearing a very embarrassed grin, said quietly, "Ships. My dream was of ships."

Judah, who had been silent up until now, merely listening as his brothers bantered, choked on his goat's milk. When he had recovered, he spluttered incredulously, "What did I hear you say? Ships?"

Zebulun answered Judah with a dreamy quality to his voice. "Remember last year when I went with you on that caravan to Joppa, Judah?"

"Yes, I remember."

"While you and Ruben haggled over the prices of the spices, I went down to the harbor." His voice was now filled with his fascination. "There were ships of all sizes there and of every color of the rainbow! Then, I got to see one come into the harbor with its sails full." His eyes looked to the others as if he were seeing something they could not. "Water poured off the front of it like a small waterfall the ship was going so fast! Oh, how I wanted to go out on one of those!" His face again showed his embarrassment. "Now, I find myself dreaming of them."

The end of Zebulun's admission was greeted with a stunned

silence. After a moment, Asher, obviously amused, said, "Personally, I'm disappointed! Here, I thought we'd be treated to a lurid tale of wanton debauchery, but you want to tell us about ships?" That was all it took. The brothers dissolved into gales of laughter.

Judah, with tears in his eyes from his laughter, said, "Well, in a way you did, Asher! Didn't you know that sailors always refer to their ships as women?"

Asher immediately shouted, "Let's hear it for Zebulun's new woman, the woman with the full sails!"

Everyone, including Zebulun, was laughing so hard that a few of the men actually fell over. Benjamin interjected, "Joseph dreamed a dream last night too!" The effect of that simple statement was immediate. There was dead silence.

Judah was stunned, his mind racing. He thought, "Oh, not now! The child's going to stir up an awful hornet's nest!"

The only thought in Joseph's mind was, "Benjamin! When I get you alone...," as he glared at his little brother.

Ruben looked from Judah to Joseph, and from the look on their faces, Benjamin had just thrown the fat in the fire. As angry as Joseph looked, it was safe to assume he had told Benjamin to keep quiet about his dream. "Why can't children listen?" thought Ruben.

Simeon was instantly angry. "So the *chosen one* has had a dream, has he?"

Joseph did his best to play it off. "Simeon, it was nothing!"

Benjamin wasn't done with the subject. His childish voice contained all the indignation he could muster. "No, it wasn't! Father says that our dreams are very important and that we need to share them!"

Joseph was desperate. He hissed, "Benjamin! Be quiet!"

Levi was even angrier than Simeon and determined to see the worst in anything that came from Joseph. He growled in a dangerous voice, "Yes! Do tell us your *important* dream." Angry murmurs of assent rose from some of the brothers.

Joseph spread his hands in a pleading gesture and said, "Levi, Simeon, brethren, I don't..."

Benjamin, unaware of the danger to Joseph, wheedled, "Come on, Joseph, you even said that you thought you knew what it means!" This innocent statement brought more angry murmurs from the rebellious brothers.

Ruben, knowing that one more outburst from Benjamin could set Simeon and Levi into an uncontrollable rage, whispered in a commanding tone, "Benjamin! Be quiet! You're not helping!"

"But Ruben. . ."

"I said, be *quiet*!"

Simeon pointedly ignored both Ruben and Benjamin. Instead, he stared dangerously at Joseph and shouted, "WE'RE WAITING!"

Ruben, in an attempt to defuse the situation, spoke to Joseph in a conciliatory tone. "Joseph, perhaps it is best you tell us." Then turning to Simeon he added, "Who knows Simeon, it may be important."

Joseph was now quite frightened. He pleaded, "Judah?"

Judah, knowing that to deny these two firebrands would create an even more dangerous situation, said resignedly, "It may be for the best, Joseph. Go ahead."

Joseph lowered his head and spoke very quietly, hoping desperately to avoid telling what he knew would enrage Simeon and Levi. "The dream may have no meaning at all, brethren."

Simeon shouted angrily, "Let *us* be the judges of *that*!"

Joseph, with a great sigh of reluctance, began. "Hear, I pray you, this dream which I have dreamed. We were binding sheaves in the field, and lo, my sheaf arose and stood upright and. . ." His voice trailed to silence.

Levi shouted angrily, "Don't stop now!"

"But, Levi, it might not. . ."

"Levi said *continue*!" Simeon's tone left no doubt that violence would follow if he were disobeyed.

Joseph, almost mumbling, said, "Behold, your sheaves stood roundabout and made obeisance to my sheaf."

Simeon jumped to his feet, his face distorted with hatred. The veins were standing out in his neck and his hands were balled into fists. "I knew it! I knew you were going to tell us you were our master! Just who do you think you are, *little* brother!"

Dan too had risen. He too was angry. "Shall you indeed reign over us? Well, you will *not* reign over *me*!"

Levi, unlike his more demonstrative brethren remained seated. He did not shout, but his voice was filled with a deadly tone when he spoke. "Shall you indeed have dominion over us? Do you flatter yourself to think this?"

"Levi, I told you. . ." Joseph began, pleading.

Leaping to his feet, Levi screamed, "SILENCE! You spoiled little fool! Do you think us idiots? We know all about your precious coat of many colors! Do you think we would permit you to *live* if you tried to rule over us?"

Levi's outburst was too much for Ruben. "Levi! You go too far! Would you bring the curse of God down upon us by shedding a brother's blood?"

Simeon did not wait for Levi to answer. "The mark of Cain could be no more galling than putting up with this strutting, bragging, treacherous little fool's leadership! You are the eldest, Ruben! He is less than nothing!"

For the first time that Joseph could remember, Ruben lost his temper. As he stood, his countenance became like their father's on the very few occasions Joseph had seen him angry. His presence was just as commanding when he spoke. "That is enough! Back to the harvest — all of you!" He paused only for a second and then shouted, "Now!"

Simeon said, "We have little choice! Come, Levi, at least I can trust you!"

"Coming, my brother. The stench of these cowards is too much for me!"

With this, the brothers began filing away from the shade of the tree under which they had eaten their midday meal. They were a sullen and grumbling group as they returned to their labors. As Joseph and Benjamin made to follow their brethren, Ruben stopped them. His voice was harsh. "Joseph, Benjamin, come here!"

Joseph, fearing his brother's wrath, answered timidly. "Yes, my brother."

Ruben stood like a statue watching his departing brothers. When they were out of earshot, Joseph noted that Ruben's countenance changed rapidly from anger to one of sympathy and that he spoke in a very kind tone. "Joseph, you did nothing wrong here today. You tried as hard as you could to prevent what happened. I will tell Father of this, but you Benjamin, when you are told to be quiet, do it! Do you understand me?"

"But, Father said. . ."

"Benjamin, do you realize that you could have gotten Joseph badly hurt or killed just now?"

"Father said. . ."

Ruben lost all patience with the stubborn child. "Father isn't here right now! I asked you a question. Do you understand what I asked you?"

Benjamin's answer was sullen. "Yes, Ruben."

"Benjamin, I think it is time you returned to camp — now!" Ruben said sternly. Benjamin glared at Ruben for a moment, then turned on his heel and began walking slowly back to the camp. As he went, every now and then, he would angrily kick a stone out of his way and mumble under his breath. Ruben watched him for a few moments with his hands on his hips and shaking his head. Finally, he muttered, "That child needs a mother!" Then, turning to Joseph, his countenance turned much softer. He pointed to the remnants of their lunch. "Joseph, I think it best if you clean up the mess here and then go back to the camp." He looked at Joseph for a few moments and then added, "It might be a good idea for both of you to eat in Bilhah's tent tonight instead of with the rest of us."

"Ruben, do you think that my brothers' anger over my dream is that serious?"

"Unfortunately, I do. Judah and I will do all we can to calm them. Just before he left with the others, Judah signaled me that he is already working on this too. And of course Father will do all he can to calm them as well. I still think that this can be worked out."

"I hope that you are right, Ruben. I'll do as you say and trust that you and Judah can ease the others' thoughts."

Joseph followed Ruben's advice and ate in Bilhah's tent that night, as did a very reluctant Benjamin. That night, young Benjamin was again awakened by Joseph's dream-troubled sleep, and again he tried to awaken his brother. "Joseph! Joseph!"

Joseph, groggy from this rude awakening answered, "What?"

"You were dreaming again, weren't you, Joseph!"

Joseph, not wanting a repeat of today's debacle, was suddenly wide awake and thought fast. "Dreaming? Oh! Well,. . .ah. . .as a matter of fact I was dreaming. . .of Zebulun's ships!"

"No, you were not! You have had another important dream! I know you have! These are things Father needs to hear!"

Joseph, angry at his brother's stubbornness, responded, "Benjamin, as far as you are concerned, I was dreaming of Zebulun's ships and that is the end of the matter! Now, *I* am going back to sleep!"

As soon as Joseph had obviously gone back to sleep, his breathing regular, Benjamin said quietly to himself, "You can't fool me, Joseph! You and Ruben are wrong! Father needs to hear these dreams. I know it. You'll see!"

Joseph decided, with Judah's help, that he would work in the camp all the next day and that Benjamin should stay in camp as well. By the end of the day Ruben and Judah had calmed the others enough that all the brothers could gather at the door of Jacob's tent for the evening meal. Joseph had decided that his best course of action tonight would be total silence and was determined to say nothing, least of all, anything about dreams.

That evening, it appeared that the plan hit upon by Ruben, Judah, and Joseph was working. Everyone, even Simeon and Levi, seemed to be in good spirits, laughing and having a good time. Jacob also directed the conversation to safe subjects. During the course of the meal, he turned to Ruben and said to Ruben, "Tell me, how is the harvest going?"

"It goes well, my father! The grain is thick and the ears full. It will be a good year! Is that not so, my brethren?" All the brothers nodded or grunted their agreement with this assessment.

"How are those new bronze sickles working out?"

Ruben responded with some excitement for he wholeheartedly approved of the new tools. "They are wonderful, Father! We are able to harvest two or three times faster than before!"

"That is good to hear! We will eat well this winter, and our larders will be filled with less work! Speaking of eating well, Judah, you have not reported to me on the caravan you led to the sea for our spices."

"We definitely got the spices," Judah began, then laughed. "If we had not, the food before us right now would be very bland indeed, my father!"

"Yeah, let's hear it for the spices!" Asher shouted with his mouth full. This brought a round of laughter from the brothers.

Jacob, laughing at the folly of his own question said, "So true, so true!" Then he turned serious. "I had heard that one of the camels was injured during the trip. Has it recovered?"

Judah seemed a bit surprised at the question. He had forgotten the incident. "Oh, that! One of the camels twisted its leg." He continued in a dismissive tone of voice. "It was lame for the return trip but not so badly lame that it could not be treated upon our return. We were able to split its load among the other camels, splinted its leg, and got the ornery beast home safely. Then Abdul and I treated it. The camel is fine now."

Benjamin, who had been silent throughout the meal, now spoke. He drew himself up importantly. "Father, I have something important I have to tell you."

"Indeed, Benjamin! Pray, continue."

"Joseph has had dreams that may be important to the family." His tone suggested a definite "There I told you so!" Judah and Ruben groaned audibly at Benjamin's announcement.

Jacob's voice was stern when he addressed his older sons. "Ruben, Judah, from your countenances, you know something of this."

Ruben, trying to avoid the inevitable scene, pleaded, "My Father, it is nothing."

"My son, you know my feeling about dreams. They are important. Where would we be if I did not heed the dreams I had while I was indentured to your Uncle Laban? We, as you in particular know well, would have nothing and be little more than slaves!"

Ruben did know this, but he also knew what the result of yet another disclosure of Joseph's dreams would bring from Simeon and Levi, in particular, more trouble between the brothers. "I do know this, my father, but. . ."

"There are no buts, my son! The dream must be shared!" Angry murmuring arose from Simeon, Levi, Naphtali, and Dan, but these were acknowledged by Jacob only with, "Hmm. . ." Then he spoke to Joseph directly. "Joseph, you have had dreams, my son?"

"I have, my father, but as Ruben says, they. . ."

"I will be the judge of their importance, my son. Tell us the dreams."

Joseph, knowing that he must obey, began in a very quiet voice. "As you wish, my father. Hear, I pray you with kindness, this dream which I have dreamed: We were binding sheaves in the field, and lo, my sheaf arose and stood upright and their sheaves stood roundabout and made obeisance to my sheaf."

Before Jacob could respond, Simeon shouted angrily, "Shall *he* indeed reign over us?"

Dan asked loudly, "Shall *he* indeed have dominion over us, my father?"

Jacob had to raise his voice to be heard over the tumult created by the revelation of Joseph's dream. "Peace! Peace, my sons! It took several minutes for the enraged sons to quiet, and when they finally did, Jacob continued, "I have yet to decide on this! Joseph, Benjamin says there were dreams, more than one. Is there another dream, my son?"

Joseph knew the effect his second dream would have on his brothers, but he responded sadly, "I have had another dream." With a heavy sigh, he continued. "The sun and the moon and the eleven stars made obeisance to me." A stunned silence filled the tent.

Jacob was thinking frantically. Benjamin was correct, these were important dreams, but he also saw Simeon and Levi's countenances. There was murder in their eyes. He knew that he must defuse this situation and quickly decided on a plan of action. "What is this dream that you have dreamed? Shall I and your mother and your brethren indeed come to bow down ourselves to you?" Jacob said in an indignant tone of voice.

"Forgive me, Father. It was just a dream."

Simeon, his expression a mix of anger and satisfaction at Jacob's apparent indignation said. "What has become of your grand dreams now!"

Dan joined in the condemnation. "Do you feel the shame of your misplaced pride?" As Joseph hung his head, Dan continued, "Well, you should be ashamed for such arrogance!"

The others joined in. "What good are your dreams now?"

"You would be master and we the slaves?"

"Shall we bow down now or wait for your greatness to grow before our eyes?"

Jacob let them unwind. He could see the pain on Joseph's face, and he shared it. *"If only Benjamin had kept his counsel?"* he thought. *"Joseph could have related these dreams to me in private."* But that was not to be. Jacob pondered the future while he watched his sons. This revelation of his son's dreams was very unfortunate. *"Poor Joseph!"* he thought. The boy was getting a lot of abuse, but he was enduring it with dignified silence. Indeed, his father knew that it was Joseph's tremendous strength and humility that set him apart. Then unbidden, these words came into his mind. *"I wonder who he is, this son of mine. What will he become?"* Jacob had much to contemplate this night.

Chapter Three
The Fateful Errand

Jacob was not the only one to ponder Joseph's dreams — his dreams occupied the thoughts of the entire family. In fact, Jacob's adult sons resentfully obsessed on the subject. Sullen conversations accompanied by angry furtive glances around the campfire were becoming common, and when Joseph walked through the camp, he was met with murderous stares from Levi and Simeon.

Judah and Ruben were worried, and Judah in particular felt that the situation was getting completely out of hand. Finally, he decided to discuss the problem with Ruben, to see if they could arrive at a plan to defuse the anger. They had agreed to meet near their mother's tent, and Judah began without preamble. "Young Benjamin stirred up a lot of trouble when he revealed Joseph had another dream, Ruben."

Nodding his head in agreement, Ruben said, "Indeed! Simeon and Levi are livid! But I think they'll cool down. It's just going to take time."

Judah, in a derisive tone, answered, "Like they did when Dinah was raped by Shechem, Ruben?"

"That was different, Judah! Shechem not only defiled Dinah but the entire family."

"But. . ."

"I know what you are going to say, that they went too far, and I agree!"

"It goes deeper than that, Ruben. Our brothers have changed since that attack on the city of Shechem. Father's wrath over the incident still burns in their hearts. If I did not know better, I would think they are ashamed and trying to hide it under all that anger they are always spitting out."

Ruben became very somber and said slowly, "My brother, I think that you are very close to the truth of the matter, but their anger is all they feel at the moment, their only thought."

"You speak the truth, Ruben, but their anger *must* be cooled at all costs for this is unbridled anger at one of our own, at one of their kin! The question is how?"

"I too have been giving this issue much thought, and I think that the older brothers, you and I included, were to take the sheep somewhere to pasture far from the camp for a time, their tempers might cool."

"That is true. I have noticed that they are far calmer in the fields and have wondered why."

"Judah, look around you, brother! All around us are slaves, servants, and even wives that were once captives from the destroyed city of Shechem! Our brothers' shame is evident everywhere here!"

Judah, hanging his head at his own folly exclaimed. "Oh! What a fool I am to not see this! You are correct, Ruben. We need to get them into the fields!"

Ruben, his countenance and voice charged with determination, said, "Come, Judah. Let us propose the idea to father. He will decide which pastures we are to use.

These two went swiftly to their father with their request. As Jacob nodded his agreement to their plan, he said thoughtfully, "Your request is a sound one, Ruben. The rams *have* been very active this winter and the ewes are fat with growing lambs. They need good pasture if those lambs are to be strong."

"Where do you suggest that we pasture them, Father?" Judah asked.

"I have heard from passing caravans that the pastures near the old city of Shechem are full and green, Judah. They also say the river there is full with goodly water. That is where I feel that you should take the sheep."

"Is that wise, Father? Are we not still outcasts there?"

"I would have thought so, Judah, but recently I found out that King Hamor of Shechem had not dealt fairly with many of his neighbors." Jacob's tone became scornful. "He often broke his oaths. No man of honor does this! His neighbors were actually glad that he was killed and his city destroyed. It should be safe enough to travel there, as none are seeking revenge for the destruction of Shechem. You should, in fact, be welcome there."

Ruben, sensing Judah's discomfort but knowing their father's determination, not to mention his temper, quickly interjected. "It will be as you have commanded, my father."

With a wave of his hand to indicate that the interview was

over, Jacob said, "It is well. Go then, prepare for your journey."

When the two brothers were outside and out of earshot, Judah turned on Ruben and his tone of voice was incredulous. "We cannot go to Shechem and you know this!"

With an odd tone of resignation in his voice, Ruben responded, "I dare not risk Father's wrath, Judah."

"His wrath? What of the wrath of Simeon and Levi? Is that not why we leave the camp? Will the situation not be worsened by our proximity to the town they destroyed?"

"It might be, but you have never incurred Father's wrath." There was a long pause, and then he said simply, "I have." He stood silent for a moment more, then continued. "If I were to anger him like that again, I would be of no further use to you, for I would no longer be a part of the camp."

"Ruben, forgive me. I spoke without thinking. You speak, of course, of the incident with Bilhah?"

"I do. I shamed my father, the camp, myself, and Bilhah. It is a shame that burns within me still, and there is little I can do to make amends except obey without question."

"Your reluctance is very understandable, Ruben." Judah paused. "All right, it is to Shechem we go then!"

"Oh, oh, I know that tone of voice! You are definitely up to something, Judah!"

Judah's voice was filled with false innocence when he answered. "Me?"

This was too much for Ruben and he broke down laughing, managing to choke out his response. "Oh, very definitely you!"

Judah laughed as well and slapped his brother on the shoulder. "Then my dear brother, you are just going to have to wait see to what it is that I am up to!"

Ruben groaned as if in pain.

"Sorry, I didn't mean to hit so hard!"

"It's not that, Judah! I'm just worried. . ."

"Fear not, my brother, you shall come out of this with your honor fully intact."

When the brothers were prepared for their journey, they herded the sheep to Shechem as their father had commanded. As expected, because of their proximity to Shechem, Simeon and Levi became very restless. Ruben was getting worried, all the more so because he had yet to see Judah's plan to avoid this growing anger.

One night around the campfire, Dan noticed something odd about Judah. Wanting to discover the cause, he called out to him. "You seem awfully content about something, Judah. You are laying there with your eyes closed and a big smile on your face."

His brothers were quick to seize upon this irregularity, for Judah was always serious in his demeanor, and they began calling out. "Oh, he's dreaming of women, again! Hey, Judah is she pretty? Has she got a sister?"

All of these inquiries were followed by much raucous laughter.

Judah, lying was on his back with his head propped up on a sack, his eyes still closed, replied in a dreamy voice, "I *was* dreaming!"

This admission was followed by much hysterical laughter from the brothers, and Asher said loudly, "Told you so!"

Dan laughed with the rest, but he eyed his older brother with a knowing suspicion and retorted, "All right, I'll bite, you old fox! What are you dreaming about, Judah?"

Judah, his eyes still closed replied in an all too innocent tone, "Ships."

This was the last response from Judah that Dan expected. He was incredulous and stammered, "Shi. . . What?" Now there was silence. The brothers knew that there was something afoot and they didn't want to miss the punch line. Dan could only weakly repeat questioningly, "Ships?"

Sitting up, and with an odd expression on his face, Judah said, "Oh, not just any ships, Dan. These are *Zebulun's* ships!"

Zebulun had expected this ever since the word "ships" was first mentioned. He groaned pleadingly, "Ohhh, come on, Judah. Aren't you ever going to let me live that down?"

Asher, who took great delight in teasing his brother, said, "Zebulun, let's face it, you *are* our shipmaster!" This brought more laughter from the assembled brothers.

As soon as he could be plainly heard, Judah asked, "Zebulun? What say you? Would you like to sit beside the sea and watch ships for a while?"

"Oh, Judah, quit making fun of me!"

"Making fun? Not at all, Zebulun! I was thinking that, if we shifted to the high pastures at Dothan, we could easily see ships in the great sea to the west from the mountaintops there."

Simeon added in an astonished tone, "Judah's right! I have sat on one of the mountains there and seen ships traveling up and down the coast, to Tyre and Sidon! It's only six leagues from Dothan to the coast."

Despite a possible trap, Zebulun was excited. "You have, Simeon?"

"I have, Zebulun! You can see them, plain as can be, from up there!"

Ruben thought to himself, *"Why that sly old fox! He gets us to move from here to Dothan and makes it* their *idea!"* He allowed himself a knowing chuckle, but then his thoughts turned to their father. "I don't know, brethren. Father specifically said that we were to come here for the fine pasture."

Judah eyed his brother sourly for a few moments. "Ruben, like Father, I talk to the caravans, and they are saying that the pastures in Dothan are even finer than the ones here. They say that the streams in the mountains are full too. Father only wants the sheep well fed and watered, and that makes Dothan better than here. He would not dispute a decision made for the good of the flock."

"I don't know, Judah. It. . ."

"Ruben, you know as well as we do that the sheep are more content up there!" Levi interjected. "They thrive in the high pastures! Judah's right, Ruben!"

Asher could not wait to speak. "Well said, Levi! And just think, Ruben. Not only are the sheep content and well fed, but Zebulun gets to dream sweet dreams about his beloved ships." Once more the brothers broke into laughter.

Ruben, still chuckling, relented. "All right, you've convinced me, Asher. We shall go to Dothan. It's for the best, if not for the sheep. . ." He lowered his voice into a conspiratorial whisper. "Then for Zebulun's sweet dreams!"

With much knee slapping and back pounding, the brothers celebrated the move. There were a number of relieved comments.

"Let's get started!"

"I will be *very* glad to leave this place!"

"So shall I!"

"Come Zebulun, your ships are waiting!"

Quickly the brothers dispersed and began making the preparations for departure. As soon as they were out of earshot, Judah turned to Ruben. "I thought you were going to overplay your reluctance for a moment, Ruben."

"I had to make it look good in case Father. . ."

"Ruben, he won't turn a hair over this!" Pointing to the rest of the brothers, who were laughing and joking with one another as they made their preparations, he continued, "See how lighthearted our brothers are? Trust me! This side trip is going to solve our problems!"

At that very moment, however, unknown to the brothers, their biggest mistake, not telling Jacob *why* they were leaving, was about to bear extremely bitter fruit. Joseph was looking through the camp for Ruben. Spying his father, Joseph decided to ask him where his brother was. "My father, have you seen Ruben? I have sought him for some time this morning and cannot find him."

"He is not here, my son."

"Not here? Where is he, my father?"

Realizing Joseph's error, Jacob continued in a gentle voice. "Do not your brethren feed the flock in Shechem?"

Laughing at himself for his own forgetfulness, Joseph said, "Now I feel the fool! I knew this, but like an idiot, sought him in the camp all morning!"

A relieved Jacob chuckled. "We have all done something like that, my son. Why did you seek Ruben?"

"It was nothing important. I just like talking to him."

"Joseph, I may be able to help you. I am hearing some rumors among those in the caravans of sickening herds in the north, and I am concerned as I sent your brothers there." Coming to a quick decision, he continued. "I will send you unto them. Go, see whether it is well with your brethren and well with the flocks. When you have done so, bring me word."

Joseph bowed to his father. "I will do so, my father. Peace be upon you until I return."

So Jacob sent Joseph out of the Vale of Hebron, and the young man went to Shechem. Oh, the plight of those who are destined by God for greatness! Their way is never easy, but it is always guided. So it was with Joseph, for even as he searched vainly in Shechem, the God of his father's sent him a messenger to speed him to his fateful meeting with his brethren.

After searching for several days near Shechem, Joseph was about to give up and return home. In frustration, he spoke out loud. "I know that Father said they were at Shechem, but I have searched

JOSEPH Ruler of All Egypt 35

for days and there is no sign of them!"

Joseph was startled by a voice behind him. "Peace be unto you, stranger."

Joseph, severely surprised, cried out, "Ahhh! Forgive me, stranger. I did not hear you come up behind me and was startled!"

The stranger merely chuckled and said, "I can see that, lad! You are as pale as a woman's wedding veil! Come, let us sit under this tree. I have food and drink. Let us rest here for a while and we can talk."

Feeling the pangs of hunger after his journey and his fruitless search, Joseph followed the stranger toward the indicated tree. As they walked, Joseph said, "I thank you, stranger. I have been wandering up and down these hills for days!"

"I know. I have watched you from a distance. What do you seek?"

"I seek my brethren, the sons of Jacob, sometimes called Israel. Tell me, I pray you, where are they feeding their flocks."

"They have departed from here. I heard them say, 'Let us go to Dothan.'" He then continued with a questioning tone in his voice. "I thought I also heard something about ships?"

Joseph laughed heartily. "They were probably teasing my brother Zebulun. He is fascinated by ships."

The stranger chuckled appreciatively. "Ah, a family joke! You will seek them then in Dothan?"

"Indeed, for my father seeks after their welfare."

"Please, tarry a short while here. It is a long way to Dothan. Eat and drink. I have more than enough, and you will need your strength."

"I thank you, stranger, for your kindness and your directions."

Joseph traveled north, and as he neared his final destination, his brothers were enjoying their new location. It wasn't only the ship-struck Zebulun who spent many hours watching ships on the distant sea or just staring into the vast expanses from the mountain tops at Dothan. On this fateful day, Zebulun, Levi, and Simeon — who had taken an odd delight in ship watching that was at least the equal of Zubulun's — were together on the peak staring out at the Great Sea beyond. Zebulun, pointing excitedly, exclaimed, "Look! See that one. It actually has two masts. See there, it has two sails, one in front of the other, Simeon!"

"Are you sure, Zebulun? That just might be two ships

travelling side by side."

"I don't think so. That is definitely a single ship, Simeon. I heard the sailors in Tyre talking about ships like that. They say that there are only two or three such vessels that come into Tyre. That must be one of them!"

Levi laughed. "You two! How you can spend endless hours discussing ships I'll never know! Me, I like looking out at the land. Look! See there. A traveler makes his way up the road from Shechem."

Curious, Zebulun turned and looked in the direction indicated by Levi. He then exclaimed, "So there is! He must be two or three leagues away!" Zebulun watched the stranger in silence for a moment or two, then exclaimed, "My, he's wearing some bright colors. They are visible all the way up here!"

This statement drew Simeon's attention, and he asked with curiosity, "Bright colors?"

"Yes. Wait a moment. He is in the shadows right now. Once he comes out. . . Yes! See, his coat is quite colorful."

Simeon sat looking at the stranger in silence, seemingly lost in thought. When he finally spoke, there was annoyance in his voice. "Humph! He reminds me too much of another with a bright and colorful coat! I'm glad we're here and *that* coat is in Hebron!"

Levi, with a disgusted gesture, added, "You know, I think I'll go back to camp. That fellow down there has ruined the view!" No sooner than he had said this than the brothers heard footsteps coming up behind them. Startled, Levi shouted. "Who's coming?"

Naphtali, having heard Levi's startled exclamation, shouted, "Have no fear it is only I, Naphtali."

Zebulun, eager to resolve the issue of the fellow in the colorful robe, called out, "Ah, Naphtali! Just the man! We need your sharp eyes!"

Groaning in mock despair, he responded, "Not another ship debate!"

Simeon chuckled. "Not this time, brother. No, we were wondering about that traveler yonder."

"Oh? Where is he?"

"Just there by those rocks, about a league from here."

"Oh yes! I see him now. . . This isn't possible!"

Simeon did not like the sound of that comment. "What isn't possible?"

Naphtali, pointing dramatically, exclaimed, "That's Joseph! I can tell by the way he walks, not to mention that accursed coat! But it can't be! No one knows where we are!"

Levi's ill humor returned with a vengeance. "Apparently *he* does!"

Simeon said angrily, "Naphtali, Levi, come! We need to talk, but not here. Let us get back to the camp." As quickly as they could, the three brothers scrambled back down the mountain to their camp. As soon as they were in shouting distance, Simeon called out angrily, "Asher, Dan, Gad! Come here!"

Ruben, who had been mending part of the camel's furniture, looked up from his work and at Judah, who was nearby sharpening a tool. Worriedly, he said, "Oh, oh, I don't like the sounds of all that angry shouting, Judah."

"Nor do I. Especially since it is Simeon doing all the shouting. We had better investigate the problem." They put aside their work and walked toward the rest of their brethren.

As they came closer, they heard Gad ask, "What is it, Levi?"

Levi's answer was filled with loathing. "Behold, the dreamer comes!"

Dan was astounded. "Dreamer? Surely you can't mean Joseph! He doesn't know where we are."

Naphtali shouted. "Oh, but he does, Dan. I saw the little snitch with my own eyes!"

"How in the world did he find us?"

Simeon, who was so angry he was grinding his teeth, growled, "I for one do not care! I say kill him!"

Levi shouted, "Yes! Let us slay him and cast him into some pit!"

Naphtali, not to be left behind in these murderous plans, added excitedly, "We will say that some evil beast has devoured him!"

Simeon, his teeth bared like the fangs of some wild feral creature, growled, "We will see what will become of his *dreams*!" The brothers all seemed in agreement.

"We'll teach that brat a lesson!"

"Kill him!"

"Strip that foul coat off him and burn it!"

"Beat him till he can't stand!"

It was at this point that Ruben and Judah arrived. What they heard saddened them. Ruben shouted to get the plotters attention.

"Brethren! Speak not so! Shed no blood!"

As Simeon turned to face him, Ruben could see that there would be no reasoning with this man. He was too far gone into his blind hatred. His next words sent a cold chill down Ruben's spine. "Ruben! You of all people should want rid of this spoiled little brat! We're doing you a favor by killing him!"

"Having the blood of a brother on my hands is no favor, Simeon! Maybe he needs a lesson, but shed no blood! Cast him into this empty pit that is near the camp, but lay no violent hand upon him."

Miraculously, something in what Ruben said reached Simeon's hate-fogged mind. Grudgingly he said, "All right, but this isn't the end of the matter!"

A very frightened Ruben thought to himself, *"It is, if I can get him out of that pit and escape with him back to Father before you can act so foolishly!"* He turned away from his violent and sullen brethren and approached Judah, who looked as scared as Ruben felt. Yet there was a calmness of potential action in his eyes as well.

This was even more evident when Judah whispered to Ruben, "This situation is getting out of hand — fast! We have to do something!"

Ruben, knowing that he could depend on Judah, whispered frantically, "Do what you can to protect the boy while I prepare the camels so that I can get him out of that pit and escape back to Father before they can catch us!"

Shocked, Judah said, "Ruben, you realize that this will result in Simeon and Levi being cast out of the camp? Father won't stand for this!"

"Would you have the blood of innocent young Joseph on your soul just to keep Simeon and Levi in the camp? They become more violent and dangerous with each passing year, and so this would not be their last murderous act, of that I am certain."

Judah hung his head and was silent for a few moments. Then, with a sigh of resignation, he said, "You are right, Ruben. Joseph's murder at their hands cannot be allowed. If they are cast out, they are cast out. However, the others cannot see what we are about or they *will* kill *us*! You will have to wait until night. Go! Prepare! I'll do what I can here." Ruben nodded and made his way toward the tethered camels.

As Joseph traveled the mere league to the encampment,

hidden from the view of the others, Ruben was preparing two camels with riding furniture, food, and water for his escape with Joseph. He was close enough that he heard Joseph's arrival. It was a reception that would haunt his dreams and that would make him weep for years to come.

Joseph, unaware of the great danger, joyously greeted his brothers. "Greetings, my brethren! I had a hard time finding you!"

Simeon, his anger now an uncontrollable demon, shouted angrily, "And you will regret to the end of your life that you *did*! Which *won't* be long!"

Ruben could hear the resulting scuffle, and with only his imagination for sight, the scene was doubly terrible for him. He listened with his head hung low and tears in his eyes as he was forced to sit and listen to his younger brother being brutalized by those that should have been his greatest friends. First came the sounds of blows raining down on the unfortunate youth, followed quickly by yelps of pain from Joseph. It was obvious that he tried to call out, but the pain of the blows prevented him. Then came the demonic, insane comments of his own brothers:

"Hit him again!"

"Hit him harder!"

Then there was a ripping sound followed by, "That's it! Strip that accursed coat off him!"

Then Simeon's voice surmounted all the others. He shouted in a voice filled with demonic and uncontrollable rage. "Who has the knife?" When no answer came immediately, he screamed, "Who has the knife? I can't slit this swine's throat without it!"

Judah's enraged bellow was like balm to Ruben's ears. "Simeon! We agreed! He is to be thrown into the pit, *not* butchered!"

The response to Judah's intervention was mixed. Some of the brothers — Simeon, Naphtali, and Levi foremost — still wanted blood, but the rest agreed with Judah. Then came another cacophony of shouted comments and all too graphic sounds.

"Hit him again!" This was followed by the sounds of more blows and yelps of pain from Joseph.

"To the pit with him!"

Ruben could hear the sounds of the struggle as the brothers tried to force Joseph to the edge of the pit to throw him in. Then came the most heart rending sound of all, as Joseph cried out desperately for help. "Ruben! Judah! Save me!" Ruben's heart was about to break and he sobbed uncontrollably. Joseph had called out to him in a desperate plea and all Ruben could do was cower behind a rock like a craven coward. Just as Ruben had grasped his knife and determined to fight to the death to rescue the lad, he heard a sound that made his blood run cold — Joseph's terrified scream. "Noooooo. . ." The boy's voice faded as he fell deep into the pit. Ruben could bear no more. He fled, running down the trail to hide behind some boulders where no sounds from the camp could reach him, and he wept bitterly.

After a time, a determination settled in his breast. He would rescue the boy as planned. Then he would tell Father all. Their father's wrath would be terrible, but so would Ruben's. Simeon and Levi now had a deadly enemy — Ruben.

Ruben did not hear the victory celebration that followed Joseph's being thrown into the pit. The first to shout was Asher, who cried joyously, "Come let us eat and celebrate! The pest is out of our hair!"

Simeon, whose voice was almost inhuman in its insanity, laughingly shouted, "That's it, Asher! We just took care of an annoying flea!" The men continued their revelries for some time. Then they sat to eat. It was then that Joseph's weakly repeated cry for help could be heard coming from the bottom of the pit.

Dan was worried. "Simeon, what if someone hears him? We could be in real trouble!"

"Bah! Who is there to hear him in this wilderness? I for one like the sound of his whimpering! The more he cries the better! It is a balm to my soul!"

Judah watched, horrified, as the murderous gleam once more appeared in Simeon's eyes and he purred, "But not half so much as killing him will be!"

Judah had watched all of this, scared to the bottom of his soul. He thought frantically, *"Oh, this is getting out of control! What am I to do? Ruben is in hiding with the camels. It is hours before dark. They are all in a murderous mood! If I try to stop them now, they will kill me! What am I to do?"*

Dan burst into Judah's thoughts when he said, "Balm it may be to you, Simeon, but I was thinking of them!"

An exasperated Levi grumbled, "Dan, what are you babbling about and what are you pointing at?"

Dan, undeterred by Levi's wrath, continued to point into the distance and said, "Do you not see that caravan in the distance, Levi? It is coming this way!"

Judah peered into the distance and recognized the caravan coming toward their camp. To his brothers he announced. "Behold, a company of Ishmeelites comes from Gilead with their camels bearing spices and balm and myrrh, carrying it down to Egypt." To himself he thought, *"This is just the thing I need! It will be bad, very bad! Ruben and father will be devastated and I may be cast out of the camp for it, but. . . "* Then he blurted out his frantic plan. "What profit is it if we slay our brother and conceal his blood? Come, let us sell him to the Ishmeelites. After all, he is our flesh."

Levi was delighted and laughed heartily. "Leave it to Judah to find a way to make a profit!"

Everyone but Simeon laughed now too. He stood staring at the traders as they came closer and his brethren ran to the pit to bring Joseph out to sell. After a few moments, he said to no one in particular, "I like the idea *very* well! As Naphtali says so often, with *him* around we are little more than slaves! Well, I call it justice that he feels the lash for the rest of his life!" Again, the maniacal gleam appeared in his eyes. Through gritted teeth he ground out a curse, "May his life be long and painful!"

Chapter Four
Valor and Deception

Ruben had crept away and wept, moving far enough away so that he could no longer hear the pitiful cries coming from the pit; as a result, he knew nothing of the traders and Joseph's sale as a slave. Once it was dark, Ruben thought that he could safely reach the pit and rescue Joseph.

Ruben advanced slowly. He had already removed the bells from the camel's furniture so he could approach the camp quite silently. When he had come as close as possible with the animals, he tethered the camels and continued on foot, listening intently as he crept forward. If his brothers were to catch him, it would be disastrous. Simeon and Levi were capable of murder when enraged and stealing Joseph away would anger them beyond all reason. Ruben wanted no part of his two younger brothers when they were in a killing frenzy!

Fortunately, there was a sliver of a moon that night that gave Ruben more than enough light to silently pick his way through the rocks to the pit where they had thrown Joseph. He crept to the edge of the cavity and listened, and then, when he was confident that there was no watch set, he whispered loudly into the shaft, "Joseph! Joseph? Joseph, answer me!"

When no answer came, Ruben's thoughts raced. *"Oh, no! He was injured by the fall! He cannot answer me! I must go down there and get him!"* Then a realization came to him. He had to go into that dark frightening hole! His thoughts raced yet faster. Oh, how he hated dark enclosed places! At the thought of entering this dreadful place, Ruben involuntarily groaned aloud. "Ohhh!" Shocked at his own folly in making such a sound, he thought to himself, *"Ruben, you fool, keep quiet!"* He stared wildly about, expecting his brothers at any moment, but no one came. Relieved, Ruben turned his attention once more to the problem before him. Staring into the pit, Ruben made up his mind. With a new determination, he thought, *"All right, so be it!"*

Before he descended, he needed to tie off the rope he had carried with him. Searching about him, he discovered a large rock that appeared to go deep into the ground, he tied his rope around it, and then threw the free end into the pit. As if to give himself courage, he whispered aloud, "Now, in I go!" There followed scraping sounds and grunting as Ruben climbed into the shaft. His fear of the place intensified as he began to descend; worse, the slight sound he made sliding down the rope was, to Ruben's sensitive ears, as loud as the roar of a hundred angry lions! Surely his brothers would hear all this racket! Finally, with a soft thump, he reached the bottom of the pit. Ruben called softly, "Joseph! Joseph?" Ruben's thoughts became more frantic. This place was so small! He felt all around the tiny space and Joseph simply wasn't there! He was gone! Unable to contain his grief, Ruben screamed aloud, "Nooooo!"

A short distance away, Asher and several of his brothers were still awake and staring hopelessly into the embers of their fire. The realization of the enormity of what they had done was becoming a reality to them. Asher's thoughts were extremely uneasy. Their deed today, when discovered, would get them all disinherited and thrown out of the camp by their enraged father. Then he heard Ruben's cry of anguish from the pit. Asher panicked and exclaimed, "What was that?"

Simeon, sitting close by, growled, "Quiet Asher! It's just that brat Joseph whining again!"

Levi added quietly, "He'll be quiet in a while, Asher, when he falls asleep." Asher was now more frightened than ever. Had his brothers lost their minds? "Simeon! Levi! Joseph isn't in that pit! He's on his way to Egypt! Don't you remember?" cried a now thoroughly panicked Asher.

Simeon looked at Asher without understanding for a moment. Then he nodded and said absently, "That's right, Asher. I forgot." Becoming aware of the situation and frightened by it he added, "But if that isn't Joseph, what is it?" Then there rose another anguished cry of "Nooo!" into the night.

Levi was also becoming frightened. He sat up from the bed he had made himself, the covers falling off of him. In a frightened whisper he said, "There it is again!"

Now, Simeon was becoming very frightened. He stared in the direction of the pit, his eyes wide in fear and whispered. "It. . . It is the spirit of Joseph come back to haunt us!"

Judah, who had managed to actually fall into a troubled sleep, sat up and looked around with unfocused eyes. He said grumpily, "What's going on? You woke me up."

"It is the ghost of Joseph come back to haunt us, Judah!"

Judah was confused. "Ghost? Haunt? What are you going on about, Simeon?"

Before Simeon could answer, Asher sat up and pointed in the direction of the pit and in a frightened whisper called out to the others. "Listen! Something comes!" In the near distance, the brothers could hear someone weeping and wailing. "It cannot be!" There followed rapid footsteps that were becoming louder, plainly approaching the camp.

The brothers were about to panic and run from this specter of the night when Judah, now completely awake, shouted, "Wait, I know that voice!"

Levi was frightened out of his wits and becoming hysterical. "It's Joseph's voice!" Shortly after this, there was a ringing slap.

Simeon, who was alarmed at Judah's swift response to Levi's terror, cried. "Judah! You didn't have to slap him!"

Judah was calm and had a definite note of command in his voice. "Simeon! Levi! Control yourselves! That's Ruben's voice, not Joseph's! After a short pause, he called out, "Ruben! Ruben? Is that you?" The sound of running footsteps and weeping got louder and then the sobbing Ruben stumbled into the firelight.

In anguish, Ruben cried, "Judah! The child is not, and I . . . Where shall I go?" He collapsed into Judah's arms and began weeping again. The remaining brothers were aroused by all this commotion and began to rise with confused comments, groans, and exclamations.

Levi, for his part, could not take his eyes off of his eldest brother. In an awed voice he exclaimed, "Look at him! Look at his clothes!"

Simeon was also shocked. "He's rent his clothes?"

A very confused Asher asked, "What does he mean, Judah? What does he mean by 'Whither shall I go?'"

"It isn't something we talk about much, Asher."

Asher was even more confused. "Yes, but what is it?"

Ruben, in anguish, cried, "It means that my shame is complete!" He then dissolved once more into uncontrolled sobs.

Simeon, unnerved by Ruben's behavior, asked in confusion, "His shame?"

Judah was angry. "Are you a dolt? Do you think that you and Levi have been the only ones to incur Father's wrath, Simeon? You think that your debacle at Shechem was the only time the family honor was besmirched? Do you?"

Simeon replied in surprise and consternation, "Oh! Ruben, I am so sorry! I forgot about the incident of which you speak!"

Ruben managed to choke out between sobs, "Some of us can never forget, even unto death!"

Asher was even more confused. "Judah, what are you talking about?"

Judah realized that Asher truly didn't understand. He said apologetically, "Forgive me Ruben, but I must explain."

Ruben seemed to be getting control of himself. "It doesn't matter now, Judah. We are now all outcasts! Forgive me if you can, brethren. Most of you are far too young to remember the incident. I. . . I defiled my father's bed with. . .with. . .Bilhah."

Dan, who knew nothing of this, was aghast and shouted, "With my mother?"

"Forgive me, Dan. I was just a boy, and I was stupid. Oh, I remember Father's wrath as though it happened just moments ago! He was angrier than I have ever seen him. He raged for hours! I sat outside the tent huddled with Bilhah awaiting his judgment and suffering the angry stares of the whole camp as Father shouted that we would be cast out. It was only the pleading of my mother Leah and Zilpah that Joseph and Benjamin needed Bilhah to care for them that prevented us from being sent away." He drew a shuddering breath and continued. "I live with that shame every day. I still see the accusations in the older servants' eyes, still feel the shame when I pass Bilhah in the camp. It never leaves me!" He began to weep softly once more.

Zebulun too had a quiet question. "Judah, what does he mean that we are all cast out?"

"Do you think Father will overlook the fact that Joseph is missing? He knows that many of his sons bear Joseph a grudge for his coat of many colors and his dreams, and he *will* act, Zebulun."

Simeon seemed to come to life. "Judah is right! We can't just sit here fixing blame! We have to think of something to tell Father or find ourselves cast out with hungry wives and children to feed and nothing to give them!" Suddenly, there was excitement in his voice. "Wait! Ruben, what is that you are holding?"

Ruben, who had been sadly staring at the garment in his hands, said, "It is all I could find of Joseph. It is his torn coat."

Levi seemed to pick up on what Simeon had in mind. "His torn coat? Let me see that, Ruben!"

"Yes!" Levi cried. Then he continued more to himself than to the others. "Yes, this could work!" He began tearing at the coat with his knife.

Judah, shocked at Levi's actions, shouted, "Levi! What are you doing to that coat with your knife?"

"Fixing it!"

"Fixing it? You're shredding it!"

"Exactly! Judah, if you were to see this coat without knowing what had been done, what would you think?"

"Well, it's pretty shredded. I suppose that an animal... Wait! I see where you are going with this! It needs one more touch, Levi! Dan! Run to the flock and fetch us a kid of the goats!"

Dan, who was still staggered by the revelation about his mother, was confused. "A kid? You're thinking of eating at a time like this?"

"Not just eating, my good brother, but *bleeding*..."

"Oh!" shouted Dan, realizing what was going to be done, and he ran to the flock and picked a young goat kid. Then they took Joseph's coat, killed the kid, and dipped the coat in the blood. They did this to make it look as though an animal had killed Joseph. The brothers now faced a serious problem. Who was going to take the destroyed coat back to their father with the false tale of Joseph's death and suffer Jacob's possible wrath?

Levi, his hands still dripping with the blood of the kid, looked up from the loathsome object in his hands and said in an unusually quiet voice, "The coat is finished."

Ruben, repulsed, said, "What a horrid object it is now! What dire images such a thing brings to the mind!"

Judah, who had been firm and decisive to this point, said tentatively, "It should be taken to father for him to identify."

Zebulun, like the rest, eyed the coat with dread. "Aye, we are all agreed as to that, but who shall take it?" There were murmured replies.

"Not me!"

"I could not face Father with such a thing!"

"Not I!"

It was Dan who tentatively suggested, "I think it should be Simeon and Levi!"

Simeon, caught unaware, said indignantly, "Us?"

Judah, once more in control, said with authority, "Hold, Simeon! Why do you think thus, Dan?"

"I confess anger at the thought of Joseph as the head of the family, but I never wanted him dead. Simeon and Levi wanted his blood, and they threw him in the pit."

Ruben's head came up instantly at this admission from Dan. There was a fire in his eyes that none of the brothers had ever seen before and those nearest backed away from him. Looking Simeon directly in the eye, he asked, "Simeon, is this true?"

Simeon answered with defiance. "Yes, Ruben. We did it. In fact, it was *I* who threw the brat in that hole, and I would have cut his throat first if the others had allowed it!"

The fire in Ruben's eyes intensified. Without wavering and completely without fear of Simeon, Ruben announced, "Then, it *will* be you who faces Father with this grotesque proof of Joseph's death!"

Simeon was deeply frightened by what he saw in those eyes, but he was loath to admit it to the others. He replied with all the impudence he could muster, "Very well, Ruben. After all, you are the eldest and your judgment is final. Come Levi, let us take this *thing* to our father!"

While it was yet dark, Simeon and Levi began their journey toward their father's camp in Hebron, and when the sun rose, they were well on their way. But, despite their early start, it was still a long journey in which to stare at the gruesome token they carried. The journey home was also an equally long time to ponder the effects of the sad, false tidings that they would carry to their unsuspecting father. The closer they got to their home camp, the more uneasy they became.

No desert dweller is ever at ease, for danger lurks everywhere, and must always be on guard for poisonous snakes, insects, ravenous wild animals, and even attacks by rival tribes or thieves. In fact, the most dangerous animal in the desert is always man, and so everyone, from the oldest to the youngest member of any desert camp, keeps a constant vigil for invaders and despoilers. So it was for Jacob's camp, and as Simeon and Levi approached, they were spotted at a great distance by young Benjamin. Immediately, he ran to Jacob, shouting, "Father! Father!"

"What is it, my son?"

"Look! See there on the far hill? That looks like Simeon and Levi coming."

Jacob stood shielding his eyes from the sun with his hand and stared in the direction indicated by Benjamin. After a few moments, he said, "My eyes are not as sharp as yours, Benjamin." Turning, Jacob looked about and spotted their sharp eyed camel driver. Jacob hailed him. "Abdul! Come here!"

"Coming, Master!" Abdul ran to Jacob's side. "What is it you require, my Master?"

"Your sharp eyes, Abdul." Pointing to the pair approaching the camp, Jacob asked, "Look, yonder upon the far hill, Abdul — are those travelers Levi and Simeon as young Benjamin here seems to think?"

Abdul stared hard into the distance and then announced, "The young one's eyes are sharp indeed, my Master! It would indeed appear to be your sons, Simeon and Levi."

"I thank you, Abdul." Jacob thought, *"I like this not! It should be Joseph returning, not these two!"*

Benjamin said innocently and in an excited tone, "They will be here in a few minutes, my father, and then you will have the news of the northern herd as you wanted."

"Indeed Benjamin, I will." Then the aged Jacob thought, *"You are innocent, Benjamin, and know not the signs I see. The way they walk tells me of grave troubles. I know not what to make of the bundle they carry so oddly."*

It was not long before the two brothers covered the distance to the camp. Benjamin, excited to see his brothers, shouted, "Peace be unto you, my brothers!" His greeting went unanswered. Benjamin was upset by this discourtesy. "Why do you not answer me?" Then, being a child, the perceived insult disappeared in the face of curiosity. "What is that you're carrying?"

Jacob quietly commanded, "Benjamin, please be quiet." With foreboding in his voice, he continued, "My sons, what is this that you have in your hands?"

Simeon's voice was uncharacteristically tremulous when he spoke, "Father, we found this. We want to know if this is Joseph's coat."

"Nooo!" Jacob shouted. His agony was evident. "It *is* my son's coat!" He began to wail the traditional cry of anguish for the death of a loved one and the sound of his mourning roused the camp. Soon anxious voices and running feet were heard as the camp rushed to their leader. The first person to reach Jacob was Leah.

"My husband! What has happened?"

"An evil beast has devoured him, Leah!"

"An evil beast? Devoured who?"

Zilpah, who had rushed with her mistress and to her husband, recognized the coat instantly. She cried in a shocked voice, "Mistress! Look at what Father Jacob is holding! It's. . . It's. . ."

Leah stared in horror at the mutilated garment for a long moment, and then she said, aghast, "But, Zilpah! It is bloodstained and rent! It is in shreds!"

Bilhah too recognized the garment and shrieked, "Joseph's coat of many colors! No! My husband! This cannot be!"

Jacob was still wailing and weeping, but he managed to answer his wife. "But it is true, Bilhah! Simeon and Levi found this!" Then, with such agony in his voice as none of them had ever heard, he cried, "Joseph is without doubt rent to pieces!"

The camp instantly dissolved into the wails of mourning for the lost son. There were also shouts of consternation and the preparation for the young man's funeral.

"Bring sack cloth and ashes!"

"Not Joseph!"

"Poor Joseph!"

"He was always so kind!"

Over all of these exclamations rose the repeated cries of the heartbroken Jacob, who repeated over and over, "My son! My son!"

Simeon was appalled. He had not known what to expect, but the scene that was now playing out before his eyes was shocking. He motioned to Levi and said quietly, "Come, Levi. I *must* get away from this!"

Levi was pale. He looked at his brother and asserted, "I too!"

As quickly as they dared, the two brothers separated themselves from the mourners. Once they were far enough from the rest that they could talk, Simeon looked back at the camp and said with a shaky voice, "Listen to them! It is as bad as when Rachael died!"

Levi stood shaking his head. "No, Simeon — it's worse! I've *never* heard them like this!"

Simeon muttered with astonishment, "He was loved by all! See how they mourn! Look at Father!"

"Look! Look at our mother, Simeon!"

Simeon was shocked anew by what he saw and cried out, "She is prostrate on the ground! I never knew that Joseph was thus loved even by our own mother!"

Levi pointed and said in a strangled voice, "Oh no! I think poor Dinah has fainted, Simeon! Ohhh! She has! See, they are carrying her toward her tent!"

"What have we done, Levi? What have we done?"

"Simeon, look! Father has rent his clothes!"

"We must go to him, Levi! Come!" Simeon said decisively. Both men rushed to their father's side. Simeon attempted to hug his father but was roughly shoved away. In agony, Simeon cried, "Father, *please* be comforted."

Jacob shouted in anger, "I will not be comforted! I will to the grave mourning my son!"

Then, despite seeing Simeon rebuffed, all his family rose up and attempted to comfort Jacob, but he abjectly refused to be comforted. He continued to wail loudly, "I will not be comforted! I will go down into the grave mourning my son!"

Chapter Five
THE HOUSE OF POTIPHAR

Thus it was that Joseph was brought to Egypt as a slave and Potiphar, an officer of Pharaoh, Captain of the Guard, bought him from the Ishmeelites. Following the sale, Potiphar and his Head of House, Inep, were walking back to officer's estate. The nobleman had come to distrust the man walking beside him for there was a nasty gleam in his eye when he looked at the servants in Potiphar's house, which disturbed him greatly. Potiphar was gone a great deal of the time attending to his duties as the Captain of the Guard for Pharaoh, and he was beginning to regret his absences. As they walked together, Potiphar again saw the odd gleam in Inep's eyes as they walked. In an attempt to plumb the depths of his servant he asked, "What do you think of the young slave we purchased today, Inep?"

"He appears strong, but..." His voice turned hard. "I suspect he will require much discipline."

Potiphar responded sadly, "Ah, yes, discipline. You do seem to have some problems with that."

There was a look of surprise upon Inep's face and a definite element of panic in his voice when he replied hurriedly, "It is nothing that I cannot handle, my Lord!"

Potiphar walked in silence for a few moments, but while his voice was silent, his thoughts were not. *"I see the scars of your whip on even the youngest slaves, but I wonder if it is necessary. I am gone too much in the service of Pharaoh. I serve Pharaoh well, but it seems I cannot protect those in my own house! However, I must. . ."* Determined to gain control of his house, Potiphar turned to Inep and continued aloud, "I do not think you are right about the young slave Joseph."

"In what way, Great One?"

"I saw much humility and honesty in him."

"You did?"

"Indeed, I did." Potiphar paused for a moment as though

coming to a decision. "See to it that he is assigned solely to the Chief Steward, Inep. I think that they will work well together." For just a fleeting moment Potiphar thought that he saw disapproval on Inep's face, but the moment passed and again he saw nothing in his servant's expression that might reveal his thoughts.

"It shall be as you command, my Lord!" After a moment he asked, "Ah, my Lord, did I hear you say earlier that you are going to a party this afternoon?"

"I am. Why do you ask?"

Inep, with a dismissive wave of his hand replied, "It is nothing, Master! It is just a small matter of discipline."

"Ah, I see." Despite the neutral tone that he had used with Inep, Potiphar's thoughts were in turmoil. Another poor slave was undoubtedly about to feel Inep's cruel whip! He wondered if the violence in his home would ever end. They traveled the rest of the way home in silence. He was very ill at ease and debated the wisdom of leaving his estate at this time, but the party was one of those numerous "must attend" functions common to one of his station, and he had no choice. To ease his guilt and unease, he saw to the placement of Joseph himself and then reluctantly departed for the party.

No sooner was Potiphar out of the estate's gates than Inep, puffed up with the exaggerated self-importance he assumed in the Master's absence, shouted to the guards, "Assemble the household at the place of punishment!" While the guards did his bidding unenthusiastically, Inep hurried to his quarters and grabbed his most prized possession, his whip, the symbol of his great power and authority. Oh, how he loved the fearful looks of those assembled mindless cowering sheep when they saw the mighty Inep with his whip!

He returned to the courtyard and watched as the slaves and the rest of the household slowly assembled, and their lack of haste enraged him. When *he* spoke, these animals were to run. They simply were not to go at their own pace! He began to shout, "Run you filthy vermin!" Then to some of those already gathered, "Stand in a line over there!" He saw one of the slaves slouching and screamed, "Stand up straight, you!" Finally, he saw a sight that filled him with indignant anger, the new slave that his Master evidently held in some regard even without knowing the man. *"What's his name?"* Inep thought angrily to himself. Instead of standing with the other slaves, he was standing by that squeamish weakling Hotem! Well, he'd see to that! Pointing imperiously at the estate's Chief Steward, he shouted angrily, "Hotem! Why is this new slave still there by you? He will stand with the rest!

"Potiphar placed him in my personal care. He will stand with me," was Hotem's immediate and calm reply.

Inep assumed the dangerous tone he used when he was about to declare judgment upon a slave. "You DARE to defy me?"

"*I* obey Potiphar." There was a strong emphasis on the word "I" in his response.

Inep was livid. This mere steward implied that he, Inep, disobeyed their common Master! His voice took on its most dangerous tone. "Very well, Hotem. You are a free man . . . for now, but I shall speak with the Master of this!" He then turned his attention toward Joseph. Inep looked at the boy with pure loathing and malice, and when he spoke there was a cruel edge and threat to his voice. "You, slave, though you think yourself protected, watch and learn what happens to the disobedient in this house!" He turned angrily upon his heel and strode stiff legged toward the raised platform that served as the "place of punishment" for the House of Potiphar.

When Inep was out of earshot, Joseph whispered frantically to Hotem, "I do not wish to cause you trouble, Master. If. . ."

Hotem looked quickly at Inep's retreating back and whispered in turn, "Think nothing of it, Joseph. I am acting on Potiphar's orders. Inep can do nothing to me! Observe, for Inep is about to speak!"

Inep had reached the top of the platform and stood before the flogging pillar that was in the center of it. He postured importantly for a moment, and then shouted, "Slaves in the house of Potiphar! Silence!" He glared out at the already silent assembly as though daring anyone to utter the slightest sound. After a sufficient dramatic pause, he continued. "Still, you have not learned! I *will* have obedience!" He gestured to his left and Joseph saw that the guards, who seemed very averse to their task, were dragging a young girl of perhaps ten or twelve years of age to the top of the platform. Inep glared threateningly at her for a moment continued, "This filthy girl was caught stealing bread from the kitchen! This will not be tolerated!"

The child, weeping and desperate, fell to her knees and cried out, "Master, please. Mercy! It was a stale crust! It was giv. . ." Instantly, Inep turned and struck the child a full force-backhand blow to the face. She fell nearly unconscious. The crowd reacted with a collective groan in sympathy for the child. Inep turned, his face a study in rage, and bellowed, "SILENCE! All of you! I shall not have *my* authority challenged by filth like you!" Pointing dramatically, he shouted, "Tie her to the pillar!" The guards complied, but it was plainly obvious they deeply detested what they were doing. The child was dragged to the pillar, tied to it, and then hoisted up by her wrists until her tiny feet were barely touching the platform. Finally her dress was ripped from her to eliminate even the tiny protection it could have offered from Inep's whip. The child cried out in desperation. "Please! Mercy!"

Inep, his face no longer human but filled with the insane lust of sadism, screamed, "Mercy? Here's your mercy!" The child screamed in agony as the whip opened her back like a knife and her blood flowed freely.

Hotem, unable to watch such cruelty, closed his eyes and groaned quietly, "Oh, how I loathe that man!"

Joseph overheard and whispered, "Master?"

Realizing his error, Hotem frantically whispered," Silence, Joseph! I fear I spoke when I meant not to. It is not safe to speak now!"

Inep was blind to all except his own sadistic lust to cause pain, and he delivered ten full bloody strokes to the child. With each blow the child's cries became weaker. The cuts were deep and went from the back of the child's legs up to her tiny neck. She was covered in her own blood as she hung limply, barely conscious. Inep turned and faced the watching crowd. With a voice filled with insane triumph, he shouted, "That is how thieving slaves are punished in this house! Now, back to your work and I'll tolerate no slackers!" The crowd turned and began shuffling off to their various chores quietly and sullenly. The guards turned quickly and would have let the poor child down, but Inep shouted, "Leave her! She will be an example to the rest!" Neither guard could hide the horror they felt at such an order, but they obeyed.

Hotem, seeing this final act of insane cruelty, turned on his heel and began walking toward the storehouse built into the outer wall of the estate. Walking slowly and sadly away, he signaled quietly for Joseph to follow. As Joseph came alongside him, he whispered, "I am sorry I spoke so to you, Joseph. Inep is a violent and dangerous man. I feared that he would hear you and have you on the pillar next." Before Joseph could respond, they were interrupted by the sound of rapid light footsteps behind them. They turned. Approaching them was a lovely young woman. Her countenance spoke of fear and concern. Hotem quietly greeted her. "Ah, Anah, what is it?"

Anah quickly matched their pace and whispered, "When will it be safe to cut her down, Hotem?"

Hotem came to a stop and stared for a moment at the pathetic young child still tied to the flogging pillar before he spoke. There was genuine anguish in his voice when he finally said, "The poor child! She bleeds badly. Those cuts on her back are deep, but I dare not let you cut her down until Inep goes back into the house. After that, he will see nothing." With a slight hesitation, he added, "Come, Inep's not looking this way. Come with me into the storehouse."

They walked quickly to the storehouse door, which Hotem opened as he signaled the other two to precede him inside. He then entered but did not fully close the door. Instead, he kept it open just a crack, and peered out through the opening it provided. After a few moments, he closed it and faced the rest of the small group. "Good! I checked through the crack in the door. He did not see us come in here! Anah, once Inep is done gloating he will go inside. Then you can cut the child down. Take her to the women's quarters and treat her wounds. If you need medical supplies, come to me and I'll get them for you."

Anah had tears in her eyes. Her response was filled with gratitude. "Thank you, Master Hotem!"

Hotem stared at the door, and it was as though he was speaking to himself. "She is going to be quite weak until all those cuts heal. She has lost so much blood! She might not survive." As he turned to face the others, his tone became decisive. "If she lives, keep her hidden. I'll speak to the cook. I have no doubt she will help us in this matter. I saw the look of horror on her face during the whipping. Now, go out the back way, Anah, so as not to arouse Inep's suspicions. Go!"

Anah bowed. "Thank you again, my Lord!" Then she ran from the room, presumably to leave by another exit.

Hotem watched her go. Again he spoke but so softly it might

have been to himself. "I hate these situations!"

Joseph said nothing, but Hotem would have been interested in his thoughts, for he was thinking, *"Oh, how this man reminds me of my great grandfather's steward, Eleazar of Damascus! He too would have sickened at such cruelty. This man is very much like the tales I heard of Eleazar."*

Hotem was unaware of Joseph's scrutiny. "Come, Joseph. We have done all we can do here." Their exit was interrupted by the sound of running feet. This time a manservant approached the pair.

"Master! There is a trader at the gate who would speak with you!"

"Thank you. Come, Joseph. Let us meet this trader. It will be good experience for you." His unspoken comment to himself was. *"It will also let me think of something other than that poor possibly dying child!"* He motioned for Joseph to follow and led him to another door in the storehouse that opened just inside the gate to the estate. Standing outside the gates were a trader, his assistants, and his laden donkeys. The trader and his attendants all bowed deeply as Hotem and Joseph approached. With a flourish of greeting and in the ingratiating tone of the desert trader, the merchant spoke the traditional desert greeting, "Peace be unto you, Great One!"

"And peace be unto you, trader. What are your wares?"

"If it pleases you, Great One, your humble servant is a wine merchant."

"Wines? What kind of wines have you?"

"My donkeys are loaded with only the finest wines from Samarkand, Great One!"

While watching this interaction, Joseph had also been looking at the animals and their cargo. At the mention of Samarkand his head snapped around. He thought, alarmed, *"Samarkand? That's not a place but a type of rug! My father has one! Worse, those aren't donkeys, they're asses!"* Very quietly he tried to get Hotem's attention. It appeared that the Steward was unaware that something was terribly wrong with this merchant. "Ahem!" He finally coughed aloud.

"Joseph? What is it?"

Joseph, leaning close, whispered, "Master, these traders are not what they seem."

Hotem, with a look of disappointment on his face, whispered sternly, "Joseph! You are here to learn, not to advise! We shall speak of this later!"

Joseph, realizing that Hotem misunderstood, whispered meekly. "Yes, Master."

Hotem turned again to the merchant and in an apologetic voice said, "Forgive, please, my servant."

The trader looked relieved. "It is nothing, Great One!"

Joseph noticed that Hotem had apparently missed this nuance and was studying the jars on the backs of the asses. "How many jars of wine are there?" Hotem asked.

"We have twenty full jars, Great One!"

Joseph thought disgustedly. *"Oh, yes! There are twenty jars, but over half of them are empty! I can see that by the way the asses are standing! Next, he'll offer Hotem a sample from a skin, not from one of the jars."*

Hotem, still apparently unaware of the swindle, said, "May I sample your wares?"

"Of course, Great One!" With a flourish, the merchant produced a bulging wineskin along with a cup from the lead ass. With an ingratiating smile he added, "Here, I have a skin open. Allow me to pour you some!" Swiftly he opened the stopper and poured some of the blood red wine into his cup and then gave the cup over to Hotem.

Hotem made a great show of sniffing and tasting the wine, and after a few moments, he announced, "Ah, this is excellent!"

Joseph was aware that Hotem was completely taken in. In disgust he thought, *"Of course it's excellent! That's all part of the swindle! Now, he will offer the skin in his hand for our supper..."*

With a flourish the false trader handed the wine skin to Hotem and bowed saying, "Permit me, Great One. Take this skin as a gift for your excellent supper!"

Hotem, surprised at the generosity, answered, "I thank you! What is the price you ask for this excellent wine?"

Joseph fought not to roll his eyes heavenward. *"Here it comes, the price that can't be resisted."*

"We ask only the humble sum of seven pieces of silver per jar, Great One."

Hotem, with the look of a man who has just made the deal of a lifetime, winked at Joseph, and said, "Who could resist a price like that, eh Joseph?"

Joseph, playing the role of dutiful servant as best he could, answered in a pleasant voice, "Indeed, Master!" In disgust he thought, *"That's the whole point of the scam!"*

His anger at the false trader roiled, and he thought, *"Ruben and Judah would have had this thieving scum staked out in the desert for the vultures by now! Now comes the payoff — the thief will insist that his attendants unload the jars as they are used to the weight!"*

Hotem then spoke kindly to the trader. "Come, trader. Come into the storehouse and I shall pay you for your wares while Joseph sees to the unloading. . ."

"Let your man supervise, Great One! My men are used to such heavy lifting! They will have it done in a moment!"

"Why, thank you, trader!" Hotem said, "Joseph! See to it that the jars of wine are stacked on the north wall where it is cool."

"It shall be so, Master." As the trader and Hotem departed, Joseph observed the unloading, and to maintain his part in this tragedy he said to the assistants, "Remember now, the north wall!" He thought, *"What actors! They are straining like those jars are overfed camels! See, I was right! The asses do not even stir as the jars are removed! They are empty!"* The obviously empty jars were swiftly unloaded and stacked according to Joseph's instructions. Thus it was that, when Hotem and the trader returned, the assistants were astride their asses and ready for a fast getaway.

Hotem observed this and completely misinterpreted their actions. "I see that your men have all those jars unloaded! They are fast!"

The trader responded smoothly, "Thank you for your compliment! May peace and prosperity rest upon you, Great One. Farewell!"

Hotem responded affably, "Farewell and peace be unto you!" As soon as the small caravan was out of earshot, Hotem spoke to Joseph in a stern voice. "Let us go inside, Joseph. I would speak with you." They quickly returned inside the storehouse by way of the gate doorway. Once inside, Hotem turned to Joseph with a stern visage and said, "Close the door, Joseph." Joseph meekly complied. Hotem began, "Joseph. . ." It was then, that Joseph very quietly, but purposefully cut him off.

Holding up an apologetic hand, he said, "Master, there is an explanation for my actions."

Hotem was surprised and even angrier, but he acted in

restraint. "All right, explain!"

Joseph looked at Hotem and sadly said, "I fear the explanation will make you angrier still, but. . ." With that he turned and walked to the north wall where the wine jars had been stacked.

Hotem was now becoming quite indignant. "Joseph, where do you think you are going!"

Joseph's voice carried an apologetic tone when he spoke. "Just here, to the north wall, Master."

"And why are we here?"

Joseph spoke in a very quiet voice. "So that I may show you this." He then grasped one of the empty jars and began rocking it to show his master that it was empty.

A very exasperated Hotem snapped, "So that you can show me. . ." Then the realization began to dawn on him. "Wait! How are you moving that heavy jar so easily?"

Joseph, very quietly said, "Because it is empty."

Hotem was confused and now even more exasperated. "Joseph, we do not put emp . . . ty jars. . . with. . . full. . . ones." His words tumbled to a halt and his eyes widened as the full import of what Joseph was trying to tell him hit home. "Oh no! That's one of the jars they just . . ." The poor man squeezed his eyes shut and then hid his face in his hands for a few moments. He raised his eyes to Joseph, took a very deep breath, and meekly asked. "Joseph, how many of those jars are empty?"

Joseph kept his answer very quiet. "I suspect about two thirds of them."

"And the full ones?"

"I have not had the opportunity to check, but I think they probably hold water."

Hotem was now panicking. "Quickly, let us open them!" he said in a strangled whisper. Rapidly, the two began opening the seals on the jars. The results were not good at all. Hotem cried, "What a disaster! Thirteen of the jars are as empty as grudging forgiveness and seven are filled with nothing but water! Joseph, how did you know?"

Joseph kept his voice low, trying to make the blow softer. "You've never been out of Egypt, have you?"

"No, why?" asked Hotem, confused.

"Samarkand is a place, but it is renowned for its rugs, not its . . . wines. My father has one." Joseph said reluctantly.

Hotem was in despair. "Oh no!" Then he became furious. "Quickly, after them! We'll use the household guard and capture them. They'll pay for this!"

Joseph had to raise his voice to be heard. "Master, don't, please!"

"Why?"

"They were not using donkeys, Master — those were asses."

"So?"

"It's an old trick. They claim they have donkeys, which are slow afoot, when they actually have asses, which are almost as fast as camels! Asses and donkeys are often hard to tell apart. Those thieves have ridden far by this time, Master. There is no way we could catch them on foot!" Then with great deference he added, "I don't think it's a good idea to arouse Inep over this, do you?"

Hotem was aghast. "Oh, I'd forgotten about him in my anger, Joseph! I just wasted 140 pieces of my Master's silver!" He paused, wringing his hands. After a moment he continued, "This is very bad!"

"Perhaps not, Master. Come, look at these jars."

"What about the jars, Joseph?" Curious, he walked over and inspected the vessels. "Oh! These are expensive jars! They are worth as much or *more* than what I paid for the supposed wine!" After a few moments, he asked, "How is this possible?"

"I would guess they stole the jars from a master potter, then, not knowing the real value of the jars, decided to use them to cheat you." Joseph then continued in a thoughtful quiet tone. "Do we have a wagon and oxen, Master?"

Hotem realized immediately what Joseph had in mind and whispered excitedly, "I like the way you think, Joseph! Indeed, we do have wagons and oxen and I like your idea! We sell these jars, buy some good wine, and make a small profit as well! My Master gains and *we* are *not* in trouble!" Turning toward the stables, Hotem shouted. "Stable boy!"

The means to salvage the wine disaster was only the first of Joseph's keen ideas born of his business sense that he shared with Hotem. However, with each example of his prowess, he always claimed that the God of his father's guided him, giving all the credit for his sharp business and leadership skills to his God. Hotem decided that, whatever guided Joseph, it guided well! Soon the House of Potiphar was more prosperous and harmonious than it had ever been. Hotem and Joseph had only one large problem remaining — Inep. Unknown to them, that problem was being addressed by none other than Potiphar himself.

The steady increase in the quality of food, service, and morale intrigued Potiphar, and he was curious as to the cause. In an attempt to divine the true state of affairs in his house, Potiphar invited Inep to dine with him; but throughout the meal, Potiphar watched his Head of House with growing concern. Surely this man was not the active agent behind all these positive changes! Finally, Potiphar decided to take a more direct approach and said, "Inep, the meal this evening is excellent and the wine is splendid! I have noticed that the household staff has more smiles, that there is more cleanliness, and well, just more happiness! How did you manage it?"

Inep looked up from his meal, confused by the question. When he answered, it was obvious that he had no idea about the day-to-day affairs of the house. His mouth barely empty of food, the Head of House attempted to bluff an answer. "Ah, well. . . My policy of strict discipline is finally bearing fruit, Great One!" The words had barely left his mouth when the serving girl in the room slapped her hand over her mouth, bowed and ran from the chamber. Inep, who had his back to the girl, was totally unaware of this.

Potiphar knew instantly that things were very amiss. It took a great effort to keep his demeanor and continue to seem impressed by Inep's actions. "Indeed, Inep. Indeed!" He thought. *"Your strict discipline has little to do with this, I'll warrant! That is undoubtedly why the serving girl just covered her mouth to prevent herself from laughing out loud and scurried out of the room!"* Aloud, he said, "Forgive my questions, Inep. Please enjoy the meal alone for a moment while I step aside for a moment."

With a bow, Inep said, "Of course, Great One. Wine does tend to do that!"

Potiphar rose from his place and walked from the room. He was fuming. Once out of Inep's earshot, he mimicked the man aloud, "Wine does tend to do that! What an idiot!" He then thought, *"Now, where did that serving girl get to? Ah! There she is! But wait! She's talking to the cook."* His thoughts turned sly. *"Perhaps it is time to simply listen."*

The slender serving girl, Anah, was standing in the kitchen with her hands on her hips as she spoke in a truly indignant tone to the cook. "It was all I could do to keep from laughing out loud!

Imagine! That fat, lazy, cruel oaf taking credit for Joseph and Hotem's hard work!"

The cook looked up from her pots and returned, "I can just hear him." She mimicked Inep's overbearing tone. "I did it with my policy of strict discipline, Great One!" She spat on the floor with contempt. When she spoke next, she acted as though the words tasted evil. "Strict discipline! Hah! Ridiculous, unjust, and inhumane torture is what he employs in this household! That poor child he whipped for stealing bread stole nothing! I gave her that morsel! She had worked hard for it, too! She tried to tell that fat sadist the truth, but he struck her down!" There were tears in her eyes when she continued. "It has taken all Joseph's persuasiveness to get the child to eat anything after she was brutalized by Inep's whip!"

Anah stared at the floor for a moment before she responded. "I know! Hotem and Joseph have her assigned to light chores in the storehouse, doing what little she can after her beating." There was a slight sob in her voice as she continued. "Despite all we could do, she's crippled. Those cuts never healed properly."

The cook nodded. "She's still too scared to cross the courtyard most of the time, and Joseph has one of the guards escort her to and from the women's quarters because of it. The poor little thing starts crying every time she sees that blasted pillar out there!"

"She isn't the only one Joseph protects!"

"Really?"

"You live here in the main house, so as to be close to the kitchen, but the rest of us live out in the women's quarters. It used to be dark out there at night, and Inep used the darkness to his advantage." She made a face of disgust and continued. "He forced himself upon many of the women after he caught them in the dark!" Her tone changed to one of awe. "I'll never forget the day Joseph found out about that. He was furious! None of us had ever seen Joseph angry until that day. Even the guards shrank from him!"

"He yelled? I've never even heard him raise his voice?"

"That was the real wonder of it. He didn't even raise his voice. The fury just radiated from him! I'll remember his fury until my dying day!"

"So what did he do?"

"He was like an angry father, and we were his despoiled daughters. He quietly ordered torches set along the path to the women's quarters at night — every night! Then he ordered the household guards to stand watch not only at the gate but along our path! Even Hotem quailed at Joseph's fury over the attacks! Joseph went so far as to find out which women had been defiled, and then he and Hotem saw to it that those girls worked together and were escorted to our quarters after dark by two of the guards." Potiphar noted the genuine awe and admiration that the girl held for Joseph.

The cook seemed surprised. "That stopped Inep?"

Anah muttered an explicative under her breath, and then said aloud, "There have been no attacks since. Joseph and Hotem say that a man who attacks a helpless woman in the dark is nothing but a filthy coward! Joseph said that such a man fears the light and the presence of real men, and Hotem agreed."

The cook nodded and said knowingly, "Ever since that swindle with those false wine merchants, Joseph and Hotem have worked together like brothers."

"I know! I shudder to think what would have happened to Hotem if Joseph had not figured out how to salvage that disaster!"

Potiphar noticed that she was actually shivering at the thought. *"So that is the answer! Joseph and Hotem, eh? I think I need to hear more of this."* Stepping out of his place of concealment, Potiphar said in a soft voice, "Girl! Come here, please."

Quickly Anah ran to him and bowed low before him. "Yes, Master! What is it you desire?"

"To know what it was that Inep said that drove you from the room trying desperately not to laugh out loud."

Falling to her face on the floor, she cried, "Forgive me, Master! Mercy! I meant no harm, Great One!"

With a gentle and reassuring voice, Potiphar said, "There is no offense, little one. I would simply like to know who is really running things around here. It certainly isn't that fat dolt Inep!"

Still afraid to look up, Anah responded, "I fear to speak, Great One!" Then, very quietly and desperately, she added, "I fear Inep's whip."

Potiphar had heard enough. He reached down and pulled her gently to her feet so that she could see his face and said in a determined voice, "My dear girl, you may be assured that Inep will hear of this conversation only when I am ready, and even then you will not be mentioned! Now, what is this I heard about a false wine merchant?"   Potiphar was not an ordinary man but Captain of

Pharaoh's guard and quite used to finding out the truth in any matter. After a lengthy conversation with both Anah and the cook, and swearing them to secrecy, he summoned Hotem to his private rooms.

It was a nervous Hotem who entered his Master's private domain. Both stern of visage and of voice, Potiphar snapped, "Do you know why you are here, Hotem?"

"No, Great One."

"You can think of no time that you allowed your Master to be swindled? Perhaps the mention of false wine merchants will jog your memory?"

There was terror on Hotem's face as he fell to his knees and pleaded, "Forgive me, Master! Joseph saw my error and together we even managed to make a profit for you!"

Potiphar was relentless in his pursuit of the truth. "Indeed? I'll let that pass for the moment. I have also heard a disturbing rumor that several of the household's women have been despoiled by force. Is that true?"

Hotem hung his head in shame and answered in a miserable tone. "It is true, my Lord."

"And exactly what has been done about these attacks?"

Hotem looked up and his tone became hopeful. "We have placed torches along the path to the women's quarters, Oh Great One! Further, we have seen to it that men from the household guard are placed along that path each night. There have been no further attacks!"

"And these actions were all your idea, Hotem?"

Once again, Hotem hung his head. Crestfallen, he said, "I cannot take credit, my Lord. The real credit goes to Joseph."

"And I suppose this Joseph lords it over you because of this?"

Hotem shook his head in the negative. Then he spoke in a voice filled with wonder. "No, my Lord! The exact opposite is true! If he does something wonderful, Joseph gives the credit to the God of his father's! He treats me with the greatest respect, not disdain!"

Potiphar's demeanor changed from stern to pleased. "You have confirmed what I have heard from others in the household. I thank you for your wonderful honesty." His voice then hardened again. "Now it is time for *real* justice in this house!" He quietly added, "Hotem, when you leave here, I want you to look crestfallen as though you were in great trouble as you summon Inep to my rooms. Then return to the storehouse and wait."

With trepidation, Hotem responded, "It shall be as you command, Great One."

"Have no fear, Hotem. Things will move very swiftly *and* to the great benefit of all!"

"I obey, my Master!" Hotem bowed, rushed from the room, and ran to find Inep, who was lounging in his quarters.

When Hotem found him, Inep looked up at him with disdain and snapped, "What do *you* want?"

Managing to sound frightened, Hotem stammered, "The . . . the . . . Master wishes to see you immediately!"

"What is this all about?"

"The Master said it was a discipline problem."

"Discipline?" Inep came alive at that word.

It took all of Hotem's self control to look as though he were the one in trouble. He hung his head and mumbled, "That's what our Master said."

"You are dismissed! I shall speak with the Master about this!" Inep was not a thin man. In fact, he was quite fat, but in his excitement, he ran to his master's chambers. This was a mistake. He was thoroughly out of breath when he wheezed into Potiphar's rooms and stammered, "You . . . you . . . summoned me, Great One?"

Potiphar had no trouble playing his part. The sight of the fat Head of House infuriated him. "Inep! Get your whip, and summon the entire household staff to the courtyard near the flogging pillar!"

There could be no mistaking the sadistic cruelty in Inep's visage and voice as he asked, "My whip, Master?"

Potiphar's voice turned cold as ice. "Yes, Inep, your whip! It shall do much good service this night as an instrument of *true* justice!"

Inep, totally unaware of what was actually to follow, responded eagerly, "It shall be as you have commanded, Great One!"

It was not long after his interview with Potiphar that the courtyard rang with the cruel voice of Inep calling the slaves to what, he assumed, would be yet another exhibition of his strict discipline. This time the experience would be all the sweeter for the Master was here to observe him in action. From the top of the flogging platform he beheld the weakling Hotem with his pet,

Joseph. Inep knew that Hotem had, at last, gone too far. This time, Hotem's blood would run. Inep knew that he would make Potiphar proud.

Inep stared at Hotem for a moment, haughtily ignoring the looks of loathing on the faces of the guards. What were they to him? He was the Head of the House and they were, by pain of the whip or worse, to obey his every command. He assumed his usual place on the edge of the platform of the flogging pillar and then shouted in his loud "official" voice, "Silence! The Great Potiphar, officer of Pharaoh, Captain of the Guard and true master of this house, comes! He will speak to you and mete out justice." Oh, how he loved that word! He savored it in his mouth for a second before repeating it as he continued. "He will mete out justice to the vile offender! All Kneel! Potiphar comes!"

All about him, the servants and the slaves bent to one knee. How Inep loved this sight! He turned and bowed while he proudly watched his master stride toward the platform. The Master's visage spoke of his wrath. He was rigid when he stood on the front of the platform, as if he were a mighty general overseeing a battle.

Potiphar then raised his arms and spoke in a commanding voice that rang through the courtyard. "Arise!" There was much shuffling as the crowd rose to its collective feet. When they were all standing, Potiphar continued in his most serious tone. "I am forced to come before you by most disturbing events. Justice must be done in this case!" There was some quiet murmuring in the crowd, but at a quelling look from Inep, the sound died out very quickly. Potiphar ignored the interruption. Looking to Inep and holding out his hand he said, "Inep! Give your Master your whip!"

"Here it is, my Master!" Inep said, and he enthusiastically handed Potiphar his prize possession.

Potiphar stood gazing at the loathsome object in his hand for a moment, and then he glared into the face of the man who had handed it to him. He was repulsed by both. He saw nothing but cruelty and sadism in that face and his blood boiled, but he had to contain himself for a little while longer.

Holding the whip so that it did not touch him, Potiphar stood silent for only a few moments more. Then he steeled himself for the farce that would follow. It would be hard playing this part, but looking into the faces of those in front of him, he knew that he had to do it somehow. They badly needed the boost to their morale.

He took a deep breath and the shouted, "Joseph! Stand forth and be judged by your Master!" This was unexpected. There was an alarmed murmur at his pronouncement.

Before Potiphar could react, Inep stepped forward, his face full of indignation at the interruption, and he shouted, "Silence!" There was a vindictive threatening edge to his voice, and the crowd quieted very quickly.

Joseph, with the look of abject surprise on his face that Potiphar had hoped for, stepped forward and humbly said, "Here am I, Master."

Potiphar, not wishing to drop his facade, glanced away from Joseph and caught a glimpse of Inep's face. What he saw made his blood run cold. Inep's face was now a study in hatred and bloody sadism and it was all Potiphar could do to maintain his composure. When he spoke there was more vehemence in his voice than he intended, but his tone served the task Potiphar had set himself well. "You stand accused, slave! Hotem! Stand forth and testify!"

Hotem stood forth, his head high and a gleam of pride in his eyes as he announced, "I am here, my Master!"

"Hotem! Answer me truthfully! Who was it reclaimed you from that incident with the false wine merchant?"

Hotem, unable to contain his pride in his friend, announced in a ringing voice, "It was Joseph, Lord!" This was neither the question nor the answer that the crowd expected. There was much confused murmuring and glancing at one another. Joseph, realizing what was happening, was having a hard time keeping a straight face. Stealing a glance to his right, Potiphar saw the look of shock on Inep's face, which fueled his determination to continue. Looking at Hotem with what he hoped was still a stern face, for Joseph's struggle not to laugh and Hotem bursting with pride in Joseph wasn't helping his acting, he continued in an accusing tone. "Tell me and tell me truly! Who was it that has been responsible for my house prospering so?"

Hotem, his voice ringing with pride, shouted, "It was Joseph, Lord!" There was even more murmuring in the crowd. Some looked confused. Others, like Joseph, having realized what was happening, were having a difficult time not laughing and were hiding their mouths so that their very broad grins could not be seen.

Potiphar, fighting to maintain the hard visage he needed for the jest, thought, *"So much for honesty and hard work — now for compassion!"* It was then that he realized a startling fact. He did not know the name of the injured girl he was going to call up next! Potiphar was furious with himself! His voice was rough and commanding in his self-degradation, but he forged ahead. "Former serving girl from the kitchen, stand forth!"

Anah, the head serving girl Potiphar had first talked to about the situation in his house, was quick to realize who it was that he wanted. She turned to a young girl standing near her and whispered a few words to her. Potiphar, to his dying day, would never forget the look of abject terror on that child's face as Anah gently urged her forward. He noticed that her posture seemed all wrong and remembered Anah saying that the child could not walk upright due to her injuries from the unjust flogging that she had received. His anger instantly became a raging tiger clawing to escape from him. He looked to his right and allowed the rage he was feeling to show on his face momentarily.

Inep visibly quailed at this glance and realized, in that moment, it was he and not Joseph or Hotem who was on trial. He frantically looked for an escape and began inching to the edge of the platform. Potiphar noticed the movement from the corner of his eye. He glanced at the Captain of the Guard and nodded discreetly toward the fleeing Inep. Instantly the Captain signaled the guards to encircle the platform. Thus it was, that the now thoroughly terrified Inep, bereft of his authority, found himself facing grim and determined guards, the same men he had so recently scorned, their spears leveled lethally at him to prevent his escape.

Totally unaware of these things, the young child made her terrified way forward to face she knew not what. Arriving at the platform that she feared so, and that held such a special terror for her, she fell with her face to the ground and in a tremulous and muffled voice said haltingly, "Here I am, Great One." As she did so, her bowing position burst open several of the deep whip scars on her back that were still festering, despite treatment, and they began to stain the crisp whiteness of her dress.

The sight enraged Potiphar. He could not even look at the quivering sadistic coward that had done this to the child, and with a voice made far rougher by his righteous anger than he had ever intended, he managed to say, "Answer me truly! Who was it brought you food and insisted that you eat after your unjust, crippling beating, and who was it who then insisted that you be

JOSEPH Ruler of All Egypt

escorted to and from your quarters because of your quite justified fear?" Terrified beyond her wits, the child could only mumble indistinctly. Potiphar saw that Joseph was no longer looking at him but instead staring at the child's back. He saw that there were tears shining in Joseph's eyes. Now utterly enraged by the cruelty that caused the injuries, he bellowed harshly, "I didn't HEAR you!"

The child, frightened and obviously weeping uncontrollably, managed to respond, "Joseph!" And then she collapsed into a weeping heap at Potiphar's feet.

Potiphar, wishing he could hold the child and wipe away her tears, continued in a tone made rough by the sobs that now threatened him, continued. "Joseph! You are proven guilty before your peers and by these witnesses! You are guilty of the crimes of honesty, hard work, and compassion! You are condemned! Your punishment will be hard to bear! You are hereby, this day, set free! You are further sentenced to be the new Head of the House of Potiphar!"

Despite his anger at the cowering Inep, Potiphar was caught up in the wild cheering that followed his pronouncement. All he could see for the moment were the happy relieved faces of people who had just been freed from a cruel oppression. It was a sight that gives purpose to the heart of any true warrior! He found himself grinning like a fool and with tears streaming down his face, and he was clapping like everyone else, everyone but Inep. The joyous occasion was marred by his whining voice, which was filled with panic and, of all things, indignation! Over the noise he whined, "Master! What of me?"

This outburst renewed Potiphar's wrath. His iron control snapped and he allowed his true feelings free reign. "I shall deal with you presently, Inep!" Turning away from the hideous quivering coward to his right, he saw, in contrast, Joseph quietly cradling the weeping child in his arms while a worried Hotem looked on. She was clutching at Joseph and weeping freely, her face buried in his chest.

For a moment, Potiphar was overcome, and his eyes filled with tears once more but this time tears of shame for the pain that he had caused this child. Bending down, he placed a gentle hand on Joseph's shoulder. Joseph looked up but said nothing. His tear stained face spoke for him. Potiphar fought the lump in his own throat. And with difficulty, he said softly, "Joseph, take the little one up to the main house. I fear I've overstressed her in my anger at Inep! Have the cook prepare a soft bed for her in the kitchen where it's warm. Then summon a physician to see what can be done about her wounds." His visage turned hard for a moment. "I have more business here this night that you and she need not see." Softening his voice, Potiphar continued gently, "I shall personally apologize to her once I am finished here."

There was an unmistakable look of relief and respect on Joseph's face. It was clear that Joseph was anxious to leave with the child by the way he responded. "I shall do so at once, my Master!" Then, before Potiphar could say more, Joseph looked around and beckoned to someone in the crowd. He shouted, "Cook! Anah! Come. Help me with this poor girl!"

When the two women arrived by his side, Joseph spoke to the child in a kind and soft voice. "Come, little one. You have had enough for one night! You need quiet, warmth, food and rest!" The women then helped the child to her feet. It was obvious she was overcome, in great pain, and still weeping; but with a woman lending support on either side, she was able to slowly make her way to the kitchen.

Potiphar watched them silently, his anger building inside him. He waited until they were almost inside before he loudly commanded, "Inep! Stand forth!" Inep did not move from his cowering position at the edge of the platform. Angered even further, Potiphar shouted in fury, "Inep! I said STAND FORTH!" Still the former Head of House cowered at the edge of the platform, shaking and staring wildly at the flogging pillar. All patience lost, Potiphar commanded, "Captain of the Household Guard! Drag that cowardly, sniveling, pile of reeking offal before me!"

"Immediately, Great One!" The Captain very rapidly put action to word and strode onto the platform. Inep, who had no intention of being punished for his crimes, shouted a weak "No!" and tried to escape from the Captain's firm grip, but the fat former overseer was no match for the powerful soldier. Swiftly he was dragged before Potiphar and forced to his knees. "Here he is, Master!"

Potiphar, without looking at Inep, addressed the rigid soldier. "Captain! I have noted that torches are set on the path to the women's quarters at night and that there are two guards there all night long now. I have even seen women being escorted by guards.

Why is this, Captain?"

"There have been attacks on the women in the dark of the night, Great One."

"And who made those attacks, Captain?"

The Captain was unable to contain his disgust and actually sputtered when he responded, "This one that cowers before you, Great One!"

Inep, unable to remain silent, now made a feeble attempt at a defense. Though he tried to sound reasonable, the terror he felt was evident in his whining voice. "Master? Of what consequence? They are but slaves!"

Potiphar snapped, "Slave or free, they are women and as such demand respect!" Then, looking out at the crowd, he asked in a loud voice, "Women of the house of Potiphar, if any of you have been defiled by this man, step forth!" To his surprise, the response was almost immediate. Many of the household's women stepped forth and not a few loudly and boldly shouted, "I!" The look of loathing in their eyes spoke volumes. Potiphar had no idea this many had been defiled.

The Captain of the guard stared about him, and in a deeply surprised and awed voice said, "Over a third of the women of the house have stood forth, Great One!"

Potiphar, still in shock, had to take a deep breath before he could speak properly. He was so overcome he could only quietly respond. "I thank you for your observation, Captain." Then the enormity of the crime before him struck home. The tiger within him that had threatened to break loose all evening made good its escape, and with his teeth grinding together in his fury, he addressed the quivering Inep. "Do you hear this, defiler?" Suddenly, his mind cleared and control returned, but his anger remained. "The evidence against you is great and indisputable! You are pronounced guilty! You are sentenced to forty full hard lashes with the same vile bloody whip with which you have so cruelly savaged others, and if you survive the scourging, you shall be sold into slavery and banished from this estate forever!"

In desperation, Inep grabbed at Potiphar's skirt. He was weeping as he screamed in panic and fear, "Mercy! Have mercy upon me, Great One!"

In disgust, Potiphar knocked the clutching Inep away. Then in a voice filled with contempt he said, "Mercy? That same mercy you showed a poor kitchen maid who had committed no crime, the same maid who is now crippled from your unjust flogging?" Unable to contain his fury any longer, he shouted, "Mercy is DEAD to you!" Remembering the whip in his hand, Potiphar threw it to the grim faced Captain of the Guard, who caught it neatly by its handle. "Captain! Carry out the sentence with his own whip! Then have this accursed pillar and its platform torn down! And burn that whip!"

Inep, his eyes staring wildly at the blood soaked whip in the strong hands of the Captain, screamed in abject terror, "Noooooo!" His plea went unheard. All eyes were on the Captain, who responded to his Lord crisply and with feeling, "At once, my Master!"

Chapter Six
JOSEPH AND POTIPHAR

Joseph found grace in his new master's sight and Potiphar had made him head of his house, and all that Potiphar had, he put into Joseph's hand. Joseph served him well, and it came to pass that the God of Joseph's fathers blessed the Egyptian's house for Joseph's sake. The blessings of the God of Abraham, Isaac, and Jacob were upon all that he had in the house and in the field. As the years passed, Potiphar knew not what he had and did not care, so great was his trust in Joseph. The God of Joseph also guided Potiphar and blessed him in his duties to the Egyptian crown, and thus Potiphar's reputation in the court of Pharaoh was also elevated.

Unfortunately, having one's reputation increase in the court of Pharaoh had its dangers. Such esteem can lead to charges of sedition. Amenemhet III was no stranger to intrigues. His grandfather fell prey to a conspiracy in his harem and was murdered, and because of this, Amenemhet was always mindful of those who served him, especially those most near. He had devised many tests of loyalty. He decided to use the High Priest of On, Potipherah, to determine Potiphar's true loyalties. Not long afterward, the Lord Chamberlain was seeking Potiphar in Pharaoh's palace.

He searched for some time, finally finding him in one of the side corridors of the palace. Upon sighting him, the Chamberlain called out, "Potiphar! Potiphar!"

The Captain turned quickly upon hearing his name. He recognized the caller immediately. "Yes, Lord Chamberlain?"

"Come here, please! I would speak with you!"

Encumbered with his armor and weapons, the officer ran as quickly as he could to the Chamberlain. "At your service, my Lord!"

The Chamberlain greeted Potiphar most cordially. "I have heard much that is good of you, Potiphar."

Potiphar, taken back by such flattery also grew wary of such praise as he responded humbly, "I seek only to act for Pharaoh."

The Chamberlain once again applied his best flattery. "Ah, then you should know, the God on earth is aware of who acts for him."

Potiphar was unsure where this conversation was going and replied simply, "I thank you."

"Do you know the Priest of On, Potipherah?"

Thoroughly confused, Potiphar replied, "I know him on sight. As I am but a humble soldier in the House of Pharaoh, it is not for me to socialize with one as great as he."

The Chamberlain seemed to find Potiphar's answer amusing. He chuckled. "Potipherah thinks otherwise and would speak with you. Come, I will take you to him." They walked back up the corridor and into one of the main chambers of the palace, a huge room with a high vaulted ceiling where numerous people were milling about. The Chamberlain looked about the room for several seconds before he spotted the High Priest and then led the way to him.

Potipherah turned at the sound of their approach. "Ah, Chamberlain! I see you have found him! I thank you!

The Chamberlain bowed. "It is always a pleasure to serve the great High Priest of the God Ra! Shall I leave you now?"

Bowing formally to the Chamberlain, Potipherah said with great dignity, "Yes, and I thank you again!"

"You are most welcome!" The Chamberlin smiled, bowed formally, and departed.

Potipherah stood silent for a moment watching the departing Chamberlain, and then he turned to Potiphar. "Potiphar, I have heard much of you and your house."

Potiphar did not like of all this sudden attention, and his worry was conveyed in his tone when he answered the High Priest. "You have, Honored One?"

Potipherah placed a reassuring hand upon Potiphar's shoulder. Then, smiling, he said, "Have no fear, good Potiphar. All I have heard is to your credit."

"My Lord?"

Potipherah found himself approving of this man more and more. "Your humility adds to your reputation. I was impressed when you discovered the assassination plot in the royal harem. Your handling of that fiasco was inspired! Then there was the theft of the royal seal ring! I shudder to think the harm that could have been done if the ring were in the wrong hands!"

Potiphar, who did not think his part in these affairs all that great, lowered his head humbly and responded, "Honored one, I truly seek only to serve Pharaoh."

Potipherah noted the humility in his voice and his manner. "Indeed, and you serve Pharaoh with great diligence! I have also heard of your just dealings in your own home."

"In my own home, Lord?" Potiphar could think of no intrigues in his home.

Potipherah chuckled. "Do you think that your servants do not boast of their Master's deeds, *especially* when those actions are to their benefit? Many have heard of your just punishment of the fool Inep and the promotion of your current Head of House from his former position as a slave!"

Potiphar was embarrassed by these tidings. "I. . . I had not thought those events were known outside the walls of my home."

"Do not think ill of your household, Potiphar. They say nothing that is not good of you. Few of us can boast of that!"

Potiphar could not help himself. He chuckled and said aloud to himself, "Joseph!"

"Joseph?"

Potiphar was taken back. He had not realized that he had spoken aloud. "Forgive me, Honored One! I did not know that I spoke aloud!"

"There is no offense, but I would know more. Who is this Joseph?"

There was no hope for it, he had to explain. "Joseph is my Head of House. He has served me for many years now. I found it humorous that you had heard no evil. If I have heard Joseph tell disputing servants 'If you have nothing good to say to one another, and then say nothing!' once I've heard it a hundred times!"

"Do you still hear it often?"

An odd look crossed Potiphar's face. He realized something and voiced it aloud. "Now that I think about it, I have not heard such a comment from him in a very long time!"

"Do you hear many angry outbursts between the servants?"

"No, they are very rare." Then his voice became introspective. "I can remember a time in my home that all one felt was fear and all one saw were sullen looks and cowering people. I confess I spent as much time away as possible because it was so unpleasant, but that was a long time ago!" Potiphar's face cleared. "Now, I look forward to going home." He continued in a thoughtful tone. "I had not thought much on this before. I enjoy the staff. They care not only for me but each other. There is much laughter and kindness in my home, and now, I often can't wait to finish my duties to return. That is especially true when there is some unsettling intrigue here! My home is like a shelter in such a storm."

Potipherah noted the expression on Potiphar's face. He realized that this man thought little of his home except that he was comfortable there and liked those he found there. He found the other's confusion amusing. He chuckled. "It sounds as though your Head of House is a genius! How does he do it?"

Potiphar's manner took on one of great respect when he answered, "He gives all the credit for his success to the God of his fathers." He became silent as he thought to himself, *"I can't count the times he has had a dream he says came to him from his God, a dream that has helped me or my house. His ability to read the dreams of the night has done much good in my home! I have felt the power of his God in him. Never more so than when he hears of a defiler of women!"*

Noting the silence and the faraway look on Potiphar's face, Potipherah said, "You seem distracted, Potiphar."

Potiphar, alarmed that he had allowed himself to drift off into retrospection when speaking to one as important as the Priest of On, abased himself and said, "Forgive me, Honored One! I was thinking of Joseph and his God."

With an approving tone, Potipherah said, "Even these thoughts of piety do you credit, *especially* in my eyes." His tone became sad. "I see so few who think of *any* God." Suddenly, he brightened. "Potiphar! Would I be too forward if I invited myself and my family to your home?"

"To . . . to my home, Honored One?"

"Indeed! I would see this home of harmony for myself!"

Potiphar did his best to keep panic out of his voice. He humbly replied, "I would be most honored, my Lord!"

Potiphar was in no easy frame of mind as he trod homeward to tell Joseph of their distinguished guests. He knew full well that, in his position, what sounds like a compliment from such a high official as Potipherah can often be a trap. By the time he reached his home he was in a fine state of nerves. No sooner had he entered the gate than he began to call out, "Joseph! Joseph!"

Joseph was working in the gardens of the estate when Potiphar arrived. Unlike his predecessor, Joseph liked to work at the tasks of the house, liked getting his hands dirty, and he was weeding a flowerbed when Potiphar entered the estate and called out. Joseph had worked and lived at the estate long enough that he knew every nuance of his Master's voice, and he sensed a level of panic in the normally calm Potiphar. He called out, "Coming Master!" Then he ran to the gate where Potiphar stood. Coming to an abrupt halt, he bowed respectfully and asked, "What is it, Master? You sound worried!"

"Joseph! I was requested to present myself before the Priest of On, Potipherah, today! He seemed to know all about our house! Then he invited himself *and* his family to dinner!"

"This could be of great benefit to you, Master."

"It could also be a disaster!"

Joseph knew something of his Master's prowess in his duties for Pharaoh and doubted the man was in any kind of trouble. He chuckled. "I think not. You are the only one who does not see your great worth to Pharaoh! I would enumerate your virtues, but you would think I only flatter you!"

"This is no time for jesting. . ."

Joseph assumed a mock sternness, and blustered, "Who says I jest about my honored Master? I would have a word with *him*!"

Potiphar could not resist Joseph in this mode. He laughed in defeat. "I surrender! But what are we to do?"

Joseph scratched his chin thoughtfully. "I think perhaps the first step is to call the entire household together." Turning from Potiphar, Joseph called out, "Hotem!"

Hotem, who was inside the storehouse, heard Joseph's call, stopped what he was doing, and ran outside. "Yes, Joseph!"

"Please call the household together in the courtyard."

"Immediately, Joseph!"

Potiphar mused aloud, "I have not heard that command since the days of Inep!"

Sensing Potiphar's discomfort with such a meeting, Joseph added reassuringly, "I assure you, Master, that this will be nothing like one of *his* meetings!"

The call went out throughout the estate for all the staff to gather in the courtyard. Unlike the days of Inep, the household gathered quickly, and instead of the dread that always accompanied such gatherings in the past, this one was marked by quiet curiosity. Hotem noted the difference and smiled. He then noticed that Joseph and Potiphar were coming and called out, "Behold! The Master and Joseph come!" Rapidly the crowd became respectfully quiet and bowed.

Joseph took up a position in the center of the group. He looked upon all present with pleasure and could see that they were politely waiting to learn the reason for this meeting. There was no fear in their faces, and this pleased him greatly. "My fellow servants! Please, stand! The Master has come home with some exciting news! The High Priest of On will be coming here to dine in a few days with his family." There was excited murmuring at this announcement. Joseph let them wind down a bit before he continued. "Now, I know that you all do your best to see to it that the estate is kept in good order at all times, but I would ask you to please make it shine! We must not let Potiphar down in the eyes of this great one!" There was much agreeable murmuring at this statement. "Now, as you all, at times, are out in the city on errands, has anyone heard anything that should be shared here that might help us make a good impression?"

After a short pause, the Captain of the Household Guard said tentatively, "I may have heard something that might help."

With a polite gesture, Joseph said, "Please, share what you have heard, Captain."

The Captain of the Guard spoke quietly as though his information would be of little value. "In my duties, I am often near the musician's hall, and I have heard them talking. Once I heard that Potipherah will only allow musicians in his home who are modestly dressed and play quietly. They say this is because he is such a pious man."

Hotem chuckled and said loudly, "Well, we have nothing to fear there! Our women are always modestly dressed *and* respected!" There was much murmuring of assent and many heads nodded approval at this statement.

Potiphar nearly cheered himself. He said proudly, "Well said! Well said indeed, Hotem! And as for musicians, I'll pit our lovely talented ladies against any of those paid harpies!" The crowd began cheering.

Joseph, with a huge smile on his face, shouted, "It is well! It is well." Seeing that there was more, the people quieted quickly. "There is more that we may learn." Turning and bowing to Potiphar, he continued, "Master, be assured, it is indeed our own who shall entertain that night, but I have a further concern." Turning back to the crowd, he asked, "Have any of you heard what Potipherah and his family like in the way of food and drink? At this statement there was much shuffling of feet and silence. Joseph knew what to do. "Hotem! Anah!

Both of them answered at the same time, "Yes, Joseph!"

Joseph assumed a sly visage before he spoke. "I think that it is time for a little market trip for our best. . ."

Potiphar couldn't help himself, and he cut in, chuckling, "Spies?"

Joseph, with a melodramatic flourish, pretended to be shocked. "Spies? Why, Master! I was going to say our most attentive people!" The staff broke into gales of laughter.

Potiphar laughed so hard he had tears in his eyes. "Joseph, which are you, a military tactician or Head of House?"

Joseph, his tone mischievous, said, "Why Master, in this job. . ."

Potiphar chimed in and together they completed the oft repeated phrase, "You have to be both!"

It was well for Potiphar that he had held a counsel with Joseph, for unknown to them; Potipherah was indeed acting upon the orders of his Pharaoh. While Potiphar was meeting with Joseph and the staff, Potipherah was informing his wife of their mission from Pharaoh.

The home of Potipherah was an estate, and like Potiphar's, it was a small estate for Potipherah felt that the ornate palaces with their flagrant display of wealth were unbecoming of one who represented the Gods. Potipherah also found the flagrant nudity among the staff of most upper-class Egyptian homes distasteful in the extreme. The servants and staff of his home were decently clad at all times, and the usually nude musicians and dancers, so very popular in many Egyptian estates, were not welcome at the home of Potipherah.

That evening, he sat with his wife and daughter after dinner in their great room, enjoying the quiet music provided by a trio of very modestly dressed young female musicians. It was during this quiet interlude that Potipherah decided to disclose the mission he had been assigned by Pharaoh. "My wife, I have arranged for us to dine at the home of Potiphar next week."

Knumah, his wife, looked at him curiously. "You have? I am intrigued, my husband. I have heard much of this Potiphar!"

"What have you heard, my wife?"

"I have heard of his fairness and courage from my sister, the wife of Pharaoh."

"She was one of those he protected, was she not?" asked Asenath, their daughter.

It was Potipherah who answered the question. "Indeed! She discovered the plot of the second wife and the Eunuch of the harem to kill Pharaoh. Their plan was apparently to place her son upon the throne of the two lands! They had no small number of followers. It was a great feat that Potiphar accomplished!" He shook his head in remembrance of the incident. "The king was devastated! His grandfather had been killed in just such an attempt! Had not Potiphar succeeded in destroying the conspiracy, the country could have dissolved into chaos!"

"My sister says that the entire harem is still frightened and the king is distrustful of all but the first wife, now."

"I know! Did you know that it was also Potiphar who found the thief who stole the Pharaoh's seal ring as well?"

His wife was surprised by the revelation. "It was?"

"Indeed, it was! In the process, he discovered nearly all the rest of the conspirators who would have dethroned our beloved Amenemhet III! That is one of the reasons that we are going to the house of Potiphar."

"It is?"

Potipherah's tone turned serious. "Yes. The Pharaoh wants a firsthand report on this man's household, which is reported to be exceptional in its harmony. If this is true, then Pharaoh is thinking of placing far more trust in him. Having talked to the man, I feel that he is genuine, but this trip to his house will be the proof."

Knumah quietly mused, "I have heard much of his Head of House too. I believe that his name is Joseph."

"That is correct, my wife. According to Potiphar, he is as exceptional as Potiphar himself, a man who gives a God the credit for his exceptional talents."

"Two righteous men in the same house! My Husband, that is

so rare these days!" Knumah paused thoughtfully for a moment and then asked, "Why do you think so many others have forsaken the Gods?"

Potipherah shook his head sadly and sighed before he answered. "Life has become too easy. The people are too used to riches, good times, extremely erotic entertainments, wine, and much food. They forget the Gods!" He paused for a moment and looked thoughtful, and when he continued, there was much conviction in his voice. "There is something coming that will shake them to their cores. The Gods will *not* be ignored!"

Knumah was used to her husband's prophetic pronouncements, which were, more often than not, quite accurate, and she asked with genuine concern, "What is it, my husband?"

"I know neither the what nor the when, my wife. I know only that an event of inordinate import comes and that Pharaoh will know of its coming, but that is all!"

Such an admission from her husband worried her. With a shaking voice, she said, "It is small wonder that Pharaoh wants to be sure of those around him! Knowing this, is it safe to take our daughter Asenath with us to this man's house?"

Potipherah, remembering the cause of Inep's demise, chuckled. "That is the one thing in this affair I *am* sure of, my wife! The maltreatment of women is answered, quite literally, with death in that household! She will be more than safe there!"

The intervening days passed quickly for those in the house of Potiphar, and they passed very fruitfully as well. The gardens were all trimmed, watered, and mulched; the spotless walls of the estate freshly whitewashed; and the already clean rooms made, somehow, even cleaner and more inviting. Flowers were everywhere, and new colorful pennants were on the flagpoles in front of the house's pylons. Hotem and Anah, having long since been successful in their culinary "spy" mission, reported to Joseph and the cook.

Finally, the special evening came! The kitchen's fires were alight and wonderful inviting smells were coming from the cooking pits! All the servants were excited and wearing their best clothes. The tables in the great room were scrubbed, shined, and set with a very modest but gleaming table service. The musicians with their polished instruments were playing softly and beautifully in a corner of the estate's great room.

The household guards were rigid at their posts, as polished, groomed, and alert as if they were being inspected by Pharaoh himself. This then was the home into which Potipherah and his family were greeted by the tall and very handsome Joseph.

Joseph had prepared well for the arrival of Potiphar's esteemed guests. The guards on the pylons kept a sharp eye for the approaching party, and as soon as they were sighted, Joseph was summoned. The gates were thrown open and Joseph himself, flanked by two resplendent guards, stood in the center of the gateway to greet their guests as they turned into the estate from the main street.

When the dinner guests stood inside the gateway, Joseph and the guards bowed low. Joseph then greeted them in a formal, but friendly voice. "Welcome Potipherah, Priest of On, the High Priest of Ra, and special friend of Pharaoh, to the humble home of Potiphar, an officer of Pharaoh and Captain of Pharaoh's Guard. Welcome also to the very lovely Knumah, wife of Potipherah and their. . ." Here Joseph paused. He had looked up and was surprised to see the loveliest young woman he had ever beheld. She had not only the external beauty, so common in many high class Egyptian families, but she also radiated an inner beauty that Joseph could actually feel. Suddenly, he realized that he had been silent and staring. Quickly he resumed, "Welcome to Potipherah and Knumah's *beautiful* daughter, Asenath!"

Asenath was charmed. This Joseph was handsome and she could sense a power in this man that she had not felt in any other man except her father. For one short moment, they looked each other in the eye, and she felt herself blushing even as she noticed that Joseph too was showing the same effect. He quickly looked away, but for that short moment when their eyes had met, they shared something neither could explain nor define.

Potipherah was amused. He too had seen the exchange, and he found Joseph's embarrassment refreshing. He decided to ignore these young people's obvious interest in each other and continued as though nothing had happened. "I thank you for your greeting. You must be Joseph, Potiphar's Head of House."

Joseph looked genuinely surprised. "I am honored that one so great should favor Potiphar so that he knows the name of his humble Head of House! May God bless you!" The young man bowed low and then continued. "Now, Honored One, if it pleases, I would escort you into my Master's house."

Potipherah continued to be impressed with this young man. When he spoke next, his tone was genuinely warm. "It would greatly please us! Please, lead on, Joseph!" As Joseph led the way into the grounds, Potipherah was even more impressed. There were flowers everywhere, well tended trees, and beautiful lily ponds. Everywhere he looked he saw the signs of well directed industry. Finally, he remarked, "The grounds are magnificently kept!"

"I thank you! I shall be glad to tell the servants who work so hard to make them so!"

Knumah was quick to notice the omission of the head gardener. "Your servants?"

Joseph understood her concern. "We have no head gardener, my Lady. Potiphar preferred, for a long time, just a utility garden, not a decorative one. Then one of the young women got the idea of making the grounds look, well, nice. Except for the flowers to make the plot decorative, what you see before you is our vegetable garden!" Joseph ended his comments with an embarrassed chuckle.

Asenath was astounded. They had a professional gardener at home and their garden didn't look half as lush as this. Then the man insisted that this is a *vegetable* garden. "Surely you jest!" she said aloud.

Joseph began to laugh in earnest. Bowing, he said, "No, my Lady! It is not a jest. Allow me to prove it." He strode to the edge of the path, bent down, and skillfully spread the leaves of a nearby garden plot. Nodding with his head for the others to look, he said, "See here, these green fill plants? Now, look at the roots."

Potipherah bent low at his side to peer into the foliage. He exclaimed, "By my word! Carrots! And those others are onions!"

Asenath had gone from disbelief to delight as she pointed to another garden plot on the other side of the path. "Look, Father. The ground cover for those beautiful irises is a combination of lettuce and cabbages!"

Potipherah was delighted. Laughing, he said, "If you had not pointed it out, I would *never* have discovered it! This is brilliant!" While Joseph had been showing them the true nature of the gardens, Potiphar had joined them.

Potipherah noticed Potiphar's approach and, still delighted, greeted his host. "Ah Potiphar! You are brilliant! I have never seen such beauty combined with such a wealth of vegetables!"

Potiphar, who had not expected the compliment, blushed and

said with an embarrassed shrug. "I see Joseph's been showing off our garden . . . again."

Knumah giggled like a school girl. "See how he blushes! You are most modest! Such genius!"

Potiphar, still blushing, laughed and answered, "I cannot take credit for the hard work of another!"

Potipherah's mouth formed an "O" as he turned from Potiphar to Joseph. "Ah the light dawns! The genius must be this Joseph!"

Joseph smiled and bowed low as he answered. "Not I either, Honored One. This garden is the brainchild of one of our servant girls, a cripple actually. She devised this as a way to thank Potiphar." There was a rustling noise from a nearby path, and everyone turned to look. From behind a large group of river fronds, a slim hunched-over young woman emerged, and Joseph waved at her, indicating that she should join them. "Ah, this is she!"

She looked like a frightened doe, and Knumah sensed the girl's embarrassment and spoke quietly and kindly to her. "Girl, you devised this garden as a way to thank your Master?"

The young woman kept her head lowered but spoke with a beautiful quiet voice. "I did, great lady. After I was . . . hurt, everyone was so kind and I could do so little. I thought that if I could add some beauty. . ." Her voice drifted away into an embarrassed silence.

Potipherah was impressed. He saw that the blushing young woman thought her contribution was a small thing. He disagreed and it was evident from the looks of pride on Joseph and Potiphar's faces that they agreed with him. "You have succeeded in adding beauty to this household magnificently! Then, he added, in a quietly conspiratorial tone, "I suspect, from the well-fed faces I see here, that your thanks go beyond the eye!" Though her head was bowed, her smile was evident and the chuckles of her Masters verified the fact that they too agreed with Potipherah that her efforts were nothing short of miraculous.

Potiphar confirmed this. "Indeed she has, Honored One! She has done so much for one who should be able to do so little! But come! Our dinner awaits!"

The party retired to the house, and Potipherah and his family were treated to their favorite dishes. The room had been decorated with flowers, and the household musicians played softly in one corner of the room as the dinner proceeded quietly and most pleasantly. After a time, Potiphar pointed to the musicians in the corner and remarked, "I have been meaning to ask where you hired these musicians, Potiphar?"

Potiphar, with evident pride in the group, said, "They are not hired, my Lord. They are a part of the household."

Knumah stared at the group in amazement. "You have a clever artist in gardening, a wondrous cooking staff, and talented musicians all in the same house! But I sense something lacking."

"What is that, my Lady?"

"Where is your lovely wife?"

Potiphar blushed. "Ah, I am a soldier, my Lady. I have no wife." He then made a sweeping gesture to include the entire household. "Yet, of late I do have a family. My servants treat me as a father and I think of them as my family. They have made this a pleasant home, indeed!"

Potipherah, knowing all too well his wife's matchmaking tendencies, said gently, "Enough, my wife!" Wagging a mock stern finger at her, he continued. "I can hear your thoughts! You are already matchmaking!" Everyone in the room, including the musicians, laughed at this comment. He then turned to Potiphar. "Potiphar, this has been a very pleasant evening. I have another question."

"What is your question, Honored One?"

"A number of times both Joseph and yourself have referred to his God, and yet I see no shrine. Who is this God?"

"Perhaps I should leave that question to Joseph." Extending his hand toward the corner of the room, he called, "Joseph?"

Joseph, who had been seated near the musicians, rose and came to the tables. Potipherah waited until the young man was bowing before his master to repeat his question. "Who is this God to whom you give the credit for all your doings?"

When Joseph spoke, there was a quiet strength and reverence about him. "He is the God of my fathers, Honored One, the God of Abraham, Isaac, and Jacob."

Potipherah thought for a moment. "I think I remember something of this Abraham. If I remember the story correctly, he and his God were quite powerful. Tell me, Joseph, what is his name?"

With great dignity, Joseph replied, "The man you remember was my great-grandfather, but as to our God's name, Great One, we do not know it. We refer to him simply as El, or Addoni. In my language, the first means God and the second means Honored One or Great One. You see no shrine because He allows no images of Himself."

Potipherah was impressed. "A god of *great* power! He retains his name that none may have power over him and allows no images that can be desecrated. Hmm . . . You have given me much to think about, Joseph." He then turned to Potiphar and asked suddenly, "Tell me Potiphar, what do you think of Pharaoh?"

Potiphar did not hesitate. "I love him with all my heart! He *is* greatness! I would gladly jump before him in battle to take any blow intended for him!"

Potipherah nodded his approval. "It is good to hear! In parting, Potiphar, may the blessing of this God of Joseph's fathers continue to grace this house, and if I may, add the blessings of Amen Ra to rest upon it and yours as well." He paused, looking thoughtful for a moment, and then continued quietly, "I doubt that Ra will be able to do much in this household, for if I remember the stories of Joseph's great-grandfather correctly, his God is quite powerful! Pharaoh has nothing to fear and much to gain from those who dwell in this house of righteousness!"

The next day, Potipherah was among those who attended the court of the great Pharaoh Amenemhet III. When he was summoned to stand before his king, Potipherah walked with great dignity to the foot of the dais and bowed deeply before he spoke. "How may I serve you, Great One?"

Amenemhet looked at the priest for a moment and then quietly inquired, "Have you a report for your Pharaoh, Potipherah?"

Once again, Potipherah bowed, and he very quietly answered, "I have, Great One. I dined at the home of Potiphar as you requested, and I found it a home most excellently kept, a home of beauty, utility, harmony, righteousness, and love matched by few households in Egypt, Great One."

Amenemhet smiled. "It approaches the perfection of *your* home, does it, Potipherah?"

Potipherah could not suppress an embarrassed chuckle. "It exceeds it in most respects, my Pharaoh!"

Amenemhet was genuinely surprised. "Exceeds it?"

"It is true, my Lord! There is only one area in which my home exceeds that of Potiphar."

"And what would this lack be, good Potipherah?"

"Potiphar has no wife, my Pharaoh. He has been faithful in your service and has had no opportunity to seek a wife."

"Well, his Pharaoh has apparently been remiss! This shall be corrected this very day!" Amenemhet turned to the Chamberlain, who stood nearby. "Chamberlain, is the Captain of the Guard, Potiphar, present today?"

"He is, Mighty One."

"Then call him forth!"

The Chamberlain's staff once more struck the dais and intoned, "Potiphar, Captain of the Pharaoh's Guard, step forth — your Pharaoh would speak with you!"

Potiphar, who was standing guard near the entrance doors with the other soldiers, was caught off guard by this announcement. He ran forward, his armaments making a loud clattering that he wished he could have silenced. His rapid advance, along with the noise, brought all eyes in the chamber upon him. He was used to being invisible and all this attention embarrassed him. Finally, he reached the dais and bowed before the Pharaoh. "How may I serve you, Great Pharaoh?"

"It has come to my attention that your house exceeds Potipherah's in beauty, utility, harmony, righteousness, and love. He says that your household is only lacking in one way, in that you do not have a wife. I shall correct this shortcoming! Kneumet, sister of my third wife, stand forth!" To Potiphar's utter astonishment, a young woman of ravishing beauty stepped gracefully from the crowd to come forward and bow low to Pharaoh. She then stood beside Potiphar, whose mouth was agape. He realized this but had no control to shut it!

While Potiphar tried in vain to regain some measure of control, his Pharaoh spoke again. "Behold this beautiful woman. I give her unto you as your wife!"

Potiphar's head was spinning. Gaining a wife was the last thing he had expected to happen this morning! All he could do was stare stupidly at the ravishing creature now standing demurely beside him. Then, finally turning to his Pharaoh with a look of pure wonderment on his face, he managed to stammer, "Gr. . . Great One, I. . . I know not how to thank you!"

Amenemhet was greatly amused and pleased at the man's reaction. All too often he bestowed such boons only to have them glibly received. This man's reaction made the gift worth the giving! Amenemhet chuckled and said, "Continue to be faithful in my service and that shall be thanks enough."

Chapter Seven
THE WIFE OF POTIPHAR

The court of Pharaoh erupted into cheers for the fortunate Potiphar as Pharaoh placed his blessing on the pair and they were dismissed from the court. As the newly married couple walked down the center of the great hall there were blessings and greetings were shouted from all sides, but Potiphar heard little of it he was in shock.

"Congratulations, Potiphar!"
"Well done, Potiphar!"
"May the Gods bless your wedding night!"
"May your union be blessed with many healthy children!"

Unknown to all, a poisonous viper had just been let loose in the House of Potiphar. Kneumet was a deadly viper indeed, she walked proudly and maintained a sweet smile on her face, but inside she was seething. Could Pharaoh have heard the train of her thoughts, he would have been shocked and furious. *"I can't believe this is happening! Why would Pharaoh give me to this man? He is so . . so . . . old and plain! Why, in the name of all the Gods, would Pharaoh make someone so unimportant as the Captain of the Guard his brother-in-law?"* Outwardly, she bowed and smiled to acknowledge several courtiers and to maintain an appearance of joy and happiness, consoling herself with one pleasant thought. He reportedly had a very beautiful home — she would have to take comfort in that.

As the couple walked out of the palace and onto the grounds, the man kept stealing glances at her, but he kept his counsel. It was as though he was afraid to speak to her. For her own safety, she had to maintain the facade of the happy bride, but she was determined to see to it that the wedding night was as short as possible.

As they continued to walk, she wondered if this man owned a chariot. Was she, the sister-in-law to Pharaoh himself, going to be forced to walk to every single function? Well, she was going to have to do something about that! She was about to say something when abruptly they turned into a nearby estate. Looking back the way they had come, she was surprised to see that his estate was literally only a stone's throw from the royal palace! No wonder the man walked! As they entered the gate, the man — she tried to recall his name — turned to her, and gesturing to the interior of the estate, announced, "We are here, my wife!"

Kneumet was honestly surprised. The estate inside those walls was beautiful, a riot of color with flowers and trees everywhere and there were lovely pools with benches along the carefully maintained gravel walks. "I had not realized that *this* was your home! It is indeed as beautiful as I was told, and so close to the Pharaoh's palace!"

Potiphar was greatly pleased with her reaction. "I must live close to the Great One's house. I am, after all, Captain of Pharaoh's Guard and must be nearby in case I am needed. The beauty? Well, that is the result of my wonderful staff. Ah, speaking of the staff, here comes my Head of House, Joseph.

Joseph was delighted to see his Master home. Only minutes before one of the palace guards had run to the estate to give them the good news, that Potiphar had a wife. Even from a distance he could see that she was beautiful, and he was delighted for Potiphar. Bowing, he said, "Master Potiphar! We just got the good news! Congratulations! And welcome unto you, wife of Potiphar!"

Potiphar was all aglow. Suddenly, he remembered that he had not introduced the young woman at his side to Joseph. "Forgive me, Joseph! I am remiss! Joseph, this is Kneumet, my wife! And, this fellow is Joseph, my Head of House!"

Kneumet was taken aback by Joseph and became quite demure. "Greetings unto you as well, Joseph." Her thoughts were nothing Potiphar would have liked to have heard. She observed that Joseph was young, handsome, tall and well favored. Oh, that this Joseph were the Captain of the Guard and this man beside her the Head of the House! She decided that she would be seeing far more of this handsome Joseph than of Potiphar in her bed.

Realizing that she had been silent far too long, she covered by complimenting the grounds again. "My! I was told that the grounds and the house were beautiful, but the seeing far exceeds the telling!"

Potiphar was too besotted by his good fortune to notice her lapse. With pride, he laughingly said, "I thank you, my wife! It is not only pleasing to me to hear this, but I am sure that Joseph will share your comments with the staff."

Joseph also radiated pleasure at her compliments. "Indeed, you may be assured I will and speaking of the staff. . ." Turning, he gestured to a young woman who was approaching them. "Anah! Come!"

She hurried to them. "You called, Joseph?"

"Indeed, Anah, I did! I would that you should meet our new Mistress. This is Kneumet, Potiphar's new wife!"

"Greetings to you, Mistress! We have just had the news of the marriage!" She bowed to Kneumet. "How blessed is Potiphar to have Pharaoh choose for him so beautiful a wife!"

Kneumet laughed pleasantly at the flattery. "My niece, Asenath, told me of the graciousness of the House of Potiphar. I had thought her simply being polite, but now I see she understated the warmth!"

Potiphar's face was flushed with pleasure. "I am greatly flattered that she spoke so highly of our home. Anah, would you be so kind as to show my bride to her chambers?"

"It would be an honor, my Master! Mistress, if it pleases you, I will show you to your chambers."

"I would be glad to, but what of my things?"

Joseph replied quickly, "I will see to it that your things are brought to your chambers as soon as they arrive, my Lady."

Kneumet loved the sound of this man's voice and responded demurely, "I thank you, Joseph."

Anah gestured toward the house. "This way, my Lady." Kneumet bowed to Potiphar and gracefully followed Anah into the main house.

Joseph watched them for only a moment. He turned to Hotem, who had joined the group in the gateway. "Hotem. Would you be so kind as to have two or three of the men take the new Mistress's belongings to her chambers when they arrive?"

"It would be a pleasure, Joseph!"

Potiphar was staring after his new bride. When he spoke, his tone was wistful. "Is she not beautiful, Joseph?"

Joseph could not resist the humor of the situation. "Indeed, she is! However, you sound like a schoolboy with his first crush!"

Potiphar looked embarrassed. "Is it that bad?"

Joseph saw the besotted look on his friend and Master's face. "You have a case of utter infatuation, and indeed, it is written on you as if on papyrus! But if it will make you feel any better, if our fortunes were reversed, my state would be worse!"

"How am I to treat a wife, Joseph? I am a soldier and have no experience with a wife."

Joseph was surprised. "You're asking me? I have no wisdom in this matter, Master. Like you, I am as a babe in this situation!"

Hotem, who had returned from detailing two men to move the Mistress's things to her rooms, joined the conversation. "What is this I hear of babes in such situations?"

Potiphar was glad this man had joined them. "Ah, Hotem. You are the man of the hour!"

"I am?"

"You're married!"

Hotem threw up his hands as though in defense. "Oh, I do not like this proclamation! It seems to me that you are promoting me to the office of Master of Husbandry!"

Joseph intervened. "Yet, it is true that you have a wife, good Hotem!"

"Yes! But it would be more true to say that she has me!" The group laughed heartily.

Potiphar's face took on a serious cast. "Yet, despite your disclaimer, it must be true that you have some knowledge of what a wife wants?"

"That, Master, is one of the great secrets of the ages! For to my knowledge, no husband knows truly the thoughts of a wife!"

Anah had come upon the group unawares and had heard enough to understand Potiphar's dilemma. She decided to have a bit of sport with these men, who seemed so at a loss about marriage. "And what is this you speak of, wives' thoughts, my husband?"

Hotem was surprised at her seeming appearance out of nowhere. "My wife! I had not heard you return!"

"So it would seem."

Potiphar, who misunderstood Anah's comments, quickly interceded. "Be not cross with your good husband, Anah. The fault is mine, for I had asked him, since he is married, how best to please a wife."

Anah wasn't through with Hotem. "Nay, good Master. *You* have nothing to fear in pleasing a wife!" Seeing the crestfallen look on her husband's face, she relented. "Or you either, my good husband, or any man of this house! For the men of this house are gentle, kind, considerate, and compassionate, and yet, they are also just, strong, and brave, especially you, Master. What more could any wife desire? You need only be with her as you are with all of the women of this house and she will love you deeply!"

Anah did not reckon in her discourse with that poisonous viper, desire. The heart of Kneumet sought not after true happiness, but rather, after those fleeting ghosts: passion, position, and possession. She looked not to the heart, but to vain appearance and fleeting sensation. She thought not of lasting loving smiles, compassion for others, the pleasing laughter of children, nor even the comforting warmth of a loving arm in time of trouble! Like the vile Inep, she had other, less wholesome appetites.

The new Mistress and her maids stayed in their quarters most of the time, but there was something about them that made the rest of the staff uncomfortable. They were forever going to parties without the Master, but it was also the nature of some of those parties and the way that the Mistress and her attendants dressed that most alienated those of the House of Potiphar.

One afternoon, six months after Kneumet arrived, Anah was walking in the gardens, trying to calm down after another silent run-in with one of Kneumet's maids-in-waiting. There was much about the Mistress and her entourage that did not please her, but perhaps least of all, the haughty stares of the woman's maid servants. Being lost in her own thoughts, she was startled by a rustling sound in the flowerbed near her. Looking down, she discovered Benar, the young woman who had so long ago been a child victim of Inep's cruelty.

Normally, the sight of Benar peacefully working in the gardens would not have bothered her, but today was different. "Benar! What are you doing? You know that the physician said that you should rest. He has just done the last of the surgeries on those horrid scars upon your back. Do you wish to undo all that was done?"

Benar lowered her head contritely. "Be not angry with me, Anah. The day is so beautiful and it is pleasant here in the shade."

"You are indeed in the shade, but I fear what Joseph or the Master will say if they find you weeding the flowerbeds!"

Benar peered up at Anah with a look of pleading in her eyes. "But I do enjoy it so! The soil feels good in my hands!"

Anah could not resist those eyes. She said laughingly, "I hear tales in the marketplace of servants who cannot be gotten to work, and I can't get *you* to stop!" Both women laughed. "Oh, very well, but be careful. If you overdo it and become ill, the Master will be truly upset."

"I will be most careful, Anah," Benar said contritely. Anah departed chuckling and Benar resumed her quiet industry. After a few minutes, she heard footsteps. Curious as to why Anah had returned, she peeked through the foliage. With a start, she realized that the person coming was not Anah but Kneumet, the Master's new wife. The woman was dressed in an extremely thin, almost transparent, shift. She sat down on a bench not five feet from where Benar was working. Benar was shocked at the woman's lack of modesty. She was also determined not to disturb the new Mistress and bent to her task as silently as she could.

Then she heard someone else approaching. Peeking curiously out through the leaves, she saw that it was Joseph walking down the path. Kneumet too had noticed Joseph and hailed him in her most seductive voice. "Joseph, would you care to join me?"

Joseph bowed and responded, "What is it that I can do for you, Mistress?"

Kneumet leaned forward in her most seductive pose and purred, "Lie with me."

Joseph, taken aback, chuckled nervously, "Surely you jest, Mistress!"

Kneumet changed her position to one even more seductive and revealing. Then, in her most enticing voice, she said, "Am I jesting? You are handsome, and am I not desirable? I want you. So, again, I say that you should lie with me."

Benar, who was a silent witness to her Mistress's bold attempt at seduction, could only sit dumbfounded at such blatant adultery! Joseph too was shocked and let it show in his voice. "Mistress! Behold, my Master has committed all that he has to my hand. There is none greater in this house than I. Neither has he kept back anything from me but you, because you are his wife. How then can I engage in this great wickedness and sin against God? I cannot do this that you ask!" Without another word, he bowed to her and, turning on his heel, hurried away from the adulterous wench.

Kneumet only smiled. She was undeterred. Her voice was still seductive when she said quietly to no one in particular. "Oh, so you're playing hard to get. Good! I like a challenge!"

Kneumet rose and made her way back to her quarters, leaving

Benar sitting dumbfounded. Unable to contain her thoughts any longer, she whispered aloud, "What manner of woman is this that has married my Master?"

Benar returned to the house, appalled by what she had seen. She was proud of Joseph for refusing the advances of Potiphar's unfaithful wife, but her heart ached for her Master. She loved him greatly for his kindness to her and could not bear to see someone be so unfaithful to him.

Sometime after this, Asenath, the daughter of Potipherah came to visit her aunt Kneumet but did not feel welcome. Oh, the staff welcomed her with open arms and seemed genuinely pleased to see her, but her Aunt Kneumet did not seem to want Asenath around and seemed to find excuses to send her on meaningless errands. One day, Asenath found herself on the way to the estate's kitchens on yet another spurious errand. She was proceeding down the long corridor to the kitchen when she heard someone weeping further along the passageway. She was unsure as to what to do. Her first thought was to leave, but then curiosity got the best of her. She crept forward quietly until she could hear what the weeping person was saying. After a few moments she recognized one of the voices as that of the cook.

"Benar, why are you weeping so?"

Benar's voice came in broken sobs. "I . . . weep . . . for the Master . . . and for poor Joseph!"

The mention of Joseph caused Asenath a moment of unexplained panic, and she thought, *"What has happened to him?"*

The Cook had the same question. "What has happened, Benar?"

The distraught girl had to take a moment to steady her voice before she continued. "It is the new Mistress! She is unfaithful to the master! She . . . she tries to seduce Joseph and chases him all over the estate! Her voice took on a scandalized tone. "The way she dresses. . ."

The cook actually snorted in disgust. "Dresses? Don't you mean undresses? I have seen her too, Benar! She may as well be naked! The slut won't leave poor Joseph alone! He literally has to hide from her!"

Benar nodded her agreement. "Then she tells the Master that she is ill when he desires her. She is so unfair to him!" Benar began weeping once more.

Asenath thought, "My aunt rebuffs her husband and plays the whore after his Head of House? What manner of a woman is this aunt of mine?" Hearing footsteps, she ducked into a corner and waited. The cook identified the newcomer.

"Ah, Anah! Welcome."

"And a fair good morning to both of you!" She hesitated for a moment, and then continued. "What is the cause of these long faces, especially you, Benar? Why have you been weeping?"

Not waiting for Benar, the cook responded angrily, "It is our new Mistress, her. . ." She paused and continued very quietly. "It is her whoring after the men of the house, especially Joseph!"

Anah's voice when she replied was sad. "I should not tell you this, but the Master is aware of her sly and unseemly ways, and he is brokenhearted."

Benar seemed to take interest in this. "He is aware? How?"

"My husband, Joseph, and few of the others that she has propositioned were angrily discussing the problem in the storehouse one evening and Potiphar overheard them. He was furious at first, thinking them disrespectful of his new wife, but when he realized that they were telling him the truth, he wept."

The cook's voice expressed her awe. "I have not seen him weep since the night, long ago, when he apologized to young Benar for not dispatching Inep sooner. What is he going to do with the adulterous vixen?"

Anah was silent for a moment or two before she replied simply, "Nothing."

Both of the other two women responded together with an astonished. "Nothing?"

Asenath too was astounded. Her aunt the woman may be, but her father would have had such a vile creature torn limb from limb by four oxen for such blatant adultery, and this man did nothing?

Anah's reply was resigned. "That is the true tragedy of it all. She is sister-in-law to Pharaoh. Exposing her for what she is would hurt Pharaoh and she knows it. I know that Potiphar tried to talk to her, and she threatened him with precisely this. She said she would go to Pharaoh and tell him — you would not believe the things she would have falsely testified to Pharaoh about our Master!"

Asenath was at once both ashamed and aghast. The idea that her aunt would use her position to blackmail the innocent so that she could continue her adulterous activities made Asenath angrier than she had ever been in her life. Her anger was shared by the cook.

"And what of the truth about her? Are you not aware of the parties she attends?" The cook's voice dropped to a conspiratorial whisper. "Parties at the house of Seneb?"

Asenath was shocked. She had heard her father angrily raving about that place, which he said was nothing but a brothel! What on earth would her aunt be doing in a place like that? Anah seemed aware of this too.

"We are aware that she goes to that horrid place! Heaven only knows in what vile perversions she indulges in there! "She goes to a house of prostitution to be . . . entertained, who knows how, and threatens to expose our honorable Master to Pharaoh with her lies of perversion!" Anah paused, and it was plain that she too was now near to tears. "The Master is at his wit's end over this!"

Asenath could feel hot tears forming in her own eyes. What must these good people think of her? She was, after all, the niece of nothing more than a common whore! It was Anah who supplied the answer to Asenath's unspoken question.

"Her personal perversions are not the worst of it. The Master dreads to expose her for another reason. She comes of a very good family. Her sister, the wife of Potipherah, is a model of grace and propriety, and their daughter, who visits us here, is as sweet and chaste as the morning dew! The Master and Joseph protect them with their silence as well. Anah paused for a moment. "They both expect some vile trick from her soon, but they have no idea what it might be or how to deal with it when it comes!"

Before she could say more, there was a piercing scream. "What was that?" Anah asked the room in general. Before anyone could answer, the scream was repeated only louder.

It was the cook who identified the source. "That sounded like it came from the Mistress's quarters!"

Asenath heard the women rush from the kitchen, and she followed in time to see the last of them depart through a corridor at the far end of the kitchen. She followed as they rushed along several other corridors and finally up a flight of stairs to rooms on the second floor. Asenath immediately recognized these rooms as her aunt's apartment, and she pushed through the crowd to the forefront. She saw her aunt clutching a white linen garment and weeping hysterically. What struck her first was the way she was dressed. The garment that she wore was so sheer as to be transparent, just as the cook had described! The combination of the woman's nakedness and what Asenath now perceived was false weeping made her very angry and apprehensive at the same time. Hotem, the Steward, had been one of the first to arrive and asked, "Mistress, what is it? What has happened?"

Kneumet, with much dramatic weeping and gesturing, held out the garment she had clutched to her and cried out, "See, Potiphar has brought in a Hebrew to mock us. He came unto me to lie with me, and I cried with a loud voice. It came to pass, when he heard that I lifted up my voice, that he left his garment with me and fled!" As soon as she concluded her speech, she began weeping and wailing once more. As if on cue, her maids joined her. The din they created filled the entire house!

Asenath was disgusted. She could have hardly missed the vile ethnic slur in her aunt's tirade, saying the word "Hebrew" as though it were an explicative. Such bigotry enraged her. Then there was the matter of her weeping and wailing. There was not a trace of a tear in her eyes! This was nothing but a vulgar and deceitful show, and even her maids were party to the deception, wailing as falsely as their Mistress. It was obvious that Kneumet had engineered the entire episode. Asenath heard the whispered dark muttering from those assembled.

"The execution of the four oxen would be too good for her!"

"The vile whore!"

"A quick death is too good for her!"

"Aye let the lying whore be staked in the desert for the vultures!"

Unknowing, or perhaps uncaring, of the dark glares and angry muttering, Kneumet continued her vile display. She had apparently prepared for this foul performance. Thus, she continued her loud false weeping, and she laid up Joseph's garment by her, where she said it would remain until Potiphar came home.

At Kneumet's command, Joseph was "arrested" and one of the guards was dispatched to the palace of Pharaoh to fetch her husband. The man returned shortly with Potiphar. Instead of going into the house, Potiphar stopped at the storehouse. After a short time, the guard came out and began assembling the household in the courtyard. Potiphar remained inside the storehouse with Joseph and Hotem until the people of the estate had gathered.

In the very midst of this household gathering were Kneumet

and her weeping maids. Kneumet had changed her clothes and now wore a very modest garment, but she still clutched Joseph's garment to her chest and was weeping loudly. As soon as Potiphar made his appearance, she began her tearful story. "The Hebrew servant, whom you have brought unto us, came unto me to mock me. It came to pass, as I lifted up my voice and cried that he left his garment with me and fled!"

Potiphar was so angry that his face was splotched and brick red. He stared at his wife darkly for a few moments. Unmoving, he seemed an angry statue. Then he called out in an oddly calm voice that was at odds with his angry visage, "Joseph! Stand forth!"

Joseph, unencumbered by any form of restraint, stood forth and calmly said, "Here am I, my Lord."

Asenath was astounded by the apparent calmness of both Joseph and Potiphar. She now knew that nothing good was going to come of this proceeding, but what struck her most was the bravery of these men! They knew the evil end that they were facing and they did not flinch.

Potiphar looked Joseph in the eye and asked calmly, "What is this that you are accused of? What have you to say for yourself?"

Joseph, who was equally calm, started to respond, "My Master. . ."

This show of utter restraint enraged Kneumet. She was being ignored and she wasn't about to stand for it. She screamed, "What insult is this?"

Potiphar refused to rise to the bait. His tone was quiet and reasonable when he answered her. "Insult, my wife? It is my task. . ."

Kneumet was in a screaming fury. "Your *task* is to uphold the honor of your wife! This servant's very appearance is an insult to me! Why is he not in chains? Where are the marks of the lash upon him? Why is he not lying upon his face in fear before me, pleading for his miserable life? No! He is boldly, proudly even, upright, and without a mark upon him; and, he is being calmly asked for his version of what happened like . . . like . . . an equal?" She stood at her tallest and assumed an imperative air. Then in a pompous tone, continued, *"I* am an Egyptian and the sister-in-law to Pharaoh himself! What is he? *He* isn't even Egyptian! He's . . . he's . . . HEBREW! He is the son of shepherds and thus barely human!"

Kneumet's outburst did not have the desired effect. She had

long since lost her audience, all of whom glared at her, murmuring and whispering.

Anah was angered and sickened. She whispered angrily to herself, "Egyptian is she? She's an insult to Egypt! Whereas Joseph has the dignity, honor, bravery, and appearance of Pharaoh himself! Yet it will be poor Joseph who suffers the punishment for *her* sins!"

Asenath overheard Anah's whispered comment. She was in tears. Anah had spoken the unspeakable truth. She too knew that Kneumet would demand the severest of punishments for Joseph, death. Unbidden, whispered angry words escaped her lips. "Who will demand such a just punishment for you, oh aunt? Who will see you rightly rewarded for your vile sins?" Then a powerful reality struck her. "The God of Joseph!" she whispered in awe.

Potiphar let the babble build for a few moments, then he shouted, "Silence!" The crowd quickly quieted, and he continued. "Very well, wife!" He turned and gestured to the Captain of the household guard. "Captain!"

"Master!"

"Bind the prisoner and secure him in the storehouse until. . ."

Kneumet was in a livid rage. She mocked Potiphar with his own words. "Bind the prisoner and secure him in the storehouse. . ." She then screamed, "What farce is this? Do you think I am an infant? Do you think that I do not know that you plan to feed him well and allow him to mock me in his bed away from my sight with the whorish sluts of your house!"

Had it not been for the guards with their spears, Kneumet would have been torn to bits by the crowd. She ignored their rage as beneath her and screamed at the top of her lungs. "I know what you are! You are nothing! *"I* am of the house of Pharaoh! Do you think that your puny impotent wrath is of importance to ME!" Turning from the household, she faced Potiphar, and pointing at Joseph screamed, "If this villain is to be merely imprisoned, then it will be in the Pharaoh's prison, where *you* have *no* control! If this is not so, then I will see your head, *Potiphar,* upon a pike and this entire household sold into slavery!"

A stunned silence followed this pronouncement, but then Asenath shouted, "Aunt Kneumet! You surely cannot mean all this! You would punish honest people. . ."

Kneumet turned on her in fury. "Silence! I will not be lectured to by a self-righteous and hypocritical child! You think that I do not know that you secretly would sleep with this . . . this *animal* and you think to lecture ME!"

Asenath's jaw dropped! She was flabbergasted. She cried indignantly, "Aunt Kneumet! I have. . ."

Potiphar interceded. He roared, "Silence!" Absolute quiet followed. The Captain of the Guard noted that the man's face was filled with rage, the likes of which he had not seen since that fateful night Inep met his much justified end. Yet this glare was not directed at the silent and dignified Joseph. Instead, he stared steadily at the willful Kneumet. The woman had been stripped of all semblance of beauty by her avarice and hatred. The Captain would not have been that wench for the entire world!

Potiphar looked at the Captain, and now the man saw pity in those eyes. He knew what the command would be when his Master spoke, and he dreaded it. Finally, Potiphar spoke slowly, "Captain, take Joseph to Pharaoh's prison."

The Captain nearly wept, but somehow he managed to keep his voice clear when he answered sadly, "It will be as it is ordered, Great One." His response, and the glare he leveled at Kneumet, made it clear who it was who desired this. Bowing to Potiphar, the Captain slowly walked toward Joseph, who merely nodded to Potiphar and turned silently to walk with the Captain toward the estate's gateway. The Captain could not bring himself to lay hands on him but simply walked beside him. As they approached the gates, he called out quietly, "Open the gates." In the stillness that had settled upon the courtyard, even this quiet command resounded as if shouted. Wordlessly, the guards at the gate complied. Unseen by the rest of the household, they bowed as though to Pharaoh when Joseph passed through the gates. They knew he had done nothing and bowed to show their respect for his courage.

The rest of the household saw none of this. They lost sight of Joseph and the Captain as they entered the gateway, but they listened silently and unmoving as the Captain called, "Open the gates." And then, just moments later, they heard those same gates slam shut with a crash like the knell of doom for poor Joseph. They all felt the sounds of the gates crashing closed in their chests.

Turning away from the gate, the household saw Potiphar standing still as a statue in the center of the courtyard. After several moments, Potiphar's agonized, quiet voice was heard. "This proceeding is concluded. All, return to your quarters."

The only sound now was the quiet shuffling of many feet sadly departing. Some stood silently and sullenly watching the proud Kneumet, her head held high and a satisfied expression on her face, sweep triumphantly from the scene to return to the house.

Hotem watched his beloved Master. He had never seen the man look so defeated, not even when his closest childhood friend, Henaket, was killed in battle. Without thinking, Hotem walked to Potiphar and whispered, "Master, please come with Anah and me to the storehouse for a while."

Potiphar seemed in a daze, and it took him a moment to realize who had addressed him. "Hotem?" He asked quietly.

"Yes, Master. It is I. Please, come!"

Potiphar seemed a broken man for the moment. He hung his head and mumbled, "Very well."

Anah and Hotem led Potiphar to the storehouse, where he sat before the fire and said nothing. Anah was worried. She whispered to her husband, "Hotem, it has been over an hour now, and the Master just sits and stares into the flames of the fire, saying nothing."

"I know, my wife, I know. This has been hard on him. Potiphar, Joseph, the Captain and I talked of the possibility that this woman would do something rash days ago, and we discussed what the results might be. Sadly, it was Joseph who foresaw it correctly."

"Joseph expected this?"

"He did. Potiphar thought that he could control the situation and keep Joseph out of prison. So did the Captain, and so did I."

"But could not have *something* been done to prevent Joseph unjustly going to prison?" Anah asked.

"You heard that whore. If we had not acted as we did, everyone would have suffered greatly — perhaps there would even have been deaths. We. . ." Unable to continue, Hotem burst into tears.

Anah, with tears in her own eyes, cradled her brokenhearted husband and said softly, "Peace, my husband. I see now that there was nothing more you could have done."

The door to the storehouse opened and closed quietly as the Captain of the Guard entered. When he saw the startled stares on those in the room, he announced, "It is only I, the Captain of the Guard." He sounded utterly exhausted.

Potiphar seemed to come alive at the sound of the man's

voice. "Captain?"

The Captain looked startled. "Forgive me, Master. I did not see you there!"

"There is nothing to forgive, Captain. What news of Joseph?"

The Captain sounded as though he would weep, but he held himself in check. "It was as we feared, Great One." Then, unexpectedly, he did break down for a few moments. "Forgive me, Master!" He took a few deep breaths to steady himself and then continued in a ragged voice. "I told the chief guard of the prison that Joseph had done nothing wrong and that he should be treated fairly. I was told to mind my own business for he was now the property of Pharaoh, and they slammed the door in my face!" He paused for a moment. "Through the door, I heard them use the lash and Joseph cry out in pain as soon as it was shut!" He lowered his head in shame. "I could bear no more! I. . . I ran from that place like a craven coward!"

Potiphar understood. He motioned to Anah, who came quickly to his side. "Anah, see to the Captain. He has been through enough for tonight." Turning and facing his steward, he said, "Hotem, see to it he sleeps, and have his second in command take the watch until he wakes. I am going out into the garden for a while. I'll return shortly, as I will sleep here." His voice turned cold. "I can't stand the thought of being in the same house with that . . . that *woman* tonight!"

Hotem understood fully. "I will make your bed myself, Master. It will be here by the fire when you return."

"Thank you, Hotem." With that, he opened the door to the gardens and stepped outside. Potiphar's footsteps sounded loudly in the freshly raked gravel of the pathway, and he found the sounds of the night, the crickets and a few night birds, quite soothing.

After a few moments, he reached a secluded spot in the garden, and he fell to his knees as he had seen Joseph do many times. Into the night air, he said his first prayer to the God of Joseph aloud: "Oh, God of Joseph's fathers, hear me! Joseph has done nothing wrong that he should be imprisoned here in Egypt! Forgive me for being so weak and allowing this to happen!" The tears he had contained all afternoon and through the evening now flowed freely. After a while, he continued. "Be with him in that awful place and, if it is possible, comfort him. Oh, God of Joseph, if thou will, be with me also that I may be an instrument to help in his rapid release." Again, he gave in to tears, but somehow they were different. He wasn't alone. These were cleansing tears. He felt warmth in his soul he had never felt before: he was greatly comforted by this unseen and unnamed God of Joseph's.

The God of Joseph heard Potiphar's humble brokenhearted prayer, and Joseph's God was with Joseph and showed him mercy, giving him favor in the sight of the keeper of the prison. The keeper of the prison committed to Joseph's hand all the prisoners that were in the prison. Whatever they did there, he was in charge of it. The keeper of the prison looked not to anything that was under his hand. The Lord was with him, and that which he did, the Lord made it to prosper. Just as Joseph's God protected Joseph and comforted the broken hearted Potiphar, his righteous wrath was kindled toward the willful Kneumet.

Thus it came to pass a few days later during the court of the great Pharaoh Amenemhet III that the wrath of the God of Joseph fell full force. The court had assembled as usual, and the business of the day was progressing swiftly. The Chamberlain was just announcing another petitioner when a tremendous flash of lightning filled the hall with light. This was followed immediately by a deafening clap of thunder. So close had been the lightening strike that everyone's hair stood on end. The day turned dark and cold, and there was a downpour going on outside. Amenemhet was awed and frightened. He seemingly asked the room as a whole, "What is this? Just moments ago it was warm and the sun was shining. Now, it is cold! It is dark enough to light the torches and we are having a cloudburst!"

Potipherah had quickly come to the side of his Pharaoh after the thunderclap. He too was frightened by the lightening and the storm, but for a different reason than the rest. He knew its meaning. "My Pharaoh, there can be only one meaning for such an event. One of the Gods is angry and is about to wreak punishment on a guilty defiler!"

There was a commotion at the chamber entrance, and one of the guards burst into the hall, ran up to the dais, and fell on his knees before the Pharaoh. Potipherah sensed something terribly amiss and demanded, "What is the meaning of this, guard? Why do you burst in upon the court in this fashion?"

The guard was badly frightened. "Forgive me Great One, but the raven has dropped a black feather at your door, Great Pharaoh!"

Amenemhet was taken aback. First, there was this unexplained storm, and then Potipherah had announced that these events were the result of a God's anger. Now, this guard brought tidings of ill omens. "An ill omen, indeed!" he said cautiously. "What has happened?"

The guard, his face pale, pointed back toward the front of the palace, then bowed low in fear. "Your sister-in-law, Great Pharaoh, the sister of your third wife and the wife to Potiphar, was coming to the court riding in an ox-drawn chariot. She was just outside the gate when the storm struck. Lightning hit one of the trees near the front gate. The ox panicked and bolted, running headlong into the canal across the road from the palace." His fear was evident as he continued. "Master! Great Pharaoh! All in the cart were killed: your sister-in-law, her serving girls, even the ox!"

Chapter Eight
THE BAKER AND THE BUTLER

The God of Joseph did not forget Potiphar. Because he had sought the Lord, his house did not suffer, and according to his request, the Lord had just put into Potiphar's hands the means to ultimately bring Joseph to the Pharaoh's attention. The Queen's jewels had been stolen, and Potiphar was now in hot pursuit of one of the suspected thieves, the Chief Baker. The man was overweight, but at the first sight of Potiphar he ran, and surprisingly fast. Potiphar had to exert quite an effort to keep up with him. Finally, the man ran into a dead end corridor and Potiphar had his quarry cornered.

Wary of armed resistance, Potiphar stopped some distance from the panting Baker and had pulled one of his daggers in case the man tried to escape by violent action. For a few moments, the Chief Baker stood looking wildly about as if trying to find an escape through solid walls. Then, with a look of desperation, he tried the only avenue he felt was left open to him. He tried to bluff his way out of the trap. Sweating profusely and still panting, he pulled himself to his full height and tried to pull rank on Potiphar. "Why do you pursue me? I am an important person in the house of Pharaoh!"

"Then why flee when I first hailed you, Baker?"

Puffing himself up with all the indignation he could muster, the man made a second futile attempt to intimidate Potiphar, barking, "I will not be spoken to thus by such as you! I am. . ."

Potiphar was having none of it, cutting the Baker off, he shouted, "Under arrest!" Pointing to his own chest with his drawn dagger, he said, "*I* am Captain of Pharaoh's Guards, Baker! When there is a threat to the Pharaoh, I have authority over any in this house!"

"What nonsense is . . . ?"

Potiphar was done with this man and commanded, "Silence!" At this point, two of the Pharaoh's guards came pounding into the corridor. Potiphar signaled to them to come forward, pointed to the panting baker, and ordered curtly, "Bind him and take him to the court of Pharaoh. I will follow you in a moment. I saw the other man I am supposed to bring in farther down the other hall."

One of the guards saluted smartly and responded, "It will be as you command!" The pair moved to the Baker as warily as had their commander. The man was quickly subdued, though he struggled with all his might. Using the point of his sword to prompt the fat man, one of the guards growled, "Come on, you! Move!"

Potiphar had rushed back into the main corridor and was now looking first up and then down the hallway. He once more spotted the other man he was to arrest, the Chief Butler. Hoping to avoid another weary chase, he called out, "You! Hold!"

The butler simply turned to look at Potiphar and made no attempt to run. He only seemed surprised at being so rudely ordered. His answer, however, was simple, dignified, and quite polite, "Sir?"

Potiphar was doubly wary at this man's reaction. Either he was innocent of any crime or he was very, very dangerous. Potiphar took no chances. Again producing his dagger, he commanded. "Hold where you are, Butler!"

The Butler stared at the exposed weapon. His fright was very evident, and yet he asked, "Sir, what is it? Why have you need of me? Why do you draw your weapon?"

Potiphar closed the gap between them and pinioned the man. "You are under arrest and will be taken to the court of Pharaoh, immediately!"

The Butler was now genuinely frightened. "Why am I being arrested?"

Potiphar's orders were specific. He was to bring the suspects to the court with as little foreknowledge as possible. To that end, he said simply, "You will know that when you get to the court."

The Chief Butler made no attempt to escape, meekly allowed himself to be bound, and walked silently before the well-armed and determined Potiphar as they made their way through the palace to the main hall. When they arrived, the place was alive with angry murmurings. People stared at the butler with loathing in their eyes as he and Potiphar made their entrance.

The Chamberlain turned when he became aware of Potiphar's entrance. "Ah, Potiphar! You have brought the Butler!"

Potiphar bowed to the man. "I have, Lord Chamberlain."

The Chamberlain returned the bow, which was not necessary

given their difference in station, but he felt that bowing was well deserved in this case. Turning, he struck his staff of office upon the floor and loudly announced, "My Lord, Pharaoh, both of the men accused with the theft in the harem have been caught and are present."

Amenemhet bowed slightly from his throne to the Chamberlain. "I thank you, Lord Chamberlain. Have them brought before me." Quickly the two men were brought before Pharaoh and both were made to lie prostrate before his throne. He studied the two men before him silently for a few moments. His look did not bode well for the accused. After a few moments, he turned to the priests who stood at the side of the hall. "Lord Potipherah, Priest of On, have you or the magicians determined who it was that stole the jewelry from my wife's room?"

Potipherah stood forth from the group and bowed to the Pharaoh. He sounded tired when he addressed Pharaoh. "We have not. The case is an odd one, my Pharaoh. Only these two were known to have been near the Queen's chambers at the time of the theft, yet the items have not been found and the Gods are silent on the matter."

Amenemhet nodded to the apparently exhausted Priest. "I thank you Priest of On and those who have assisted you." He then turned to Potiphar. "Captain of the Guard, what is the report from the guards?"

Without a preamble, Potiphar reported. "The rooms of both of these men have already been searched thoroughly, but nothing was found. The search continues, my Pharaoh."

Amenemhet again nodded his thanks. "You have done well, Potiphar. I know you will leave no stone unturned in this matter. Place these two in my prison while the investigation continues."

Potiphar bowed low to his king, and then responded, "It shall be as Pharaoh Commands." He then turned to the men who had brought the still weakly struggling Baker before Pharaoh. "Guards, bring those two and follow me!" One of the men, the Baker, was roughly manhandled by the guards into motion, but the other moved without any prodding. Pharaoh observed this silently. Then noted that Potipherah had, rather surprisingly, stepped forward from among the priests.

He bowed to the Great One and announced, "Great Pharaoh, I have just had a premonition."

Amenemhet was definitely surprised at this. "What is that?"

Again Potipherah bowed and then said, "This investigation is going to take some time, but the Queen's jewels will be returned before they are needed at your birthday celebration at the end of the spring barley season."

It was not like the High Priest of On to make such predictions. Indeed, Potipherah was inclined to be very conservative in speaking any predictions so openly, let alone one of such import. Thus Amenemhet took his words very seriously. "I thank you. I will inform the Queen of your words. They are most comforting."

Not long after Potipherah made his prediction, Potiphar arrived at the prison with his captives. It was Potiphar himself who beat on the doors to get the attention of those inside the prison. From within they heard a muffled voice challenge, "Who is it that seeks entrance to the prison of Pharaoh?"

"It is I, Potiphar, Captain of Pharaoh's guard." The door creaked open, and a lean man in an official headdress appeared in the doorway. Potiphar recognized the man as the Warden himself.

The Warden, recognizing Potiphar, bowed and asked, "What may I do for you, Captain of the Pharaoh's Guard?"

"I have two prisoners for you. They are important men. This one is the Chief Baker and the other is the Chief Butler. Pharaoh orders that they be kept in your charge until evidence is found concerning the guilt of one of them."

The Warden rubbed his chin thoughtfully for a moment before responding. "Then one of them is innocent of any crime and the other guilty? This is indeed a delicate situation. Fortunately, I have a good solution for it." He turned and shouted into the prison, "Joseph! Come to the gate!" One of the prisoners in the courtyard turned at this summons. He, unlike the other prisoners, was dressed in clean linen. The moment he turned, Potiphar recognized him. The man in the courtyard focused on the sound of the Warden's voice, and turning, ran to him.

Coming to a halt a respectful distance from the Warden, Joseph bowed and asked, "You called, Master?"

The Warden acknowledged Joseph with a small nod of his head. Then he indicated the new prisoners with a nod in their direction and said, "Indeed, I have a delicate situation for you to handle. One of these two men is guilty of a crime against Pharaoh and the other is innocent, but we know not which is which."

Potiphar nodded to Joseph as well and then said in a gentle tone, "Joseph, I know that you will do well in seeing for the care of these men."

The Warden had not been looking at either Joseph or Potiphar but at the baker. The fat man was looking at Joseph with disgust on his face. It was obvious the Warden was angry when he spoke. "I see the look of loathing upon your face at this proclamation. Who are you, prisoner?"

The baker puffed himself up and answered arrogantly, "I am the Chief Baker to Pharaoh himself!"

The Warden was not impressed. His tone was filled with loathing and great authority. "Well then, 'Chief Baker to Pharaoh himself,' your Pharaoh has placed you in prison, not in your kitchen!" The Baker glanced at Joseph once more with disdain as the Warden spoke. This made the Warden angry and he waved in Joseph's direction adding. "Whatever is done here, *he* is in charge of it." Still seeing the look of disdain on the Baker's face, he added sternly, "You would do well to heed my warning and do all that he tells you to do." He then turned to Joseph and continued in a calm, but commanding voice. "Joseph, do as you see fit with these two." Finally, he bowed to Potiphar and added, "Potiphar, you may be assured all is cared for."

Joseph looked at the prisoners for a moment. He saw the rebellion and hatred in the Chief Baker's eyes, and turning to the Warden said in a quiet simply, "Indeed, my Master." He then turned and gestured to one of the nearby guards, who came to his side immediately. "Guard, take these two prisoners to the old guard barracks on the south wall. I shall be with you shortly."

The guard bowed to Joseph and answered crisply, "At once, Joseph!" Then, leveling his spear at the two new prisoners, he ordered, "You two, move!" Glaring haughtily at the guard and at Joseph, the baker moved in the indicated direction. The butler, on the other hand, walked with his head bowed without comment or a display of any kind.

Joseph and the Warden bowed to Potiphar and were turning to go when Potiphar interjected, "May I step inside and have a word with Joseph?"

The Warden seemed unsurprised at the request, but his answer was wary. "Does it concern the prisoners?"

Potiphar bowed and said, "It does."

The Warden seemed satisfied. With a small bow of recognition to the friendship between Joseph and Potiphar, he said simply, "Certainly." Turning to the remaining guard he ordered, "Guard, close the gate and then, when Lord Potiphar has finished speaking with Joseph, let the Captain of the Pharaoh's Guard out."

The guard bowed. "As you have commanded, sir!" He then saw the two guards that had come with Potiphar out of the gate and closed it.

After the gate was closed and the guard resumed his post, Potiphar looked at his friend with great concern in his eyes. Quietly he asked, "How are you, Joseph? I worry and I must carry word of you to all your friends in my house. They ask about your condition almost daily!" He chuckled. "If they find out that I had seen you and bring them not word of you, I might not get my supper!"

Joseph smiled and good humor showed in his eyes. "I would most certainly keep your supper secure! Tell them that I do well enough and I think of them often." His eyes held a faraway look for a moment, and then he continued most reverently. "The Lord my God is with me here in this place. You have heard the Warden — God has given me favor in his sight — he has committed to my hand all of the prisoners. Whatever they do here, I'm in charge of it."

Potiphar placed a brotherly hand on Joseph's shoulder. His eyes were wet with tears. "Truly, Joseph, your God *is* God! The night that you were committed to this terrible place, I prayed to your God that he would be with you, and now. . ."

"You prayed to the God of my father's?"

Potiphar's voice showed the depth of his emotions. "Aye, that I did, and many times since!"

Joseph was taken totally by surprise. He was dumbfounded. "Master, I. . ."

Potiphar shook his head. "Joseph, don't call me Master. I miss your friendship, our talks, and your wise counsel. You are my equal, a free man, and my friend. Call me by my name, Potiphar." He dropped his hand from Joseph's shoulder and stared at the ground. "It is to my eternal shame that I used my authority so poorly that I failed you and let you be imprisoned in this horrid place!"

Joseph waited until Potiphar looked up to speak. "I have had dreams since I have been here. I know from them that it was neither your failure nor the treachery of Kneumet that put me here. It was the Lord, my God."

"Why?"

"I know not, but the Lord will reveal the reason in his own due time. Until then I must be patient, and you must be patient as well. Our path will be revealed when the time is right."

Potiphar stared in the direction that his two recent prisoners had gone. Then he said thoughtfully, "I think that these two prisoners may have something to do with my request of your God to be the instrument of your release, but I have no idea how."

"If it is permitted, may I know why they are here?" Joseph asked.

"One of the two stole the Queen's jewels. Pharaoh is furious! Yet he wants to be fair, and thus he has these two in custody here until the guilt of one of them can be proved."

Joseph's face reflected his determination. "I will do my best to serve them!"

The prisoners that Potiphar had delivered were a season in the prison when they dreamed a dream, both of them, in the same night. When the early morning hours had arrived, while it was still dark and most of the prisoners were quietly sound asleep, in the old barracks that served as the cell for the Chief Butler and the Chief Baker, things were neither quiet nor untroubled. The Butler was tossing and turning in his sleep. Groans were escaping him as he rolled restlessly. Finally, with a loud cry he bolted awake and sat up in his bed.

The Baker, who was already wide awake and sitting on the edge of his cot, looked over at the Butler and asked in a shaken tone, "What is it?"

The Butler looked about himself wildly for a moment or two before answering. When he did so, it was obvious that he was still shaken from whatever had awakened him. "I have dreamed a dream!"

The Baker seemed shaken by this and said, "You as well?"

"You also had a dream?"

"Indeed! I have been awake for some time now because if it! It is most troublesome to me. I know it is important but have not the wit to unravel its mystery! Can you interpret a dream?"

"No! I, like you, know that the dream I had, which was vivid indeed, is of great importance. Curse it! We are in a place that is removed from the priests! There is no interpreter of dreams here!"

They both paused at the sound of footsteps coming from outside their cell and the Butler asked the Baker, "Who is this that comes?"

The Baker, whose cot afforded a view of the outside, peered out of the tiny window. "It is Joseph who waits upon us with our breakfast." Looking at the floor for a moment, he continued. "I for one have no appetite until the mystery of this dream is revealed."

The Butler nodded his agreement. "Nor I."

Joseph undid the lock to the door to their cell and entered. He greeted them as he always did. "Peace be with you, my Masters." It was then that he noticed that these two men seemed ill at ease. He therefore asked, "Why do you look so sad today?"

It was the Butler who answered. "We have each dreamed a dream, and there is no interpreter of dreams here."

Joseph was intrigued. "Do not interpretations of dreams belong to God? Tell me the content of your dreams, I pray you."

The Butler regarded Joseph silently for several moments, then slowly he said, "You are not a Priest, but I have heard it said of you that your God has revealed the visions of the night to you." Joseph, who was not aware that his gift from God was common knowledge, was greatly surprised at this statement by the Butler, but he kept his silence and simply nodded. After several moments, the Butler seemed to come to a decision. "I will tell you my dream." Taking a deep breath, he began. "In my dream, a vine was before me. In the vine were three branches. It was as though it budded and blossoms shot forth. The clusters of it brought forth ripe grapes. Pharaoh's cup was in my hand, and I took the grapes and pressed them into Pharaoh's cup and gave the cup into Pharaoh's hand." The Butler then sat quietly, staring at Joseph hopefully.

Joseph was quiet for a full minute, then said thoughtfully, "This is the interpretation of your dream: The three branches are three days. Within three days will Pharaoh lift up your head and restore you unto your place. You shall deliver Pharaoh's cup into his hand, after the former manner when you served him."

The Butler's face shone with the hope that he could be returned to his former station. "Your interpretation is good! I had not dared to hope for such an outcome!" He paused with an odd look on his face for a moment, and then added, "I know not how, yet I know your explanation is correct!"

Joseph added with caution, "I thank you, but it was God that told you, not I. Think on me when you are restored to your position, and show kindness, I pray you, unto me. Make mention of me unto Pharaoh and bring me out of this house, for indeed, I was stolen away out of the land of the Hebrews and in my role as Head of House for Potiphar did nothing for which they should put me into the dungeon."

The Baker, who had been silent until now, spoke in an ingratiating tone. "Your interpretation is indeed pleasing. Hear my dream also, I pray you, and perchance your God will give you the interpretation."

"Tell me your dream, I pray you."

The Baker looked at the Butler in an odd way, and then with his eyes closed, he began speaking. "I had three white baskets on my head. In the uppermost basket were all manner of bake meats for pharaoh. The birds did eat them out of the basket upon my head." He paused, then he opened his eyes and in a pleading tone asked, "Can you interpret this dream?"

Joseph looked at the man for a long time before he spoke. When he did there was pain in his voice. "I fear to tell you."

The Baker's face went pale and he began to shake. After a moment or two, he pleaded, "Please, tell me the meaning."

Joseph saw no way out of the situation. He responded sadly, "Very well. This is the interpretation of the dream: The three baskets are three days, and within three days will Pharaoh lift up your head from you and will hang you on a tree. The birds will eat the flesh from your corpse."

The Baker said nothing for some time. He simply sat wide-eyed, pale, and shaking. Finally, he buried his face in his hands and began sobbing. The Butler tried to comfort him, but to no avail.

That evening, one of the prison guards, a friend of Joseph's, stopped by the estate of Potiphar. Quickly he related the story of Joseph's reading of the Baker's dream and the Butler's dream, and the Captain of Potiphar's Household Guard wasted no time in rushing to his Master with the information. He found him in the gardens puttering in one of the flowerbeds.

"Master! There is news of Joseph!" he called out in a rush.

Potiphar rose from the flowerbed instantly and asked, "What sort of news?"

"You spoke of the Butler and the Baker. You said that one of them was the thief that you are seeking?"

At the mention of the two men he had placed in the prison,

Potiphar's excitement rose. "What about them?"

"Apparently they both had strange dreams in the night. Joseph interpreted their dreams!"

"And?" Potiphar asked excitedly when the man paused.

"He said that the Butler would be restored to his butlership in three days, but that the Baker would be hanged in three days!"

"Yes! I knew I didn't like the looks of that arrogant Baker! We have him!" Then Potiphar began to pace. "The problem is proving it. In three days, Pharaoh is going to celebrate his birthday with a grand party, and that is when God will reveal the thief, but I know that it is up to me to find the proof!" He paused in thought for a few moments. "I must think on this very carefully. Thank you for the information, Captain, but now I must be alone for a time."

"Of course, Master!" the Captain responded. He quickly saluted and left Potiphar to ponder this dilemma and to work toward Joseph's release.

As soon as the Captain was gone, Potiphar once more knelt in the flowerbed, but this time he picked up no tool; instead, he folded his arms, bowed his head as he had seen Joseph do many times, and addressed the God of Joseph. "Oh, God of Joseph I pray, hear me! Thou hast been kind to Joseph in his prison and thou hast been kind to me and my house. For these things I thank thee! Now thou hast given Joseph the sight to read the dreams of the Butler and the Baker. Thanks to thee, we now know who the thief is! Sadly, it is I who have failed. I have not found the evidence needed to convict the Baker. Grant me the sight that has failed me for so long to discover the evidence! Grant this I pray thee that not only the Baker may be brought to justice but that thy faithful servant, and my friend, Joseph may be freed from that awful prison."

Joseph's reading of the dreams and Potiphar's prayer bore fruit quickly. Two days later, in the palace of Amenemhet, Potiphar, who was staring quietly out at the gardens of Pharaoh's palace, was met by the Chamberlain.

"Potiphar, why stare you out at the gardens so intently?"

Potiphar only glanced at the Chamberlain. "Of late, I have been spending much pleasant time working in the gardens with one of the young women of my house. She tends them and has taught me much as we work together in the plant beds."

The Chamberlain misunderstood Potiphar's meaning. "She has helped you after the loss of your wife?"

Potiphar, who was not expecting this answer to his comment, said simply, "Greatly." Then he pointed to the object of his intent scrutiny. "I was looking at that flowerbed over there."

The Chamberlain, curious, asked, "Why so? It is unremarkable."

Potiphar pointed. "Notice that the flowers in that one bed do not flourish like the others."

"You have a sharp eye for detail, good Potiphar! I had not noticed this! I will speak to the Chief Gardener immediately!"

"I do not know why, but I feel compelled to send one of my men with him when he investigates that plot."

"You say you do not know why you should send a guard with the Gardener?"

Potiphar's brow wrinkled at the question. "I do not know now, but I will!"

The Chamberlain looked at Potiphar with a curious expression on his face. After a slight hesitation, he said, "Be it as you desire, good Potiphar." He noticed a movement out of the corner of his eye. Turning, he saw the Chief Gardener entering the gardens. "Ah! What luck! See, the Chief Gardener comes!" Raising his hand to get the man's attention, he shouted, "Gardner! Please, come here!"

Seeing that it was the Lord Chamberlain that had hailed him, the man hurried to his side. "My Lord Chamberlain! How may I be of service to you?"

"Do you see that small flower plot yonder?"

"I see it, my Lord."

"Lord Potiphar has noticed that it grows poorly and would have you investigate it."

The Chief Gardener stared at the indicated plot and then at several of the others. "Very well. Now, that you have pointed it out, that plot *is* weak. Let us see why." They walked swiftly to the indicated plot, where the gardener stooped down and began looking at it quite carefully. After a few moments, he mumbled, "Hmm. . . Look at this. This area is disturbed. I think something has been buried here."

Potiphar, looking over the man's shoulder, asked, "Can you see what it is?"

"Indeed! It appears to be buried quite shallow it will take but a moment." The man bent to the task. His trained hands quickly unearthed something that did not belong in a flowerbed. "There is something here, Lord Potiphar! Let me just pull it free. . ." He applied his strength, and with a mighty pull, the object came free of the ground. The force of the release almost tumbled the gardener. Undeterred, he announced proudly, "Here it is!

Potiphar was excited. "Unwrap it!" he exclaimed.

The Chamberlain was the first to recognize the objects within the decorative box thus revealed. "Those are the Queen's jewels!" The Chamberlain seemed puzzled. "Why would something like this simple box cause the flowers in this plot to grow poorly?"

The Gardener looked at the cloth that the jewelry box had been wrapped in. He then sniffed at it and wrinkled his nose at the odor he detected. "This cloth has been treated with embalming tar to keep it dry while it was buried. That tar is a poison. The plants were affected by it."

Potiphar was quick to see the implications. "Who tends these flowers, normally?"

"One of my servants, Ahmed. . ." The Gardener hesitated, looked about the gardens, and then pointed to a man working not too far from where they stood. "It is that fellow, working near that date palm tree."

"Call him here."

"Ahmed! Come here!"

As Potiphar turned to talk to the Gardener once more, the Chamberlain proclaimed, "Potiphar! He runs!"

Potiphar, feeling foolish because he had looked away, shouted to the guards at the edge of the gardens. "Guards! Seize that man and bring him here!"

The guards quickly grabbed the man as he tried to flee and dragged him before Potiphar, the Chamberlain, and the Chief Gardener.

As the man was forced to his knees before them, he shouted, "I did nothing!"

Potiphar stood over the man and glared at him. "You did nothing? Then tell me, why did you run? Would it have something to do with the jewels that were just unearthed here?"

The man fell on his face and began to weep. "Please, Lord! He made me do it! He said that, if I did not, he would kill me and then sell my wife and children into slavery!" Ahmed said between his sobs.

Potiphar' excitement rose. "He? Who is this 'he' of whom you speak?"

Ahmed's mouth worked for a few moments, but no words came out. He was as pale as death. Finally, he managed to say, "I fear him even now!"

Potiphar understood. The man and his family really had been threatened. "If what you are telling me is true, and can be proven, then you have nothing to fear."

Ahmed's next words confirmed Potiphar's suspicions. "My wife and child were there when he threatened us. They will tell you the truth of the matter!"

"Very well. We will talk to them, but first, you need tell me who it was that is behind this."

The man lowered his head. It was obvious that he was struggling with the safety of his family. In a halting voice he said, "It. . . It was the Chief Baker, my Lord"

Tears came to Potiphar's eyes. Here was the proof of the Baker's crime and the vindication of Joseph's reading of the dreams. Once more the God of Joseph had answered his prayers!

As Joseph had interpreted the dream, it came to pass the third day, which was Pharaoh's birthday that Amenemhet made a feast for all his servants. The throng at the party was large and colorful. Among those present were Potiphar and Benar. Potiphar beamed each time Benar was complimented.

The Lord Chamberlain spotted Potiphar in the crowd and came to his side. After bowing formally to Benar, who blushed prettily at such a courtesy, he whispered to Potiphar. "Pharaoh would speak with you privately."

Potiphar nodded and responded, "Of course." Then he turned to the lovely young woman at his side. "Benar, would you mind waiting for me here?"

Benar, still blushing, said quietly, "Certainly, my Lord." Potiphar nodded to her and turned to go with the Lord Chamberlain.

As they walked, the Chamberlain said, "That young woman is striking, Potiphar! Who is she?"

Potiphar's pride in her was evident. "She was raised in my house. It was she who taught me so much about gardening, and it was her instruction that allowed me to see those wilting plants that led us to the Queen's jewels."

"So you rewarded her by bringing her to the Pharaoh's birthday party!"

It was Potiphar's turn to blush. "You should be one of the magicians! You read my mind!"

The Chamberlain made a dismissive gesture. "Oh, it's all just part of the job. Ah, we are here!" Bowing to Pharaoh, he said, "My Pharaoh, I have brought him."

"Potiphar, it is good to see you. I wanted to thank you. It is astounding that you found the Queen's jewels in that flowerbed. We all walked by there every day and did not notice what you did."

Potiphar bowed and said humbly, "God guided my eyes, Great One."

Amenemhet nodded his approval of this answer. "It is good to hear one speak who still gives the Gods credit! Are you ready to bring the Butler and the Baker forth so that justice can be done in this case?"

"I am, Great One!"

Pharaoh turned to the Lord Chamberlain and ordered, "Assemble the house."

The Chamberlain bowed. "Immediately, my Pharaoh!" He then turned and faced the party, striking his staff on the flagstones to get their attention. He waited until they had quieted before he loudly announced, "All gather at the feet of Pharaoh! Justice is to be meted out this day!" The music stopped. There was a shuffling for positions followed by a quiet that was broken only by some birdsong in the distance and the very faint sound of the breeze in the trees. Seeing that they had everyone's attention, the Chamberlain turned to Pharaoh, bowed and said, "All are gathered, Great One."

Amenemhet viewed the crowd silently for a few moments before he began to speak. "All those of the house of Pharaoh know there was a heinous crime committed here at the beginning of the spring barley season. The Queen's jewels were stolen." There was much murmuring at this statement. Pharaoh added quickly, "It is well! It is well!" With this assurance, the crowd quieted and Pharaoh continued. "The jewels have been recovered, and the thief is in custody and will be tried before you this day. Potiphar, bring forth the accused!"

Bowing to acknowledge the order, Potiphar replied, "It will be done, Great One! Guards! Bring in the prisoners!" The guards rushed from the party and soon returned accompanied by the sounds of clanking chains. Between them the two prisoners could be seen. There were a few whispered comments.

"Those two!"

"The Butler?"

"I knew that the Baker was a no good!"

When these two men were standing before their Pharaoh, the Butler prostrated himself immediately, but the Baker hesitated, frozen in place as though with fear.

Potiphar instantly noted the failure. "Kneel before your Pharaoh!" The Baker then too prostrated himself.

Amenemhet directed his next question not to the prisoners but to Potiphar. "Are there any witnesses?"

"There are, Great One!"

"Call them forth, Captain!"

"At once, Great One!" Turning he called loudly, "Ahmed, servant to the Chief Gardener, come before your Pharaoh and testify!" Ahmed ran forward and quickly prostrated himself before Pharaoh.

Before the man could speak, Amenemhet demanded, "Tell your Pharaoh what you know."

Ahmed, his face close to the ground, answered in a muffled voice. "Great One, as I was working in the garden, the Chief Baker came to me and asked me to help him bury something there. I did not like the idea and said I could not, that he would have to ask the Chief Gardener. The Chief Baker became furious and threatened to have me flogged to death and my family sold into slavery! I did not answer him. Then he came to my quarters that night and threatened my whole family, saying that, if we told of his visit, we would all be flogged and, if we survived, we would all be sold into slavery. I was terrified and so was my wife. I. . . I did as he requested. Forgive my weakness, Great One!"

Amenemhet looked questioningly at Potiphar, who quickly responded. "Great One, if it pleases you, his story is confirmed. He is telling the truth."

Amenemhet nodded his appreciation. "I thank you, Potiphar." Turning to the prisoners, he called out, "Chief Butler, stand forth before your Pharaoh!" The man struggled to rise but was encumbered by his chains and so could not stand fully. "Raise up your head! Stand forth and give my cup into my hand! You are restored to your butlership!" The assembled crowd broke into cheering. "Loose his chains, Potiphar that he may do as his Pharaoh commands!"

Potiphar jumped forward to comply, almost shouting in his delight in the task.

The Butler seemed in shock, but as soon as the chains were released, he struggled to the table on the dais where the wine and Pharaoh's cup were sitting. He shakily poured some wine into the cup and carefully placed it in his Pharaoh's hands. He then bowed low before him, and said, "Here is your cup, Great Pharaoh, receive it and my great thanks. May this cup of wine refresh you, and may your wisdom and mercy be spoken of forever!"

Amenemhet raised the cup in salute to the Butler, and then said very quietly, "I thank you, good Butler. Now, get yonder! I see your weeping wife there. She has far more need of you than I do at the moment. Go."

The Butler looked in the direction indicated by Pharaoh, and tears sprang into his eyes. "At once, my Pharaoh!" Despite the cruel marks of the chains upon his ankles, he rushed as best he could toward the weeping woman and a small child waiting at the edge of the crowd.

Pharaoh Amenemhet III watched this tender scene for several moments. His pleasure at the sight was very evident. Then he sighed deeply and directed his attention toward the still prostrate Baker. His visage changed instantly. Handing the cup the Butler had given to him to his valet, he addressed the Baker in a very harsh voice. At the very sound of it, complete silence filled the courtyard. "Baker, raise up your head before your Pharaoh!

The Baker failed to move and was prodded to his feet by the guards attending him. "You are accused and proven guilty of theft and blackmail! You are not worthy to live! Therefore, you will be taken from this place and hanged from a tree until you are dead. No man will remove your bones from there. You will be without a grave in Egypt! Your bones will be scattered by the hyenas and your flesh consumed by the fowls of the air that there will be nothing of you left to stain Egypt!" He paused and directed his next command to Potiphar. "Have your men take this man out and carry out the sentence!" Then, over the wailing of the Baker, he said quietly to Potiphar, "You may remain here with us."

Potiphar, grateful not to have to attend to such a foul task today, answered gratefully, "It will be as you command!" Turning to his soldiers, he commanded, "Guards! Take this man out to the place of execution and carry out the sentence pronounced by

JOSEPH Ruler of All Egypt 125

Pharaoh!" The guards were quick to obey and moved forward rapidly. The Baker collapsed on the step of the dais and began to weep uncontrollably.

One of the guards, disgusted by the display, said angrily, "Stand on your feet and die like a man!"

This only resulted in the Baker screaming, "No!" He actually began clutching the dais to prevent being dragged to his death.

Thoroughly disgusted, the first guard called out to two more of their number standing close by, "You two come here! We'll have to drag the cowardly scum!" The extra guards rushed forward, grabbed the wailing and screaming Baker, and dragged the man from the party. The guests, with expressions of disgust mixed with horror, made a wide avenue for them to pass. Soon the wailing and clanking could no longer be heard.

The Chamberlain spoke into the silence that prevailed after the scene of fear and anguish played itself out. "The justice of Pharaoh is true justice! The justice of Pharaoh is guided by the hands of the Gods! The Justice of Pharaoh is final! This proceeding is concluded. Pharaoh invites those remaining to enjoy his hospitality on this his birthday! Musicians, pray, continue playing!" The party was quite subdued for some time, but finally, a semblance of normality prevailed.

Benar was one of those still having trouble with the scene that she had just witnessed. Potiphar noticed and came to her side. When she spoke to him, her voice, indeed her entire body, was trembling. "It was good to see the Butler restored, but the scene with the Baker was hard to bear!" At this, she dissolved into tears.

Potiphar placed a comforting arm around her. "Forgive me. I am an old fool! I forgot about your injury at the hands of Inep. With you standing beautiful, tall, and straight now, it is hard to remember you as a cripple!"

Benar, unused to such tenderness, laughed nervously through her tears. "I know what you mean! I find it hard to believe that I can stand erect now. It is still strange to me!" She noticed a hard look on her kind Master's face. "Master, your face is troubled. What is it that troubles you? Have I embarrassed you?"

Potiphar turned to her, and in an embarrassed tone, he said. "Fear not, gentle Benar. You have done nothing. The lacking I find sad is the fault of the Butler." His face reflected his disappointment. "He failed to tell Pharaoh that it was Joseph who interpreted both his and the Baker's dreams!"

Benar realized what this would have meant and asked, "Master, can you not inform Pharaoh? Such a wondrous thing would bring Joseph out of the prison."

Now there were tears in Potiphar's eyes. "I cannot. Everyone here knows that Joseph was Head of my House. If I were to do this in the place of the Butler, it would seem as if I were taking advantage of the Butler's innocence to promote Joseph from the prison, which would anger Pharaoh, and that would do much harm. No, Benar, we must wait, still."

Chapter Nine
Pharaoh's Dreams

Events had come to pass just as Joseph had predicted, but it had been two years since the Chief Butler failed to remember Joseph to Pharaoh. Now Pharaoh was having dark and troubling dreams.

The hour was late, and Pharaoh was in his bed chamber tossing and turning. Behind his closed eyelids, Amenemhet's eyes could be seen shifting wildly. His dream began peacefully enough. He was standing by the river. While he was admiring the view, seven cattle came up out of the river. The beasts were serene, well favored, and fat fleshed. They quietly joined the Pharaoh and began to feed on the lush grass of the river bank. Oh, what a peaceful pastoral scene they made! Then seven more cattle came out of the river that were horrid to look upon, their hides moth-eaten. These creatures were so lean that one could count the bones inside them. These animals stood near the other cattle that were already feeding. Suddenly, the moth-eaten beasts opened their mouths. Never had Pharaoh seen cattle with teeth like fierce lions! Without warning, they attacked and consumed the fat cattle. Although they had eaten much, there was no change in them, and the cattle looked as wretched as before.

When they turned their hungry eyes upon Pharaoh, he was frightened beyond words. It was then that he awoke, sat bolt upright, and screamed, "Ahhhhhh! Nooooooo!" His eyes were wide with fright and he was soaked in sweat, his breathing rapid and irregular. He stared wildly about as if expecting to see the frightening monsters there in his room. He jumped when the door to his room was thrown open and two armed guards rushed in with their weapons leveled. They rapidly looked around the room for an intruder but found none. Wary, and with his weapon still at the ready, the lead guard asked, "Are you in danger, my Pharaoh? We heard you cry out."

Amenemhet had covered his face with his hands and sat

unmoving for several moments. When he removed his hands, he said, "No. No, I am fine. I have just dreamed a frightening dream. Thank you for coming to me, my loyal guards." With a kind tone, he added, "Please, it is nothing. You may return to your most excellently kept posts."

The guard was worried for Pharaoh, but he bowed and responded, "It shall be as you wish, mighty Pharaoh!" The guards lowered their weapons, and as they left the room, Pharaoh heard the door close and the bolt slam home, securing it once more.

Amenemhet, still shaken, said aloud to the empty room, "I must get back to sleep for there is much for me to do tomorrow." Before he lay down again, he made a great show of readjusting the bed covers, and when he did nestle within them, he lay in a fetal position. He was still badly frightened and this position somehow made him feel more comfortable. After a time, he stretched out and his breathing became slow and steady.

When he was once more asleep, again he dreamed. He was in one of the grain fields, and as he looked upon the rich field, seven ears of corn appeared upon one stalk, rank and good, promising a grand harvest! Then seven thin ears, blasted with a hot east wind, sprang up after them. Suddenly, the withered ears sprouted teeth, and as he watched, the seven thin ears devoured the seven rank and full ears! Then, as with the kine in his previous dream, the ears of grain began to turn their attention toward Pharaoh. Once more he awoke screaming.

Again, the door flew open and the alarmed guards rushed into the room to protect their Pharaoh only to find the room empty and their beloved Amenemhet sitting in the middle of his bed looking extremely frightened. The lead guard was even more alarmed than he had been previously. "Are you in danger, my Pharaoh? We heard you cry out again."

Amenemhet, not wishing to frighten the man further, said, "No, I am fine. I have just dreamed yet another disturbing dream. Thank you for coming to me again, my loyal guards. Please, it is nothing. You may return to your most *excellently* kept posts."

The guard bowed, but it was evident from his tone that he was anything but assured. "It shall be as you wish, Mighty Pharaoh!" Again the guards retreated from the royal chamber, closing and bolting the door behind them.

As soon as the men had departed from his room, Pharaoh

reached behind him and grabbed one of his pillows. Clutching it to his chest, he rocked back and forth for a few moments. Amenemhet was no coward but a seasoned warrior who had distinguished himself in battle many times, but these night visions and the terror they instilled were beyond his experience. He was frightened through and through. Then, burying his face in his pillow, he did something he had not done since he was three years old — he gave in to the fear and wept like a child.

Outside the chamber, the senior guard was now listening intently at the door, and the guard could hear the Pharaoh's sobs despite his attempts to cover his weeping with his pillow. The lead guard was frightened and he needed help. He quietly commanded his companion in a strained whisper, "Quietly! Quickly! Go to the house of Potiphar! Something is amiss with Pharaoh! Potiphar will know what to do! Go!"

The other guard wheeled and ran down the corridor. He too was badly frightened. He had been with his Pharaoh in battle and had never seen him look so much as mildly discomfited let alone afraid. For Pharaoh to be this frightened was not a good omen! The other guards in the palace stared in disbelief as he raced past as swiftly as he could. He was challenged only by the officer of the watch.

"Where are you going?"

The man turned and shouted as he ran past, "I go to the house of Potiphar. There is something amiss with Pharaoh! He is safe, but he weeps and has frightening dreams. Potiphar will know what to do!"

Since the man was one of the personal guards, one of the Medji, there was nothing the Officer of the Watch could do but let the man go. However, to see one of these extremely brave, wholly dedicated men in such a state was very disquieting. He stared after the man for a moment and said to his already retreating back, "Go!"

The man raced out of the palace gate and down the street to the gate of Potiphar's estate. The man pounded on it with the butt of his spear, making a terrific din. The Captain of Potiphar's household guard happened to be on the pylon as the man pounded, and annoyed, he shouted down to the man, "Who is it that beats upon the gate at this hour?"

Pharaoh's guard shouted in return, "One of those who guards the Pharaoh's chamber. Something is wrong with the Great One!"

Alarmed, the Captain rushed down the steps to the gate and opened it himself. The man rushed in, but before he could speak, the Captain cautioned, "Keep your voice down! Would you panic the entire city? Now, what troubles the Pharaoh?"

The man made an effort to get control of himself and to catch his breath. And then he responded. "He has twice awakened screaming tonight. We rushed into his sleeping quarters on both occasions, and both times, Pharaoh said it was nothing but a bad dream and returned us to our posts. We listened at the door the second time and could hear him sobbing like a child within. Something is terribly amiss, Captain! The Pharaoh is a brave man. He would not weep over nothing. We need Potiphar!"

The Captain agreed. He was now as frightened as the other man. "Return to your post. I will awaken Lord Potiphar. He will be with you shortly."

The man's face plainly showed his relief. His response was more firm. "I thank you!" He turned and raced back the way he had come.

The Captain stood silently in the open gate and watched the man go; pondering these events for several moments more before he could move. He did not like these happenings! It was a bad thing for Pharaoh to be so troubled by foul dreams. What was bad for Pharaoh was bad for Egypt! Turning to one of the guards on duty inside the estate who had been attracted by the commotion, he said, "Guard! Close the gate! I must awaken the Master."

"At once, Captain!" the man responded crisply.

The Captain walked swiftly into the house. He decided to walk to avoid panicking the household, but he was still badly frightened. He worked hard to clear his mind of his own panic as he ascended the stairs and came to the curtained entrance to his Master's rooms. Quietly pushing the curtains aside, he entered and found the sleeping Potiphar on his cot. Gently reaching out and touching Potiphar's shoulder, he said softly, "Lord Potiphar, awaken!"

Potiphar, being a soldier and quite used to coming instantly awake, was startled at the first touch of the Captain's hand but soon gained his bearings. "Huh? What? Who? Oh, it is you, Captain. What is the hour of the watch?"

"It is the tenth hour, Master. It will not be long before the Goddess Nut welcomes the God Shu to her domain in the sky, bringing the day."

Potiphar rubbed his face and took a deep breath. "Very well. Why did you awaken me?"

The Captain did his best to cover his own panic and reported crisply, "One of the guards from the Pharaoh's chamber came to the gate. He said Pharaoh awoke screaming twice this night. The guards rushed into the chamber at the sound and Pharaoh told them on both occasions that it was nothing but a bad dream. He then told them to return to their posts. After the second incident, they could hear Pharaoh sobbing inside his chambers. They were concerned and called for you."

Any vestige of sleep was gone from Potiphar. He was now wide awake and very concerned. "As well they might! This is not good, Captain. Pharaoh having bad dreams cannot be good for Egypt! Quickly, awaken Hotem and have him send our swiftest runner with this information to the house of Potipherah, the Priest of On. He will need to be at the Palace when the Great One awakes." The Captain saluted and swiftly left the room and Potiphar arose and dressed.

He was just coming out of his rooms when he bumped into Benar in the corridor outside his personal chamber. In the dim light of the passageway it was plain to see that she was in her nightdress and wore a worried expression. "What has happened, Master that causes you and the Captain to converse in the middle of the night?"

Potiphar was surprised to see her. "Benar! Why are you awake?"

"I heard the Captain as he passed the kitchen, and then I heard worried voices, and so I came to see if all was well with you, Master."

Potiphar shook his head and smiled. "Your concern for me never ceases to amaze! It is nothing. Pharaoh has been awakened twice by bad dreams. I need to go to the palace in case I am needed."

Benar was not fooled. "Bread, boiled eggs, and onions left from last night's supper await you in the kitchen. I believe that there is even some mulled wine on the hearth. I will fetch you some that you may go to the Pharaoh stronger for having eaten."

Potiphar still worried about the girl's health and strength. "That is not necessary, Benar. You are tired and need. . ."

Benar's eyes filled with tears and she pleaded, "It is no bother! It will only take a moment to fetch the food and you can eat on the way!"

Potiphar could not resist the girl, especially with tears in her eyes. "Very well, Benar. I still have a few things to do before I depart, and as you say, I can eat it on the way."

It was well for Potiphar that the ever faithful Benar had insured that he ate. The palace was in an uproar. For it came to pass that morning that Pharaoh's spirit was deeply troubled and he had called for all the magicians and wise men of Egypt. Pharaoh had then told them his dreams, which none of them could interpret.

The effect of their failure was like electricity. Many people were moving about and nervous conversations were everywhere. None of the Priests, including the venerable Potipherah, had a single clue as to what Pharaoh's dreams could possibly mean.

Through the maze of restlessly moving bodies, Potiphar spotted the Butler, who was apparently on his way to the kitchens to get something for Pharaoh. This seemed the perfect opportunity. Here, at last, mused Potiphar was the means to bring Joseph to the attention of the Pharaoh. He hailed him. "Hold for a moment, good Butler."

The Butler seemed distracted but stopped none-the-less, "What can I do for you, Lord Potiphar?"

Potiphar decided to act as if he knew nothing in order to nudge the Butler into the action he desired. "Good Butler, would you please tell me the current state of affairs in the throne room."

The Butler began to wring his hands and his voice was filled with worry as he answered. "All is not well! None of the magicians or the Priests can tell Pharaoh the meaning of his dreams. Pharaoh is deeply troubled and the whole court with him."

Potiphar then asked, "Where are you going, good Butler?"

The Butler was still distracted. "To fetch mulled wine from the kitchen. When Pharaoh is troubled, he often calls for mulled wine."

Potiphar leaped at the opportunity. "Can you think of nothing stronger that would ease your Pharaoh's mind?"

The man looked genuinely puzzled for a moment, and then with a wrinkled brow answered, "No, I cannot."

"Are you sure of this?" Potiphar pressed.

The Butler was confused. "What could I, a humble Chief Butler, possibly know that could ease the mind of Pharaoh? I am not a physician or one of the learned Priests!"

Potiphar pounced. "You do not remember a time when you

dreamed a dream and there was no interpreter of it?"

The man's eyes widened in fear. He began to shake. Finally, he answered in a frightened whisper. "You would have Pharaoh reminded of my sins when he is in such a troubled mood?"

Potiphar pressed the man mercilessly. He whispered urgently, "What are your sins in comparison to the dangers that Egypt could face if these dreams are not interpreted? You know that Joseph can give Pharaoh his answers."

The man seemed to wilt. His long frightening days in the prison still terrified him, and even the merest reminder of them would cause him to weep. His dreams were still filled with terrifying images of his imprisonment. Now, here was Potiphar, boldly reminding him of his time in those dank walls and demanding that he bring it up to Pharaoh! The Butler stood silently staring at Potiphar in fear and amazement for some time. Finally, he realized that Potiphar was right. Without another word, his head bowed in abject fear, the poor man retraced his steps to the dais where Pharaoh sat staring into space. Bowing low, the Butler approached Amenemhet and very quietly said, "Great Pharaoh, may I speak with you?"

Amenemhet was startled out of his distraction, and then recognizing the speaker, said, "Speak on."

His head still bowed in shame and fear, the Butler took a deep breath. His voice shook with the emotions flooding through him as he spoke. "I do remember my faults this day. Pharaoh was angry with his servant and put me in the prison along with the Chief Baker. We dreamed a dream one night, he and I, and there was with us a young man, a Hebrew, who had been the servant of the Captain of the Guard. We told this man, and he interpreted our dreams. And his interpretations of both our dreams came to pass, for he had told us that my dream portended that I would be restored unto my office and the Baker would be hanged."

Amenemhet's brow wrinkled for a moment. "I remember that incident. It was at my birthday party that year, was it not?"

"It was, great Pharaoh."

"This Hebrew who interpreted your dream, you said that he was a servant to the Captain of the Guard? Do you mean, Potiphar?"

"The same, my Lord."

Amenemhet sat looking thoughtful for a few moments, and then he smiled and said, "I thank you for this information, good

Butler." Please, would you go to the kitchens and fetch me some mulled wine?"

Greatly relieved, the man bowed low, and with tears of gratitude in his eyes, responded, "I would be most honored, Great One!"

Amenemhet watched silently as the man quickly left the chamber to fetch the wine he desired. He then turned to the Chamberlain who stood nearby and declared quietly, "Chamberlain, call forth Potiphar to stand before me."

The Chamberlain bowed then struck his staff to the floor and called out, "Potiphar, Captain of the Pharaoh's Guard, stand forth! Your Pharaoh would speak with you."

Potiphar had been expecting the summons and responded quickly. "I am here, my Pharaoh." He rushed forward to the dais and bowed low.

"Arise; I would speak with you, Potiphar."

Potiphar rose. "What is it you desire, Great One?"

"I have heard that your former servant has the ability to interpret the visions of the night, Potiphar. Is this true?"

"It is true that he correctly interpreted the dreams of the Baker and the Butler as you have just heard, Great One."

Surprisingly, Amenemhet became angry. "If you have known these things, why have you not brought this before your Pharaoh?"

Potiphar quickly bowed once more. "Great Pharaoh, be not displeased with your servant. Joseph is held in your prison house. He was placed there on false charges. I was unable to effect his release, as it is only you who can release a prisoner from that place."

Amenemhet was still angry. "False charges? Has the person responsible for the injustice been brought before me?"

Potiphar remained with his face to the floor and said apologetically, "That is no longer possible, Great One. Nor has it been possible for several years. The God of Joseph, being angered with the offender, struck her and her handmaids down with a bolt of lightning."

Amenemhet was startled. "A bolt of lightning, you say?"

Potiphar rose from his genuflection only far enough to nod. "Indeed, Great One."

Amenemhet seemed thoughtful for a moment, then, turning to the High Priest, said, "Potipherah, do you remember the day when

Kneumet, my sister-in-law, was killed along with her handmaids, when their ox was frightened by a bolt of lightning before the very door of this palace?"

Potipherah, who had been standing in his place near the dais, responded quietly, "I remember it well, my Pharaoh!"

"Did you not at the time declare that the lightning, so sudden and strange, was the punishment of some God?"

Potipherah nodded and bowed, "I did, my Pharaoh. It was not until later that my daughter Asenath brought Kneumet's evil report to my ears. I knew not of her immoral nature at the time of her death and did not wish to speak ill of her after her passing."

"Is this Asenath present here today, Potipherah?"

"She is, Great One. This is she who stands at my side"

Amenemhet regarded the young woman for a moment or two, then asked, "Asenath, daughter of the Priest of On, how came you by this report?"

Asenath was surprised at being called upon to speak by the Pharaoh himself. She was even more surprised at the honor of her father's title being used in addressing her. She blushed and bowed deeply. "It came from the lips of the defiler herself, my Pharaoh. I was there when she used her position as your sister-in-law to threaten Potiphar with death and his entire household with slavery if Joseph was not imprisoned, my Pharaoh. For his part, Great One, Joseph was completely innocent but went willingly to protect not only Potiphar's household but that of my father as well." The court had become totally silent during this disclosure but erupted into whispers at the report of such blatant treachery.

The Chamberlain was forced to act. "Silence! Silence in the court of Pharaoh!"

Amenemhet used the interruption to think a moment, and then he asked, "Why would your father's household need to be protected?"

Asenath lowered her head in shame and said quietly, "The vile jade was my aunt, Great One. Her sister is my mother, who is unfairly shamed by the association."

Amenemhet was exasperated. "Why have you not come before your Pharaoh with this injustice before now?"

Potipherah saw that his daughter could not answer the question and interjected, "Forgive me, Great One, but this was the work of some God, not the frailties of man."

"Why do you say this?"

"Forgive me, Great One, but had not this Joseph been in prison he would not have been available to interpret the dreams of both the Baker and the Butler, and thus his skill in the visions of the night would not have been known and therefore not available to Pharaoh in this current extremity."

Amenemhet was astounded. The truth of what Potipherah said hit him like a hammer blow. He looked at the trembling young woman and her worried father and felt ashamed. He held up his hand to indicate that he spoke to all the room and announced, "All of you have the apology of your Pharaoh for the hand of a God *is* evident in this matter!" He turned to the scribe seated on the dais and continued. "Scribe! Make a writing for the release of this Joseph from the prison and do it quickly! Then give it to the hand of Potiphar." Pharaoh then turned to the waiting Potiphar. "Bring this man before me as swiftly as you can!"

"It shall be as you command, my Pharaoh!"

Surprisingly, Asenath stepped forward, and bowing gracefully, she asked, "If it pleases you, Great One, may I accompany Potiphar on this errand? I have some skill in the arts of the physician and it may be that some such may be required."

Amenemhet bowed to her. "Be it as you have requested."

* * *

"My father?" A child's voice broke the spell of the story and the members of the court of Merneptah, which had been reliving the events of hundreds of years before, were drawn back to the present by the sound of a child's inquisitive voice. Everyone in the chamber blinked and looked at the child. "My father, is not Pharaoh all knowing? How is it he erred in the case of this Joseph?"

Merneptah looked at his son, then quietly answered, "Ah, my son you have asked the question of the ages. A Pharaoh *is* all knowing, but only so long as he listens to the Gods. As with Amenemhet III, there are times when even Pharaoh must wait upon the Gods' pleasure! Amenemhet III did listen in this instance, and thus he made no error. He immediately sent for Joseph, who was brought hastily out of the dungeon. He shaved himself, changed his raiment, and came unto Pharaoh." Once more, the spell of the story fell upon the court of Merneptah, and they were drawn back into the events of the past.

***

It had been some time since Potiphar departed to the prison to fetch Joseph to the court of Pharaoh. Finally, he and the handsome young man returned to the court accompanied by the daughter of Potipherah. Potiphar approached the Lord Chamberlain and said, "My Lord Chamberlain, the man Joseph, is here as Pharaoh requested."

"It is well, Lord Potiphar. I shall inform the Pharaoh." As the Chamberlain began walking toward the dais, Potiphar leaned toward Joseph and whispered. "Joseph, may your God be with all of us this day!"

Asenath also whispered to him, "May He bring an end to your suffering and bring you peace." She lowered her head and added. "You have suffered greatly because of the sins of my aunt."

Joseph looked at them both and smiled. "My God has been with me always. It will be well this day for all of us."

At the far end of the chamber, the Chamberlain's voice rose clearly, ringing throughout that great space. "Joseph, servant of Potiphar, come forth! Your Pharaoh would speak with you!"

Joseph bowed to Potiphar and Asenath. Then he walked slowly toward the dais. He walked like one of the Priests, with great dignity and authority, and there were many whispers in the audience remarking his strange manner. When he reached the dais, Joseph bowed deeply and said, "I am here, Great Pharaoh. How may I serve you?"

Pharaoh ignored the man's unusual approach and said without preamble, "I have dreamed a dream, and there are none here who can interpret it. I have heard it said of you that you have skill in the interpretation of night visions."

Joseph did not rise. From his bowed position, he said with great humility, "It is not in *me* to do so. God shall give Pharaoh an answer of peace."

"You are as humble as I have been told! Therefore, hear you then my dreams. In my dream, I stood upon the bank of the river. Behold, there came up out of the river seven kine, fat fleshed and well favored and they fed in a meadow. Then seven more kine came up after them, poor and very ill favored, lean fleshed, such as I never saw in all the land of Egypt. To my horror, the lean and the ill favored kine devoured the seven fat kine! Worse, they remained as ill favored as at the beginning. So I awoke.

"After a time, I slept again, but only to dream of seven ears of grain upon one stalk, full and good. Then seven ears that were withered, thin, and blasted with the east wind sprung up after them. The thin ears then devoured the seven good ears. Once more, I awoke. These dreams I have told the magicians and none could declare the meaning to me."

Joseph was silent for a few moments, and every eye in this great room was upon this young man. Finally, he spoke. "These two dreams of Pharaoh are one. God has shown Pharaoh what He is about to do. The seven good kine and the seven good ears are seven years. The seven thin and ill favored kine that came up after them and the seven empty ears blasted with the east wind are also seven years — seven years of famine." The word "famine" brought startled exclamations from many in the chamber.

Once more the Chamberlain had to restore order. "Silence in the court of Pharaoh!"

Amenemhet looked thoughtful and said, "There is a great ring of truth to your words, but *seven years* of famine?"

Joseph only nodded and continued. "What God is about to do, he has shown unto Pharaoh. Behold, there come seven years of great plenty throughout all the land of Egypt, and there shall arise after them seven years of great famine. All the plenty shall be forgotten in the land of Egypt as the famine shall consume the land and be very grievous."

Amenemhet asked anxiously, "When shall this come to pass?"

"Inasmuch as God has shown Pharaoh these things twice, He will shortly bring it to pass."

"What is to be done?"

Joseph, who had unconsciously risen, was now facing Pharaoh. "Now, therefore, let Pharaoh seek out a man discreet and wise and set him over the land of Egypt. Let Pharaoh appoint officers over the land and take up the fifth part of the land of Egypt in the seven plenteous years. Let them gather all the food of those good years and lay up grain under the hand of Pharaoh, and let them keep food in the cities, stored against the seven years of famine so that the land perishes not."

Once again there was murmuring in the court. This time the Chamberlain did not intercede but was staring at Joseph in astonishment. The interpretation was so simple when this man spoke!

Potipherah, unlike the Chamberlain, knew the source of what he was hearing. "If it pleases you Great One. That which this man speaks is great wisdom. It comes from God!" This pronouncement from one as influential as Potipherah set the court into a frenzy of whispered and mumbled comments.

During this babble, Asenath whispered to Potiphar, "He has done it!"

Potiphar, leaning close, whispered in her ear, "Nay, not he, little one! As Joseph would tell you, what you have just witnessed is the power of the God of his father's! But, quiet! Pharaoh speaks."

Amenemhet had risen from his throne and was addressing the crowd. "Can we find such a one as this man in whom the Spirit of God resides?"

There was a tremendous roar of "No!" from the assembled crowd.

Turning to face Joseph, Pharaoh continued. "Because God has shown you all this, there is none so discreet and wise as you are! You shall be over my house, and according unto your word shall all my people be ruled. Only in the throne will I be greater than you." Then moving to Joseph's side, Pharaoh said quietly to Joseph alone, "See, I have set you over all the land of Egypt."

Joseph, taken back by the proximity of the Great King, said in an astonished whisper, "Great One, I know not what to say. I am but a humble servant! God, not I, has given you peace!"

Amenemhet actually chuckled very quietly a moment, then whispered, "I shall share with you a great secret. Even Pharaoh is nothing but a servant! He serves your God as well as those of Egypt, *and* he serves all the people of Egypt, just as you will henceforth. We shall not be so different in our tasks, you and I!" Then he removed a ring from his finger, held it aloft for all to see, and announced loudly, "Hold forth your hand, Joseph. Before all present, I place my ring upon the finger of this man. This shall be his signet and his official seal."

Everyone in the chamber bowed and intoned, "So shall it be, Great Pharaoh!"

Amenemhet was not finished. "Chamberlain, fetch from my own wardrobe vestures of fine linen for Joseph. Also bring my second pectoral upon its gold chain. This shall be his badge of office." Then he turned and spoke to the waiting Potiphar at the end of the hall. "Potiphar, may Joseph retire to your house to prepare for his formal installation?"

Potiphar smiled and bowed deeply to the Pharaoh. "It will be my great honor to have him once more beneath my roof, Great One, even if for so short a time."

Amenemhet nodded and turned to the Chamberlain. "See to it that he rides to Potiphar's and then returns to his formal installation in my second chariot. Have the escort cry before him, 'Bow thy knee!' Because I have made him the ruler over all the land of Egypt!" As Joseph and his party left the chamber to the cheering of the assembled courtiers, Pharaoh turned to the Chamberlain and asked quietly, "Does this man have a wife?"

"He does not, my Pharaoh."

"Who would make this man a good wife in your estimation?"

Potipherah, who had been privy to the question, bowed and interrupted, "My, Pharaoh, if it pleases you, I would recommend my daughter, Asenath."

"Why do you make this recommendation?"

Potipherah smiled. "She has long been smitten with this man, but unlike her adulterous aunt, she has kept her silence and conducted herself with the utmost propriety around him."

"Very well then! His wife she shall be!" announced the pleased Pharaoh.

A very humble Joseph rode in state to the house of Potiphar preceded by the royal guards, who shouted, "Bow thy knee! Here comes Joseph, the ruler of all Egypt!" Once there, his greeting was jubilant indeed! The staff was overjoyed at seeing him again and mobbed him. He was almost smothered in hugs and kisses from his former friends. They were also ecstatic that he had been made the ruler of all Egypt. Hotem had even shouted, "If he cares for Egypt the way he cared for us, they will sing the praises of Amenemhet III for a thousand years!"

All in that house took great pride in preparing Joseph for his installation, the least task considered a high honor! It was not long before Joseph again stood before the Great Pharaoh, but this time resplendent."

This time, they did not meet in the Grand Hall of the Palace but stood upon the balcony that was built into the pylon on the outside of the palace. While Joseph had prepared for the presentation, a huge crowd gathered at the palace gates and it was thus "before all Egypt" that the installation was to take place. With

Joseph and the rest of the party already in place, Pharaoh walked to the center of the balcony. The crowd instantly became silent and bowed in respect.

Amenemhet raised his scepters and shouted, "All Egypt, hear! I am Pharaoh, and without this man, no man shall lift up his hand or foot in all the land of Egypt. He is to be known throughout all the land of Egypt by his title, Zaphnath-paaneah!" He paused and motioned to Asenath to step forward. Once she had done so, he placed her hand in the hand of Joseph and held their joined hands aloft for the crowd to see. "Be it also known that I give unto him as wife, Asenath, daughter of Potipherah, the priest of On."

The crowd shouted. "Hail Zaphnath-paaneah! Long live Zaphnath-paaneah!"

The couple was dismissed by the Pharaoh and made their way down the stairs in the pylon to the gateway, where Potiphar joined them. After hugging them both, he said to Joseph, "I am on the verge of tears, my old friend! Your God has saved us all! Now, I think it is time you spoke to this blushing maid at your side for she is now your blushing bride!" Potiphar started laughing and pointed at Joseph. "Look at your face!"

Joseph, who was blushing fiercely and had been staring wide eyed at Asenath, said sheepishly, "I told you once that, if I were to receive a beautiful wife at the hand of Pharaoh, my state of astonishment would be greater than yours was with your wife!"

Asenath, who was also blushing, asked, "Are you displeased with me?"

"Displeased? Nay, fair one. I am simply astonished beyond measure at my good fortune!" He then said softly. "I have loved you since the first time I saw you at Potiphar's gate! I. . . I thought you forever beyond my reach."

Asenath reached out and, caressing his face with her hands, said, "It is strange! For I have loved you from that very same moment!" After a short pause, she cocked her head prettily and said, "I like the title that Pharaoh has given you."

"You do?" Joseph was confused at the apparent change of subject.

"Indeed. 'He Who Reveals that Which is Hidden' describes your relationship with your God and to *my* heart!"

Chapter Ten
THE RULER OF ALL EGYPT

Joseph faced an interesting problem. He was made Vizier, ruler of all Egypt, based on a dream that *he* had interpreted! In the eyes of the unenlightened, this fact made his appointment, and thereby everything he said or did, false. He had to convince each and every Nomarch, the provincial governors, of the correctness of his mission — and that would be no easy task. They would be giving up one fifth of all they grew to Joseph and Pharaoh to store for the time of the famine, and this had never been done before. They would also need to build multiple huge storage vaults in each Nome for all the grain. This meant not just a loss of wealth but a large expense to the Nomarchs, who already thought they stored sufficient grain in the event the Nile failed to provide the water needed for abundant crops, a fairly frequent occurrence. These precautions had served Egypt and the Nomarchs for centuries, and the extreme precautions outlined by Joseph seemed suspicious, especially to the rulers of the outlying Nomes.

Egypt was having exceptionally good crops, as foretold by the dreams, which only served to compound his problems. Famine would not be recognized as a real threat until the people were staring a hungry vulture in the eye. Joseph had one great advantage over almost all the other men to hold such a vaunted position. He had the protection and guidance of the God of his fathers. He also had the help of friends, capable men all, who helped him in everything.

Joseph went about his new duties as he always had, with dedication and fairness, and nowhere were these attributes more evident than in Diwan, the court of the Vizier. This morning was no exception. Joseph was already seated. He turned and asked his scribe, "Has Potiphar reported this morning?"

Bowing low, the man replied, "He has, my Lord! He asked that you be informed that he is coming to meet with you late this afternoon after his inspection of the flood gates of the Fayum. He begs your forgiveness for his absence this morning."

Joseph nodded. "Thank you. There is nothing for which he needs forgiven! I myself must journey there upon his return. I await only his report before departing." Turning, he asked, "Chamberlain who is first to be seen today?"

The Chamberlain consulted the list that the scribe had given him. "The Nomarch of the Fifth Nome that of the Two Falcons has sent his representative, Ti, to discuss the granary you have required of him."

Joseph asked, "Is this he that kneels before me?"

The Chamberlain said very quietly. "He is not, Great One. That is he seated on the bench at the rear of the hall."

Joseph looked in the indicated direction and saw a well dressed young man sitting politely on the rear bench. Nodding in the man's direction to acknowledge his presence, Joseph said, "The Court of Pharaoh and his Vizier bid the Nomarch of the Fifth Nome's representative welcome. I will meet with you in due order, but it is the rule of this Diwan that an audience is not given to the man in the back before the man in front is heard."

The young man stood, bowed, and said politely, "This is as it should be, oh Vizier. Forgive, please, my impatience and impertinence."

"I thank you. Know that I understand your impatience, for the matter to be discussed is undoubtedly one of importance and will receive its full due." He bowed slightly to the young man. Then Joseph turned his attention to the man lying prostrate on the floor before him. "Now, who are you that kneels before me and what do you require?"

The man, who had remained quietly prostrate before Joseph until now, raised his head slightly and said, "If you it pleases, Great One. I am Khep, a simple farmer."

Joseph's brow wrinkled at the strange and difficult dialect, but he asked politely, "What is it you desire of this Diwan, Khep?"

Khep bowed to the ground, and then, raising his head, so that he could be heard, began. "If it you pleases, Great One. My brother elder became like the panthers of southern Egypt! He made sharp his dagger and took it in his hand. Then my brother stood behind the door of my stable to stab *me*, his younger brother, when I returned at eventide with my cattle! Now, when the God Shu was setting, I was loading myself with green herbs of all kinds of the fields, according to my habit of every day, and I was coming home."

The Chamberlain, who had obviously lost patience with the man's involved story and strange dialect, snapped, "Cowherd! Your speech is strange and you waste the time of the Great One!"

Joseph held up his hand and got the attention of the Chamberlain. He signaled him to come close, then very quietly said, "Have patience, good Chamberlain. His speech is quite rural and difficult, but a man with a grievance likes his tale of woe to be heard even more than he wants it put right!" Turning back to the prostrate Khep, Joseph said, "Pray Khep, continue."

Khep, worried about the Chamberlain's complaint, said, "I do not the time of the Great One wish to waste!"

"Hearing your grievance *is* the business of this Diwan! Pray, continue."

Khep's tone became even more humble. "If. . . If it you pleases." Clearing his throat nervously, he continued. "The cow leading entered into the stable, and she said to her keeper, 'Verily your brother elder standeth in front of you with his dagger to stab you. Run away from before him.' I harkened unto the speech of my cow leading. The next entered and she was saying unto me likewise. I looked under the door of my stable and saw the legs of my brother elder as he stood behind the door, his dagger in his hand. I set my load upon the ground, and then I betook myself to flight rapid!"

Joseph quietly whispered to the Chamberlain. "What say you now, good Chamberlain? Do you still think this hearing is a waste of our time?"

"I am ashamed, my Lord."

Joseph, still whispering said, "Be not ashamed. Patience is not an easy virtue to cultivate! It will come." Turning to the side of the room, Joseph addressed a burly young man standing there. "Constable! Go with this man. Arrest his elder brother and bring him hither! He must account for his murderous anger at the next Diwan."

The Constable bowed. "It will be done as you have commanded, Great One! Come, Khep. Let us find this elder brother who would do you harm."

Khep looked at Joseph with unmistakable gratitude in his eyes and stammered, "Thank you, Great One!" He then quickly followed the constable out of the room.

Joseph heard many other cases while the representative of the

Fifth Nome sat quietly listening. He had been told what to expect when he came before Joseph, but he was not prepared for the patient and fair man he encountered, a man who, unlike so many, followed the traditional charge of his office. He listened as each case was presented with dignity and respect. Some cases, like Khep's, were serious matters, while others were frivolous. But whatever the case presented, it was dealt with fairly. This was not the self-important greedy individual he had been told to expect. Finally, Ti's turn came.

The Chamberlain announced, "Ti, representative of the Fifth Nome, come forward. The Vizier would speak with you."

Ti walked forward and bowed before the dais. "Great Zaphnath-paaneah, I come as the representative of Satsobek, the Nomarch of the Fifth Nome."

Joseph nodded his acknowledgment of the greeting. "In the name of Satsobek, we greet you. You have been greatly patient. There were many before you."

"I thank the Gods for it, Great One. It was time well spent and highly informative," Ti said.

"You have come far, and I suspect that your mission is not only imperative but complex. If it pleases you, let us adjourn to my residence. It is the time of the noon meal. We can, perhaps, defeat two demons at once — hunger and complexity."

Ti could not help but chuckle at the man's sense of humor. "I would be honored, Great One!"

Joseph turned to the Chamberlain. "That will be enough for this morning, I think. Would you be so kind as to bring Ti to the residence after you have dismissed the Diwan for the day?"

The Chamberlain bowed. "It would be my pleasure to do both of those things, Great One." He then faced those gathered and announced, "This proceeding is adjourned. All rise! Lord Zaphnath-paaneah departs!" The entire assembly rose and bowed. Joseph rose from his chair and departed from the hall while the crowd continued to genuflect. As soon as he had left the hall, everyone stood upright and a lively babble broke out as they began discussing the day's cases. The Lord Chamberlain approached Ti and said formally over the din, "Lord Ti, if you will follow me, I will escort you to the Master's home."

"I thank you, Chamberlain." They left the hall and proceeded down the street. After a few moments, they came to the pylon and gate of a sizeable estate. Once inside, Ti was struck by the colorful place. "The grounds here are beautiful! I have never seen such lush flowerbeds!" Ti exclaimed.

The Chamberlain smiled as though he were enjoying some private joke. Noticing Ti's hurt reaction, he quickly apologized. "Forgive me please, my Lord, but I think I will have to let the Great One and his Lady explain the beauty of these gardens to you. It is something of which both are rightly proud!"

They continued down the beautifully raked gravel walk into the estate's residence. Like so many Egyptian residences of the high born, this one was colorfully painted, but absent were the usual depictions of the Gods of Egypt. Instead, the walls had intricate geometric designs and pastoral scenes. Despite the lack of depictions of the Gods, the effect was beautiful. They walked along the highly polished stone floors enjoying the coolness of the halls. Finally, they came to the inner hall, where Joseph and his wife were waiting. Joseph rose to greet them as they entered the room. "Lord Ti! Welcome to my home!" He extended both his hands in the Egyptian handshake. Then he turned to the Chamberlain. "Would you please join us as well?"

"I would be greatly honored, Noble One!"

Gesturing to the lovely lady who was already seated, Joseph added, "Before we sit, gentlemen, may I present my lovely bride, the Lady Asenath!"

Both men bowed deeply to the smiling lady of the house, and together they said, "My Lady."

Joseph indicated the two remaining tables in the room and said, "Gentlemen, please, sit!"

As soon as he was seated, Ti began. "Lord Zaphnath-paaneah. . ."

Asenath, raising a hand in mild protest, laughingly said, "Please, Lord Ti. This is our home. Call my husband Joseph."

Ti, unused to such informality, was unsure how to proceed and stammered, "I fear that would be rude, as I am but a humble servant. . ."

Joseph, smiling, held up a forestalling hand and said confidentially, "Let me share a secret that a good friend of mine once shared with me – we are all but servants! You serve your master, the Nomarch, and I serve the Pharaoh, who serves everyone else!"

Ti was frightened. He had never heard such blasphemy! Every Egyptian knew that all were born to serve the Pharaoh, not the other way round! Pale faced, he blurted out, "How can you say such a thing of the Great Pharaoh?"

Joseph leaned forward, and in a conspiratorial, dramatic whisper said, "It was *he* who told that to *me*!"

Ti's head was swimming! Who was this man? If what he had just said was true, he was a confidant of Pharaoh himself! He sat with his eyes wide and his mouth open for several seconds before it dawned on him that this Joseph was indeed the ruler of all Egypt. Of course he was a confidant of the Pharaoh! Totally abashed at his own lack of understanding, he meekly said, "Oh!" He then silently thanked the Gods that, before he could continue and make a bigger fool of himself, the meal was delivered by the servants with much shuffling of feet and clanking of dinnerware.

Joseph, who seemed to take no offense at Ti's remarks, was looking happily at the dishes set before him. "Ah Knut!" he announced happily. "The meal looks wonderful! You have outdone yourself!" Taking the cover off one of the dishes and sniffing at the steaming contents, he added blissfully. "It smells even better!"

Ti was again taken aback when Knut, the serving woman, actually giggled and, blushing, replied, "Master, you say this at every meal!"

Joseph laughed heartily. "It is true — at every meal!" Knut giggled even harder and then turned to run from the room.

Ti watched these exchanges with a growing sense of wonder, even astonishment. He had never seen the like. If one of the serving women had acted thus in the hall of Satsobek, she would have been flogged! Looking around the room, he discovered that everyone was actually relaxed. Only he seemed to see something amiss.

Joseph sensed his discomfort. "Ah, this is one of my great joys, Ti. I am home so seldom that I truly relish the time I have within these walls, especially now that my beautiful wife is with child." To his left, the beautiful Lady Asenath smiled and blushed prettily. Ti noticed for the first time that indeed the seated lady was pregnant. His attention was abruptly drawn back as Joseph spoke once more.

"That is not why you are here, though. Your Master, the Nomarch, has serious concerns about the tithe and the granaries he has been ordered to construct. He doubts the interpretation of the dreams, and he doubts my appointment, does he not? He fears I intend to glut myself on the hard work of the good people of his excellent Nome. I will do what I can to set his concerns at rest, good Ti."

Now Ti was genuinely astounded. "You have expressed each of my master's concerns! How . . .?"

Joseph smiled and raised a dismissive hand. "He is not the first to express them. May I ask you a question?"

"Ask on."

"Why does your master think that he has been commanded to construct such large granaries so close to his capital city and then in each of the towns and cities of his Nome?"

Ti's expression was of one who has heard this argument many times. "He understands this not. He is concerned that they can only be opened by your command and will have your seal upon them and troops to ensure that only your representatives have access to the stores."

Joseph noted a look of distrust on the man's face. Thoughtfully he said, "Perhaps I can best answer this with another question. If the Nile were low in the extreme, could heavy cargo ships, filled with food, make passage from the Lower Kingdom to the Upper?"

Ti was taken by surprise by the question. "They . . . could not." Then the distrustful expression common to dwellers of the Upper Nile returned. The look of distrust the dwellers of the Nomes reserved for all those from the better favored lower Nile. He continued. "Such an extremity would not affect the Lower Kingdom. The flow of the Nile from the Fayum down is fed by the great lake. You would not suffer."

Joseph did not let the man bait him. He simply looked the man in the eye and said the very thing he didn't expect. "Nor would you, for the grain to feed your people would already be in place. There is no need to transport that which is already available."

Ti had obviously been prepared for his mission. With a dismissive gesture, he said, "My master is no fool, Great One. He understands mathematics. You have set back one fifth of the grain for this 'supposed' seven-year famine from each of the seven hypothetical 'good' years. Even if the crops were double the normal harvest in those years, this plan would set back only enough grain for two and four fifths years. It is not enough! My Master suspects a deeper purpose."

Again Joseph did not rise to the implied slur. "Tell me Ti, have you been in the fields this season?"

Ti simply shrugged as if to suggest that this was of no importance to their discussion and said, "No, I have not."

The Chamberlain, who had been growing agitated at the young man's obstinacy, blurted, "The crops are more lush than any of the farmers can remember! The yield could easily triple the normal harvest!" Realizing that he had spoken out of turn, the Chamberlain then turned to Joseph, and bowing low to him, said with a gasp, "Forgive me, Great One! I meant not to intrude upon this conversation!"

Joseph signaled the man to rise. "There is nothing to forgive. Your spirit does you credit!" There was a reassuring mildness to his voice and the Chamberlain relaxed. Turning back to Ti, Joseph continued. "Ti, with normal plantings the amounts set in reserve would indeed yield only enough for four and one fifth years, but the plantings are not normal but fully one third greater. That should bring the total to six and one quarter years of food in storage."

Still unconvinced, Ti replied, "That is still three quarters of a year short of the seven years of dirge you have predicted and leaves nothing for the planting of the eighth year!"

Joseph simply smiled as one who has a secret and said, "You have not taken something into your accounting, Ti."

Ti, slightly angered at what he perceived as smugness, snapped, "What is that?"

Joseph, still smiling, asked, "Have you not mentioned the Great Lake at the Fayum?"

This time Ti was caught off guard. He answered cautiously, "I did?"

Joseph nodded and then calmly said, "With the water that flows down the Nile for the extra one hundred days that the lake will supply, there are now two full growing seasons possible in the delta. As you know, the growing area of the Delta is fully twice that of the Upper Nile. If the crops are only doubled, then this alone would make the difference, but since they are triple, we will have enough grain for all of Egypt, food for our families and our livestock and seed for fourteen years!"

Joseph could see Ti running the numbers in his head. Then, in a surprised tone, he said, "Is that possible?"

The Chamberlain could no longer contain his enthusiasm. "Yes, it is! And that is not counting the reclaimed fertile lands at the mouth of the Fayum that can produce an astounding total of *three million measures* of barley a year and that is in a normal year!"

Joseph nodded his agreement. "All of that excess will be spread between the Nomes in proportion to their populations, Ti. It will be shipped while the Nile is high and can support the shipping. That is why the huge granaries were commanded to be built."

Ti had never in his life considered such events. In an astonished tone, he said, "We had not taken this into account, but -."

Joseph held up a forestalling hand and said, "Have patience until the end of this year's harvest. If this plan is not borne out, then your master is free to ignore my commands."

Ti's astonishment was growing. With wide eyes he said, "Do you mean this?"

"Indeed I do! Now, I believe that this excellent meal is getting cold. Let us apply ourselves to prevent such a disaster!"

Ti was caught off guard and disarmed. He could only laugh. *"That* is a disaster I will gladly help you prevent!" A look of curiosity passed over the young man's face and he asked, "Lord there is a personal question I would ask of you."

"Ask on."

"As we were coming into your estate, I noted the beauty of the flowerbeds, and the Chamberlain said that I would have to ask you about them. The flowers are familiar, yet unfamiliar."

Asenath giggled and covered her mouth. The action brought a funny look from Ti and broad grins from both her husband and the Chamberlain. It was Joseph who spoke first. "I think it should be you who explains your amusement, my wife."

Recovering, Asenath looked at the young Lord and said apologetically, "Forgive my outburst, but you are not the first to ask about the gardens and I am afraid it is something of a family joke. The garden was a gift from our friend Potiphar and his lovely new bride Benar. She is an excellent gardener and manages to raise a great deal of our food in those flowerbeds!"

Ti's jaw dropped and he exclaimed, "Food?"

Asenath's smile widened at his astonishment. "With the exception of the boiled barley, everything on the table before you came from that 'flower garden!"

Ti stared at the huge meal spread before him, the great variety of vegetables on the plates and in the bowls, and then, looking at Joseph with true amazement and admiration in his eyes, he said, "My amazement knows no bounds! If you can do *this*, you are capable of the miracle of feeding all of Egypt for seven years with nothing but a fifth of the harvest!"

Joseph's expression indicated that he was pleased by the compliment. But there was a very serious shade to his voice as he responded. "No, good Ti. It is not I that will feed Egypt. It is God."

Joseph, though he did not know it at the time, was not through with the Fifth Nome. Although Ti was thoroughly convinced of the need for the commanded food storage, his Nomarch definitely was not. When he heard Ti's report, he became furious and began plotting the overthrow of Joseph — and perhaps of the Pharaoh himself. Joseph was to find this out sometime later, when, once more, he and his wife were entertaining. This time the guests were Potiphar and his beautiful wife Benar.

Potiphar sat looking thoughtfully at Joseph as he interacted with Asenath. This was good to see. Benar had told Potiphar how lonesome Asenath had been during Joseph's absence. How good it was to see them both smiling and joking with one another. After a time, he said, "It is good to see you home, Joseph! You have spent several months touring the Nomes of the Upper Kingdom. You were missed here."

Joseph looked at his friend and smiled. "I must confess that I am very glad to be here. However, I did receive a large shock when I got home."

"What was that?"

Joseph pointed laughingly to the very gravid Asenath. "I was not prepared to see my wife so great with child. She was just a little thing when I left."

Asenath, with the defensiveness of any pregnant woman, was definitely put out at Joseph's mention of her current size. "My husband, you were gone for three full months and I was almost three months along when you left!"

Joseph, holding up his hands as though to ward off an attack, said defensively, "I complain not, my wife. I only said that it was a surprise." Turning to his guests, he pointed to her swollen stomach and said, "I must confess, I fear she is going to give birth to an ox! The child must be huge!"

Asenath exclaimed, "Oh! So you are one of the midgets of the

Pharaoh's court and your child will be tiny? Then the small size of the child within will be a great blessing when it comes my birthing day!" She had to wait to continue, as all three members of her audience were laughing unto tears. When she could be heard, she continued. "What did you expect? You are a large and powerful man, and your son will undoubtedly be like his father!" There was unmistakable pride in her voice.

Potiphar gazed at Asenath for a few moments, and then suddenly said, "Benar and I have good news as well. We too are with child!"

Asenath trilled her delight at this news. "That is wonderful! How do you feel, Benar?"

Benar blushed and stole a sideways glance at her new husband. "I am fine. Potiphar worries though. He is afraid bearing the child will injure me."

Joseph's face suddenly wore the identical expression of concern that was on Potiphar's face. "I for one can share that fear. I remember all too well the horrid injuries you suffered as a child!"

Potiphar now had a pained faraway look. "I only saw them after the fact, but that was terrible enough! All those years that she could not even stand upright! I know that the physician says that she will be fine, but I still worry."

Asenath, with a smile on her face and mock sternness in her voice, said, "Both of you are a pair of old worry warts!" Making a dismissive gesture she added, "She will be fine!"

Joseph sighed heavily and, staring at the floor, said distractedly, "It is pleasure to worry about something so pleasant for a change!"

Potiphar's tone matched Joseph's when he spoke. "You are thinking of Satsobek the Nomarch of the Fifth Nome?"

"Indeed I am. Through his messenger, Ti, I told him that he was to wait for the harvest, and if it were poor, or indeed normal, he was released from the orders I had given him previously."

Potiphar's tone was incredulous. "The harvest is huge, and it's not all in! In the Fifth Nome the yield is almost fourfold the normal year! Yet still he doubts?"

"He not only doubts but is quite vocal that I, 'like all false magicians,' faked the interpretation of Pharaoh's dreams to gain my position. He is spreading this as a fact through the Upper Nomes. The Nomarchs are all beginning to show reluctance at the requirements set by the Pharaoh for the survival of Egypt in the event of the famine. Potiphar, how did Satsobek come so quickly to your mind?"

"Joseph, forgive me. I have also been traveling about the land for Pharaoh. He too is concerned by the rumors that are reaching the court. I had to report to him before I could report to you, and by the time I had given him the news, you had departed on your harvest tour of the country. I heard a report that Satsobek was murmuring rebellion against your just demands." Potiphar paused for a moment, carefully weighing his next words, then said slowly, "It is reported that he intends to sell all the tithe grain in order to buy a large quantity of tin."

Joseph was alarmed. "Tin?" His visage then turned a dangerous color. He was becoming exceedingly angry and it was showing on his face. "There could only be one purpose for such a purchase!"

Asenath, who seldom saw the anger in Joseph, was alarmed. "Why so angry, my husband?"

Joseph, looking quite contrite for upsetting his wife, answered, "Forgive the outburst, my wife. Tin is critical ingredient metal in bronze. The only reason he would need large quantities would be to forge weapons, weapons that could only be used for a standing army in a single Nome!"

Potiphar too was showing his disgust at the Nomarch's actions and spat out, "He would bring back the days of incessant civil wars and attempts on the throne itself. Such nonsense was stopped by the wisdom of Sesostris III, who disallowed the Nomarchs their own standing armies!"

Both women were alarmed at the implications and said the dire word they feared together: "War?"

Potiphar took his bride's hands in his own, and in the most reassuring voice he could muster, said, "Have no fear! Have no fear! Joseph has ample time to stop the fool before he can do any real harm. The harvest is not yet finished. He has only just approached the Phoenician traders about the purchase, and they have not had time to acquire the metal. Nor has Satsobek shipped the grain for payment down the Nile."

Joseph, who had remained silent, asked thoughtfully, "Is young Ti involved in this?"

"It was he who made me aware of the Satsobek's treasonable

activities, Joseph."

Joseph nodded at this comment and his face showed his content at what he had just heard about young Ti. Then his countenance hardened and he said. "The time has come for you and I to speak to Pharaoh. This man must be stopped, and quickly!"

Indeed, Joseph and Potiphar met with their Pharaoh, who wisely elected to hold a conclave of Nomarchs in the capitol. All the Nomarchs were required to attend this special meeting, and here, behind closed, locked doors, the traitorous Satsobek was to be exposed.

The Nomarchs gathered on the appointed day in the great hall of the Pharaoh, and each of the thirty-three Nomes was represented by its Nomarch along with some members of their staff. It was a large and colorful party, and only a few noted the large number of Pharaoh's personal body guards, who literally ringed the walls of the room. Those who did notice were ill at ease but helpless to alter the situation for they had been ordered to leave their own personal guards outside the audience chamber.

When Pharaoh entered the chamber, the doors, surprisingly and most unusually, were locked. All present bowed, and Pharaoh wasted no time, personally addressing those assembled as soon as the Chamberlain had raised them to their feet.

"I thank you great Nomarchs for coming to meet in conclave this day. I know it is a long journey for most of you, and the effort is appreciated. Unfortunately, it is a sad duty that has forced me to call you together. There is the stench of rebellion in the land. One Nomarch would, by force, alter the affairs of the kingdom. Is that not so, Satsobek?"

With the mention of a specific Nomarch, the assembly began to buzz excitedly. For his part, Satsobek stepped forward, and with a tone filled with innocence, declared, "I know not of what you speak, Great One. I am, as always, your most faithful servant!"

Amenemhet's tone, when he responded, made it clear he did not believe a single word the man was uttering. "Is that so? Then, my 'loyal Nomarch,' why are you negotiating with the Phoenicians for large quantities of tin? Why was the payment for the metal to be the tithe grain that you were to set aside for the survival of your people in the famine to come?"

Satsobek, in an oily and deceptive tone, replied, "My Pharaoh, you have been misinformed. It is true that I buy the tin and that I use the grain to pay for it, but it is to your salvation that I do this."

Amenemhet's tone when he responded was rife with derision. "My salvation? Do you not know that it has been against the laws of the land for a Nomarch to maintain or recruit a standing army since the days of my father, Sesostris III?"

Satsobek bowed, and with words intended to confuse, he intoned soothingly, "Indeed! I know this, Great One, but I do it in desperation! I would save *you* from a vile creature, he who has deceived you." As he talked, he warmed to his subject and began shouting. "I would save you from he who is nothing more than a lying, deceitful, and false magician — this . . . this . . . Joseph! I would save you from the one who lords it over us with his self-proclaimed title of 'He who reveals that which is hidden!' It is HE who would defraud you, Oh Great Pharaoh! It is HE, not I, who would glut himself on the labors of this people then use the very grain of their supposed 'salvation' to overthrow you!"

Amenemhet sat nodding as though Satsobek were making his point. When Satsobek had finished, Pharaoh said reasonably, "I see." Then with a wrinkled brow as though thinking very hard, he asked, "How, good Satsobek, will he glut himself on grain that is stored hard by the cities where it will be needed?" Holding up a hand to forestall an answer, Amenemhet turned to the Chamberlain, who was standing beside his king, and asked thoughtfully, "Chamberlain, who was it gave the name 'He who reveals that which is hidden' to Joseph?"

The Chamberlain, unlike Pharaoh, was literally staring daggers at the oily Satsobek. In a hard voice that clearly showed his dislike of the man, he said, "It was you, Great One."

Amenemhet nodded pleasantly, as though the answer had been equally pleasant, and asked further, "And what is the report of this year's harvest?"

The Chamberlain bowed but his malignant glare was still fixed on Satsobek. He replied, "It is reported that this year's is the largest harvest ever recorded in the history of the nation, in most places threefold the normal and in some fourfold. The second planting in the Lower Kingdom is already showing the blade, and it is reported that this crop too is full and more lush than ever seen before. The harvest from the reclaimed area of the Fayum was also fourfold the normal harvest and is lush with its second growth."

Amenemhet once more nodded as though being reminded of

forgotten facts. "Ah, yes, I see. I thank you, good Chamberlain." Then, turning to Satsobek, he said calmly, "How do you answer all of this, Satsobek?"

Satsobek, realizing that his deceptions were not working, replied in desperation. "The man is a foul magician, Pharaoh! He can alter the mind! How he will advantage himself of the grain, I know not. I know only that he will! As to the harvest, it is nothing but a coincidence. Such a thing could happen in any season!" There was a quiet murmur of agreement among the assembled Nomarchs to this last statement.

Amenemhet looked thoughtful for a moment, and as the Nomarchs agreed to Satsobek's last comments, he had nodded as though he himself agreed. Then, after scratching his chin thoughtfully for a moment, he pointed to Joseph. "So, this man, Joseph, while he was in chains in the prison, interpreted the dreams of *two* of Pharaoh's servants correctly. Then, while still in the prison, he forced his Pharaoh to have not one but *two* dreams that only *he* can interpret! Then, once released from confinement, he devised a plan by which the people of this land could survive *any* famine, a plan that increased the amount of farmland, and in his spare time, he has acted as one of the most just Viziers Egypt has ever seen — and he has achieved all this as a deception?" The room erupted into gales of laughter.

Satsobek was beside himself. He was being ridiculed by Pharaoh himself! Worse, his humiliation was before all the Nomarchs of Upper Egypt. Unfortunately for him, his lying words were also being disproved. He sputtered, defeated for the moment. "I. . . I. . . That is. . ."

Amenemhet pounced. His voice became like an avenging whip. "You seem to have lost the use of your tongue, which of late has been so vocal. Pray, find the use of your tongue once more and answer your Pharaoh this: Why did you not inform your Pharaoh of your concerns instead of buying the materials for which there could have been but a single purpose, to enforce your views by the edge of the sword?" Stunned by the sudden change in their Pharaoh, the assembled Nomarchs were as silent as if in the tomb. Into this profound stillness, Amenemhet shouted, "Answer me!"

Satsobek, his nerve beginning to fail, made one last attempt at a defense. "Great Pharaoh, I did send an emissary to this Joseph, but he returned with nonsense about water flows, increased harvests, and such. It was all double talk meant to deceive!"

Amenemhet, his voice still hard, replied, "So you decided, in your great wisdom, that your next best option was force of arms and not direct communion with your Pharaoh?"

Satsobek stared about himself in desperation. He could see in the eyes of the other Nomarchs that he had completely lost their support. He made one last hopeless attempt to sway them back to his way of thinking. He shouted, "Do you hear this, my brother Nomarchs? Do you not hear the results of this . . . this . . . *Hebrew's* treachery? He has bewitched the Pharaoh himself! He. . ."

He had gone too far! Total pandemonium erupted in the court. Angry shouts rent the air.

"Blasphemer!"

"Vile usurper!"

"Whose Nome would you have conquered first, mine?"

"He speaks treason!"

"Cut out his lying tongue!"

"I was here! I saw and heard all! Do you call ME bewitched?"

Amenemhet let the Nomarchs vent for several moments, and then he bellowed, "Silence!" At his shout, the Nomarchs slowly regained some measure of composure, but if their glares could have been given sound, the resulting din would have been quite deafening!

Turning to the numerous guards, Amenemhet shouted "Guards! Bind that man! Then gag the foul traitor's mouth!" The guards moved with almost blinding speed. In a trice, they had the man bound and wound a gag over his mouth. Still, he attempted to shout through the gag. Amenemhet was furious. "Traitor! You would have built a standing army to forge rebellion, a rebellion that would have cost the blood of many, many innocent Egyptians. Bloodshed simply for your own aggrandizement? You are condemned by the words that have come out of your own mouth! Potiphar!"

Potiphar, who had already stepped forward to assist the guards, replied crisply, "I am here, my Pharaoh!"

Amenemhet, pointing to the prisoner, said, "Stand ready, Potiphar." Then in a voice as grim as death itself he proclaimed, "Satsobek, hear your full sentence! For treason most foul, you will be taken from this place and hanged from a tree by the neck until you are dead! No man will remove your bones from there. You will be without a grave in Egypt! Your flesh will be consumed by the fowls of the air and your bones will be scattered by the hyenas that there will be nothing of your foul person that will remain to stain Egypt!" Turning to Potiphar, he said, "Potiphar, carry out the sentence!"

Potiphar saluted. "Immediately, my Pharaoh!" He then turned and motioned to the guards to follow him with the prisoner. Satsobek began to struggle. Falling to the floor, he tried everything in his power to escape. Although he was a large and powerful man, Satsobek's best efforts were to no avail. He was ultimately dragged from the chamber. The Nomarchs stood silently and watched the drama play itself out. Those who had backed Satsobek looked frightened, while others were righteously indignant.

Amenemhet let the silence drag on for some time. Then he turned to Joseph and said calmly, "Joseph is there another that would be suited to fill the post of the Nomarch of the Fifth Nome?"

Joseph, not taken by surprise, answered smoothly, "I would recommend Ti, the young noble from that Nome, my Pharaoh."

Amenemhet, forgoing the usual amenities, beckoned imperiously for the young noble to approach and ordered, "Ti, come forward!"

Ti nervously stepped to the dais with a stunned expression on his face. He bowed low to his king and nervously said, "I am here, my Pharaoh!"

"Ti, from this day forth, you are the Nomarch of the Fifth Nome!" Then to the chamber as a whole he shouted, "It is done! Hear me, my Nomarchs! There remain only six years to garner enough food to feed our people during the predicted seven years of famine. Pray, you take heed to Joseph's commands. He has the grace of his God with him, and with the help of God we will survive that which is coming!"

So it was that, with the great help of Joseph's God, Pharaoh and Joseph solidified the Nomarchs behind the food storage project. They all cooperated from that time forth, and in the seven plenteous years, the earth brought forth grain by the handfuls. Joseph gathered up all the tithe grain of the seven years and laid up the food in the cities, and the harvest of the fields round about every city was stored in the same city. Joseph gathered grain as though it were the sand of the sea, until he quit counting for it was without number!

However, not all Joseph's duties involved the coming famine.

There were more pleasant duties as well. Three months after the elevation of Ti to the position of Nomarch, Joseph, who was holding a Diwan, turned to his Chamberlain and asked, "Who is the next petitioner?"

The Chamberlain leaned forward and consulted the scribe's list. "That would be the messenger from the Eighth Nome. He. . ." As he began to explain the man's needs, they were interrupted by a messenger bursting into the Diwan chamber.

The man laid prostrate before Joseph, then said through his labored breathing, "Great . . . One. . . You must . . . come at once!"

Joseph was naturally alarmed. "Why? What has happened?"

"Your wife has just given birth to your firstborn son!"

Joseph was flabbergasted. "What?" Before he could say more, the room erupted into cheers! Everyone seemed to shout in unison, "Long live the House of Joseph!"

The now smiling Chamberlain pounded his staff loudly and shouted over the din, "This Diwan is concluded and will continue tomorrow. God has intervened! Let all cheer the arrival of the Great One's firstborn son!" The room went wild! The grinning Chamberlain turned to Joseph and shouted over the noise, "Master! All Egypt celebrates with you! Now, go and greet your new son!"

Joseph, who was grinning broadly, laughed and shouted in return, "So let it be written, and so it WILL be done! Still laughing Joseph rushed from the chamber.

In no time he was running up the stairs to his rooms. As he hurried down the hall, he could hear the soft cries of a newborn infant coming from the room he shared with Asenath. Entering carefully, a wonderful sight greeted his eyes. There, lying on the bed, her face all aglow, was Asenath; and in her arms was the source of the crying — Joseph's firstborn child. He remembered that the messenger had said it was a boy. He stood there numbly staring at his wife and the child, the words, *"My firstborn son!"* repeating over and over in his head. Unbidden, tears of joy filled his eyes. When he tried to speak, he found that there was a rather large lump in the way. "My. . . My wife why did you not let me know your time had come so that I could be with you?"

Although Asenath was smiling, it was obvious that she was exhausted from childbirth. Her voice was tired when she spoke, yet it was filled with humor and love. "There was nothing you could have done, save wring your hands, my husband." She looked down upon the wailing infant and smiled. "He is a fine strong boy, our son!"

Joseph, still fighting tears, choked out. "He has good lungs!" With tears streaming down his cheeks, he declared. "I think his name shall be Manasseh, which means 'forgetting' in my language, for God has made me forget all my toil and all my Father's house."

Two years later, a second son was born, Ephraim, which in Hebrew means, "fruitful." He was thus named, because, Joseph said, "God hath caused me to be fruitful in the land of my affliction."

Chapter Note:

The text of Khep's story was a translation of the ancient Egyptian story, "The Tale of the Two Brothers." It was adapted into the first person for use here. The original was taken from Sir E.A Wallis Budge's book *Egyptian Language*, pages 38-42 (Copyright 1993). The transcript was left in a literal translation state to create the impression of a primitive rural dialect.

Chapter Eleven
THE DEARTH BEGINS

It is a sad truth, but the death of Satsobek did not completely stop the self-serving attitude of the Nomarchs of the Upper Kingdom. With the exception of the loyal Ti, the sedition spread across the entire region. The reason for the disloyalty and disbelief was simple. For six years after the death of Satsobek, Egypt enjoyed huge crop yields and the granaries were full to overflowing. Such plenty stood in stark contrast to talk of famines. Several of the Nomarchs used this to quietly foment rebellion, but the harvests were also beginning to change.

After seven years of unparalleled plenty, a drought was beginning, and everywhere in Egypt eyes were fixed on the river gauges. In every marketplace, shop, and even in the halls of the government the main topic of conversation was the lack of water in the Nile. This was the most discussed issue in the home of Joseph.

Once more, Joseph and Asenath had dinner guests, including his father-in-law, Potipherah, and his wife, Knumah. Joseph knew that something was bothering the man, but he kept his counsel. Finally, late in the evening, Potipherah spoke what was on his mind. With a look of concern on his face, he said, "My son, the summer solstice has passed. There is much anxiety in the land."

Potiphar and the lovely Benar were also guests in the house of Joseph, and Potiphar nodded his head and added, "Indeed, I have even seen the peasants staring at the water levels at the river gauges."

Potipherah nodded in agreement. "Indeed, Potiphar, so have I. Even the meanest peasants know that Egypt is a gift of the Nile, and this year, the Nile rises little." Turning to Joseph, he asked, "What is the status of the great lake at the Fayum, my son?"

Joseph had remained silent as the other spoke, but he now answered, "It too is low, my father-in-law. There will be water to drink, but there will not be sufficient water to raise crops this season. The time of the great dearth has finally arrived."

Asenath's face showed the worry that only such a word as "dearth" could create in a desert community. "You mean the seven years of famine that you predicted to Pharaoh?"

"That is exactly what I mean, my wife."

Asenath looked abashed. "I had forgotten about that."

Joseph, taking her hand, said gently, "Some of us are not permitted to forget it, my love."

Potiphar gave a derisive snort and said scathingly, "That cannot be said of the Nomarchs of the Upper Kingdom, Joseph."

Joseph, ever aware of his friend's keen insights, asked, "What do you mean, Potiphar?"

"There is still rebellion in the Upper Kingdom. The death of Satsobek just drove it underground. The dearth has begun exactly as you said it would, but the Lords of the Upper Nile claim this is just a bad year and cite other years when the flood was insufficient. They say that this lack of water will pass and next year we will again see large yields in the harvest, that such things are common. They continue to quote Satsobek and insist that you are a false seer, that you have glutted yourself all these years on the excess grain that could have gone to 'worthy' projects and not into 'your' storehouses."

"What are they doing about the possibility of famine?"

Potipherah answered the question. "They are doing as they have always done, my son — planning to ration the grain they normally set aside in case of a bad year. I know also that all of them are having every square cubit of land possible tilled. Many boast that next year will be the 'mistress of wheat, barley, and all things.'"

Joseph's look became thoughtful. "What of young Ti? Is he joining this sedition?"

Potiphar's tone indicated his strong approval of the young Nomarch. "He has not. He remains loyal to the crown."

Joseph asked hopefully, "Does he know who the new leader of this sedition is?"

"He is not sure. The southern Nomarchs do not talk much in his presence for his views make him suspect to the other Nomarchs, but he has kept his ears open and the name of Qebu, the Nomarch of the Third Nome, seems to be spoken all too often."

Joseph turned to Potipherah and asked thoughtfully, "My father-in-law, was it not the Nomarch of the Fourth Nome who led the rebellion against Pharaoh Mentuhotep III?"

Potiphar was slightly surprised at the question, but at the same time was filled with pleasure at Joseph's knowledge. "It was indeed!" He replied happily. "I see that you have profited greatly from all those evenings of study in the Temple Library!" He then became serious and thoughtful. "You are thinking that it has been the last five Nomes before the first cataract that have led the most recent rebellions against the throne, are you not?"

"Indeed." Joseph paused for a moment, staring thoughtfully at the floor before he continued quietly, "I have reports from caravans that the weather in all the lands around us is bad. Other countries are going to be very short of food this year."

Potiphar gasped. Then he got a faraway look on his face and said, apparently quoting from something unfamiliar to Potipherah, "'And in all the land of Egypt, there will be bread!' This is a serious problem, Joseph! Every one of our neighbors will want to raid Egypt for the stored food supplies."

"I know. That may, however, work to the advantage of the crown," Joseph added thoughtfully. Potiphar said nothing. He simply nodded his agreement with Joseph's assessment.

Potipherah looked from Joseph to Potiphar and then at Joseph again. They often finished each other's sentences, so in accord were their minds, and this appeared to be one of those times. He could not follow their rapid thoughts. Thus, he asked, "How is that?"

Potiphar respectfully replied, "This will allow Pharaoh to station large garrisons in all the Nomes to protect the food stored for the people of Egypt. It will also give us the means to control the Nomarchs themselves."

Joseph's visage was hard. "That was indeed my thought, my brethren!"

Another year passed after the dinner at Joseph's house. All crops had failed in the previous year. While the Nile rose normally the following spring, there had been a hot and scorching east wind during the critical part of the growing season. Once again there was no harvest. The Nomes had fared reasonably well during that first year of the dearth, but now their food reserves were either critically low or totally exhausted.

Pharaoh had called a meeting of his closest advisors to discuss the situation and to make plans for the welfare of Egypt. This meeting was not in the great hall, but in the Pharaoh's private chambers.

The Chamberlain, as usual, was conducting the meeting and rose to announce the Pharaoh. He did this without his normal staff. He simply stood and said quietly, "All rise. Pharaoh comes!"

Amenemhet entered the room. He was simply dressed in a plain white kilt and a bead collar. Gone for the moment were the crowns, the pectoral, the cheetah skin, the flail, and the crook of his office. Among the men gathered here, such trappings were unnecessary. As he entered, he smiled a greeting and with a friendly wave of his hand said, "Please be seated, my friends!" The men had been summoned quickly and thus knew this meeting was grave. They did as they were bidden. Amenemhet seated himself on one of the floor cushions provided for all and began. "I have called you together to discuss the situation in the Upper Kingdom. I do not like the reports that have been coming to me. Potiphar, what are the current reports from the twin fortresses of Semneh and Kummeh in the south?"

Potiphar nodded to acknowledge the request and said, "They remain secure, Great One. They have reported several recent attacks by Nubia, but these were repelled easily." At Pharaoh's questioning look, Potiphar added, "The Nubian troops were ill fed and unable to put up much of a fight."

Amenemhet asked with concern, "What is the state of *our* garrison there?"

Potiphar answered reassuringly, "They are well supplied and those installed there in good spirits, my Pharaoh. Joseph foresaw the possibility of an invasion due to the famine in all the lands around Egypt, and as you know, moved troops to the border outposts. He also saw to it that the granaries built into those fortresses were filled to capacity before the dearth began."

"Will the grain stored there be sufficient?"

Joseph answered this question. "The storage bins in the old fortresses were increased in size fivefold during the years of plenty, Great One. Prior to the increase, the stores there were sufficient to see a garrison through a two-year period. They now have more than enough for the duration of this emergency."

"Again, your foresight astonishes me!"

"It is not in me to do these things, my Pharaoh — it is the Spirit of my God that inspires them."

Pharaoh smiled and shook his head. "As always, you give credit to your God, Joseph!"

Potipherah quietly interjected, "I praise all the Gods of Egypt and the God of Joseph that he does!"

Amenemhet, turning to the aged priest, asked, "Why is that Potipherah?"

"Each time he listens to his God, the Land of Egypt benefits, my Pharaoh!"

"I agree, my Priest! I agree!"

Joseph, who seemed embarrassed and as if he wished to change the subject, said quietly, "The time is at hand that the granaries will have to be opened and the grain distributed to the people, Great One. Famine grows in the land and the reserves of the Nomarchs are either exhausted or nearly so. There was no harvest last year and there was none again this year."

"Was nothing raised?"

Joseph spread his hands in resignation. "Only some table vegetables from small gardens that were sheltered from the strong east wind and required little water."

Amenemhet looked thoughtful for a few moments. "Ah, like that fine garden inside the walls of your estate. Several of us have those now and the food produced is excellent!" With a furrowed brow he continued. "I was not aware that gardens like that were the only ones producing."

Potipherah nodded in support of the fact and added, "My son-in-law saw to it that I too have one of these gardens at On. They are a wonder! I can still feed my entire household out of mine!"

Joseph, who looked very concerned, said unexpectedly, "During this time of national emergency, I intend to cut back my garden for a while."

Amenemhet was very surprised at this decision. "Why do you do this, Joseph?"

"If I do not, it may appear that I am glutting myself on food that should have gone to the people, and this subject brings me again to the grain in the special storehouses, Great One."

Amenemhet looked at Joseph quietly for a few moments. He then shook his head as though trying to rid it of unpleasant thoughts and said, "I was not ignoring you, Joseph. I was thinking of a few unpleasant incidents of which you might not be aware."

"Not aware, my Pharaoh?"

"I have been using the garrison commanders and some . . . special individuals to gain information on the status of the Nomes. I have been particularly worried about the Third Nome and Qebu its Nomarch."

Potiphar became animated at the mention of that particular Nomarch. He asked sharply, "He still foments rebellion?"

"I think so, but in such a way that it cannot be proven. He isn't the fool Satsobek was. There have been several aborted raids on the royal granaries in several of the southern Nomes but never such an attack in the Third Nome!"

Potiphar's tone was angry. "He tests the defenses of the granaries!" Suddenly, his eyes widened and he turned to Joseph. With awe in his voice he said, "Is that why you constructed garrison forts into each of the granaries, Joseph?"

Joseph simply shrugged and said, "I was impressed to do so by my God and to man them, but that was all."

With sudden realization, Potipherah exclaimed, "With access to the stored grain, Qebu could enlist armies from other countries to defeat the crown!"

Amenemhet nodded his agreement. "That is what I fear, Potipherah. The man seems to have a strong ambition for the crown. He may be thinking of using the stored grain to further that aspiration." He was silent for a moment, and then, turning to Joseph, he said, "Joseph, see to it that the granary garrisons are fully manned at all times."

"I shall do so, my Pharaoh!"

Amenemhet looked at Joseph thoughtfully for a few moments before he spoke again. "Joseph, I know you to be an honorable, truthful, and compassionate man, but I do not want the granaries opened until the Nomarchs beg for food."

"Until they beg?"

Seeing the look of disbelief on Joseph's face, Amenemhet held up his hand to forestall comment and continued. "Forgive me, Joseph. You are compassionate, and I will not command you in this. Ask your God. If He gives you confirmation, then we will proceed as I have said. If not, return and bring me word. We shall make other plans."

Bowing low, Joseph responded, "I will do so, my Pharaoh."

Joseph went directly to his home and retired to his room to seek his God. He prayed all that night and for the next three days. His household became worried as they anxiously waited. Chief among those disturbed by his long period of meditation and prayer was Asenath. As she sat in the large common room of their home sewing, she looked anxiously at the Captain of their household guard and asked, "Khu has my husband come out of his room yet?"

"No, my lady. I have heard nothing since he cried out in the middle of the night, when I was making my final rounds as the Captain of the household guard two nights ago."

"Cry out?"

Khu had the look of one who was reluctant to admit to what he had seen, but the anxious look on his Mistress's face convinced him to speak. "He was weeping, and I mistook the sound for an attack and rushed in. He had tears in his eyes as he told me it was nothing and I could return to my post. I. . . I placed a guard outside his room after that. The men have reported nothing since that evening."

Asenath wore a truly worried expression but said nothing, only nodded to acknowledge Khu's report. As she returned to her sewing, albeit somewhat distractedly, Knut, chief maid, and Nakhti, the cook, entered. Knut looked about the room expectantly. Not seeing her Master, she asked, "Why is the Master in his room so long"

Asenath put aside her sewing. "I know only that he was commanded to seek his God about something Pharaoh wants Joseph to do."

Nakhti the cook was carrying several bowls and plates of food on a tray. She wagged her head and intoned, "The last time he sought his God, he fasted and prayed for three days!"

Senbi, their Head of House, chuckled and commented, "Only Nakhti would remember that detail!"

"The Master likes my cooking!"

Knut, her hands on her hips, replied humorously, "He must! He brags about it at every single meal!" Despite her worry Asenath had to laugh at this.

The quip was made doubly funny because it was absolutely true! Yet the comment made her aware of something Joseph had once told her. She turned to Knut and said in a very serious tone, "He once told me that he remembers all too well his time as a slave and as a prisoner in the dungeon. He wants no innocent man or woman to suffer as he did. That's why he loves all of you so much. He says that, between the children, myself and all of you, he has a loving family here in Egypt and is always thanking his God for all of us."

Asenath's disclosure stirred a strong memory for Senbi and he found tears coming to his eyes. A long time ago he had inadvertently stumbled upon Joseph while he was praying to his God. Senbi had heard almost those exact words pass from his Master's lips. He had known Joseph to be kind, but this had been something new to his experience — a Master thanking his God for the kindness shown him by his servants! He had even asked a blessing upon them in that prayer! Senbi remembered his resolve to be a better servant to Joseph from that day forward.

Now, seeing the worry on the Mistress's face was almost too much to bear. Senbi did his best to comfort her. "Have no fear, my Lady! I know that all is well with the Master." He said this as encouragingly as he could. To his surprise, Asenath replied, "It is not for Joseph that I fear, Senbi. I worry when Pharaoh asks such a thing of Joseph. It means that there is a real danger facing Egypt. It means that something is terribly wrong. It also means that he has asked Joseph to repair something very difficult to fix."

They all turned toward the hallway entrance to the room at the sound of running footsteps. One of the household guards burst into the room, skidded to a halt and bowed to all, then faced Asenath and announced, "Forgive me Mistress, but the Master comes." He then turned to face his superior officer, saluted and said, "Captain Khu, the Master said that I was relieved and could get something to eat."

Khu returned the salute and confirmed Joseph's orders. "Then you are relieved. After you have eaten, get some sleep." Turning to the cook, he politely asked, "Nakhti, would you be so kind as to get this man something to eat. He's been on duty all night."

Nakhti smiled and took the young man by the arm. "I would be glad to!"

Once again the man saluted and said with feeling, "Thank you, Captain!" He might have said more, but the smiling Nakhti was already steering the man out of the room. As they were leaving, a very worn looking Joseph entered. Asenath leaped to her feet and came to his side. "My husband! You look so tired! Knut, run to. . ."

Joseph held up a forestalling hand and in a very tired voice said, "Nay, stay Knut. I have no need of anything at the moment, just your company."

Asenath clutching his arm as though to hold him up, and with great worry in her eyes, asked quietly. "Joseph, if you can tell us, what is it that Pharaoh has asked of you?"

Joseph was silent for a moment and simply looked at his wife. Then, nodding his head as though coming to a decision, he said, "I can tell you, but for the moment it must not leave the walls of this estate. Is that agreed?"

Everyone in the room nodded their heads and almost as one said, "It is agreed."

Joseph took a deep breath and stared at the walls as he spoke. "Pharaoh has asked me not to open the storehouses until those who need the grain beg for it." He then sighed deeply before continuing. "Once the granaries are open, I am to sell the grain, not give it freely as originally planned."

In horror Asenath said, "Why would he do such a thing, my husband?"

Joseph laid a comforting hand on her shoulder and said gently, "The common people will not be doing the begging or the paying, my wife. It will be the Nomarchs."

Senbi realized the import of the statement and blurted out, "The Nomarchs? They are too proud to beg! The people will starve!"

Joseph began weeping. After a few moments, he regained enough control to say, "I know this, Senbi! I know this. Pharaoh does not target the people in this action, but the Nomarchs, and many people will suffer because of the foul ambitions of a few men. This is especially true in the southern Nomes. Some of the Nomarchs there are still bent on taking the throne, or at the least, removing me as the ruler of Egypt. Qebu now apparently leads them in their rebellion, but none of us can prove it."

Asenath found her voice. "I cannot believe that young Ti would be involved in such a disgraceful thing!"

"He is not, my wife. He has remained loyal. His people will be fed, for he will ask for the grain when it is needed, and without false self-serving pride. This will be done before there is any real problem in his lands. It is for the others that I weep. The deaths in their Nomes will be awful!" His voice became nearly a whisper. "God has shown it to me. They will rob temples, raid the tombs, and strip the mummies of their dead kings. They will even try to get food by force of arms before they will beg. There will be so many dead in some Nomes that there will be no time to bury them. It will be called the year of the hyena!"

A full year passed following that fateful evening in Joseph's home. The people of all the lands of Egypt were famished and cried to Pharaoh for bread. Finally, a huge crowd had gathered outside the palace walls. Most were commoners, but prominent among the crowd were several Nomarchs of the Upper Kingdom.

The Chamberlain stood on the balcony of the palace and stared at the crowd. The household troops had them under control, but the sight was worrisome. The people gathered were quiet, and most showed signs of starvation. It was not a pleasant sight. Looking to his left, he saw that Pharaoh was ready to meet the people. He stepped to the rail of the balcony, and after pounding his staff on the floor as hard as he dared he shouted, "Silence! Silence before the Great Pharaoh!" The crowd slowly quieted as they realized what the Chamberlain had said. Then, majestically, Pharaoh entered their view from the side of the balcony. The common people, struck with fear at the sight of Pharaoh, quickly prostrated themselves and became utterly silent. The Nomarchs, fearing the anger of the crowd, followed suit.

Amenemhet shouted, "What is it that you desire of me? Who is it that is your spokesman?"

Qebu boldly stood. He bowed and announced, "I, Qebu, am their spokesman, Great One."

Amenemhet stared hard into the face of the man. He did not like what he saw there. After a long silence, Amenemhet finally asked, "Very well, Qebu. What is it that this vast company desires of me?"

Qebu, bowing once more, said, "Our grain is spent. There is no more. Many die for lack of bread. We appeal to you, oh Pharaoh! Give us bread that we may feed our little ones!"

Pharaoh wondered if the man's request was genuine and decided to leave the matter to Joseph. Amenemhet said simply, "Go unto Joseph. What he says for you to do, do it!"

The Chamberlain stepped forward and forestalled any more words from Qebu by quickly intoning, "The Pharaoh has spoken! So it has been said. So it has been written, and so you shall do!"

Qebu wasn't that easily put off. As Pharaoh left the balcony, Qebu shouted, "Chamberlain, Where is this Joseph that we may speak with him?"

Although Amenemhet had walked out of sight on the balcony, he had remained to covertly observe the crowd and heard Qebu's remark. Once more he noted the southerner's choice of words. Qebu was acting as if he had never heard of Joseph. It was a studied insult. Pharaoh waited quietly for the Chamberlain to speak in his place. He would continue to observe and see how this drama would play itself out.

The Chamberlain too had noted Qebu's insult and did not rise to it. Simply pointing to the entrance of the palace, he shouted so the entire crowd could hear, "Joseph stands yonder upon the stair to the pylon of the Pharaoh's house. Go to him!"

Before he could say more, many in the crowd had turned to look in the direction indicated. There behind them, in his official splendor and surrounded by Pharaoh's personal guards, stood Joseph. There were several shouts.

"There he is!"

"I see him on the stairs there!"

"Let us go to him quickly before he departs and we know not where he goes!"

These statements were followed by a mad dash by the crowd as they rushed forward like a giant wave of the sea. At their head was Qebu. When they reached the foot of the stair upon which Joseph stood, Qebu decided to play to the crowd and in mock humility prostrated himself as he shouted, "Joseph! *Great* Zaphnath-paaneah! Give us bread! Why should we die in your presence? The granaries in the cities have failed."

Unseen by the crowd, Amenemhet had quietly returned to the balcony so that he could see as well as hear what was going on. He had removed the crowns, cheetah pelt, and other symbols of his office, and thus "disguised" he stood watching the drama before him. With none standing near him, no one heard him mutter disgustedly, "*Great* Zaphnath-paaneah?" Amenemhet was angered for Joseph's sake. Was it not this same Qebu who only recently bragged to Pharaoh's spy that he would never stoop to using the "false Hebrew's" equally "false" name? Now he was crawling like a worm before the very man whom he normally slandered!

As he listened, Pharaoh's eyes narrowed. There was more to this. There was still a nameless something in the man's words that deeply bothered Amenemhet. This man was hiding something, and he was obviously playing to the crowd and not to Joseph.

Joseph, by contrast, was making his Pharaoh proud. He stood silent for a moment, and then with scorn in his voice, he said, "You have asked for bread. Why have you waited so long, Qebu, to make this desperate request? Others have long since gotten the grain they need to feed their people."

Qebu knew instantly he was in deep trouble. He therefore lied. "We knew not what to do!"

"Very well!" Joseph shouted. "This I will do. I will open the royal granaries in your cities and *sell* you the grain that you need."

There was an outraged outcry from somewhere in the crowd. "Sell?"

Joseph turned toward the sound of the voice and snapped angrily, "Yes! I said SELL! I hear the outcry of the dead in your kingdoms! You come to me as beggars, but what is the outcry I hear from the tombs of your kingdoms? What is the outcry I hear from the temples? I hear the voices of your dead kings calling for their funerary to be returned! You have defiled even their very bodies to STEAL! You have stolen their gold!"

There was a profound silence in the courtyard. Many were hanging their heads in shame as Joseph continued relentlessly, "Well, with that gold you shall *buy* your bread, and the gold shall be returned to the dead from whom it was stolen. You have raided the temples. You have stolen that which belongs to God! You shall use that gold to buy your bread! Then it shall be returned to where it belongs! Deny, if you can, Qebu, that these things are not true!"

Those who had not known of the crimes Joseph accused him of were murmuring dangerously. Those who had done them were simply staring at the ground guiltily. Qebu knew he had lost the crowd and could think of no way of regaining it. There was genuine anger building in those about him. In defeat, he bowed his head and said loud enough for Joseph to hear it, "It is true." The crowd now grew furious, and Qebu knew he was as good as a dead man, and if not by Joseph's command then at the hands of this angry mob. What astounded him most was Joseph's detailed knowledge of all that had happened. In his mind the words came unbidden: *"He is a seer! He was truly named by Pharaoh, 'He who reveals that which is hidden.' My life is forfeit just like that of Satsobek!"*

Joseph had heard the man's admission, but it had not been loud enough for the entire crowd to hear. Joseph shouted, "I did not hear you, Qebu!"

Qebu let the agony he was feeling show in his voice as he shouted in a strangled voice, "It is true!"

Joseph did not let the situation get out of hand. He had no

intention of allowing the crowd to tear the man limb from limb inside the walls of Pharaoh's palace. He shouted above the din, "So be it, Nomarchs! Bring forth the gold you have stolen and you will have bread. Then, after that is returned, you shall use your own gold, and when that is spent, your livestock and even your lands will be used for more grain. These crimes demand *four-fold* payment!"

There was silence in the courtyard at this statement. Qebu bowed his head. He then raised it, and with tears in his eyes, said loud enough for all to hear, "Your judgment is guided by the gods. We will do as you say."

The Chamberlain too had remained on the balcony and stood silently beside his Pharaoh watching as Joseph dealt with the crowd. In an awed but quiet voice he said, "Great Pharaoh, I have never seen Lord Joseph as angry as he is this day!"

"Nor have I, Chamberlain. Nor have I, but I understand it! I have seen the reports from the worst of the offending southern Nomes. There are reports of the moldering remains of the dead lying not only unburied but uncovered all over those Nomes. Do you know what they are calling this past year in the Upper Kingdom?"

"No, my pharaoh, I do not."

"The year of the Hyena'. The bones of the dead have been scattered all over the land by those foul creatures!" They both turned at the sound of footsteps coming from the stairway. In moments they were joined by both Joseph and Potipherah.

Amenemhet looked quickly out into the courtyard and noticed that the crowd was leaving. He then turned and addressed his guests. "Ah, Potipherah and Joseph, welcome!"

Both men bowed and said as one, "My Pharaoh."

Amenemhet looked at his Vizier and friend for several moments before he spoke. "Joseph, I have never heard you raise your voice until this day, my friend."

Joseph's face darkened. "I learned of the thefts, and more, from my honorable father-in-law, the venerable priest of On, just before the crowd came to the palace. I was devastated by what I heard!"

The Chamberlain, a normally mild man, said harshly, "I was surprised that you did nothing to the traitorous Qebu, Joseph."

Amenemhet placed a calming hand on the man's shoulder. "He could not have more fully condemned him, my good

Chamberlain! In robbing the tombs, he has stolen more than gold. He stole the people's chance to follow their kings into the afterlife! I am not the seer Joseph is, but I foresee that Qebu will not live to see the end of this famine!"

Joseph nodded. "That is so, Great One. Nor will it be by command of either Pharaoh or I that he meets his fate. God will smite this man!"

The Chamberlain, still indignant at the traitorous behavior if the Nomarchs said, "At least they can now feed their people."

Potipherah, who was looking out at the few remaining stragglers in the courtyard, said quietly, "They will, but I am worried that, with the thefts, the priests will not have enough grain to see us through the famine."

Amenemhet said simply, "You and yours will be *given* your portion as it is right!"

Potipherah was taken aback. "I thank you, but. . ."

Joseph interjected. "You and yours have remained loyal to your king and to the Gods you serve. Many of the priests fell, a bloody sword in hand, defending the temples, did they not?"

"They did, but. . ."

Joseph smiled and pointed to Potipherah's side and said, "And you also. For are you not wounded in your side and conceal it with your cloak?"

"How did you . . .?"

Joseph laughed heartily. "I needed not God's gift of divining! Your wife talks to her daughter and her daughter talks to *her* husband!" Even Pharaoh joined in the laughter that followed this revelation.

Amenemhet was still chuckling when he added, "It was Joseph who made me aware of your wounds and your bravery. The order to apportion to the priests stands!"

Potipherah gave in with a smile and a bow. "So it shall be, Great Pharaoh." Then, turning to Joseph, his tone changed. "However, my son-in-law, my daughter also talks to her father." There was awe in his voice as he continued. "She told me nearly a year past of the terrible death that would stain the Upper Kingdom. She also said that your God had revealed the name that the people of those Nomes would call this year past." He continued in a very quiet voice. "The year of the Hyena!"

Amenemhet was astonished. "The year of the Hyena?' I have

just had a report in which this is confirmed! You truly are 'He who reveals that which is hidden!'"

Joseph held up a denying hand. "As always, Great Pharaoh, it is not in *me* to do these things — they are a gift from God." None broke the profound silence that followed this statement.

Chapter Twelve
MEMORIES AND DECISIONS

A soft spring-like evening had settled upon Egypt. The night birds were cooing quietly and there was a reassuring sound of crickets in the gentle night air. The sky above was filled with a beautifully brilliant display of stars, and yet, for Senbi, these things did not exist. He was looking for his Master. Asenath had sent him to fetch the Master for supper; unfortunately, the task was proving to be a difficult one. Finally, Senbi spotted a form sitting in a dark corner of the garden; and coming closer, he saw that perhaps it was his Master and called out to him.

"Master, Joseph! Is that you? The Mistress was worried and sent me to look for you." The form under the tree turned and looked at Senbi, but said nothing. The silence troubled the Head of House, and he asked, "Why are you sitting here all alone under the trees in the night? Your supper is getting cold." The form under the tree sat silently for several moments more. It was a pause that worried Senbi. Had he hailed the wrong person in the dark?

At last, the person under the tree spoke. "Forgive me Senbi. I'm very tired. Pharaoh decided today that it was best to open sales of grain to those from other countries."

Senbi, who was used to sharing such confidences, was still surprised at the disclosure. "Pharaoh authorizes the sale of grain to others during a time of famine?"

"It solves a major problem, Senbi."

"A major problem, Master?"

"Yes. The countries around us have no food either. If we keep what we have to ourselves, they will attack us and try to take it. The loss of life would be very high in Egypt as a result."

"I had not thought of that!"

Joseph chuckled. "Many people had not. The decision caused quite an uproar in the court, until it was explained, and then it was accepted readily enough."

Senbi thought for a moment and asked, "What of the border

guards?"

"Ah, they have been a big problem in the past. Reports of their thievery came up in the court all the time." Joseph actually chuckled for a moment. "I was astounded when someone actually shouted, 'What is the point of selling grain to avoid wrath and then angering everyone even worse as the border guards steal it back again!'" Joseph shook his head at the memory. "It took time to convince them that the border garrisons are well fed and are under orders to stay within their forts as much as possible. With full bellies, they are less likely to turn to thievery. The garrison commanders are also under special, extremely strict, orders to prevent such actions by common soldiers." His voice became intense. "Honesty is absolutely vital in this time of famine."

"Again, Master, you astound me!"

"Why is that?"

"You see what others do not! None of us would have thought of these details! How rightly you were named by Pharaoh!"

Joseph's voice contained a mild rebuke. "Senbi, you know my answer to that."

Senbi answered hesitantly, "The power to do those things is not in you, but it is the power of your God?"

"Exactly! Now, what was it you said about dinner?"

"Dinner? Oh, dear! The Mistress is going to be very upset with me! I was to bring you straightaway, and instead I stand and talk with you!"

Joseph laughed heartily. "Have no fear. I shall take all the blame! However, we had indeed best make haste or we may both be sleeping in the kennel!" With that, the two men made their way laughingly toward the warmth and light of the estate's main house.

They were stopped short at the entrance, their way barred by none other than Asenath herself, the perfect picture of an irate housewife. She stood with her arms folded and her foot tapping impatiently as the two made their approach. She wasted no time in venting her frustration. "Where have you been? I was getting worried!"

Joseph, holding up both his hands in a placating gesture, said, "I was sitting in a quiet corner in the garden, love. It took Senbi some time to find me."

Asenath's face took on a shrewd look as she asked, "And just how long did the two of you talk before someone. . ." She stared hard at Senbi. "Before someone remembered the request of his Mistress? Hmm?"

Senbi assumed a look of pure innocence. "Mistress?"

Joseph, who was likewise looking as innocent as possible, interjected, "Whatever would make you think that, my love?"

Asenath gave up and burst into laughter. "You two! I swear you are worse than a pair of mischievous brothers!"

Joseph gave his wife a huge hug and then asked, "What is that I smell? Is that savory meat?"

Asenath snuggled into him. "It is!"

"What's the occasion?"

Asenath looked up at her husband with mild reproach and asked, "Don't you remember what day this is?"

Joseph, utterly confused, stammered, "Ah, it is the 15th day of the second month."

Asenath, obviously disappointed, said, "It is our anniversary."

An abashed Joseph very quietly said, "Oh."

Asenath sensed that her husband was truly sorry for his lapse. Under normal circumstances he would have surprised her, but these were not normal times. "Don't be so ashamed, my husband! You have a great deal on your mind! Come, sit and have your supper." She then took her husband by the arm and led him into the main room of the house.

No sooner than they had entered the room than they were hailed by Nakhti, the cook. "Here you are, Master! I made savory meat, and I made it the way you like it best! Joseph beamed as he sniffed the air in the room. "Nakhti! It smells wondrous! Ah savory meat. He thought, *"Oh, how I remember the first time I had this dish! It was at the tent of my father.* In a moment, he was transported into his memory of that event. In his mind's eye, he could see plainly his father's camp, Jacob's camp.

He could see once more the pleased expression on his father's face as he sniffed the fragrant air of the camp and asked, "Leah! What is this you have made?"

Leah, aware that her husband knew full well what he was smelling, answered happily and playfully, "You know full well, you old fraud! It is your favorite dish, savory meat, and such as your father liked." With this pronouncement everyone laughed, then shouted, "Happy birthday, Father!"

Jacob, holding up his hands in delight at the surprise, shouted over the din, "I thank you, Leah! I thank you! I thank you all! Now, let us enjoy Mother Leah's fine meal!

Joseph, who was only five at the time, was sitting on his brother Ruben's lap. Curious, Joseph looked up into his big brother's face and asked in his small childish voice, "Ruben, what is savory meat?"

Ruben smiled down at his small charge and said, "This is your first time seeing this, isn't it, Joseph." The child nodded in the affirmative and Ruben smiled kindly at him. "Here, try a little of mine." He reached into his own bowl and selected a small piece of the spicy meat for his little brother, and all conversation stopped. Everyone was watching Joseph's reaction to the treat. The silence was broken only by a few of whispered comments:

"Oh, oh!"

"Watch this!"

"This ought to be good!"

Joseph ate the tiny morsel. Then a smile of delight lit his face and he said, "Mmm. This is good!"

Ruben roared with laughter, and then after a few moments managed to say, "Well, Father, there's no denying it — he *is* his father's son!" This brought gales of laughter from everyone.

Well, almost everyone. Mother Leah was frowning and said thoughtfully, "Most children would find that far too spicy!" She saw Ruben about to give Joseph a larger piece of meat and warned, "Ruben! Don't you dare give him too much of that! He's only five and Rachael doesn't need to be up all night with him!"

Jacob, still chuckling, held up a forestalling hand. "Now, Leah, it is a party. Let the child have a small portion of his own. He'll be fine."

Leah looked furious. She turned away to the cook fire, but everyone plainly heard her mutter, "Just like a man! He doesn't have to spend the night walking with him to fight off indigestion!"

Rachael, her sister, responded sweetly, "Do not worry, Leah. If Joseph becomes fretful, I know just the person to awaken to walk with him — my husband."

This sally brought gales of laughter. As the laughter died down, Leah turned to her husband. With an all too obvious innocence on her face, she asked sweetly, "Forgive me, my husband, but I've forgotten. How big a portion did you want Joseph to have?"

Once more the camp dissolved into laughter. A blushing and contrite Jacob held up both his hands in surrender. "A small one, and if he takes ill I shall take my punishment like a man!"

Joseph sat musing to himself as the vision of the past closed, *"But I did not take ill. I slept fine that night and had far more of the wonderful meat than the tiny portion Mother Leah gave me!"*

He grinned to himself and thought conspiratorially, *"Neither she nor Father saw the amount my brothers kept sneaking to me when no one was looking!"* He sighed out loud and thought wistfully to himself, *"How I remember that night! There I sat on Ruben's lap, eating with my big brothers, listening to Father's stories, and having my hair tousled by Ruben. Then, while the family talked far into the night, I fell asleep cuddled up next to my sister Dinah."* The longing he suddenly felt was almost overwhelming. *"Oh, how I miss them all!"*

As he sat musing, he noticed two things. First, that there were tears streaming down his face, and secondly, he became aware of someone calling to him. "Joseph? Joseph?" He discovered that it was his lovely wife who was calling to him. He turned to her and saw a worried expression on her face as she spoke to him. "Joseph? What is the matter? There are tears in your eyes?"

Joseph felt foolish for having slipped into his memories in public. He sputtered as he hastily wiped the tears from his eyes, "What? Oh! Sorry! I was just remembering the first time I had this dish in the camp of my father in Canaan."

Senbi stared at him a moment and said, "It must have been a painful memory!"

"No Senbi, quite the contrary. It is a cherished memory!"

Senbi looked at his Master questioningly for a moment and then asked. "When I found you in the garden, you were staring up at the sky with great intensity. Were you thinking of Canaan then too?"

Joseph had to laugh at this. "And they call *me* 'He who reveals that which is hidden!'" Everyone was relieved by the return of Joseph's normal sense of humor. Everyone except Asenath laughed heartily at Joseph's humor. After chuckling for a moment or two she asked, "What was it you were thinking of in the garden, my love?"

"I was just looking at the stars."

Khu, the Captain of Joseph's personal household guard spoke up for the first time. "The stars reminded you of your home in

Canaan, Master?"

Joseph could not help being amused at the incredulous tone in the man's voice. Chuckling, Joseph replied, "Oh, yes!"

Khu, confused, asked, "Are they not the same stars, Master?"

"Oh, they are the same stars, Khu; but I was remembering an incident involving them."

Asenath, who loved to hear her husband's stories of his home in Canaan, asked, "What incident would that be, my husband?"

Joseph, smiling at the request, replied, "I was perhaps six at the time, and I was out with my brothers at night tending the flocks." As he spoke, he transported them into his memory of the event. They could all hear the small child, Joseph, as he said, "The stars are so bright and clear tonight, Ruben!"

"So they are, Joseph! Do you know any of them?"

"No."

Ruben carefully pointed to a particular spot in the sky. "Do you see that very bright star over there toward the east, the bluish one?"

Joseph dutifully looked in the indicated direction and saw plainly the star he thought Ruben meant. "That big bright blue one there?"

"That's the one! That is called Vega. If you look below it, you will see four other stars." Noticing the confused look on Joseph's face, he paused and then said, "Wait. Look here. I'll draw it in the dirt." He began sketching in the dirt to show Joseph what he was trying to explain. When he had finished, he continued. "Here's Vega and the others are set like this, see?"

Joseph stared at the drawing in the dirt and then answered simply, "Yes."

Ruben pointed skyward once more. "Now, look up in the sky and see if you can see the same pattern there."

Suddenly, Joseph became excited. "Yes! I can see them!"

Ruben smiled. He was reminded of the first time he had recognized one of the constellations. Seeing Joseph's reaction was like reliving the event himself. Beaming, he said, "Excellent! That is a constellation and it is called the scales."

Joseph was confused again. "The scales?"

Ruben understood the confusion. Pointing to the drawing in the dirt, he said, "Look here, Joseph. If I add these lines to our drawing in the dirt, what do you see now?"

Joseph was delighted. "A set of scales like the ones father uses to measure the money when we sell things!"

"Exactly! Now look higher up in the sky, almost directly overhead. Do you see that whitish band that runs all the way from the southern horizon to the northern one?"

"Yes! I do!"

"That is called the Great Sky River."

"River? But why is it white, Ruben? Water isn't white."

For a moment Ruben was at a loss for words. "Uh, well. . ."

Before he could continue, Judah, who had been listening quietly to the lesson, chimed in. "Some say it is made of milk, Joseph."

Joseph stared at his brother for a moment, then asked, "Really, Judah?"

Judah shrugged his shoulders. "That's what they say."

Ruben watched his little brother quietly, and after a few moments, confused at his antics, he asked, "Joseph? Why are you jumping up and down like that?"

Joseph continued his jumping and seemed to be trying to grab something as he jumped. He gasped, "I... am... trying... to... get... some... of... the... sky... milk!"

The past dissolved into the present, where the brightly lighted room was filled with the sounds of delighted laughter. After a few moments, Asenath interjected, "What a precious memory!"

Senbi, who was wiping tears of laughter from his eyes, said, "Indeed it is, but I'm sure it was some time before you heard the end of the teasing!"

"Oh, you are correct, Senbi! Thereafter, whenever I was in the fields with my brethren, I heard, 'Joseph, fetch us some sky milk!'"

Asenath looked at her husband questioningly and asked, "Why are you remembering your brethren so much of late?"

Joseph's face became quite serious. "I do not know, my love. Perhaps it is because of the famine, which is in all lands, including Canaan!"

"You have had reports of Canaan?"

"I have, and the famine is as dire there as it is here."

Asenath's voice was filled with concern. "Do you think that they are in trouble?"

"I do not know." Then he added in a voice filled with confidence, "I do know that, if father is still alive, he will take action before it is too late for the camp and for the animals."

Asenath, who had always wanted to meet Joseph's father, asked, "Do you think that he would come here?"

"Most likely not, but he would send some of my brethren once the word reached him that there is grain for sale in Egypt."

Unknown to Joseph, his father was indeed still lived, and word was soon to reach him that there was food for sale in Egypt. The famine had reached Canaan, and pastures that had always remained green were now scorched by the constant hot east wind that was plaguing the region. For shepherds, the lack of forage was a constant worry, even in good times. Ruben, the eldest of Jacob's sons, stood silently looking at the scorched hills around him with his brothers Dan and Judah. After some time, Ruben spoke. "Dan, you have been to the northern Pastures?"

"I have."

Ruben did not look at his brothers. Instead, he continued to gaze steadily at the ruined pasture before him. "What are the conditions there?"

Dan shrugged and said sadly, "There is fine water there, but with this miserable hot east wind blowing, the grass is parched. There is graze, but it will not last the season."

Ruben finally looked at his brothers. Shaking his head and with a heavy sigh, he said, "We will have to move the sheep there then. How long do you think that the grass will hold?"

"Possibly until the fall rains." Dan's tone indicated that he did not think the possibility all that likely.

Ruben stared out at the devastated fields once more and then asked. "What do you think, Judah? Where will we take the flocks once that grass is gone?"

Shrugging his shoulders, Judah said, "Well, once the fall rains come, there will be grass in the Jordan valley and elsewhere. Anywhere near the valley should do, unless the fall rains fail."

Asher, who had seen the three older brothers talking, joined the group. He now voiced his own worries. "That's all fine and well for the sheep, but what about us? What are we going to eat?"

Dan had no patience for his whining brother today. He snapped, "There you go again, Asher! We are not out of food! Father and the steward do well for us!"

Judah, who had apparently been looking at the fields, pointed. "Speaking of Father, look yonder. Is that not a caravan that approaches?"

Asher was confused and asked, "What has that to do with Father, Judah?"

"He always entertains the members of the caravans and gets the latest information from them of the conditions they have seen on their travels."

"So?"

Ruben could bear no more and spoke rather sharply to Asher. "Where do you think the food has been coming from all these months? Father learns from the caravans where there is food to be had and then sends us to buy it."

Unaware of the scrutiny of his sons, Jacob came out of his tent to greet the caravan as it entered the camp. He hailed the caravan leader. "Peace be unto you, traveler! Welcome to our camp!"

The trader executed the formal bow of the desert traveler and responded, "Peace be unto you, Oh Sheik of Canaan! Might a weary caravan of travelers find shelter with you for a short time?"

"Indeed! There is ample water for your camels and some provender. Come, join me at my tent." Turning, Jacob gestured to his veiled wives. "Zilpah! Bring water that I may wash our guest's feet. Leah! Have the men slay and make ready a kid of the goats; then, would you and Bilhah, please make some bread? We have guests!"

The women scampered rapidly to accomplish the tasks that Jacob had assigned them. In moments, Zilpah returned carrying a large pitcher, a foot bowl, and some towels. She placed the pitcher and the bowl on the ground before her husband, and handing him the towels, she said, "Here are the water, the bowl, and the towels, Father Jacob!"

Jacob bowed slightly to her as he accepted the towels. "I thank you, Zilpah!" She bowed again and hurried away. Jacob then turned to the caravan leader, and indicating some pillows on a rug in the shade of his tent, he said, "Please, stranger, sit!"

The trader turned toward the welcome shade, and removing his sandals, sat down. His exhaustion was obvious, and there was deep gratitude in his voice when he spoke. "Ah, the hospitality of Canaan! It never ceases to amaze me!"

Jacob, who had already begun to wash the feet of the stranger, looked up, curious and asked, "In what way, stranger?"

"The country is parched. There can be little food here, and yet every camp offers us food and water! How grateful we are for it! Our trip has been long!"

"From whence came you?"

"We have been traveling many months, from Basra near the sea. We carried a load of last year's Basra dates to Nineva to trade for spices. We then followed the river up to Harran and took the old trading trails from there to here."

Jacob, who had finished washing the stranger's feet, now sat in the shade of the tree. With a tone of wonder in his voice, he said, "Yours has been a long and tiring journey! No doubt you have had many dry and uncomfortable camps."

Nodding his head in agreement and with a far off look in his eyes, as though seeing each of the difficult camps and the trials he had suffered through on the trip, the trader responded, "Indeed! Indeed! Water is scarce in some places, but worst is this incessant wind! It parches everything! Food is getting scarce in the north as well as the south now. Even in Basra, I suspect the dates are withering on the trees this season!"

"Where are you going?"

"To Egypt. Despite this terrible famine, it is said that there is bread in the land of Egypt!"

Jacob was genuinely surprised to hear this. "How is that possible?"

"I asked the same question. It appears that several years ago their Pharaoh was troubled with frightening dreams. None of his priests or wise men could interpret them. Finally, a young man, a Semite like yourself I'm told, understood these dreams and predicted this very famine!"

"That allowed the Egyptians to prepare for it?"

"Yes! It appears that the same young man knew what to do, and Pharaoh put him in charge of the entire land!"

Jacob shook his head and said sadly, "I doubt that the food in Egypt will do us much good here!"

"Ah, then you would be wrong. The young man is wise beyond his years! He knows that those in countries surrounding Egypt are hungry, even starving, and he knows that, if they could, these countries would take the Egyptian food stores by force. He prevents this by selling grain to all who come openly and honestly, and at a fair price too!

"Yes, but what of the border guards? They are the worst

thieves in Egypt!"

The trader's tone became quiet and confidential, as though he feared the guards could hear him even this far from the border of Egypt. "No truer words were ever spoken, friend! But not just now. It is said that this leader of Egypt apparently controls the guards. They no longer molest travelers buying grain!"

On the far side of the camp, the sons of Jacob had been silently watching their father and the caravan leader. Ruben broke the silence. "Father and the traveler seem in a deep conversation, Judah."

Judah nodded. "That is true. I hope the news is good."

Asher was annoyed. "All I see is another free meal being handed out and me with an empty stomach!"

Dan was quick to seize upon Asher's comment. "When has *your* stomach *ever* been full?" The rest of the group whooped in delight at Asher's discomfiture and Dan's very timely sally. Ruben then brought something else to their attention.

"Look! Father is beckoning us! Come, let us make haste!"

Asher, who definitely had a one track mind, asked, "We get to eat?" He found himself last to move as the brother's trooped in the direction of their father.

As they approached, they all bowed in respect, not only for their father but in deference to the stranger in their midst. Jacob acknowledged their silent greeting with a small bow of his own. "Ah, my sons! This good trader tells me that there is ample grain in Egypt."

The trader added, "It is of the best quality and at a fair price."

Ruben bowed to the stranger, and with disbelief in his voice said, "Forgive me, trader, but a fair price from an Egyptian dealing with an outsider?"

The trader laughed heartily, looked at Jacob, and gesturing toward Ruben, he said, "Good Sheik, this son is no fool!" Turning to Ruben, he continued. "You do not deal with the merchants there. The grain is purchased from the government alone, and the ruler of the land oversees and approves the sales."

Judah was as incredulous as his brother. "And this ruler is fair?"

Turning to face this new inquisitor, the trader responded, "Indeed he is! And you won't be robbed at the outposts, either. He's apparently put a stop to that too!" Silence followed this remark for some time. No one seemed to know what to say. Finally, Jacob came to a decision. "Why do you look one upon another? Behold, you have heard that there is grain in Egypt. Go there! Buy food for us that we may live."

Ruben responded to his father's command. "Who of us do you desire should undertake this task, my father?"

Jacob looked thoughtful for a moment. "I think that it is best if you all go. It is a long and dangerous journey, and the larger your numbers the safer you will be."

"So it shall be, my father. I shall go to the steward for supplies for the eleven of us and depart immediately." Ruben bowed to his father and turned to go.

Jacob stopped him. "Wait, my son! Do not take Benjamin with you. He is all that is left of Rachael. Do not take him, lest mischief befall him by the way."

Thus it came to pass that ten of Joseph's brethren went to Egypt to buy grain, but Benjamin, Joseph's brother, Jacob sent not with his brethren.

Chapter Thirteen
THE BROTHERS COME TO EGYPT

The granary plaza was filled with people. The place was a riot of color, movement, and sound. People tended to group according to their manner of speech, but their manner of dress differed as much as their languages. The Nubians were distinguished by their dark skin and bright feathered headdresses, while the Babylonians could be easily spotted with their high hard-formed hats, bright fringed robes, and long black plaited beards. The Egyptians were quite visible among the crowd in their wigs, bright colored bead collars, and spotless white tunics. The desert dwellers stood out as well in their drab, dark colored, hooded robes designed for utility and protection not decoration. Among these stood the sons of Jacob.

These men of the desert and field stood out despite the plainness of their dress. They were tall and each carried a shepherd's staff in his hand. Unlike their chattering neighbors, they stood silent except for a few whispered or muttered comments among themselves. They seemed to be observing everything around them.

These were men used to the open spaces and the solitude of the desert, where silent vigilance was necessary to survive. Despite the apparent calm they exuded, however, they were very ill at ease. Judah was the first to give that discomfort voice when he stepped close to his brother and whispered, "Ruben, have you ever seen so many people in one place?"

Ruben barely moved, turning slightly to his brother. "No! It is like a sea of People! It is so noisy you can barely think! "

Simeon, who was clutching his staff so tightly that his knuckles were turning white, stared out at the crowd and growled quietly, "The sooner we get the grain we came for and leave this madhouse the better!"

Judah glanced at Simeon and noted the white knuckles. He too felt trapped by so many people crowding into them from all directions. "For once Simeon, I could not agree more!"

Asher, as usual, was thinking of food. He leaned close to Ruben and whispered, "Do you think that we will be able to get the grain that we need, Ruben?"

Ruben stared at the mass of people and had to admit that he too wondered about their chances. Ruben could not help but worry that there would not be enough grain to sell to so many. He then silently glanced down at the tiny slip of papyrus in his hand. The scribe who had registered them for the sale had given it to him for identification, but the papyrus gave him no comfort. Looking at his worried brother, he said simply, "I have no idea, Asher. We will just have to wait and see."

Unknown to the worried and nervous sons of Jacob, their brother Joseph was the Governor of all Egypt and sold the grain to all the people who came from distant lands. Being the Governor, many rumors about him abounded, which were often bandied about by those who waited to buy grain. Some in the crowd entertained themselves telling and elaborating upon such rumors while they awaited an audience. The result was often outrageous, resulting in unnecessary fear.

Joseph's brothers had gravitated to an area in the crowd dominated by peoples from Canaan. Thus it was that they were near an excited group of city dwellers from their homeland who, unlike their desert brethren, were chattering constantly. The brothers ignored the talk until one of the men in the group said, "You should hear the tidings of this man that we have to deal with here!"

Taking up the topic right away, another in the group asked, "What have you heard?"

The first speaker looked about as though what he was about to say was confidential, and then said in a voice that all around him could hear quite easily, "Whatever you do, treat this one with respect! I've heard he has had many whipped to death for just a slip of the tongue!"

Immediately, another man added, "Oh, hear me well friends. It goes far deeper than that! His name fills me with dread!"

"His name?"

Dropping his voice to a loud, and easily overheard, dramatic whisper, he croaked, "Zaphnath-paaneah."

One of the group, apparently unsure of what he had heard, repeated loudly, "Zaphnath-paaneah?"

Waving his hands wildly for this speaker to be quiet and with a loud shushing, the first speaker whispered loudly and dramatically, "Shhh! Not so loud! The guards would have your tongue for misusing his name!"

"You fear the guards?"

"I fear more than the guards! I fear the man! His name means 'He who reveals that which is hidden!'"

"I don't understand."

"He reads minds!" came the urgently whispered reply.

"No!"

Thoroughly warming to his topic, he continued the gossip. "Oh! That is not all! I have heard. . ."

Far beyond this chattering hysterical group, at the far end of the plaza, stood a raised and canopied dais where the Governor would sit during the sale of grain today. This dais was joined to the main building of the granary by a small bridge that allowed the Governor to observe the plaza from within the granary building without being seen and to hold private meetings with the officials that would actually run the sale. Just out of sight at the end of the bridge stood Joseph and Senbi, who had just arrived. Senbi, who was plainly dressed and drew no attention, looked out the doorway at the assembled crowd. Turning to Joseph, he said in an astounded voice, "Master Joseph, the crowd is huge today!"

Joseph, though he remained in the shadows and out of sight, stepped to where he too could see the mass of humanity gathered in the granary plaza, and after a brief look, he readily agreed, "Indeed!" Then after another moment of silent observation, he asked, "Senbi, do these people seem frightened?" Before Senbi could answer there was a loud chuckle from the doorway. Khu, the Captain of Joseph's personal guard had been standing nearby unnoticed and was the source of the mirth.

Surprised at this behavior, Joseph asked, "Khu, what is so funny?"

Khu, still smiling, bowed and responded, "A thousand pardons, my Lord, but the fear you see is the fault of the crowd itself."

"They are frightening themselves?"

Khu's grin became broader as he gestured toward the crowd outside with his thumb and continued. "They are scaring themselves silly with all kinds of wild rumors, Master. Several of the guards have shared these rumors back in the barracks, and they are hilarious! Some say it is all that they can do to keep a straight face while standing guard here in the plaza."

Intrigued, Joseph asked, "What kinds of things have you heard?"

Khu, rubbing his chin thoughtfully said, "Hmm. Where to start? Let's see, ah yes! You can read minds. That's why you were given the name: 'He who reveals that which is hidden.'"

Joseph wasn't sure he liked the sound of this and asked warily, "Are there any more of these . . . rumors?"

Khu's face lit with a delight that, for some reason, sent a shiver down Joseph's spine. Then Khu excitedly began, "Ah, oh yes! At Pharaoh's command, you built the pyramids using only your magic wand."

Joseph's jaw dropped! He could only gasp a strangled, "What?"

Khu, ignoring his Master's astonishment, was obviously now in full form. "Oh yes! You would walk all the way up to the quarry in the western wall and tap the granite cliff and a huge block would simply pop out of the cliff! Then, again with your powerful wand, you would tap the huge cut stone and it would fly all the way to Giza and plop itself perfectly into place!"

The mere shiver in Joseph's spine was now full-sized block of ice! For a moment he was reduced to sputtering, but he finally managed, "Magic wand . . . pyramids? Please! Tell me none of this has reached Pharaoh's ears!"

Senbi answered his question. Although he was a bit hard to understand as he was laughing rather hard at the time. "Actually, Pharaoh started that one, Master."

Joseph's spine was no longer frozen — it had suddenly turned to jelly! He managed a weak, "What?"

Senbi was still laughing but had managed to get a bit more control. "I found out at the court yesterday, Master." Senbi paused, took a deep breath to steady himself and continued. "The Chamberlain pulled me aside and told me privately. He was laughing so hard he almost couldn't tell the tale. Pharaoh thought it was a good joke."

Joseph, who was recovering rapidly, replied with a rather acid, "Oh hilarious! Small wonder Pharaoh looked so pleased with himself in yesterday's meetings! Are there more of these outrageous stories floating about?"

Khu replied happily. "Yes, sir — we all contributed."

Joseph didn't know whether to be annoyed or panicked. His shocked reply was, "All . . . contribu . . . Pray what was your contribution Khu?"

Khu's face lit like the sun in his excitement. He blurted excitedly, "Well, when we are in a battle, you can turn yourself into an eagle and fly over the foe to see the enemy's array. That is why you are undefeated in battle."

This was too much! Joseph cried out, "Eagle? Battle? I've never been in a battle!"

Senbi, who was now holding his sides he was laughing so hard, managed, "That explains the undefeated part!"

Joseph didn't know whether to throw something at these two laughing hyenas or hide somewhere! In the end, he simply buried his face in his hands and groaned.

Khu, sensing things had gotten out of hand, said helpfully, "Such things can be very helpful, Master."

A thoroughly distressed Joseph nearly shouted, then restraining himself, asked, "How? They're not true!"

Khu held up his hands. "The truth is, I agree, the best. Forgive us for having sport at your expense, but we have no control over the rumors that are started by the people out there, and they do serve a purpose."

"What purpose could such falsehoods possibly serve?"

Senbi had recovered himself, and sensing his Master's real distress added, "It is a time of famine, Master. People are scared, desperate, and hungry. They are coming here for food but they need magic as well. These rumors must be supplying something vital as they could easily riot. The guards fear this, and yet all who come for grain are quiet. Instead of violence, the crowd spreads rumors of your magical powers and come before you in polite, though perhaps frightened awe."

Khu added quickly, before Joseph could speak, "The guards are thankful for the rumors. There has been no cause to use deadly force. That is a part of the magic!"

Joseph was worried about these falsehoods, but there was nothing he could do. The situation was out of his control. With a resigned sigh, he said, "I would feel far better with less magic and more truth! I do not want to incur the wrath of my God!"

Senbi, who knew quite well his Master's reverence and fear of his God, said soothingly, "You need not fear, Master. You have always given the credit for all the wonderful things you have actually done to your God."

Out in the plaza, Joseph's brothers were having problems with what they were hearing as well. The gossip next to them was still in high form. "And then he turned himself into an eagle and flew. . ."

Simeon had heard enough. Turning to his brothers, he quietly grated, "What a load of . . . of . . . I know not what!"

Ruben shook his head in disbelief. "There certainly do seem to be a lot of wild rumors about this Zaphnath-paaneah!"

Judah, on the other hand, looked thoughtful and said to no one in particular, "Did not the traveler back in our father's camp say that this man interpreted the dreams of the Pharaoh?"

Ruben nodded his agreement. "Aye, now that I can believe. Remember Joseph and his dreams?" This comment was greeted with silence. The brothers stared at each other, their guilt evident on their faces. Then they began shifting positions or staring at the ground.

Simeon, who was still staring at the ground, asked quietly and with obvious pain in his voice, "Why did you happen to think of that, Ruben?"

Unlike the others, Ruben was looking about at the crowd. After a few moments, he said, "He has been on my mind ever since we reached Egypt. Somewhere here in this land, if he still lives, he is a slave."

Levi saw that Ruben was obviously looking to see if he could find his younger brother in the crowd. Then he realized that Ruben had been doing this silently ever since they arrived in Egypt. With genuine sadness in his voice, he turned to Ruben and said the thing none of them really wanted to hear. "Even if we could find him, we have only enough money to buy food, Ruben."

Ruben turned, tears in his eyes. "I know, but the thought still hurts."

Simeon, who was still staring at the ground, said what they were all thinking. "The thought still hurts us all."

Asher looked at his brothers and then up at the raised and still empty dais at the end of the plaza. With no small amount of fear in his voice, he said quietly, "If this man can really read thoughts, we are in real trouble!"

Judah, surprised at a comment from Asher that did not involve food, asked, "Why is that, Asher?"

"He would sense our guilt and heaven only knows what crimes he would accuse us of!" This comment brought some nods of agreement from the brothers.

Ruben, who was still scanning the faces in the crowd, was the first to notice a change, and nodding in the appropriate direction, he said quietly, "Look, the crowd is moving forward."

Judah brought his attention to the front of the plaza and saw what was undoubtedly the reason for all the movement. Pointing discretely, he said, "There is why. Look up on the dais at the far end of the plaza. See that fellow with the fancy headdress and the ornate gold medallion around his neck? That must be this Zaphnath-paaneah everyone's talking about."

Judah was correct. Joseph had come out into the open upon the dais. Once he was seated upon the throne that had been placed in the center of the dais, he called out to those who helped him in the grain sales. "Scribes! Come to me!" Having been alerted by Khu that Joseph was about to make his entrance, the scribes had already mounted the dais and quickly assembled themselves at Joseph's feet. As soon as they were in place, Joseph addressed the nearest of them. "Anet, what was the total tally for this granary?"

Bowing to his Lord, Anet responded immediately. "At the beginning of the famine there were one million measures of grain in this granary, Master. At the present time, six and eight tenths of the sixteen silos in the granary are empty, my Lord!"

Joseph nodded. "We agreed on 2,700 measures as the maximum amount sold on a sale day, did we not?"

"That was the agreed amount, Master, and that ration is holding true for the duration of the famine as you predicted."

"Excellent!" Joseph then turned to another of the assembled scribes. "Naket, what is the count of those buying today?"

"There are 523 individuals and families represented here this day, Master."

"None of those present has been here for at least a lunar cycle?"

"None, my Lord! The few that were have been instructed to wait until it has been a full lunar cycle, Great One."

Joseph beamed. Raising his scepter in salute, he added, "Excellent, Naket! You have been quite diligent!" Then, settling back in his chair, he looked thoughtful. As always, Joseph was worried about making the food stores last through the famine while still feeding all those who came to buy. Turning so as to include all those gathered before him, he instructed, "Try to keep the sale to 2,500 measures, but if required, we shall exceed that to the 2,700 measure limit — but only at my order." Turning to his right, he addressed his Head of House, who had special responsibilities during a sale. "Senbi."

"Yes, Master."

"The interpreters know the requirements?"

"They do, Master!"

"Very well. The interpreters will proceed as they see fit." Turning once more to face the entire group he continued, "Scribes, you will keep me informed as to the progress of the sale and the amount totals. I shall observe and intervene only where requested, such as for very large families or if there is a problem." The scribes all bowed to indicate that they understood. Joseph's unusual trust in his staff was something that made working for him a great privilege, and none of these men would knowingly do anything to disappoint him. "Khu, you and Senbi will remain here on the dais with me." Both men bowed deeply to their Lord. Joseph then raised his scepter as a signal and announced loudly, "Let the sale begin!"

All the scribes quickly rose to their feet and bowed. As one they intoned, "At once, Master!" Then they scurried to their various stations about the plaza. The only people remaining on the dais were Joseph, Senbi, Khu, and the six armed men who served as Joseph's personal body guards.

All of this activity was noticed by the crowd. Rapidly they began surging forward, but there was little confusion. Ruben was among those noting the beginning of the sale. "Look, the crowd is moving forward toward the tables."

Judah, seeing the huge number of people there to buy, said, "Let us hope that we can get the grain that we need to feed our families!"

Simeon, who as always was impatient, grumbled, "After all the questions that the scribe asked us, we should be able to get something!"

Judah turned to the eldest and asked, "Ruben, which table was it the scribe told us to go to?"

Ruben glanced about. "He said to go to the table labeled 'Large Families.'" He then held up the scrap of papyrus he had been unknowingly clutching very tightly. Holding it up for the others to see, he said, "See, here is the scrap of papyrus that he gave us with the symbols on it."

Asher became excited. He was pointing and said, "Wait, Ruben, isn't that the table over there. Aren't those the symbols on the paper?"

Ruben, who had been searching for the symbols everywhere, asked, "Where, Asher?"

Asher continued to point. "There. The one in the center. I think it is the table right in front of the ruler's dais."

Simeon, who like the others had looked in the direction Asher indicated, shuddered. "That man on the dais makes me very uncomfortable!"

Judah shared Simeon's apprehension but put it aside for the more important matter of getting food for their family. "Uncomfortable or not, if we are to get the food that we need to survive, we have to go to that table!" He began striding toward the indicated table, his brothers following immediately.

While his brothers had deliberated, hesitated and finally acted, Joseph sat quietly on the dais and watched the proceedings. He was very pleased with what he was seeing. Turning slightly to his side, he commented on this to Senbi. "This is going very well today! Naket's idea of using those small slips of papyrus to let people find the right lines to stand in was brilliant! There's a bit of milling about, but people are lining up very rapidly and there is less confusion than there has been at other sales. I am very pleased! Make sure to let him know, will you, Senbi?"

"It will be a great pleasure to do so, Master!"

As Joseph watched, he could not help thinking what a wonderful sight this was. Oh, how thankful he was to be here! He could not help himself — he was in awe. God had brought him here as a slave and then made him an instrument to save the lives of so many people! His thoughts were suddenly interrupted by Khu, who was pointing out something to him very discretely. "Master. Look there at the Large Families tables. See that large group of men near the end of the line? Are they not in Canaanite dress?"

Joseph came out of his reverie and peered in the indicated direction. He asked distractedly, "Canaanite dress?" Focusing on the indicated group, he saw the group that Khu had been referring to. He nodded and said, "Why, yes, they do seem to be dressed that way." As he looked at the familiar form of dress on these strangers, he could not help noticing that the big fellow in the group, the one with the graying hair, stood like his brother Ruben. How strange, he thought, but that other fellow near him was wearing a red, white, and black striped robe like the one Levi took to wearing in rebellion after their Father gave Joseph his coat of many colors. The one next to him even had a red beard like Judah's. Wait! Could this be? Those looked like his brothers! If they were, then Simeon and that huge cudgel he liked to carry as a staff should be nearby. Joseph looked at the group more carefully. Suddenly, he started. There he was! There was Simeon and his huge staff! These *were* his brothers! Quickly, he counted them. There were ten of them. Looking even more carefully, he decided that all of his brothers were there. Well, almost all. All were there with the apparent exception of Benjamin.

Khu noticed his Master's tense posture. "Master, is everything all right?"

Joseph, looked at Khu for a moment and then said in a rather distracted voice, "Ah . . . fine . . . Would you please ask Senbi to come here?"

Khu knew that something was amiss. He bowed and responded, "Certainly, my Lord!" He then ran quickly to where Senbi was talking quietly to one of the scribes. Tapping him on the shoulder, he said, "The Master needs you!"

There was something disturbing in Khu's voice, and looking over his shoulder, Senbi could see that Joseph was not his normal self. Nodding to Khu, he ran to Joseph's side and bowed. "Yes, my lord?"

Joseph did not even glance Senbi's way, but simply pointed discreetly to the group of men at the table in front of the dais. Speaking in almost a whisper, he said, "Senbi, do you see those men in Canaanite dress by that table?"

"Yes Master, I think that I do."

"Those are my brothers!"

Of all the things that Senbi could have expected his Master to say, this was not among them. Turning to face his Master, he asked, surprised beyond measure, "Your Brothers?"

Joseph's voice remained a whisper as he said, "I'm quite sure. See that big fellow there, the tall one with the graying hair?"

"Yes, I see him."

"That is Ruben, the oldest."

Senbi suddenly remembered something and asked, "Are these not the same brethren that sold you into slavery?"

There was definite pain in Joseph's voice as he answered. "Yes, they are and I do not know if they have changed since they committed that crime."

Senbi did not know what to do or say. After a moment of confused silence, he managed to ask, "Do you wish to speak with them?"

"Not yet. I must think of a way to find out if they have changed. I must know if they still hate me."

"They all hate you?"

"One does not sell someone one loves into slavery, Senbi."

Senbi, who had come to respect the men whose names he had heard so often in stories of Joseph's youth, said timidly, "They can't all hate you. I remember all the stories that you have told about them, and it always seemed to me that Ruben and Judah loved you."

Joseph's eyes filled with tears. "Perhaps, but the day I was sold into slavery, they did little." He paused and said nothing for a moment or two. When he continued, there was pain in his voice. "Oh, how I remember that awful day!" No sooner than he had said this than he was transported into his frightening memories of the events of that fateful day. In his mind, he could still hear Simeon's nearly insane screams. "Who has the knife? Who has the knife? I can't slit this swine's throat without it!" Then there was a terrified piercing scream of "Noooooo!" in his mind that Joseph recognized as his own when he was thrown into that horrid pit.

Thankfully, the horrid memory faded and Joseph found himself sitting quite safely on his chair upon the dais. With a shudder of the remembered terror of that day he said aloud to Senbi, "They may have loved me, but on the day that Simeon and Levi took their revenge, Ruben was nowhere to be found and Judah. . . Well, Judah seemed desperate. At least that is the way I see it in my mind now."

Senbi had never seen Joseph like this, and it both frightened and angered him. He loved Joseph and was instantly angry at the men who had treated his kindhearted master in such an awful manner. Yet, he remembered the stories Joseph often told of his brothers and said, "From what you have told me, Simeon and Levi would have killed you on more than one occasion, only to be stopped by either Judah or Ruben. I find it hard to believe that Judah would have stopped protecting you. Ruben might have simply been outnumbered."

Joseph looked at Senbi. He knew the man was correct. Then he remembered something and shared it. "He is younger than both Levi and Simeon. To them, he is a little brother, like me. What you say makes much sense, Senbi. That still leaves the question of how to deal with them."

Senbi could see that Joseph was not able to cope with this, but he had the germ of an idea. "Perhaps the best way is not to deal with them directly. Use me as an interpreter. Don't let them know that you speak the Canaanite language. That way you will be strange to them."

"That is fine if only I wish to remain unknown to them." Suddenly Joseph had an inspiration. "But wait, I have an idea! Not only will I be strange to them, but harsh with them. I'll accuse them of something. Ah, let me think. Perhaps of being spies and in that way I can see what they have become."

Senbi, thinking out loud, said slowly, "The idea sounds good . . ."

Khu, who had heard only a small part of the conversation, interjected, "Forgive me, Master, but I overheard you. Are those your brethren? The men that sold you into slavery?"

"They are."

Khu, who like Senbi, was instantly angered at these men for their treatment of his Master, said, "Perhaps if you were to place them in our dungeon for a time. . ."

Joseph was startled at the suggestion. "Dungeon? We don't have a dungeon! Besides, why would I do that? I only wish to see if they still hate me, not punish them! If they are here, that means that Father and the others are short of food. I can't leave them in want!"

Khu thought fast and said, "Men in prison talk, my Master. They're scared and much could be learned. It only takes a day or two. We could use one of the empty store rooms at home for that short a period of time. Surely, that would not be harmful to those remaining in Canaan."

Joseph regarded Khu in silence for a few moments, and then said thoughtfully. "Hmm. There is much sense in what you say, Khu, though it seems harsh." Then, in a flash, Joseph saw what he must do. Looking Khu in the eye, he said firmly, "So it shall be!"

Senbi, who had been staring at Joseph's brethren, saw the

scribe from the table in front of them coming. "Master, here comes Naket from the table with your brethren."

Bowing as he came to Joseph's throne, Naket said, "Master, forgive the intrusion, but I have ten brethren at my table who represent a family of seventy people in the land of Canaan. They appear forthright. May I fill the order? It will take thirty-one and one tenth measures of grain." To his surprise it was not the Master but Senbi who responded to his request.

Senbi, his tone harsh, barked, "Have them come forth and stand before the Master!"

Naket, surprised beyond measure at the anger in Senbi's voice and the stern visage of the Master, stared first at Joseph and then at Senbi. After only a slight hesitation, however, he responded, "It shall be as you command!" He then hurried back to his table where the men from Canaan stood quietly waiting. Without preamble he said hurriedly, "You are to stand before the Great One." He saw the look of confusion on their faces and added, "He will decide whether you receive grain or not!" The men seemed transfixed. They stood motionless and stared stupidly at him. Exasperated, Naket shouted, "Go!"

Ruben was the first to come out of his shock, and he responded, "Be it as you wish." At the sound of Ruben's reply, the brothers seemed to come out of their shocked trance and slowly began moving. They were in fact herded by numerous guards that had suddenly appeared beside the steps that led to the Governor's raised dais. These guards were not friendly guides. The brothers knew that something was definitely wrong; for the soldiers were grim faced and their weapons were at the ready. Troops from inside the granary had also come out onto the large dais. They were now outnumbered almost three to one by armed, apparently angry, and ready Egyptian soldiers.

As they moved, Simeon edged closer to Asher and whispered, "What did we do? Everyone else just paid for grain and was given a paper to retrieve it. Why do we have to go before this man? Why all the armed troops?"

Asher whispered back frantically, "I don't know, but I don't like it!"

Judah, who had heard the exchange, now spoke. "I agree with Asher! Look at that man! He appears upset, and from what we have heard, that can *not* be good!"

Khu had not been idle as the faithful Naket returned to his table. He had called his aide to his side and ordered extra troops out to the stairs and onto the dais. Among these were some of the best archers in Egypt. They had come with their bows at the ready and arrows already nocked. Khu approved. He now took the time to observe the men as they silently approached. Each was armed with a staff.

One staff in particular drew Khu's attention, the one in the hands of the man the Master had identified as Simeon. How many evenings had he listened, enthralled at the stories of this man and his able use of that staff. How many heads had that huge staff cracked? Khu did not know, but he was determined about one thing — his head was *not* going to be added to the list!

At the moment, these men seemed in a daze, but from what Joseph had told him, that could change in an instant. Warily, Khu brought his shield to the ready and drew his sword. None of these men would harm his Master, Joseph, *this* day! The betrayal of his Master by these men burned in his chest. Brothers or not, if they raised a hand to Joseph today, they would die!

After what seemed an eternity, the men finally shuffled to a stop a respectful distance from the Master. They were looking all about themselves. It was obvious that they realized that they were outnumbered. Simeon, in particular, stared apprehensively at the ready bowmen and then at his brethren. These men were clearly confused and frightened.

Their disrespect before his Master enraged Khu even further. Stepping forward with his sword ready to strike, he barked angrily, "Foreign dogs! You dare to stand in the presence of the Great One! Bow! Bow with your faces to the ground!" Khu's command had an instant effect. The troops who had been standing at the ready now shifted, almost as one, into fighting stance, shields up, weapons either drawn or leveled for combat. The bowmen drew their bows and the creaking of them as they were extended was heard plainly over the crowd noise. Each bowman had taken aim at one of the brothers and had a reserve arrow in his bow hand for a rapid second shot should any of the brothers survive the first volley.

Knowing that they were as good as dead if they did not comply instantly, the brothers fell to their faces as rapidly as they could with weak protestations:

"Forgive us!"

"A thousand pardons, Great One!"

"We meant no disrespect!"

Joseph could only stare at the sight before him, dumbfounded. He could not believe what he was seeing. Could this be? Could this be the fulfillment of his dream from so long ago? He was transported to that fateful night in the camp of his Father. He was no longer sitting on a throne but upon a humble sheepskin by the common fire that the family shared. Gone were the sounds of the granary, and in their place came the angry echo of his brother Simeon's terrifying voice from years before: "So the *chosen one* has had a dream has he?"

Joseph felt once more the fear of revealing his dream to his brothers that night. Then Joseph returned to himself and was once more sitting rigidly on his throne, but despite the heat of the afternoon sun, Joseph sat shivering and was covered in cold sweat. In his wildest dreams he had *never* envisioned a situation like the one now before him: his elder brethren bowing in fear before him with their faces to the ground! It was what he had seen in his dream of the sheaves! He did not know what to do. Groping in his mind for something to say, he finally turned to Senbi and said in Egyptian, "Senbi, ask them from whence they come?"

Senbi bowed to Joseph and then turned to the brothers. In Hebrew, he asked, "Where are you from?"

Ruben raised himself from the ground only enough to answer the question. He looked at Joseph pleadingly as he answered the question asked of him. "We come from the land of Canaan to buy food, Great One." There was no sign of recognition in that beseeching gaze, only fear.

Joseph was taken by surprise. They did not recognize him! Ruben was looking him straight in the eye and there was not even a trace of recognition! While he was still digesting this, Senbi turned to him and said in Egyptian, "As you heard, they come to buy food as you had surmised."

Joseph was suddenly angry. He could not have explained the sudden hostility he felt, but his tone reflected it as he spoke. "Very well. Tell them I think that they are spies."

Senbi showed no surprise at Joseph's outrage, and in truth he felt great satisfaction at his Master's anger. His tone was filled with no false indignation when he translated this to the brothers. "The Great One says no! He says that you are spies! You have come to see the nakedness of the land!"

Ruben was desperate. Falling once more to his face, he cried, "Nay, my Lord. Your servants come to buy food."

Simeon looked about in abject fear. This was a grave situation! They were surrounded by armed men and they had no chance of survival if they resisted. He turned to Joseph and pleaded, "We are all one man's sons. We are true men. Your servants are not spies!"

Senbi sensed their fear, but he had no desire to do something Joseph would be angry about. Turning, he looked at Joseph and asked in Egyptian, "What do you wish me to say to them?"

Joseph was angrier than Senbi had ever seen him. Joseph looked him in the eye and said simply, "Tell them again that they are spies."

Once more Senbi spoke in Hebrew. "My Master says that you have come to see the nakedness of the land!"

Judah, sensing the situation was out of hand, pleaded, "Nay Master! Be not so disquieted. Your servants are twelve brethren, the sons of one man in the land of Canaan. These before you are not all of us. Behold, the youngest is with our father, and one is no longer among us."

Senbi turned once more to face Joseph. "Master?"

Joseph spoke very quietly, but very clearly. "Tell them this. You are spies and this is how you shall be proved. By the life of Pharaoh, you shall not go forth from here unless your youngest brother comes to Egypt. Send one of you to fetch your brother. The rest of you shall be kept in prison. Thus your words may be proved; if indeed there is any truth in you. If your brother does not come to Egypt, by the life of Pharaoh, surely you are spies."

The brothers stared at one another, and then at the powerful man on the throne. The great man's tone was frightening. They knew that something was terribly wrong and felt that they were in severe trouble. They knew it for fact when Senbi faced them once more. The man seemed to swell before them. He was filled with authority as he spoke in a loud and commanding voice. "Hear the words of Zaphnath-paaneah, the ruler of all Egypt! Hear you he who is second only to Pharaoh! Hear him that reveals that which is hidden!" He then repeated Joseph's words as loudly as he could, then turning to his right, Senbi signaled to the alert and ready, Captain Khu. He pointed at the brothers and shouted dramatically,

"Captain! Take them! Place them in the Master's dungeon!"

Khu actually smiled. This was no friendly smile, but that of a soldier who agrees fully with an order given and is anxious to carry it out. He replied loudly and with satisfaction, "At once!"

Chapter Fourteen
THE BROTHERS ARE TESTED

Ruben was scared. He had faced wild animals with nothing but his staff, been in a war in Canaan, and had suffered the wrath of his father over the incident with Bilhah — but nothing had prepared him for this. For hours he and his brothers sat helplessly in the granary, tied up and guarded closely by grim-faced armed troops as all the tales he heard in the plaza ran through his mind like his own private play. He did not like the show! Now, he was weak and covered in cold sweat, shaking, and his stomach was threatening to embarrass him. He looked over at Levi and Simeon. If anything, they looked even worse than he felt.

Finally, the grain sale appeared to be over and they were being herded toward Ruben knew not what. Again he was forced into the intimidating presence of the man that ruled the country. The sight of him sent shivers down his spine. The man walked with his head slightly bent as though he was lost in thought — the possible nature of those thoughts scared Ruben most.

They didn't go far before they arrived at what, Ruben supposed, was the prison where they were to be held captive. However, if this was a prison, a shocked Ruben wondered what Egyptian homes looked like! The place had high walls, to be sure, and armed guards at the gates, but that was where any resemblance to a prison ended. There were lush fruit trees, flower gardens with beautiful gravel paths winding between them, and decorative ponds everywhere. To a desert dweller, this was more like a vision of paradise than any idea of a prison that Ruben could imagine.

They were led to a building set into the wall of the grounds. Here the guards untied the brothers, shoved them into a room, and slammed the door behind them. The place looked more like a storeroom than a prison cell. There was fresh straw strewn thickly on the floor, and there were some wide barred windows set high in the wall above them. At least they had light instead of languishing in the dark. After a short time they were brought food and water, delivered by attractive, well-dressed serving girls. The food was even quite good, though none of them could eat much. Ruben had to admit that this was a strange prison, but it *was* a prison and they still had to wait to find out what their fate would be.

When they were alone, the brothers talked quietly. Simeon said what Ruben suspected they had all been thinking. With an ashen face, Simeon looked at the solid walls and said, "I wonder if this is how Joseph felt?"

Joseph thought that he could now finally bring closure to his past, but he had yet to deal with an unexpected obstacle, Asenath! As they sat at dinner that evening, Asenath noted that all the men, Joseph and Khu and Senbi, seemed much quieter than usual. They ate in silence, which was definitely *not* their usual behavior, and Asenath decided that there was something wrong.

She had seen prisoners being led to one of the storerooms as the men returned home and suspected that this might have something to do with the solemn mood that had settled upon her home. She decided to take action. "Joseph, I saw the guards bringing a large group of men into the estate, and it looked like they were detained in one of the storerooms."

Joseph only glanced at her for a moment, but uncharacteristically, he did not look at her when he answered. "That's correct, my wife."

"Would it not have been better that they were placed into Pharaoh's prison?"

Again, Joseph stared at his food and did not look at his wife when he answered. "No. I wanted them where I could make a better determination as to their fate, my love."

"Are they dangerous?"

Joseph, still staring at his mostly uneaten food, replied with a shrug, "No, just scared at the moment."

"But. . ."

Joseph finally looked up and asked, "Why are you so interested in these men, my love?"

"They were in Canaanite dress, and I may be mistaken, but they looked like you." Suddenly, all the men seemed very interested in their food, staring at their plates and saying nothing. In fact, they looked like children who had been caught doing something wrong. "Why, my husband, do you suddenly look so guilty?" Glancing at the other two, she added, "The same goes for you Khu and you as well Senbi!" Still, they said nothing. Asenath wasn't going to stand for this. Assuming the tone all husbands fear, whether they admit it or not, Asenath said imperially, "Joseph?"

Joseph tried to look surprised but failed miserably. He only managed to look very sheepish as he asked, "Asenath, what do you mean?"

Asenath was furious. She could tell that she was going to get nothing more from Joseph, but she still voiced her frustration. "You know perfectly well what my meaning is!" Swiftly, she turned on poor Khu. "Khu! Who are those men?"

Khu could easily handle armed assaults, bandits, and even armies without flinching, but this tiny woman with her arms folded and her stern look was more than he was prepared for. He stammered, "Mistress, I. . . I mean. . ."

Asenath wanted an answer, and she wanted it now. "Khu, answer me!" she snapped.

Khu, with his head hung low like an errant schoolboy, answered very quietly. "They are Joseph's brethren."

Asenath was astounded. "Joseph's brethren?" Turning to Joseph, she demanded incredulously, "You have put your own brethren in prison in OUR STOREROOM?"

Joseph held up both hands as though warding off a physical attack and said quickly, "I can explain!"

She was angrier than Joseph had ever seen her. "You, who abhors the prisons of Egypt, make your own home a prison?"

It was Joseph's turn to look like the errant schoolboy. He muttered meekly, "It's not a prison — it's our home."

She was exasperated at the same time. "Since when is the guestroom a dungeon?"

Senbi interceded in a pleading tone. "Mistress, please. It is more complicated than that!"

"Really? Good Senbi, I would be greatly appreciative of an explanation." The look on her face and her tone of voice made it plain that the explanation had better be a good one.

Senbi took a deep breath. "It is really quite simple. The Master did not know how to discover if his brethren still hated him. Khu and I came up with several ideas, and it seemed like a good plan to place them in custody and see what they say there."

Turning toward her husband in disbelief, Asenath asked, "You put them in a dungeon to see if they still hated you, Joseph?"

Joseph, now hearing the plan from her point of view, felt he had erred and said weakly, "That's right."

"Oh, and when they find out who you are, they are going to love you all the more for placing them in a filthy dungeon?" she said with great sarcasm.

Khu couldn't help himself. He blurted, "It's not filthy! I had that storeroom specially cleaned and had fresh clean straw put in there!" He quickly wished he had remained silent.

"Oh, that's going to make *all* the difference!" Her look was scathing, and all poor Khu manage in response was to hang his head. Asenath was far from finished. She turned to her husband, and with a voice choked with angry tears, she said, "Joseph! I can't believe that you could be so cruel!" She stood and gestured to the other women in the room. "Come ladies! We will dine in private in my rooms! These *men* can dine alone!" She then swept out of the room followed en masse by the rest of the women of the house.

It was very quiet in the room after their departure, as even the musicians had departed with Asenath. After a few moments Joseph, looking in the direction the women had gone, said weakly into the profound silence. "Well, at least she didn't insist that I sleep in the kennel!"

Senbi, his tone both somehow chastened and weary at the same time, said resignedly, "I'll make beds for us on the floor of the storeroom, Master."

Joseph was surprised at the plural. "I'm the one in trouble."

"I got a good look at Knut's face, Master. We've both been consigned to the kennels!"

Khu was crestfallen. He looked at Senbi and his Master, and then said sadly, "I'll join you. I feel like this is my fault." No one contradicted him.

Joseph sat looking at the other two, and after pondering for a moment, he said quietly, "This brings back memories. The last time I had to sleep on the storeroom floor was with Hotem. I was in trouble then too." Seeing the questioning looks on his friend's faces he continued. "That was before I was made the Head of Potiphar's House and before Hotem married Anah."

Senbi smiled weakly. "I'll make the bed pads extra thick, Master. I'm no longer used to sleeping on stone floors either!"

Joseph, Senbi, and Khu got little sleep that night, and they looked the worse for wear the next day when they were met by Potiphar in the street. Joseph was glad to see his old friend, and

Potiphar was delighted at the chance encounter. He waved and rushed to meet Joseph and his party. As he joyfully clasped Joseph's hands, he said, "Joseph! You are well met!"

Joseph was quite pleased to see Potiphar but his lack of sleep betrayed him. Before he could speak, he had to stifle a huge yawn. Embarrassed, he quickly said, "Forgive me Potiphar! I got little sleep last night."

Potiphar looked closely at Joseph. "Now that I pay attention, both you and those with you look exhausted. Is there sickness in your home?"

Joseph shook his head sadly. "No. Just discord that I, unfortunately, created."

Potiphar knew that tone. He had been married for some years now. He too had "created discord" in his home from time to time. "What have you done?"

"It is a long story."

Potiphar smiled, and then placed a friendly hand on Joseph's shoulder. "The day is young and I am not pressed for some time."

Joseph looked at Potiphar for a moment, and then with a sigh, he said, "My brethren have come to Egypt."

"Why should that be grounds for discord, Joseph? I would have thought that would be cause for a celebration."

Senbi could not restrain himself. "Oh, that our fortunes were such! Instead we spent the night on the storeroom floor!"

Potiphar looked at his old friend and asked quietly, "Joseph?"

Joseph looked at the ground as though embarrassed. When he spoke, his voice was filled with misery. "My brethren are not my house guests, Potiphar. They are under guard in one of my storerooms."

Potiphar was taken aback. "Why did you imprison them, Joseph?"

Joseph, still staring at the ground, shrugged and said quietly, "I did not know if my brothers still hated me. Khu felt we might find out their hearts better if they were in prison for a few days, and I agreed."

"I take it that Asenath did not agree, or you would have slept in your own bed and not upon the storeroom floor."

"You have guessed correctly."

Potiphar turned and bowed slightly to Khu. "You have served your Master well!"

Khu looked miserable. "If you mean he has slept most uncomfortably because of my *wisdom*, you are correct!"

"No, that is not my meaning." Potiphar then turned to face Joseph. "Joseph, if you had revealed yourself to your brethren at the time, how do you think that you would have been received?"

Joseph shrugged. "I know not."

"They would have fawned upon you."

Joseph looked even more miserable. "Your words bring no comfort, Potiphar"

"You mistake my meaning."

"In what way?"

"You are the second most powerful man in the world. Do you believe the greetings you receive while sitting in Diwan?"

"No, of course not! The majority of those greetings are uttered simply to garner my favor and nothing else!"

"So it would have been for your brethren. They would have truckled before you simply to insure that they received sufficient food for their families in Canaan. They would have kept their true thoughts to themselves. Such men can be dangerous enemies, for they appear as kin and thus harmless. Witness the often violent doings in the harem of the Pharaoh, an institution infamous for its treachery. He can trust none of his wives unless he tests them most severely. The action suggested by Khu is no different."

Joseph looked at his old friend for some moments in silence. He knew Potiphar had the situation figured rightly. Still, he had his wife to deal with. He finally said sadly, "I wish Asenath could be made to see this!"

Potiphar looked thoughtful for a few moments and then said slowly, "Perhaps there is a way that she can be made to so see. I am meeting later today with your father-in-law. I shall have Potipherah speak to your wife. He has been a witness to many foul traitors who appeared to be innocent as lambs. He would understand the need to test your brethren and should be able to convince your wife of the need, despite the apparent cruelty."

Joseph was relieved. "I thank you, my old friend. I was doubting my decision to treat my brethren as I have. I knew that the decision was right, but having my cherished wife angry at my apparent cruelty was more than I could bear."

Potiphar looked serious and said, "I should warn you that there may be some repercussions of this action later, as your brethren will fear you, but at least you will know their true minds."

Joseph made a dismissive gesture. "Those repercussions, which are to be expected, can be dealt with as they arise, but not knowing their minds could have deadly results. That I cannot afford."

Potiphar's face showed his relief. "Thus speaks the Joseph that I know so well! Thus speaks the second most powerful man in the world! Farewell, my friend. I shall speak to your father-in-law as I have promised."

As they parted, Joseph clasped hands with Potiphar and said with great feeling, "May the blessings of the God of my father's go with you, my friend." Joseph was relieved for he knew that the situation would be resolved.

After Potiphar spoke to Potipherah as he had promised, the venerable priest, understanding Joseph's dilemma, took his wife and rushed to Joseph's house. Their arrival caused no small stir.

Asenath had not left her rooms at all the day following the arrival of Joseph's brothers, and she had spent much of that time weeping. From time to time she would venture out onto the porch outside her rooms. There, she would stand staring at the storeroom in the west wall of the estate where Joseph had locked up his brothers. She could see the guards that Joseph and Khu had placed there, and once she saw food and water being delivered to the prisoners and the sight sickened her. She could only think of those poor men huddled inside their prison and not knowing their fate. As soon as this thought occurred to her, she returned to her room and began weeping anew.

It was now late in the afternoon, and Knut was loath to disturb her mistress, but the arrival of the most powerful priest in Egypt, who also happened to be her mistress's father, demanded her Mistress's attention. Knut hesitated at the door, but finally, she worked up the nerve to enter. The sight that greeted her was not a pleasant one. Her mistress had been weeping on and off all day, and it showed in her normally beautiful face, which was swollen and red. Hesitantly, Knut called out to Asenath. "Mistress?"

Asenath did not seem to object to the interruption. She simply looked at Knut and asked in a tearful voice, "What is it, Knut?"

"Your mother and father are here to speak with you."

Asenath bowed her head and sighed deeply. She was silent, but her manner seemed to say, "When it rains it pours!" After a few moments of silence, she said in a weak voice, "Tell them I am ill and ask their forgiveness. I cannot see them now."

Knut understood, but she had been carefully instructed by Potipherah. She took a deep breath and continued. "Your father said that you would most likely answer thus, and he commands you to come to him. He knows of your concerns, Mistress. He comes to help."

Asenath snapped, "Oh, very well! I will wash my face and come to them, as they command."

Knut knew it was time to leave, and without another word, she bowed deeply to her mistress and hurried from the room. She then returned to the great room of the estate, where the parents of her Mistress waited. Upon entering, she bowed low to them and said, "Honored Ones, my Mistress says that she will be with you shortly. May I get you something to eat or drink while you wait?"

Nodding his acknowledgment, Potipherah said, "We thank you, Knut; but we will simply wait. We require nothing else."

Bowing once more, she said, "As you desire, Great One. Good day to you."

"And a good day to you as well."

When the young woman left the room, Knumah turned to her husband, and with deep concern in her voice, she asked, "Potipherah, are you sure of this errand? Our interference could simply make the situation worse."

"I must make an effort, my wife. Joseph is too valuable to Egypt, to all of us, and I would not see my daughter in pain if I can help it." He stiffened at the sound of approaching footsteps. Making a shushing noise at his wife, he nodded toward the door as Asenath entered.

Asenath, bowing deeply, said in a rather dead voice, "Greetings my parents."

Knumah was quick to observe the swollen and reddened face and blurted out, "You have been crying!"

Asenath looked embarrassed and said quickly, "It is nothing, my mother."

Potipherah, in that wise voice used so often by fathers, the same tone of voice that infuriates daughters, replied, "One does not cry over nothing, my daughter. What has happened?"

There was indeed anger in her voice as Asenath answered, "I suspect that you already know and that is why you are here."

"Tell us anyway, my child."

Knowing that there was no way out of the situation short of a tantrum, Asenath said simply, "My husband's brethren have come from Canaan."

Knumah looked at her daughter in some confusion and asked, "Why is this a reason for weeping, my daughter? I would have thought that this would be reason for rejoicing."

Asenath's answer was filled with frustration. "I thought so too, but my husband has placed them in prison in our own home!" Then her control failed her and the tears she had held back returned. Weeping, she said, "I thought I knew him! I never dreamed that he could be so cruel!"

Knumah was taken aback, and in an astonished voice, she asked, "He placed them in prison? Surely he explained himself!"

With a dismissive gesture, Asenath replied, "He said something about finding out if they still hated him. It makes no sense! Placing them in a prison is going to make them love him?"

Potipherah said quietly, "Let me ask you a question, my daughter. Who is your husband?"

"I thought I knew, but now. . ."

Holding up a hand to forestall her reply, Potipherah then said, "Let me ask that question in another way: *What* is your husband?"

The question caught her by surprise. With a wrinkled brow, she replied, "I am not sure what you ask."

"To all of Egypt and to the rest of the world, who and what is your husband?"

Asenath was flustered. She sputtered in her confusion, "I suppose he is the governor of Egypt, but. . ."

Holding up his hand once more, Potipherah said, "Let me help you. He is the governor of *all* Egypt, second in power only unto Pharaoh. As such, he is the second most powerful man in the world!"

Asenath was now very clearly confused. She said hesitatingly, "I understand that, but what has that to do with. . ."

"A great deal, my daughter, a great deal. Have you been to Diwan with your husband?"

Asenath replied warily, "Yes. . ."

"How do those who come for judgment treat Joseph?"

Asenath shrugged. "With respect, but. . ."

"Have patience with me just a few moments more, my

daughter. Have you ever heard someone there address your husband with long accolades and protestations of loyalty?"

"Yes, of course."

"Do you think that these declarations are from the heart?"

Asenath replied scornfully, "No! Most are feeble attempts to mislead Joseph and to gain some advantage in the court!"

"Do you remember the coup that was attempted in the royal harem a few years ago?"

"The one that my aunt helped to expose?"

Nodding, Potipherah said, "That is the very one I allude to — Pharaoh did not know until the last minute that his favorite wife was plotting his death. He trusted her because of the false way she acted. He had not looked beyond her flattering words and actions."

"All right, but. . ."

Potipherah did not give her a chance to continue. "How do you think Joseph's brethren would have treated him if he had revealed himself to them at the grain sale?"

"I do not know."

"Put yourself in their position. This is the brother they sold into slavery in Egypt. That is a grave crime. Now, these many years later, they find that he is the second most powerful man in the world. If you were guilty of such a crime, against such a man, how would you act?"

Asenath's hand went to her mouth as the realization dawned upon her. In an awe filled voice she said quietly, "Oh! I would fawn upon him, just as those trying to gain favor in Diwan! I had not thought of this!"

"It is fortunate for all Egypt, and perhaps for the world in this terrible famine, that Khu *did* so think!" Potipherah concluded with great force.

Knumah turned to her husband, and there was real fear in her eyes and voice as she asked, "Do you think that they are a danger to Joseph, my husband?"

Potipherah nodded sadly. "It is a real possibility, my wife. Some attempted to murder him in the past. If not tested, these men could be very dangerous enemies indeed, but that is for Joseph to decide. I suspect that he will trust his God to make the final decision." He was silent for a few moments and then continued with some conviction. "That is what I would do if in his place. *His* God makes no mistakes!" The meeting with Asenath and her parents ended her opposition to Joseph's actions with his brethren.

Joseph waited a full three days before he again approached his brothers in their makeshift prison. He did not do so without trepidation. As much as he hated to admit it, he still feared these men. As he slowly walked toward the storeroom that held them, he called the ever faithful Senbi and Khu to his side. "Senbi, as before, I want you to speak to my brethren for me. This way, if they think I do not understand their tongue, they may say something important. Khu, you and your guards will accompany us."

Senbi understood. "I will be glad to help you in this, Master"

Khu said with feeling, "As always, your will is a command for your servant!"

Inside the storeroom, the brothers were scared; and, it was Asher who gave voice to this dread when he moaned aloud, "How long have we been in this awful place?"

Simeon, who was sitting with his back against the wall, gestured to some scratch marks he had made there. "I make it to be three days, Asher."

Asher shook his head in disbelief. "It seems like three months!"

Simeon leaned his head against the wall and stared at the ceiling. Still gazing upward, he said simply, "I know."

Judah was fidgeting with the straw at his feet. Without looking up, he said sadly, "I am not concerned with how long we have *been* here, but how long we *will* be here! Food in our camp is running short."

Ruben glanced at Judah. "I know what you mean. I have small children, as do all of us. Are they eating or starving?" Suddenly the frustration and helplessness burst out of him. Pounding the wall with all his might, he shouted, "We know not in this . . . this hole!"

Levi, like Simeon, was staring at the ceiling and seemed oblivious to Ruben's outburst. Without looking down, he said quietly, "I have been wondering if this is how Joseph felt in that pit we threw him into in the wilderness."

Simeon stared at his brother and then sadly asked, "Levi, must you add to our misery?"

Levi bowed his head. "Sorry, but it has been on my mind a great deal of late."

Before anyone else could comment, the sharp-eared Asher hissed, "Quiet! I think I hear people coming!" No sooner had he said this than they heard the sounds of the lock to their prison being opened. The door was flung open with a bang and several armed men entered.

Senbi and Khu were the first to enter. Senbi shouted in Hebrew, "All rise for the Great Zaphnath-paaneah, ruler of all Egypt and second only unto Pharaoh himself!" There was confusion for a few moments as the brothers scrambled to get to their feet. As soon as the noise and movement stopped, Senbi continued, "My Master, the Great Zaphnath-paaneah, says, 'This do and live, for I fear God. If you are true men, let one of you be bound in the house of your prison. Then carry grain home for the famine of your houses. But bring your youngest brother unto me. This way shall your words be verified, and you shall not die.'"

At this pronouncement, the brothers stared at one another. There was much shuffling of feet. Then Levi, in agony, said, "We are guilty concerning our brother. We saw the anguish of his soul, but when he asked us for mercy, we would not hear. This is the reason such distress has come upon us."

This was too much for Ruben, who turned on his brother and snapped angrily, "I said to you, 'Do not sin against the child.' You would not hear but demanded his blood."

Joseph heard everything and was stunned. Ruben had not abandoned him, and from the look of anger and indignation on Judah's face, neither had Judah. Tears began to well up in his eyes. Quickly, and to the surprise of all, he fled from the room. Once outside, he broke down, wracked by sobs. It took some moments to regain his composure.

Ruben was the first to comment after the sudden departure of Joseph. He bowed to Senbi and asked hesitantly, "Did we do something wrong? Why does the Great One depart so?"

Senbi recovered quickly. "You did nothing. He shall return in a moment."

Then everything in the room seemed to stop for a few moments, but one thing that Senbi had said was buzzing in Judah's head like an angry bee: "let one of you be bound in the house of your prison." He could not contain himself. As quietly as he could, he whispered to the others, "Who shall we leave behind? One of us has to stay!"

Levi, his eyes wide with fear, whispered, "Father isn't going to like it, whoever it is!"

JOSEPH Ruler of All Egypt

Asher looked wildly at the others. Then, with genuine panic in his voice, he squeaked hoarsely, "I don't want to stay! I'm going mad already! I would not last long."

This angered the already seriously worried Ruben, who snapped, "No one is asking you to!"

Simeon was filled with a growing dread and had been watching the door. Suddenly, he whispered urgently, "Quiet! The Great One comes again!"

Joseph had returned. He approached Senbi and whispered in Egyptian, "Senbi, see the big fellow against the wall, the dark-haired one?"

Senbi looked in the indicated direction and saw the biggest of the brothers pressed against the back wall with a look of abject fear on his face. "Yes, Master. I see him!"

"That is Simeon. He is the one who will remain as our prisoner."

Senbi needed no further orders. Turning to Khu, he commanded loudly, "Captain Khu!"

Khu snapped to attention. "Sir!"

Pointing to Simeon, Senbi ordered, "By the Master's orders, take that one, the tall one with the black hair next to the wall. Bind him in full view of the others. He will be our prisoner!"

Khu saluted sharply to acknowledge the order, and then gestured to several of the soldiers. He then pointed to Simeon and shouted, "Guards! Take that one and bind him in full view of his brothers!"

Simeon tried to flee, but there was nowhere to run. He shouted helplessly, "Me? Wait!"

Levi tried to help, but he was pinioned before he could do anything. All Levi could do was shout helplessly, "No! Not Simeon!" Out of instinct, the rest of the brothers tried to come to Simeon's aid and a scuffle broke out.

"Guards! Level spears! Keep the rest back! Force them to the wall!" Khu shouted. The soldiers responded instantly and the brothers were quickly forced against the wall at spear and sword points.

Senbi took charge. "Khu! Remove that prisoner to the other cell! Then retreat and close this one!"

Khu nodded and replied, "It shall be done!"

Simeon was then dragged from the cell and the troops

retreated. The door was slammed shut and relocked. Khu approached Senbi while his troops held the struggling Simeon and whispered urgently, "What other cell? We don't have another one!"

Senbi thought fast. "Take him to the main storeroom. Have some of the guards hold him there until his brothers are gone. Then we can bring him back here."

"So it shall be done!" He saluted, and he and the guards escorted Simeon to the main storeroom.

Joseph had watched all of this in silence. As soon as Khu left, he waved Senbi to his side. "Senbi, fill their sacks with corn, enough for full rations for seventy people for a lunar month. Then restore every man's money into his sack and give them provisions for the way."

"Do you want them to have full or half rations for the journey, Master?"

Without hesitation, Joseph replied, "Full rations. At least three or four days' of baked bread will be in those rations, and enough flour that they can bake their own for the rest of the trip." He paused and looked thoughtful for a moment. "Check their equipment and make sure that they have a baking stone, salt, and enough animal fat to do the baking."

"It will be done. Is there anything else, Master?"

"Yes. Include a large bag of onions, enough that they may each have one daily, and enough beer that they may also have a daily ration of that as well."

A huge grin was on Senbi's face as he replied slyly, "Would it be appropriate to include some dates as well, Master?"

Joseph couldn't help himself. He started chuckling. "Yes! I can see that you understand my plan, Senbi! Such kindness following such harshness will be utterly confusing to them."

In mock seriousness, Senbi replied, "Of course, the fact that they are your brothers has nothing to do with the plan?"

"No! Of course not!" Joseph replied in kind. Then he added, "Oh! Before you ask, there is no need to include any dried meats. They are all expert with the bow and the sling. They will provide themselves with meat."

Senbi could hold it no longer and began laughing in earnest. He finally managed to say, "It will be as you command, Master! I wish I could see their faces when they open their grain sacks!"

The brothers loaded their pack animals with the grain and

departed, and when they stopped for the night, they discovered the extent of their provisions. As usual, it was Asher who was first into the foodstuffs. After only a short look, he shouted to the others, "Brethren! Have you seen what the Egyptians gave us to eat along the way?"

Judah, who had seen Asher head for the food, had followed him. He too looked into their provisions and called to the others loudly, "Yes! It is astounding!"

Ruben, attracted by Asher's and Judah's calls, came to investigate. As he too rummaged through the foodstuffs, he marveled aloud, "There are onions, baked bread, salt, flour, fat, dates, beer, and they even included a small hearth stone that we may bake bread along the way!"

Asher was delighted. "We eat like kings!"

Dan stood with his hands on his hips in mock seriousness, then pointing at Asher, said, "Yes, but you, *oh king,* will eat *only* your share and no more!" After the strain of the last few days, gales of laughter flowed from all of the brothers except Asher, who looked a bit miffed.

Levi said, wiping the laughter tears from his eyes, "All this talk of food has reminded me that my donkey is overtired from the journey and needs more than scrub graze. I'd give her a small portion of grain." He got to his feet, still chuckling, and made his way to the stack of grain bags. He went to the one that had his mark upon it and opened it. Then, he went to his pack and got his bowl to portion out some grain for the animal. As he dipped the bowl into the grain, he heard a definite "clunk" as the bowl struck something in the bag.

Curious, Levi reached into the bag and felt about until he found the object, a leather bag, and it chinked like it had money in it. Opening it, Levi found it was indeed money, his money! He realized that this was his own money sack! Frightened, he called out to the others, "Brethren! Come quickly!"

The brothers rushed to Levi's side. "What's wrong, Levi?" asked Ruben.

Holding out the offending money bag, Levi gasped, "My money is restored! Lo, it is even in my sack!"

This comment sent a few of the brothers rushing to their own sacks, and they discovered that their money was also returned in the mouths of their sacks. They were badly frightened and stood in a tight group. Several cast furtive glances back the way they had come, as though expecting the Egyptian army to be pursuing them. Finally, it was Ruben who said what they had all begun thinking. In a small frightened voice, he asked aloud, "What is this that God has done unto us?"

Chapter Fifteen
DECISIONS AND DILEMMAS

The gloom that had hung over the House of Joseph for the past three days seemed to have lifted. Asenath noted that the men were smiling again and joking at the dinner tables, but Joseph still seemed a bit withdrawn. In an attempt to draw him out, Asenath said, "I saw your brethren leaving early this morning, Joseph. Have you found out what you needed to know?"

Joseph looked at his wife in silence for a few moments and then said quietly, "Not all, my love."

"Not all?"

Joseph was again silent, as though considering his words carefully before he answered his wife. "As we were telling them the conditions upon which they could return home, one of them said, 'We are guilty concerning our brother. We saw the anguish of his soul, but when he asked us for mercy, we would not hear. This is the reason such distress has come upon us.'"

"That would seem to indicate that they are repentant, would it not?"

"On the surface, perhaps." He seemed to be watching the scene he had witnessed previously, not just remembering but living it again, as he added quietly, "Ruben was angry and said he demanded of the others that they not sin against the child. He said they would not hear but demanded my blood."

Asenath remembered something and replied, "You once told me that Ruben was absent when they sold you into slavery."

"That is true." His eyes filled with tears and then, with an emotion choked voice, he continued. "I had. . . I had always . . . thought Ruben had simply abandoned me. He didn't!"

Asenath leaned forward, and placing a comforting hand on his arm, she said, "What more could you need to know?"

Joseph lovingly placed his hand on hers to acknowledge her support. Then taking a deep breath, he responded, "There is still conflict, Asenath. Why else would Ruben have to say such a thing?"

"Conflict?"

"My father's house is divided. He has two wives and two concubines."

"So many?"

"He is a sheik in Canaan, my love, and a very important man there. He was at one time feared as well."

"He has an army?"

Joseph looked sad and weary as he answered. "No, but my Uncle Essau has an army of over four-hundred men-at-arms and was trained to lead them by my grandfather. My grandfather was trained by my great-grandfather, who was an expert warrior in Canaan."

Asenath was puzzled. "If he is not the one with the army, why is your father feared?"

Joseph looked very uncomfortable for a few moments. Then, still holding her hand and staring at the floor, he very quietly told the story. "We were camping outside the town of Shechem. My sister Dinah went into the town to commune with the girls there." Here, he paused for several seconds before he could continue. "She was raped by the prince of that city."

Asenath's free hand went to her mouth and she gasped, "Oh no!"

"Unfortunately, yes! My brothers and my father were livid! Then the king, Hamor was his name, came and talked with my father. They agreed that Dinah would marry prince Shechem, but all the men of the town had to be circumcised to meet with the customs of our people."

"You had that done to both of our sons."

Joseph nodded his agreement. "Yes, as I said it is an important custom with my people. Sadly, for adults it is very painful, and after about three days, the pain and the fever are at their peak. The men of the city would be helpless. That was the plan devised by my brothers, Levi and Simeon. On the third day they attacked the city and slew all the men of the city and burned it to the ground!"

Both of Asenath's hands flew to her mouth. "That's terrible!"

Joseph agreed. "My father thought so too! I will never forget his anger or his words: 'You have troubled me to make me to stink among the inhabitants of the land, among the Canaanites and the Perizzites! They shall gather themselves together against me. I shall be destroyed — I and my house!'"

"What did your brothers say to this?"

Joseph snorted his disgust. "They were not all that impressed. They said to my father, 'Would he deal with our sister as with a harlot?'"

"Those two sound dangerous!"

"Indeed, they are! They hated me so. They threatened to kill me on a number of occasions."

"What has this to do with the conflict you mentioned?"

"Ruben and Judah were always my defenders. Levi and Simeon were the violent ones. I fear that they have not changed." He paused and then thoughtfully added, "I wonder how they treat little Benjamin."

Asenath seemed relieved. "Well, at least they are all on the way back to your father."

Joseph looked at her in silence for a few moments, and then, looking at the floor as though embarrassed, said quietly, "Not all. One remains."

Asenath did not like the looks of this. "One? Which one?"

Joseph did not look up. He spoke to the floor as he replied, "I had Simeon bound before the eyes of my other brothers and taken from their cell. Then I sent the rest home."

Asenath was aghast. "Why Simeon, my husband? Why one of the dangerous ones?"

Once again, Joseph got a faraway look in his eyes. "It was he who threw me into the pit in the wilderness just before I was sold into slavery."

Asenath stared at her husband in stunned silence for a moment. "You kept him for revenge?"

"No, I did not . . .," Joseph began. He did not finish the statement. For, just as he had begun, Captain Khu entered the room and bowed before Joseph. Joseph welcomed the interruption. "Ah, Captain Khu! You have returned from your mission. Please, report!"

"As you ordered, we followed your brothers as far as the Pithom outpost." He paused, and then hesitantly continued. "I was concerned. We actually passed them and arrived at the outpost before them."

Joseph nodded knowingly and said, "I take it that you distrusted the border guards?"

Khu, who had been worried about this deviation from his

original orders, was greatly relieved. "That is correct, Master. However, the guards now know that these men are under your special protection and they will not be molested in *any* way!"

"Excellent! Truly excellent, Captain! Your men are resting?"

"They are. It was an arduous journey and we got little sleep."

"Have they eaten yet? "

Gesturing in the general direction of the kitchen, Khu responded, "Nakhti, is fixing them something now."

Joseph smiled. "See to it that they get an extra ration of beer. They are tired and they will need it!" Khu bowed as though he were about to leave, but Joseph stopped him and added, "Unfortunately, I have one other thing that I need you to do before you can rest."

"What is that, Master?"

"I need you to move my brother, Simeon, from the storeroom up to the main storehouse where he will be comfortable."

Khu was surprised. "Master, he will escape from there very easily!"

Joseph smiled. "There is a way to prevent that, Khu."

Despite himself, Khu blurted out, "What? Chain him to the wall in there?"

Joseph, rather than becoming angry at the outburst, began to laugh quite heartily. After a few moments, he continued, still chuckling, "No. It is far simpler. All you have to do is get him to swear an oath that he will not escape, come into the main house, or attack anyone here and he will be no problem at all."

Khu was astounded. With disbelief in his voice he asked, "Just get him to swear an oath?"

Joseph became quite serious as he continued. "It is a part of desert life, Khu. One simply does *not* break an oath. To do so means your death, and worse, dishonor for your family. Oaths are taken *very* seriously in the desert regions!"

Asenath was afraid of this man Simeon. She feared for not only her husband but her children. This seemed a very foolish thing and she gave her fear voice. "This is a man who has tried to kill you and all you require is an oath."

Joseph understood. Taking his wife by the hand, he said gently, "My brother Simeon may be many things, my wife, but an oath breaker is *not* one of them!"

"What of his treachery at Shechem, my husband? Did he not break his oath there?

Joseph looked at her quietly for a moment, and then responded, "No they didn't, at least not strictly."

"Not strictly?"

"They helped Father get the men there to agree to be circumcised, but they made no comment as to what would happen afterward." In the silence that followed, he added, "So they made no oath that was broken. That is why I was so specific in the conditions of the oath, my love."

The look on Asenath's face said that the conversation definitely was not over, and Khu sensed that this was time to leave. He saluted and said crisply, "It shall be as you command, Master!"

As he turned to go, Joseph remembered something else and called out, "Oh! Khu, make sure that Simeon gets a generous portion of what the guards are having, except for the double portion of beer. We don't need him even slightly tipsy let alone drunk!"

Khu realized what Joseph was up to. With a huge smile on his face as the realization dawned, he laughingly replied, "It shall be as you command, Master!" With that he saluted once more and left the room.

Asenath had listened to the exchanges, at first in fear, then like Khu, she finally realized what Joseph was doing. As soon as Khu was out of the room, she turned to the still smiling Joseph, wagged her finger at him and scowled as though he were a naughty child. "You scoundrel! You're doing it again!" Unfortunately, she could not maintain the facade. Both she and Joseph burst out laughing. After a few moments she finally finished. "So much kindness after what he has been through! This is exactly what you did to the others! Oh, he is going to be *so* confused!"

Captain Khu was also thinking of the brothers as he made his way to the kitchens. He chuckled to himself over their reactions to the rations that had been provided and was even more amused to think of their fright over finding their money in their sacks of grain. He found himself chuckling out loud. Then he heard the noise of his men in the kitchen. It was obvious that they were not only eating but enjoying themselves. He entered to see every man with food in his hand and a jar of beer nearby. Smiling, he turned to the cook. "Ah, Nakhti! I see you have wasted no time in feeding my men."

Nakhti, who was in the act of handing out even more food, said teasingly, "If you didn't run them all over Egypt, they might not be so hungry!"

Placing his hand over his heart in mock sadness and looking at his men, Khu said dramatically, "Ah, the soldier's lot! We run all over Egypt and the cook complains that we get hungry!" His troops began laughing so hard that one or two actually fell from their seats.

Nakhti scowled but continued to hand out food. Despite her scowl, it was obvious to Khu that she was fighting to keep from laughing herself. Then he remembered Joseph's commands about extra rations. "Oh, before I forget. The Master has commanded that these men get a double ration of beer tonight." This pronouncement brought a loud cheer from the tired men.

Nakhti looked thoughtful for a moment and then said, "A double portion of beer, eh? Perhaps *I* should have been a soldier!"

One of the men pointed a cone of bread at Nakhti and said laughingly, "Indeed, Captain! Her tongue would be the deadliest weapon in the troop!"

Nakhti turned and glared at the offender as the rest of the troop laughed hysterically. After a few moments, she shouted over the din, "See how big *your* second helping of beer is!" This pronouncement made the men laugh even harder. Shaking her head, she turned to Khu and asked, "Is there anything else the Master required?"

"Yes there is. I am moving the prisoner to the storehouse. The Master wants him given a generous portion of whatever you are feeding my men, except the beer. He gets just a normal ration of that."

Nakhti rolled her eyes and stared at the ceiling as though pleading to the gods. "Now I make deliveries," she complained. Making a dismissive gesture, she continued, "So be it. I shall see to it that this prisoner is well fed." Khu turned to go, but Nakhti stopped him. "Aren't you eating too?" she asked in a worried tone.

"I thank you, Nakhti," Khu replied. "I will have to eat a little later. Now, I must do as the Master commands."

"You will not eat first?" There was real worry in her repeated question.

"There will be plenty of time to eat once my duties are done, Nakhti," Khu responded gently. "Now, I must see to the Master's commands." As Khu left the kitchen, he smiled to himself. The woman had an acid mouth but a heart of gold! She complained, but never once had she shorted his men on their portions, even when they had to be fed in the middle of the night because of some emergency.

His thoughts turned far more serious as he approached the makeshift prison. Inside was a man who had once tried to kill Khu's master. He was none too comfortable with the notion of this oath. It seemed far too simple. Yet, Joseph always seemed to know things others did not. He would do as he had been told, but if this man made any hostile move toward Joseph, it would be his last. Brother or no brother, it would be Khu's own hand that ended his treacherous life!

Just as he had ordered, there were two guards outside the cell and two bright torches fixed in the brackets on the wall. This added light gave Khu great comfort. It would be hard for the prisoner to escape or attack in all this light. Taking no chances, he drew his weapon, and then signaled the guards to do the same. He knew that this man and only a few others had slain an entire town. Even if all the men in that town were as ill as Joseph had said, it was quite a feat, and it made this man very dangerous.

Khu ordered one guard, "Open the door." Then to the other he said, "Pull down one of those torches and lead the way into the cell." Both men did as they were ordered. The prisoner made no move when they entered. He simply sat with his back to the wall and glared at them.

Khu glared right back. "You prisoner, your name is Simeon, I think."

Simeon continued to glare insolently at his wardens. After a moment or two he replied sullenly, "That's my name."

"I have been commanded by my Master to require an oath of you. If you swear this oath, then you may have freedom to roam the grounds and sleep in a room in the storehouse with the staff instead of here in the dungeon. Will you so swear?"

Simeon stared at them in disbelief for a moment and then asked warily. "What is the nature of this oath?"

Khu noted the change in attitude. "You must swear that you will not attempt escape, that you will roam the grounds only during daylight hours, and that you will not enter the main house at any time or attempt to harm anyone here. Will you so swear?" There was genuine surprise in Simeon's voice as he answered, "I. . . I had not expected such in Egypt! I will gladly so swear!"

Khu nodded. "Very well. Follow me. I will take you to your new quarters. The cook has been instructed to feed you once you are in the storehouse. You will eat the same food as the household as long as you remain outside the dungeon."

Simeon walked in silence behind the Egyptian. He was still in a mild state of shock. Slowly realizations began to dawn on him. Oddly, at the mention of eating, his mind went to Asher. Guardedly, he smiled to himself. He had seen what the guards got to eat here. They were very well fed! They often had meat, cheeses, or eggs. Things like, beer, boiled barley, onions, cucumbers, fruit, bread and even sweet breads were always in their rations! Asher would be very pleased! It appeared that he would eat and drink like a king! Even the food he had been given in his cell had been quite good. This realization caused Simeon to frown in confusion. He turned and stared at the house thoughtfully. Who *was* this man who held him a prisoner? First, he was confined in a stinking dungeon, but then he gives an oath and is treated like royalty. He did not understand any of this.

Joseph thought the oath would put an end to his problems with Simeon. Unfortunately, he was wrong on one rather touchy point. Several evenings later, Joseph and his family were relaxing in the great room of their home. Such evenings were becoming ever rarer as the drought and the famine deepened. As he watched his two sons frolic on the floor, he turned to Asenath and said with great feeling, "It is good to be home and away from the chaos that was this morning's Diwan!"

Asenath, aware as always of the nuances of her husband's voice, knew that something was bothering him. Hiding her concern, she asked, in what she hoped was an offhand manner, "This morning's Diwan was more trying than usual?"

Joseph nodded. "Indeed! One fellow became so wild that he had to be removed!"

Captain Khu, who had just come into the room and had heard the comment, added from the doorway, "It took four strong men to remove him from the chamber!" He then bowed to Joseph and reported, "We did with him as you suggested, Master. We took him to a physician."

"What did the physician say?"

Khu looked worried. "The man was ill as you suspected, and he may not recover fully. The physician said he has seen a number of cases like this since the beginning of the famine, Master."

Joseph shook his head sadly and asked, "Another case of

madness caused by eating moldy rye bread?"

Khu looked sadder than Asenath had ever seen him when he replied, "That is exactly what he said."

Asenath remembered something. She realized why things were being handled the way they were in Joseph's household. In amazement she said, "That is why you will not allow bread kept! If it molds it can make us ill?"

Joseph made a disgusted sound. "More than ill, my love — utterly mad. It is not a pleasant sight. The victims are abnormally strong and hard to subdue."

Asenath was silent for a moment or two. Once again she was thankful for the man that Pharaoh had given her to. So many women complained about the practice of arranged marriage, but she could only admire this man. She did not hide the admiration in her eyes or her voice as she said, "I will tell Nakhti. She has been complaining that such good food is going to the animals. Now, I know why!"

Khu, who was still standing in the doorway, turned and looked down the hallway outside the room. "Speaking of Nakhti, I believe she is coming now."

Within moments Nakhti entered the room and bowed to Joseph. "Yes, Nakhti, what is it?" asked Asenath, who normally handled the affairs of the house.

"I have once again been out to the storehouse and took food to the prisoner, Mistress."

"Your tone of voice indicates that there is a problem, Nakhti," Joseph noted.

Nakhti looked very uncomfortable. She chewed her lip for a bit and then began hesitantly, "I hesitate to speak of this, my Master, as the man is your brother, but. . ." Here her courage seemed to fail her.

"Go ahead, Nakhti. what is the problem?" Joseph prodded gently.

Nakhti, her hands flailing in desperation, blurted in a panicked rush, "He stinks!"

Joseph sat silently for a few seconds and his face began to turn red. Everyone in the room thought that he was about to explode in anger, but to everyone's surprise, he suddenly snorted loudly and burst into an uncontrolled fit of laughing! It took a minute or so for him to calm down. Then, pointing to Nakhti, he sputtered, "He. . . He stinks!" And he collapsed back onto the cushions behind him in another fit of laughter. Finally, he arose painfully, and still trying to regain control, he said, "Oh! You have made my evening merry, Nakhti! Forgive me! After the stress of this morning, that was just too choice!" Seeing the questioning look on his wife's face, he said, "It is something that I have forgotten in all these years in Egypt."

"What is that, my husband?"

"Desert men do not bathe, my love."

"Ooh! No wonder he stinks!" Asenath said in disgust.

This comment sent Joseph into another bout of laughter. Noting Asenath's annoyed look, he waved an apologetic hand and explained. "You do not understand, my love. In the desert, where there is no water to spare, bathing is impossible. However, it makes no difference. For some reason, in the desert these men have no body odor . . . at all!"

Asenath was astounded. "None?"

"None!" Joseph asserted. Then looking at all of them and dramatically holding up a warning finger he added, "Ah! But bring them indoors and feed them a rich diet and they begin to stink so badly that a pig would run from them holding its nose!" They all burst into laughter.

Khu was the first to recover. "I don't have to be told your next command, Master. Give him a bath."

Wagging a warning finger at the Captain, Joseph warned humorously, "You may find the command easier to issue than to accomplish, my dear Khu."

"Oh? Why?" Khu questioned warily.

"Desert men believe that bathing is bad for a person. They simply won't do it unless they are forced."

Khu made a dismissive gesture. "My men should have no problems with him!"

Joseph, with the look of a devilish imp on his face, replied, "Really? I should warn you that Simeon, chief among all my brothers in this, loves to brawl. Fist fighting was his favorite sport!"

Khu had a puzzled expression. "What of his oath not to harm anyone here?"

Joseph smiled. "To his mind, he would only be defending himself."

Khu stood silent for a moment or two. Then with an evil grin on his face, he said slowly, "Hmm. It's funny that you should mention that this man likes to brawl, Master. Your brother may solve a problem for me."

It was Joseph's turn to look curious. "In what way, Khu?"

"I have several men who have taken to brawling in the barracks just for fun. This may be a good release for them."

The look on Joseph's face was unreadable as he asked, "How many men do we have that have been involved in these evening . . . ah . . . barracks activities?"

"Seven, my Lord," Khu replied, unsure of what Joseph was up to.

The look on Joseph's face changed to pure delight: "I like the idea!"

Asenath was horrified. "Joseph! You can't possibly mean that you will allow all seven men to brutalize your brother!"

Joseph snorted and raised a dismissive hand. "My love, Simeon is huge and has been known to easily defeat as many as five men in a fist fight without receiving so much as a scratch!" He paused, dramatically rubbed his chin thoughtfully, and continued slowly. "I would call seven to one just a good fair fight! With luck, he might just get a bath in the process!"

Asenath sat up straight and put her hands on her hips. She looked for all the world like some strict old maid school teacher. With thin disapproving lips, she asked reprovingly, "Joseph? What are you thinking?"

Joseph, his eyes dancing with mischief and a comically thoughtful look on his face, said quietly, "Selling tickets."

Outraged, Asenath shouted, "Joseph!"

While Joseph and Asenath debated the merits of combining hygiene and the pugilistic arts, Joseph's brethren arrived at the camp of their father in Canaan. Desert dwellers are always on the alert as the desert is filled with dangers — bandits, ravenous wild animals, rival tribes, and sandstorms. Thus, when the sons' caravan approached the camp, it was detected at some distance, but it was not long before they were identified. Jacob, resting in his tent, heard the commotion created by the approach of the returning sons and went to the door of his tent to investigate. He had barely achieved the doorway when Leah, his first wife, came running toward him. Before she could speak, Jacob asked, "Leah! What is all this commotion in the camp?"

Leah was beaming. "Your sons have returned with full packs of food upon their animals!"

"Full packs?" Jacob asked. This was joyous news indeed! They had hardly expected so much.

Leah pointed in the direction of the approaching caravan. "Look, see for yourself. The poor creatures are so laden that they stagger under the load!"

There could be no mistake. The staggering gate of the animals and the bulging sacks on their backs were very plain. Raising his hands high and looking up into the sky, Jacob shouted thankfully, "Praised be the name of the God of my father's! He has provided for us in this time of want!"

Despite the hot sun, everyone stood in the center of the camp until the group arrived. Ruben approached his father, and bowing, he said in a subdued voice, "Peace be unto you, my father."

"Why are you so sad, Ruben?" Pointing to the bulging grain sacks, Jacob said happily, "You and your brethren have brought a miracle into the camp!"

Ruben hung his head. He did not want to ruin his father's joyous mood, but the tragic truth had to be told. With his head still lowered, he said quietly, "These are not all my brethren, Father."

Jacob had been so overjoyed at the sight of the life-giving food that he had failed to count his sons to see that all was well. He was immediately deeply alarmed. Seizing Ruben by the arms, he asked, "Who is missing?"

"Simeon is no longer with us, my father. He. . ."

"Is he dead?" asked the now thoroughly panicked Jacob.

"No, he is prison," Ruben said simply.

"Prison? How did *that* happen?"

Ruben began their sad tale. "The man who is the lord of the land spoke roughly to us and took us for spies."

"How did you answer the man?"

"We said to him, 'We are true men! We are not spies!'"

Levi saw that their father was getting angry and he quickly added in Ruben's defense, "Then we said, 'We are twelve brethren, sons of our father — one is no longer with us and the youngest is this day with our father in the land of Canaan.'"

Judah too, felt he had to speak. "And the lord of the country said to us, 'Hereby shall I know that you are true men. Leave one of your brethren here with me, take food for the famine of your households, and be gone. When you bring your youngest brother unto me, then shall I know that you are not spies and that you are true men. Then will I deliver you your brother, and you shall traffic in the land.'"

Jacob listened to all of this in silence. Now he was indignant. "You left Simeon with him?"

Ruben was stung by the accusation. "We did not *leave* him; they *took* him by force, Father!"

Jacob's indignation disappeared. He was now thoroughly confused. "Then this man sent you away with full food sacks?"

Asher was excited and shouted, "Yes, Father. Come look at mine — it is bulging!" He ran to his animal and let down one of the bulging sacks it carried. Everyone crowded around to see what was there. Asher happily opened the sack, and reaching in, he pulled up a fist full of the grain and then let the grain fall back into the sack. He shouted, "See? There is plenty!"

A very sober Levi said, "That is not all we found in our sacks, Asher. Show father what else was in our sacks."

Suddenly, Asher looked pale and slowly reaching inside his robes produced what appeared to be a money bag.

Jacob was frightened. He pointed to the money in Asher's hand and asked. "Your money was in the mouth of your sack, Asher?"

"Yes, my father."

"You failed to pay for the grain?"

Before the abashed Asher could respond, Ruben came to his defense. "Father it's not Asher's fault. We paid for the grain in full, but . . ." At this point he held out his own money sack. Silently, each of the eleven brothers produced their leathern money bags.

Jacob stared at the money bags in the hands of his astonished sons. "What is this you have done? You did not pay for the grain?" he shouted.

Ruben stared at the money sack in his hand and then at his angry father. "But we did, Father! We paid full price for it! We cannot explain this!"

It was too much for poor Jacob. Pounding his chest, he shouted, "My sons have betrayed me! Joseph is no longer with us, and now Simeon is not with us either!"

Ruben ran to his father and tried to comfort him by taking him by the arm. "Father, we can get Simeon back! All we have to do is take Benjamin with us!"

"You will take Benjamin away? All these things you do are against me!" Jacob shouted, and he wrenched his arm out of Ruben's grasp. He backed away from Ruben and shouted, "No! You shall not take him! He stays with me where he will be safe!"

Ruben was frightened and desperate. The grain would not last all that long. He pleaded with his father. "Send Benjamin down with me when we need to return, father. Slay my two sons, if I bring him not to you! Deliver him into my hand at that time, and I will bring him to you again!"

Jacob was adamant. "My youngest son shall not go down with you! His elder brother is dead already! If mischief befalls him, then I will stumble under the weight of the sorrow to the grave!" With a final decisive chop of his hand he shouted, "He shall NOT go with you!"

Chapter Sixteen
The Brothers Return

The camp of Jacob, like any other in the land of Canaan, was made up of large black goat hair tents and numerous open-sided fly tents. In the center of the numerous tents forming the camp, was a never-failing well that Jacob had dug many years before, and surrounding the encampment were the large flocks of sheep, goats, camels, and asses. Normally, such a camp would be a beehive of activity. People would be visible moving about, tending livestock, working at cook fires before the tents, or sitting in the shade of a fly tent working on some project or other.

With the coming of the famine, that had changed. Very few people were visible. It was hot, and an almost continuous hot dry wind blew from the east. People were staying indoors, away from the scorching wind and the gritty sand that it carried, at the least they were in the shade of a fly tent where they were shielded from the blistering desert sun. Even the cooking was delayed until after the sun set, when the wind died and the chill of the desert night set in.

It was nearly midday, and for all intents and purposes, the Jacob's camp looked deserted, except for the lone figure of a woman walking rapidly from one tent to another. Her shawl was up over her head and she had her veil over her face, not out of modesty but to protect her face from the incessant oppressive wind, the blowing grit, and the merciless hot sun.

She now disappeared into the largest of the tents in the camp. As she entered the second, inner set of tent flaps she was relieved to feel the coolness of the place. Here there was no hot wind or blowing grit. Usually, it was quiet in the tents, but now the wind rattled the sides and shook the tent poles. Over the months of the famine, the desert dwellers had gotten used to the constant sound. Like all the tents, this one was not illuminated inside, and it took a few moments for her eyes to adapt to the semi-darkness inside.

While she waited for her eyes to accommodate themselves, she removed her shawl and the hot veil, and for a few moments, she simply relished the coolness of the place. Soon, she could see her husband, Jacob, sitting quietly, facing away from her in the center of the tent reading from a scroll. He did not realize that she was there. The noise of the tent's movements had covered the sounds of her entering the tent's outer flaps. She called out quietly, "My husband?"

With a start, Jacob turned toward the sound of the voice. "You startled me, Leah! I did not hear you come in."

"Forgive me, my husband, but I forgot about all the noise the wind makes. I came at your request."

Confused, Jacob asked, "My request?"

"My husband, you said that you should be informed when we had eaten most of the grain that your sons brought back from Egypt."

Jacob was shocked. "It is nearly gone already, my wife?"

Leah bowed her head as though this was in some way her fault. It was not. She had been very frugal with the precious grain. She said humbly. "It is my husband."

Jacob knew his wife well. She was extremely responsible. He had no way of telling her, no way of telling her that she would accept anyway, that it was not her fault. Instead, he asked gently, "How long do you think the remainder will feed us?"

Leah did not want to say this, but the truth had to be told. "For just over one lunar month if we reduce to quarter rations, my husband. Then we will have nothing to eat."

Jacob looked thoughtful, and then he said, "It is a long way to Egypt, about eighty leagues. It took my sons over a full month the last trip."

Leah sounded frightened as she replied, "That means that we will have eaten nearly all the food they brought the first time before they return with more."

Jacob shared her concern. "Then they must go again, and quickly! Leah, see to it that my sons come to me at once."

"I shall do so immediately, my husband!" She ran from Jacob's tent without bothering to replace the shawl or the veil in her haste. She did not waste time in looking for her eldest son but instead ran to the general area of the sons' tents and called out in a loud urgent voice, "Ruben! Ruben, come to me, my son!"

Ruben, who had been lying down in the cool of his own tent, heard his mother's cry and the urgency in her voice was plain. He jumped up and ran out of his tent. Looking about, blinking in the intense sunlight and blowing grit, he spotted her and called out, "Coming, Mother!" He then ran swiftly to her side and skidded to a stop before her, alarmed. Breathlessly he asked, "Yes . . . my . . . mother. What do you need?"

Leah took hold of his arm in her urgency. "Bring all of your brothers. Your father would speak with you."

Ruben was more alarmed. "Do you know why he summons us?"

"The food is running critically short, and he needs to send you immediately to Egypt to buy more."

Ruben's alarm settled into despair, but when he saw the unwavering trust in his mother's eyes, he felt some determination not to disappoint her. He knew she felt that he could do anything. In this instance, however, Ruben had serious doubts. Keeping his uncertainties to himself, he replied simply, "I will call my brothers as he has asked." Then, bowing to his mother, he left her in search of Judah. As he searched, he hoped fervently that their father had changed his mind about sending Benjamin. If he had not, they would starve, for they could not return to the Egyptian without him.

He did not have to go far. He spied Judah sitting under one of the fly tents talking quietly with some of the shepherds. As Ruben approached, Judah looked up and saw him.

"What is it, Ruben?"

"Father has called for all his sons to come to him."

"Why?"

"He wants us to go back to Egypt to buy more food."

Judah instantly shared Ruben's apprehension about this mission. "I certainly hope that he has changed his mind about sending Benjamin!"

"I was just thinking the same thing!" Ruben looked into the distance, and with some surprise, he said, "Oh! Look, here come Dan, Levi, and Benjamin!" Waving his arm to get their attention, he called out to them. "Come here, brothers!"

The younger brothers were soon with them. Dan greeted them. "Peace be unto you, my brothers!"

Judah and Ruben gave the traditional reply, "And peace be unto you!"

Dan, noting their somber countenances, asked, "Why do you look so serious?"

Ruben answered, "Father has just called for all of us to come to meet with him."

Judah added, "He wants us to return to Egypt to buy food."

Levi snorted in disgust. "Not without Benjamin, we don't!"

Benjamin, who had not been present when the others had returned from Egypt, asked excitedly, "I get to go to Egypt with you?"

Ruben held up a warning hand and looked at Benjamin. "Don't get excited just yet, little brother! Father is completely against sending you to Egypt!"

Benjamin looked hurt. "Why? What did I do wrong?"

Levi placed a reassuring hand on Benjamin's shoulder and said quietly, "You did not do anything wrong, little brother!"

Benjamin looked confused. "Then why would father not let me go?"

Dan took a deep breath. "You are the last son of Rachael, Benjamin. He loved her greatly, and he loved your brother Joseph greatly too. You are all he has left of her."

"Oh," Benjamin said looking at the ground at his feet dejectedly. Then, looking up, he asked, "But why then did Levi say he would not go without me?"

Judah explained further. "The ruler of the land demanded that we bring you as proof we are not spies."

This was all news to Benjamin. Confused, he asked, "Spies?"

"It is a long story, Benjamin," Levi said wearily. "It is sure to be *well* discussed in our meeting with Father. We need to get there quickly. Benjamin, please run down to the goat pens to fetch the rest of our brothers to Father's tent. We'll wait for you there."

Benjamin's eyes showed his excitement. "I shall do so immediately, Levi."   He then turned and ran toward the goat pens.

Ruben smiled and shook his head at his youngest brother's enthusiasm. Then he turned serious. "I hope that this meeting with Father goes better than the one we had with him when we returned with the grain. He was adamant. . ."

Before he could finish the statement, all of them quoted their father in unison, "He shall *not* go with you!"

Judah's countenance was very serious. He said worriedly, "Let us hope that we can change his mind. If we cannot, we are *all* dead men!"

They stared after Benjamin in silence for a few moments, each of the brothers wrapped in his own thoughts. Finally, Ruben broke the silence. "Come; let us go to the tent of our father. Our brothers will be with us shortly. We can only pray that the God of our fathers will soften Jacob's heart that we may live and not perish in this famine."

Jacob was waiting in his tent when they arrived, and he nodded to each as they entered. When they had all come into the tent, he said, "My sons. Now that you are all gathered, I will tell you what I desire of you. I need you to go to Egypt once more. We have eaten nearly all the grain you brought and are in great need of more. Go again to Egypt to buy us a little food."

Ruben, being the oldest, was the spokesman. Very quietly he said, "We cannot go unless Benjamin is with us, Father."

Jacob was instantly angry. "I have already told you that Benjamin will not go to Egypt!"

"He must, Father, or we cannot traffic there," Levi pleaded.

Unconvinced, Jacob demanded stubbornly, "You have said this before, but why must he go?"

Judah knew that failure in this argument meant starvation, but he also knew that he had to be as diplomatic as possible. Using his softest voice, he said, "Father, the man who rules the country did solemnly protest unto us, saying, 'You shall not see my face, except your brother is with you.' If you will send our brother with us, we will go to Egypt and buy food. But if you will not send him, we will not go down, for we will not be able to meet with the man who sells the grain in Egypt."

Jacob was furious. "Why did you deal so ill with me as to tell the man that you had yet another brother?"

Ruben, his hands spread in pleading, said, "The man asked us of our state and of our kindred, saying, 'Is your father yet alive? Have you another brother?'"

Before Ruben could finish, Levi added, "We told him honestly, according to the tenor of his words."

Jacob steadfastly refused to understand and demanded, "Why? Why did you tell the man of Benjamin?"

"Could we have known that he would demand that we bring our brother to Egypt?" Dan asked reasonably.

Jacob, almost in tears, wailed, "Rachael is no longer with us and Joseph is not with us! He alone is left!"

Judah approached their father, and kneeling down before him, he said, "Send the lad with me, and we will go. We will get the food we need that we may live, that our little ones might live. I will be surety for him. If I bring him not unto you, if I set him not before you, then let me bear the blame forever!"

"The food is running out, Father! We need food or *none* of us will be left!" Asher pleaded.

"If we had not lingered, surely by now we would have returned a second time!" Ruben added very quietly.

Jacob sat silently for some time, tears running freely down his face. Several times he tried to speak, but he could not utter a sound due to the tremendous emotions flooding through him. Finally, after a long time and several steadying breaths, he said slowly and quietly, "If it must be so, do this, but also take the best fruits of the land in your vessels, and carry the man some presents, a little balm, a little honey, spices, myrrh, nuts, and almonds. Take double money in your hand. Take also the money that was brought again in the mouth of your sacks. Maybe it was an oversight. Take your brother and go again unto the man. God Almighty give you mercy before him that this man may send away your other brother and Benjamin."

It was as though he could bear no more and Jacob dissolved into tears once again. He was wracked with his sobs, and his sons stood with their heads hung in shame before their father's grief. After a time, Jacob managed to croak, "If I am bereft of my children, I am bereaved."

The men then left silently to prepare. They took the presents that their father had commanded, and they took double the money for the grain they could carry. Then they took Benjamin with them down to Egypt to stand before Joseph.

The day of yet another grain sale had arrived in the land of Egypt. As had become usual, the granary's courtyard was filled with milling people. Devoid at the moment of his vestments, Joseph stood in the doorway of the granary looking out at the ever moving crowd. After a few silent moments, he turned and said, "Once more we begin a grain sale, Senbi." He had an odd tone in his voice

Looking knowingly at his master, Senbi said quietly, "I know that tone well, my Master. You are worried about your family in Canaan."

"I am, Senbi. I am. It has been almost two months since my brethren came the last time." Joseph once more looked out at the sea of people before him. "They should have returned long since."

JOSEPH Ruler of All Egypt

Senbi then did something very few Egyptians could have done. He placed a reassuring hand on Joseph's shoulder and said very quietly so no other could hear, "They will come, Master. They will come."

Joseph looked at his friend and with tears in his eyes said simply, "Thank you."

Khu, unseen, had joined them. He too saw the worry on Joseph's face and then he looked out at the huge crowd. Shaking his head in disbelief, he said, "The numbers keep increasing, Master! There must be close to one thousand people here today! Your brethren will be hard to spot in all of this!"

Senbi, his voice filled with excitement, said, "Perhaps not as hard as you thought, Khu! Look, Master!" He pointed into the crowd. "There is a group coming to the front with the guards. I think they are your brethren!"

Joseph looked where Senbi was pointing. There could be no doubt that the men coming with the guards were his brothers. He could not contain his excitement. "They are! Those are my brothers . . . and I see a young man with them. Could that be little Benjamin?" he asked, astonished at the size of the man.

Senbi looked at the stranger. The resemblance to Joseph was undeniable. "Most likely, Master. He definitely looks like you. Remember, it has been twenty-two years since you have seen your little brother. He would have grown into a man."

"Indeed, he would have." The excitement in Joseph's voice was plain. Realizing this, as well as remembering his responsibilities and station, he took a few deep breaths and continued in a calm voice, "Bring these men to my home, and make ready for these men to dine with me at noon."

Senbi smiled. How many times had he seen his wonderful master exercise such tremendous control? He could not count them. He heard stories of others in power in Egypt. Many officials threw temper tantrums, shouted, and lost control generally. How proud he was of Joseph. He had the bearing of Pharaoh himself! "It shall be as you have commanded, my Lord!" Signaling to the captain of the guard, he said, "Khu, come with me, and bring a few men with you."

Khu turned to the small troop of soldiers that had accompanied him. Pointing to the seven largest and most scarred of his men, he commanded quietly, "You men stay here with the

Master." To the rest he commanded, "You six, come with me!"

Joseph smiled at the men left to guard him as he turned and began putting on the vestments of his office. As he did so, he chuckled aloud, and thought to himself, *"Typical, Khu! Typical! He left me the brawlers!"* He looked at the men as they stood their posts. They were alert, and each had his hand upon his weapon, ready to strike if any should try to molest Joseph. Nodding his approval of them, Joseph thought, *"They may have been nearly defeated by Simeon in a friendly fight, but few others could do it! He left me in excellent hands!"*

While Joseph chuckled over Khu's precautions for his safety, Senbi and Khu approached Joseph's brethren. Senbi understood his part well. While Joseph was thrilled to see his brothers again, he still did not trust them. They had to be tested further. Thus, when he approached the men, he guarded his countenance. When he spoke, his voice was curt. "You, men of Canaan! Come with us!"

Ruben spoke. He bowed and said, "Master! We have brought our younger brother as you have asked. We need to see the Great One to prove our innocence that we may get the food we need for our house."

Senbi, maintaining a facade of curt indifference, said, "You shall see him shortly. I am to take you to his house. You will be dining with the Master at noon. Come, follow!"

Levi, staring at the armed troops and at the grim-faced Khu, grabbed Judah by the arm in his panic and whispered frantically, "Judah! This is bad! This could be a trap!"

Judah understood Levi's fear. This looked like a capture, not a dinner invitation. He began thinking rapidly. In an urgent whisper, he said to Levi, "Quiet! Keep your eyes open and your mouth shut! Be ready! We may be able to escape if we use our wits; but make too much noise, and we won't have a chance! Whatever happens, we have to get Benjamin back to Father!" At this comment, Levi simply nodded his full and fervent agreement.

Senbi, who spoke Hebrew, heard these comments, and moving slowly, he leaned close to Khu. "Keep a sharp watch as we travel, Khu. These men are badly frightened and are libel to bolt."

"I shall do so! I have never seen such terrified men." Nodding discretely in the direction of the brothers, he added, "See how they cluster about the young one."

"That is the younger brother of which the Master was

speaking. One of them just called him Benjamin. They certainly seem determined to protect him!" Senbi observed.

"That they do, Senbi!" Pointing ahead, he added, "We are here. What are your orders?"

Senbi glanced at the sorely-afraid and protective brothers, and then at the walled estate. He thought for a minute and then said, "Once they are inside, shut the gates and double the guards. I would not want to face the Master if they run off or attack the household in their fear!"

Khu actually shuddered. "Nor would I!"

Senbi waited until they were actually inside the estate, and then he stopped and faced the brothers. As he did so, he noted that Khu was having the gates closed and that guards were pouring out of the barracks. Loudly he said, "Men of Canaan, welcome to my Master's home!"

Asher heard none of this. He was staring back the way they had come. In a strangled, frightened whisper, he said, "They have closed and locked the gate!"

Ruben heard Asher, and looking about frantically, he whispered to the others, "That isn't all! There are armed guards moving into position everywhere!"

Dan too was looking about, a frightened expression on his face. "It is because of the money that was returned in our sacks the first time we came! He does this that he may fall upon us and take us for bondmen!"

Ruben agreed and was thinking fast. Urgently, he said quietly to Judah, "Come Judah, let us commune with the Steward! Perhaps we can prevent a disaster."

Senbi was also thinking rapidly. Urgently he whispered to Khu. "Quickly, go and find Simeon and bring him hither. That may calm these men."

Khu saw the wisdom of this instantly. Thinking out loud he said, "He likes to help with the gardening and is usually among the plants at this time of day. He should be easy to find. I shall hurry."

As the ever faithful Khu turned to go, Judah and Ruben approached. They bowed low to Senbi, and Judah spoke. "Oh sir, we came down the first time to buy food. When we opened our sacks, we discovered every man's money was in the mouth of his sack in full weight. We thought this was perhaps an oversight, and we have brought that money again."

Before Senbi could reply, Ruben held out a money sack and added, "And we have brought more money to buy the food to take to our family too. We do not know who put our money in our sacks before!"

Senbi actually smiled. Holding up a reassuring hand he said, "Peace be unto you. Fear not. Your God, the God of your fathers, has given you treasure in your sacks. I have your money."

Before anything else could be said, Khu arrived and spoke to Senbi. "Here is the brother."

The brothers spotted Simeon instantly and rushed forward. Almost in unison they shouted, "Simeon!" Each had to hug their missing brother. As they did so, they tried to ask questions:

"Are you all right?"

"How have they got you dressed?"

"Have you gained weight?"

"How come you smell like . . . flowers?"

Simeon was thrilled to see them and hugged them fiercely. Then he nearly shouted, "One at a time! One at a time! Levi, I'm fine! I've never been better! Dan, this is what they wear in Egypt. It's hotter here than in the desert, and this is cool. Asher, yes, I have gained weight. I eat like a king!" Then he turned to Benjamin, who had asked the last question. With a red embarrassed face, he said, "Ah, Benjamin. Well, it is the . . . soap I use to . . . bathe every day."

Benjamin was appalled. "They make you take a bath . . . every day?"

Simeon cleared his throat. Then he looked at one of the nearby guards who spoke Hebrew and saw he was grinning broadly. With a wry grin, Simeon said, "Yes, well it appears that a shepherd indoors eating rich food . . . well . . . stinks!"

Ruben was having trouble keeping a straight face. Fighting the grin that threatened to break into a full-blown belly laugh, he said knowingly, "Uh huh. So you calmly started taking daily baths?"

Simeon grinned even more, and looking quite sheepish, he said, "Well, not all that calmly."

The guard, who spoke Hebrew, and had been silently smiling now, began laughing. He said, "That is truth! It took ten of us to get him in the water! Then another four to soap him up!"

Simeon turned on the guard with his hands on his hips and said in mock indignation, "The ones doing the soaping didn't count.

They were women. I don't hit women!"

The brothers thought this was hilarious. Gone was their fear. They were laughing hysterically. Ruben, recovered and pounding his brother on the back, said, "It sounds like you have had a *terrible* ordeal here in Egypt, my brother!" Once more they dissolved into gales of laughter.

Senbi broke into the revelry. "Speaking of bathing, we have brought water that you may wash your feet and hands before you eat with the Master. We have also brought food for your animals."

"Did you say we will eat with your Master?" Ruben asked.

"Indeed! This is a great honor. Most Egyptians feel it is an abomination to eat with outsiders." Turning to Simeon, Senbi continued, "Before you ask, Simeon, your pledge to not enter the house is revoked for the meal. You may enter to dine with the Master as well."

Simeon bowed. "I thank you!"

"You are welcome. Now, excuse me. I must make ready for my Master's coming."

Ruben watched the man go, and then suddenly realized that haste was called for. This man's Master would be home soon, and there was much to do. "It is nearly noon! We must prepare! Brethren, run to the animals and get the presents that we brought with us. We must make sure all is as it should be! We cannot insult this man!"

So it was that the reunited brethren prepared to meet Joseph when he returned at noon. After Joseph had come home, they were taken to the dining area and presented to him.

They were escorted into the house by Senbi. The house's interior was quite cool and bright, unlike their tents in the desert, which were also cool but dark inside. The walls were covered with paintings of birds and scenes of life along the Nile. A number of people were already gathered in the room, and musicians were playing softly in the corner of the room. They had just enough time to notice these things when Senbi announced loudly, "Kneel. Bow before the great Zaphnath-paaneah. Pay homage to him who is second only to Pharaoh and rules all Egypt!" The brothers quickly prostrated themselves before the great man.

Joseph was still arrayed in his official garments and trappings. He entered and sat on a raised dais at the end of the room. As soon as the brothers had bowed before him, he signaled silently to Senbi to have them rise. Senbi said, "Arise and stand before the Great One." As the brothers were standing, Joseph again gestured to Senbi, who quickly went to Joseph's side. Joseph whispered into Senbi's ear for a moment. Then Senbi turned and faced the guests. "So, you have returned," he translated.

Ruben bowed respectfully and said quietly, "We have, Great One."

Again, Joseph used Senbi to translate and asked, "How are you?"

Ruben bowed and answered politely, "We are all well, my Lord."

"Is your father well, the old man of whom you spoke? Is he yet alive?" Senbi translated.

"Your servant, our father is in good health."

Joseph waited for Senbi to translate, but he really wasn't listening. He thought, *Once again they bow before me and make obeisance! Once again, I see my dream fulfilled!* He then noticed the younger man. Motioning to Senbi, he whispered his question.

Senbi rose and translated. "Is this your younger brother of whom you spoke?"

Judah, taking Benjamin by the arm and leading him forward, bowed and said, "Yes, my Lord. This is Benjamin."

Joseph could see his mother's face in that of the younger man! He knew he was about to lose control. Choking back his tears, he rose, and without thinking, croaked in Hebrew, "God be gracious unto you, my son!" Then, knowing that the tears and sobs were coming, he fled from the room.

Ruben was alarmed and asked Senbi, "Have we done or said something wrong?"

Senbi was polite but distracted. He was shocked that Ruben had seemingly failed to notice Joseph's inadvertent use of the Hebrew language. Reluctant to draw attention to his master's unfortunate lapse, and confused by Joseph's sudden departure, he focused on Ruben's question and answered absently, "I do not think so. All is well for you." Then, holding up an apologetic hand, he said, "Would you please excuse me?" He went quickly to the door through which Joseph had fled. Captain Khu was there standing guard. Senbi whispered frantically to him, "What is it, Khu? Why has the Master fled?"

Khu leaned forward and whispered so that no one else could

hear. "It is like when he first saw his brothers. He has gone to his room to weep. He will be with us again very soon." He straightened suddenly and looked down the hallway outside the doorway. Holding up a hand for quiet, he listened for a moment. "I think I hear him coming. Yes, it is he!" Senbi rushed back to his place.

Joseph entered and returned to his seat on the dais. Motioning to Senbi, he said loudly in Egyptian, "Set out bread, Senbi."

Senbi bowed and then motioned to the serving girl standing at the doorway to the kitchens. She nodded and went to have the food brought in. Then he turned to the brothers, who were still standing. "Men of Canaan, sit here at this table."

Benjamin had been looking around the room in wonder. He asked, "Why are there so many tables set up?"

Senbi paused and smiled at the young man. "You are observant. The Master sits alone on the dais — his is the place of honor. These. . ." He waved his arm in the general direction of the other diners, "are those of the household and other guests that are Egyptian. You will sit apart at this table."

Benjamin was impressed. "Is this an honor?"

Senbi realized that Benjamin did not understand. Motioning him to come close, he whispered in Benjamin's ear, "It is so that the Egyptians might not eat bread with outsiders. It is an abomination to the Egyptians to eat at the same table with foreigners."

An abashed Benjamin exclaimed, "Oh!"

Joseph again spoke in Egyptian from the dais, "Senbi! They are seated incorrectly! Ruben is the eldest, and he should be seated there, then Simeon next to him, then Levi."

Senbi immediately began reseating the brothers. Judah noticed the seating order and thought, *"What is this? He knows our birth order! How could he know these things?"*

Finally, Joseph concluded, "And lastly, young Benjamin there."

Judah was astounded. He tried to signal Senbi unobtrusively. "Pssst! Senbi. How is it this man knows our birth order?"

Senbi. "You do not know the meaning of my Master's name?"

"No."

Senbi seemed to swell with pride as he said proudly, "It is the title given to him by Pharaoh himself: His title is, 'He who reveals that which is hidden."

Judah was astonished and said simply, "Oh!"

Chapter Seventeen
THE FINAL TEST AND JOSEPH IS REVEALED

The meal was a very festive affair. The wine flowed freely, and people began to mix openly despite Joseph's brothers being non-Egyptian. To everyone's surprise, the brothers turned out to be quite charming. Judah, with his full head of red hair and powerful build, was quite popular, and Dan was quite the storyteller. Ruben's whooping laugh amused everyone and Benjamin, who like his older brother Joseph, was quite handsome, quiet and somewhat shy, became a favorite target for the girls present.

After a time, Asenath noticed something disturbing and brought it to Joseph's attention. Leaning close, she whispered in his ear. "My husband, why are you favoring your younger brother so? You have given him five times as much food from your mess as you have sent to your other brothers. Will this not cause them to be jealous of their younger brother?"

Joseph looked at his wife in silence for several seconds before he responded. "It may. I wish to see if they will treat him as they treated me."

"I do not understand my husband."

Joseph became very serious. He looked at his brothers in silence, and then at Benjamin before he answered his wife. Then he said slowly, "I am the son of Jacob's favorite wife. After she died, he tended to favor me in all things. He went so far as to give me, the next to the youngest, the birthright."

"The birthright?" This was a new term to Asenath and she was curious.

Joseph explained. "The position of head of the family when Father dies. The birthright, in our family, also carries with it the right to the priesthood, which only the eldest or his chosen son may hold."

Asenath, whose father was the high priest of On, was intrigued. This was something that Joseph had never mentioned to her before. "The priesthood? To which God, my husband?"

Joseph smiled. He understood her curiosity. "To the God of my fathers. The chosen son would also inherit the scriptures, or sacred writings of our God."

"An important responsibility!"

"Indeed!" Joseph agreed. Then, holding up a warning finger, he continued, "It was the source of much jealousy. The birthright normally passes to the eldest son. That would have been Ruben, but since I am the son of his favorite wife, father considered me the eldest."

Asenath was shocked. Her face mirrored her surprise. "Oh! That explains much, my husband!" She quietly surveyed the brothers for a moment, and then, her voice echoing her realization, continued. "I take it that, with you gone, the birthright falls to Benjamin?"

Joseph's face was grave, but he was proud of his intelligent wife. Placing a hand on her arm, he said emphatically, "Yes! He is the only remaining son of Rachael, my mother."

"So now you are favoring him to see if they will become angry as they did with you," Asenath said slowly.

Joseph squeezed her lovingly. "You have surmised correctly, my wife! You are as intelligent as you are beautiful!"

Asenath playfully batted at his hand. "Flatterer!"

Joseph, in mock indignation, sat up straight, and with a greatly exaggerated dignity said, "No, truthful!" He and Asenath dissolved into laughter. Wiping the tears of laughter out of his eyes a few moments later, he turned to the ever faithful Senbi. "Senbi, you have undoubtedly heard what your mistress and I have been discussing?"

Senbi bowed low, and he said in a worried tone, "I meant no offense, Master!"

"None is taken," Joseph said with a dismissive gesture of his hand. Then, looking his servant and friend in the eye, he asked, "What do you think? Is this test enough or should there be something more?"

Senbi returned Joseph's scrutiny. Then he looked out at the brothers thoughtfully for a moment before he turned again to Joseph. "They seem amicable enough here, my Lord, but they may be putting forward a false face for your benefit despite the preferential treatment shown to Benjamin." Senbi paused in thought for a moment. "Perhaps, if he were accused of some crime, they would show their true natures?"

"Hmm . . . some crime?" Joseph stared at the floor for some time before he spoke again. Then he said slowly, "Senbi, fill the men's sacks with food, as much as they can carry, and put every man's money in his sack's mouth. And put my cup, this silver cup. . ." He held up the beautiful silver cup in his hand, the one that Pharaoh had given him for his birthday. "Put this cup in the sack of the youngest, along with his grain money."

Senbi bowed solemnly, and taking the cup from Joseph's hand, said, "It shall be as you command, Master"

Asenath stared at the two of them. She understood the need to test these men, but this was too much! Horrified, she said, "Joseph! What a terrible thing to do!"

Joseph held up a reassuring hand. Then he said quietly, "Fear not, my wife. No harm will come to Benjamin or my brothers as a result of this, even if they fail. I feel in my heart that they will pass this test, but it must be administered or I have no definitive proof that they have changed."

Joseph's and his brothers celebrated late into the night and then sought their beds. Very early the next morning, Joseph, who could nap an hour or two and then work a full day, had the brothers awakened and their animals loaded with the grain for their families in Canaan.

While Joseph was capable of arising early after such a night of partying, the majority of his brothers could not. This was very evident by the way they walked as they very slowly made their way out of the estate and into the city.

Asher, who was holding his head, groaned as they walked. "Oh! Why must we leave so early? I am still feeling the effects of all that wine last night!"

"If you had not tried to drink the Great One's wine cellar dry last night, you would be feeling better this morning!" chided Dan.

Ruben, who was normally robust and loud, said quietly, "Not so loud, Dan! I did not drink as much as Asher, but I too could do with much less noise!

Judah started laughing and pounding Ruben on the back. He said in mock sympathy, "You never could withstand much wine, Ruben."

Asher made a disgusted noise and said wearily, "Ugh! That is fine for you, Judah! You always could drink a river of wine and feel nothing the next morning!"

Ruben, who was now holding his aching head, agreed. "You speak truly, Asher! He has the stomach of a goat!"

Dan, who was also clear headed and leading their small caravan, turned chuckling. "Goat or no, we must be back to our father!" He then changed his tone to one of false sympathy and said, "I will set a slow pace for you, Ruben."

Ruben made a sour face, and with a dismissive gesture of his hand, said scathingly, "Ha, ha. Just go!"

Unseen by the brothers, Knut the chief serving woman and Joseph were watching them depart from the roof of the main house. Knut stood hiding her face with her hand for several moments as she watched the brothers slowly, and with exaggeratedly careful steps, leave the estate. Finally, she giggled quietly, turned to Joseph, and said, "Master, your brethren seem to be moving rather slowly this morning."

Joseph made no attempt to conceal his grin. He chuckled and said, "Yes, some of them *are* moving a bit slowly, aren't they!"

"I never saw the likes of the big one with the red beard! He drank enough for five men and barely showed it. Now, this morning, he's the one slapping the others on the back!" Knut added in amazement.

Joseph actually laughed at this comment. "Judah always could do that!" he said, shaking his own head in amazement. He then turned to Khu and Senbi who had just joined them. "Khu, Senbi, please come here."

Both men stepped forward crisply, and in unison said, "Yes, my Lord!"

Smiling, but somehow serious at the same time, Joseph ordered, "Both of you, up, follow my brethren. When you overtake them, Senbi, say unto them, 'Why have you rewarded evil for good? My Master's silver cup is stolen, the cup from which my Lord drinks, and where indeed he divines? You have done evil!'"

Senbi immediately responded, "It shall be as you command, my Lord!" Then he and Khu left the estate in pursuit of Joseph's brethren.

Khu was silent for some time after leaving Joseph's presence. As he and Senbi rode in the chariot alongside the rapidly moving troops, he simply stared ahead and said nothing. Senbi could tell that he was mulling something over in his mind. Finally, after some time had passed, Khu spoke aloud what was bothering him. "Why is it that we chase after the Master's brethren? Would they be so foolish as to steal from him?"

"No, they would not! However, the Master must continue to test them. He and I talked during the banquet. He wants to see if they will defend their little brother," Senbi explained.

Khu's brow wrinkled in his confusion. "How is this a test if they would not steal?"

"I placed the Master's silver cup in the mouth of the sack of the youngest. It will make it appear that he is a thief."

Khu's face cleared instantly. "Ah! I see! Will they support their brother or leave him to his fate? This is a fine test of brotherly loyalty!"

Senbi's face showed his serious intent about this mission. "We shall soon know. We are upon them," he said, pointing ahead. Then, turning to Khu, he asked, "Khu, you know what to do?"

"Indeed I do!" Khu asserted. He then jumped from the chariot and ran ahead. He ran until he had passed the small column made by Joseph's brothers. He spun to a stop in front of them with his sword drawn and shouted, "Halt! You there, men of Canaan, stop or we will use our spears!" The entire troop that had followed Khu, split into two columns, and was now flanking the small caravan with their spears leveled. The brothers were surrounded, completely surprised, outnumbered, and out armed. They were also confused. Confused shouts and exclamations were heard.

"What is going on?"

"You there, don't move!"

"What did we do?"

"Keep your hands where we can see them!"

Ruben was the first of the group to spot Senbi in the chariot. "What is this? Why do you pursue us?"

"Why have you rewarded evil for good?" Senbi challenged without a preamble. Ruben was confused. "I do not understand, my Lord!"

Senbi did not soften. He could see the confusion and fear in the men's faces. Yet the test had to continue. "My Master's silver cup is stolen! The cup from which my Lord drinks, the same cup he uses to prophesy.' He paused for a moment and then growled, "You have done evil!"

Ruben was astounded. He glanced at his brothers; who from

the oldest to the youngest, showed his confusion and declared his innocence. He had heard of such traps from travelers who had been accosted by the border guards, and he was now thoroughly frightened. "Why do you say these things, my Lord? God forbid that your servants should do as you have accused us!"

Judah tried reasoning. "Behold, the money, which we found in our sacks' mouths, we brought again out of the land of Canaan. Why then should we steal silver or gold out of your Lord's house?"

It was all Senbi could do to maintain the facade he had been assigned. "We shall see!"

Simeon was indignant and confidently shouted the traditional desert oath. "With the one among us it be found, let him die, and we also will be my Lord's bondmen!"

To an outsider, this would seem a rash statement, but Senbi noted that every brother nodded his agreement to Simeon's oath. Senbi knew they were serious. "Now, let it be according to your words." He added, "He with whom it is found shall be my servant and the rest of you shall be blameless."

Ruben, in full confidence of their innocence, shouted to his brothers. "Quickly! Every man let down his sacks! Open them so that this man may search!"

Young Benjamin had lowered his sacks of grain and had already opened them. He was standing respectfully beside them when he noticed something odd, and he thought, *"He is searching in the order of our birth! And he only searches superficially! What is going on?"*

Finally, Senbi arrived at Benjamin's pack animal. Although the young man's sacks were already open, he commanded harshly, "You, Benjamin! Open your sack!"

Benjamin did not question this unnecessary order. He also did not notice that the man had called him by name. Had he been less frightened, he would have noticed that his was the only name the man seemed to know. Swiftly, the terrified young man bent down and held open the mouth of one of the already opened sacks. As he did so, he said politely, "At once, my Lord!"

Senbi searched the sack and found nothing. Then he did something that he had not done before. He stood and pointed to another of the young man's sacks and commanded, "Now that one!" Benjamin rushed to the indicated sack and held it open. Senbi reached inside and rummaged about for a second or two, then with a great flourish, he stood and held Joseph's silver cup aloft, shouting dramatically, "What is this, thief!"

Benjamin's blood froze. He was dumbfounded and shouted, "What! A silver cup? I did not put that there!"

Simeon was incredulous. "What have you done?"

Benjamin turned and stared wildly at Simeon for a moment, then cried, "I have done nothing! I did not put that there!"

Senbi was in full dramatic mode. Pointing at Benjamin, he shouted to Khu, "Seize this one and bind him! He is our prisoner!" Swiftly, several of Khu's men rushed forward. Before the confused and frightened Benjamin could react, he had been tied up and was being led roughly back the way they had come with the entire troop surrounding him.

The Egyptians' actions had been so swift that the brothers were taken by surprise. They stood transfixed for a few seconds saying nothing and not moving. Ruben stood in shock. "We are undone!" he groaned.

Judah too was in an awful state. With tears in his eyes, he shouted, "Our lives are forfeit! Rend your clothes and get up quickly — follow them!" Each man rent his clothes, repacked his animal, and quickly followed the guards who were taking Benjamin back to Joseph.

Joseph was still at home, which was unusual, and Asenath noted this anomaly. Unexpectedly seeing Joseph standing quietly on the roof of their home, she approached him and asked, "My husband, why tarry you at home today? You are normally gone before the sun is fully up. It is midmorning! Are you ill?"

Joseph, who looked unusually thoughtful, turned to her and answered quietly, "No, I am not ill, my wife. I am expecting guests."

This was a surprise to Asenath. It was she who normally prepared for guests, and she knew of none coming today. "Guests? Who are you expecting?"

"My brethren," Joseph said simply.

"Your brethren?" Asenath asked, confused. She had seen them depart only this morning. She thought for a few moments, and then, remembering, she exclaimed, "Oh! That business with your cup! I had forgotten!"

Joseph only nodded. Then quietly he said, "They should be here shortly." He continued to stare out at the road. After only a few moments, he said, "That should be them!" He pointed to a dust cloud just visible on the road. "Let us go into the courtyard and make ready to receive them."

It was some little time before the troop arrived. Asenath had not gone with Joseph to challenge the brothers, but instead, she had stayed on the roof to observe. What she saw when they entered the courtyard was a sorry sight. The scared and dejected Benjamin was bound and guarded in the midst of part of the troop that led the way into the estate. Behind them came the brothers, and bringing up the rear came the rest of the troops and Captain Khu. All of the troops had their weapons at the ready, and the brothers looked terrible. They walked with their heads lowered, their clothes torn in the front, their faces tear stained, and each wore a terrified expression.

Senbi, entering the estate first in the chariot, dismounted and approached Joseph, who was standing on the front steps of the main house to receive them. Senbi bowed low and handed Joseph his silver cup. He said loudly, "Your servant has returned with the culprit. The cup was indeed in the sack of the youngest, as you said it would be."

With an imperious gesture, Joseph signaled Senbi to rise. Then, in Egyptian, he said, "What deed is this that you have done? Know you not that such a man as I can certainly divine?" With a submissive bow, Senbi turned to the brothers and translated Joseph's words into Hebrew.

Judah listened intently to the Steward's words. Then shaking his head in wonder and shame he said, "What shall we say unto my Lord? What shall we speak? How shall we clear ourselves? God has found out the iniquity of your servants. Behold, we are my Lord's servants, including he who was found with the cup."

Joseph reacted in mock horror when this was translated to him, "God forbid that I should do such a thing!" he shouted. "Only the man in whose hand the cup is found shall be my servant, and as for you, go in peace to your father." Once again this was said in Egyptian and the faithful Senbi translated it into Hebrew.

Judah stepped closer and pleaded, "Oh my Lord, let your servant, I pray you, speak a word in my Lord's ears. Let not your anger burn against your servant. My Lord asked his servants 'Have you a father or a brother?' And we said to my Lord, 'We have a father, who is an old man, and a younger brother whose only brother is dead, so he alone is left of his mother and his father loves him."

Before Senbi could translate this, Ruben continued desperately, "And you said to your servants, 'Bring him to me that I may set my eyes upon him.' And we said to my Lord, 'The lad cannot leave his father. If he should leave his father, his father would die."

Ruben paused for a moment and then continued, "And you said to your servants, 'Unless your youngest brother comes to Egypt with you, you shall see my face no more.' When we came to your servant, my father, we told him the words of my Lord."

When Ruben paused again, Dan continued, "And our father said, 'Go again, and buy us a little food.' And we said, 'We cannot go down without Benjamin. If our youngest brother is with us, then we will go to Egypt because without him we cannot see the man's face."

Ruben, nodding vigorously to agree with Dan, added, "And your servant, my father, said to us, 'You know that my wife bore me two sons. The one left me, surely torn in pieces for I saw him not since. If you take Benjamin from me, and mischief befalls him, my sorrow would ride me into the grave."

Judah moved even closer and bowed to the earth before Joseph. "If I come to your servant, my father, and the lad is not with us, the old one will die. I, your servant, offered myself as surety for the lad. Therefore, I pray you; let me be bondman to my Lord. Let the lad go with his brethren. For how shall I return to my father if the lad is not with me? I cannot! I cannot stand to see the evil that shall come on my father."

Looking at his brothers, Joseph saw that they were all nodding in agreement with Judah, all apparently desperate to see to it that Benjamin was returned to their father, regardless of the cost. It was apparent that any of them would have made the same plea. Joseph could bear no more. With tears streaming down his face, he shouted in agony, "Senbi! All but these men are to leave my presence!"

Senbi understood — the test was over. It was time for the Master to reveal himself, and he needed to be alone with his brothers. "At once, Master! Everyone of the household, away from this place!" Seeing the look of determined defense on the faces of the soldiers, he added, "That includes the guards! Establish your posts elsewhere in the courtyard!" Turning to Joseph, he asked, "Am I included in your order, Master?"

Not unexpectedly, Joseph replied in Egyptian, "You, as well. I must be alone with my brethren!"

Simeon had watched all of this in silence. He, of all the brothers, spoke some Egyptian. Not much, but he understood sufficiently to know they were to be left alone with the Great One. Glancing to his left, he saw the seven brawlers from the troop barracks and knew plainly what was on these men's minds! He could see it in their eyes. They were ready to rebel because they were torn between obeying the order to retreat and their sworn duty to defend their beloved Master. Then, one of them, the unofficial leader of their group, caught Simeon's eye. These two knew each other. They had become friends during his stay at the estate. The unspoken plea in the man's eyes was plain. He wanted a promise from Simeon that no harm would come to Joseph. Simeon understood, and he nodded his answer in the affirmative. Then, and only then, did the seven leave their Master. In honor to his oath, though unspoken, Simeon moved unobtrusively to the front of the group, where, if necessary, he could defend the Great One. He had barely gotten into position, when, unexpectedly, the great man let out a great cry of agony and began weeping loudly.

Ruben's blood froze in his veins. Terrified, he thought to himself, *What is this?*

Levi groaned aloud, "We are all dead men!"

Dan, always the tactician, shouted, "This man's cry will surely bring more troops and they will slay us!"

Even those in the house of Pharaoh heard Joseph's cry, as it was quite loud. Everyone in the gardens stopped what they were doing and stared in the direction of Joseph's house.

The Chamberlain stood and stared, alarmed, just like the rest and nervously asked, "What was that?"

Potiphar, who stood nearby, knew both the voice and some of its meaning. He shouted, "It is a cry of pain!" Then pointing in the right direction, he added, "It comes from Joseph's house! " He turned to a contingent of the Pharaoh's own guards, and running as he did so, he shouted. "You men follow me!"

With their weapons drawn, they swiftly followed Potiphar. In moments they were skidding to a stop before the closed gates of Joseph's estate. Potiphar was livid and shouted, "In the name of Pharaoh! Open the gates!" As the gates opened, he and his troop rushed into the estate only to see the guards standing idle and staring in the direction of the group standing before the house.

Infuriated at their inaction, he growled, "Why are you just standing here! Your Master is in trouble!" Turning to his own men, he started to shout, "Men! Follow. . ."

Before he could finish the command, Senbi ran forward frantically waving his arms. In a panicked voice, he cried, "Not so! Hold! Not so! All is well!"

Potiphar was stunned. Pointing emphatically in the direction of the group at the front of the house, he cried, "Are you mad? Heard you not your Master's cry of pain?"

Senbi, holding up his hands in a pleading gesture, cried, "I heard! I heard!" Then taking a calming breath, he continued. "It is not the kind of pain you think! My Master's brethren have come! He was testing them. They passed the test and it caused my Master great pain that he has treated his brethren thus!"

Potiphar was stunned. "His brethren? The men who sold him into slavery?"

Senbi nodded. "The very same. He had to test them to see if they were now true men. The test was severe, but they passed." Still seeing the determination in Potiphar's face to defend his beloved friend, Senbi repeated frantically, "They passed!"

Potiphar felt like a fool. He had responded correctly to such a cry from a friend, but it had been his own recommendation that these men be tested. Now they had been, and they had passed the tests! He knew such actions would be hard for Joseph, and now he could see just how hard it had been. With a great sigh he put his sword away, turned to his men, and signaled them to stand down. Staring out at the scene he could just barely see, he said quietly, "Knowing Joseph, he is in tears right now. I wish I could be with him! He is like a brother to me!"

Senbi looked in the same direction. "That is how we all feel, Great One. We all wish we could be with him, but it is a time he *must* be alone with them!"

Potiphar looked at the man and saw the truth of his words written plainly upon his face. Then, chuckling in self-deprecation and placing a comforting hand on Senbi's shoulder, he said quietly, "You are so much like your Master!" Taking a deep breath, he added, "I shall tell Pharaoh. He will want to meet these men." His eyes took on a faraway look and he said thoughtfully, "Were it not for these men, Joseph would not have come to Egypt. The famine would have come and all would have been lost." Then his face took on a look of astonishment and realization. Looking Senbi in the eye, he said very quietly, "This has all been the work of Joseph's God!" Potiphar gazed across the courtyard at the group of men standing on the steps of Joseph's house for a few moments. Then he silently turned and signaled his men to follow him and led them quietly back to the house of Pharaoh.

The coming of Potiphar and his troops, all determined and well-armed men, did not go unnoticed by Joseph's brothers. The brothers were in a state of panic that was impossible to describe, but the shocks of this day were not over. As they stood in confusion and fear, the ruler of the country surprised them once more. He removed his headdress, and with tears in his eyes, he addressed them in their native Hebrew. If this were not shock enough, his words compounded it. "I *am* Joseph. Does my father indeed yet live?"

Simeon stared at the man and thought numbly,"*Joseph? How does this man know our brother's name?"*

Levi stood shaking his head, unable to accept what he had just heard. The thought that ran through his head was, "*Joseph? That is not possible! Joseph is dead!"*

Ruben, who for years had felt the guilt of not saving Joseph, was feeling very mixed emotions. His thoughts ran like a roller coaster: *"Is the man mad? Can he be? Is not Joseph dead?"*

Joseph stood with his arms outstretched toward them. "Come near to me, I pray you." Not knowing what else to do, or perhaps just because they were too numb to do anything else, they came near. Then Joseph very softly said, "I *am* Joseph, your brother, whom you sold into Egypt."

They were stunned. The sale of their brother as a slave was a dark secret known only to the ten who had been at the dry well in Canaan that fateful day. To everyone else, Joseph had been killed by a wild beast. This was the final straw. Frightened, guilty, and confused, the ten of his brethren who were guilty fell down before Joseph with their faces to the ground. Benjamin mimicked his brothers, but it was plain he was confused.

Joseph understood. He stood silent for a moment with fresh sobs and many tears. Then, after a time, he said quietly and kindly, "Be not angry with yourselves, those of you who sold me here. God sent me before you to preserve life. For two years the famine has been in the land, and for five years more there shall be no harvest. God sent me before you to preserve your posterity in the earth, and to save your lives by a great deliverance."

Simeon raised his head, his face just as tear stained as his younger brother's. There was something else in his features too, pain. The pain of unresolved guilt. In agony he said, "But we beat you and sold you into slavery!" He could say no more. He dissolved into body-wracking sobs.

Joseph knelt and placed a comforting hand on Simeon's shoulder. He said quietly and with great kindness, "It was not you who sent me here, but God. He has made me a father to Pharaoh and Lord of all his house, ruler throughout all the land of Egypt."

Ruben, seeing his lost brother before him, had only one thought, and he said it out loud, "What of Father?"

Joseph smiled. He too had been thinking of his father. "Go to our father with great haste and say to him, 'Thus says your son Joseph: God has made me Lord of all Egypt. Come to me quickly and tarry not. You shall dwell in the land of Goshen to be near me, you, and your children, and your children's children, and your flocks, and your herds, and all that you have. There will I nourish you for there are yet five years of famine. Come to me, lest you and your households come to poverty."

Simeon could see problems and worriedly asked, "How shall we convince, Jacob, our father, that these words come from you, Joseph, he whom he believes lost? I can barely believe it and you stand before me!"

Joseph tightened his grip on Simeon's shoulder, and looking him in the eye, said, "Behold what is before you and tell my father of all the glory God has given me in Egypt, and of all that you have seen."

As soon as he had said this, his brethren rejoiced. Then he fell upon his brother Benjamin's neck and wept, and Benjamin wept upon his neck. Then he kissed all his other brothers and wept upon them. Unseen by the brothers, all the House of Joseph rejoiced and wept with them.

Chapter Eighteen
THE STORY ENDS

Potiphar and his troops quietly reentered the royal estate. The troops marched in unison, standing tall with their faces proud, but Potiphar seemed withdrawn, stooped, and subdued, all the more so in comparison to the soldiers. The Chamberlain and the high priest Potipherah, who had waited for his return, noticed this and were worried at his downcast demeanor. The Chamberlain approached the seemingly dispirited Potiphar and asked, "What happened at the house of Joseph, Potiphar?"

Potipherah, whose interest was familial, asked anxiously. "Is my son-in-law well?"

Potiphar seemed to come out of his reverie and responded in an amazed voice, "Joseph's brethren have come!"

Immediately concerned, the Chamberlain asked, "The same men who sold him into slavery?"

"They are, but Joseph tested them quite severely, and they passed the tests! They are true men and no longer his enemies!"

The Chamberlain's brow wrinkled. "Then why that cry of pain we heard?"

"That was indeed Joseph," Potiphar replied. At the worried looks on the faces of the other two, Potiphar held up a forestalling hand and said quickly, "They had not harmed him! He was in agony over the pain *he* had caused his brethren with the tests!"

Potipherah shook his head in wonder. "How like Joseph! He is such a kind man. Such testing would have caused him as much pain as those being tested!"

The Chamberlain added, "That is true. I remember the agony he went through with the Nomarchs! He wept as he reported to Pharaoh."

There was silence following this statement. During that silence, Potipherah turned and stared thoughtfully out of the gate that Potiphar had just come through. After a few moments, he said quietly, "He has often spoken of his father." He turned and looked questioningly at the Captain. "Do you know if his father still lives, Potiphar?"

Potiphar showed his delight and smiled broadly. "He does! Senbi said that was the first question Joseph asked of his brothers."

The Chamberlain was delighted. "This is wondrous news! We must inform the Pharaoh!" Waving the others to follow him, he led the way into the royal palace to share the news with their king.

The interview with Pharaoh was short but quite joyous. Pharaoh was very pleased at the news and immediately summoned Joseph to come before him.

In a very short time, this message was delivered to Joseph, who washed himself and rushed to the royal residence. He was greeted by the Chamberlain, who conveyed his congratulations to Joseph and then hurried to announce him to Pharaoh. Upon entering the royal chamber, he bowed low and announced, "My Lord Pharaoh, Joseph is here as you commanded."

Amenemhet smiled at this announcement. "Excellent! Send him to me!"

Smiling, the Chamberlain bowed once more and said, "Immediately, Great One!" Turning and walking the few steps to the antechamber, he bowed. "Joseph, he will see you now."

Joseph said, bowing in his own turn, "I thank you, Lord Chamberlain." He then walked into the presence of the Pharaoh, and after genuflecting said, "Great One, you called for me?"

Amenemhet signaled that Joseph should stand. "Indeed I did, Joseph! I have heard that your brethren have come. Is this true?"

"It is, Great One!" Joseph said. He bowed his head in an attempt to conceal his delighted smile.

"I have also heard that your father still lives. Is this also true?"

"It is true, Great One. I was worried that he had suffered during this famine, but he has not."

Amenemhet's face showed surprise as he asked, "Isn't the famine as sore in Canaan as it is here?"

Joseph's face also changed for indeed the famine was getting worse. "The conditions there are far worse, but he sent my brothers to buy food earlier and thus avoided much hardship." He paused for a moment before he continued. "At least here, the river flows yet and small sheltered vegetable gardens are still possible. We also have the grain that was set aside for this very emergency. There is bread in all of Egypt. The same cannot be said of Canaan or the other lands surrounding Egypt, Great One."

"Everything you say is most definitely true, Joseph! The conditions elsewhere must be terrible indeed." He paused. "You are undoubtedly preparing to send food once more to your family in Canaan, but the way is long, and due to the famine, filled with danger." The Pharaoh paused in thought for a moment more and then continued. "Say unto your brethren that they are to bring your father and all their households and come unto you. You will give them the good of the land of Egypt, and they shall eat the fat of the land."

Joseph was greatly surprised. This was the very thing he was going to request of Pharaoh later (as he had already told his brethren he would settle them in Goshen) and Pharaoh was ordering him to do it without being asked! He was delighted and responded quickly. "I shall do so, my Pharaoh!" Joseph turned and made as though he was going to leave to carry out Pharaoh's command, but Amenemhet wasn't finished and held up a hand to prevent Joseph from leaving. He then assumed his official voice of command and said, "Now *you* are commanded, Joseph. Take wagons out of the land of Egypt for your brothers' little ones and for their wives and to bring your father. Regard not their possessions, for the good of all the land of Egypt is theirs." When Joseph left the presence of Pharaoh, he felt more pleased than he had in many years.

Several hours later, the brothers stood staring in amazement at the hustle and bustle that had erupted in the courtyard of Joseph's estate. Ruben, staring at the intense activity, made a sweeping gesture with his hand. Looking at Judah, he asked, "What *is* all this?"

Judah could only stammer, "I don't know, Ruben. There are wagons, troops, oxen, asses, and supplies everywhere!"

Ruben began looking around more intently. He pointed. "There is Senbi, Joseph's head man — let's ask him." They walked quickly over to the Head of House and Ruben said, "Greetings Senbi."

Bowing respectfully to them, Senbi said, "Greetings to you, my Master's brethren. What may I do for you this afternoon?"

Ruben made a questioning gesture at all the activity. "What is the meaning of all this commotion? There are wagons, troops, asses, and supplies everywhere!"

Senbi smiled. "They are for you and the house of your father."

Judah was stunned. "For us and our father?"

Before Judah could question him more, Senbi held up his hand, and pointing behind Judah, he said, "The Master and the Mistress come. They will explain all."

Judah looked in the direction that Senbi had indicated, and there, indeed, were Joseph and Asenath walking toward them. Joseph was all smiles, and as he walked, he spoke to this or that person involved in the preparations. Finally, he and his wife arrived where Judah and Ruben were standing with Senbi.

Raising a hand in greeting, Joseph saluted them. "Brethren!"

Ruben responded, "Joseph! Mistress Asenath! Greetings to you both!"

"Greetings to you as well, my brother-in-law," Asenath said graciously, holding out her hands to Ruben in the greeting reserved among the Egyptians for family. Taking her hands, Ruben simply bowed and smiled.

Judah was still stunned by all of this. "I still cannot take it in! Our little brother, the ruler of all Egypt! He, who lives in a beautiful mansion, has servants, soldiers at his command, and an absolutely stunning wife is our brother?" He then too took Asenath's hands in the familial greeting.

Asenath giggled as she returned the gesture. "Flatterer!" Her tone caused the entire group to break into laughter.

Still chuckling, Ruben made a sweeping gesture to indicate everything in the courtyard and asked, "What *is* all of this, Joseph?"

Judah nodded. "Yes! Senbi said that all of this is for us and the house of our father?"

Joseph held up his hands, and with a smile he said, "He has spoken truly, and that is not all." He turned to the ever faithful Senbi. "Senbi! Have you the gifts for my brethren?"

Senbi bowed at his Master's request and signaled to another servant standing near the storehouse. This servant and two others ran to Senbi, each carrying numerous large wrapped bundles. Turning to Joseph and bowing, he said simply, "Here they are, my Master, all eleven bundles."

"What are these, Joseph?" Ruben asked.

Joseph smiled. "A change of Egyptian clothing for each of you."

Judah was surprised. "That is most generous!" Then he pointed curiously at the largest bundle that was in the arms of one of the servants. "Whose is that last bundle? It is easily five times as large as the others?"

"Ah! That is Benjamin's." Seeing the look on his brother's faces, Joseph added conspiratorially, "His contains several years of back birthday presents!"

Judah chuckled. Then shaking his head, he said in a good humor, "Like Father like son!" He then clapped a friendly hand on Joseph's shoulder.

Ruben missed all of this. He had been staring intently at the pack animals. "What are in all the bundles we see on the backs of all these asses?" he asked, pointing to the heavily laden beasts.

"There are ten asses laden with the good things of Egypt, and ten she asses laden with grain and bread and meat for our father by the way," Joseph said happily.

"By the way?" Ruben asked, confused.

"I act not alone in this. This has been done by Pharaoh's command. He said that you are to take these wagons out of the land of Egypt for your little ones and for your wives and to bring our father. He also said that you are to regard not your possessions, for the good of all the land of Egypt is yours."

Judah was surprised. "We are to come to Egypt to live?"

Joseph's face lost its joviality and he became very serious. "Yes. There are five more years of famine. You and the house of our father would not survive in the land of Canaan, and even if you did, there would be great loss of life and you would be in extreme poverty. This I cannot allow!"

Ruben pointed to all the armed men standing about. "But what of all of these soldiers?"

"A contingent of Pharaoh's own household guard. They protect Pharaoh and myself. They will go with you to prevent thieves from attacking you, and indeed, if such should be so foolish, to repel such an attack."

Judah snorted in derision. "Huh! With these along, none would be so witless!"

Joseph was silent for some time. He stood regarding the troops and then his brothers. Then he said very quietly, "I have one last admonishment, my brethren: you must not fall out among yourselves along the way but return speedily and harmoniously to our father."

Ruben placed both his hands on his brother's shoulders, and

looking Joseph straight in the eye, said with great feeling, "To this we agree without reservation, Joseph!"

Jacob's camp lay on one side of a fairly deep valley. It had been moved to the east side of the dell recently to shield it from the constant hot east wind. Because the well was in the center of the valley, the condition of the settlement was greatly improved and even this slight shielding meant that more people were out and about during the daytime as the wind was not as bad. Thus it came to pass that one of the children, who was supposed to be sitting outside his mother's tent smashing some pottery shards into powder for pottery glaze, was instead watching the hill behind their old camp site. Suddenly, he stiffened as he had seen something. Then he ran swiftly to tell his grandfather, Jacob, what he thought he had seen. He skidded to a halt before the door of his grandfather's tent and shouted, "Grandfather! Grandfather! Look there, on the hill! I think I see my father coming!"

Jacob, who had been awake, came to the doorway, and looking down at the child, asked, "What did you say?"

The child pointed to the opposite hill and repeated, "I think I see my father coming!"

Smiling at the child's excitement, Jacob looked down at the pointing child. Then in mock seriousness and trying to look stern but failing miserably, he said, "Let me look." Jacob then used his hand to shield his eyes from the sun and looked in the indicated direction to study the approaching group. "Well! I do believe that it *is* your father and his brethren! Let's see." He then began counting the distant figures aloud, "One, two, three, four, five, six, seven, eight, nine, ten . . . eleven! They have *all* returned." Then, dancing in his glee and spinning the delighted child round and round, he shouted, "They are *all* returned!"

The commotion had drawn a large number of the camp to see what had excited Father Jacob so. Among these was Mother Leah, who stood watching her cavorting husband for a few moments and then asked, "What is all this excitement, my husband?"

Jacob stopped twirling the child around, and before she could resist, he grabbed the very startled Leah and danced about with her. As he picked her up and twirled her around, he shouted gleefully, "My sons have all returned unharmed from Egypt!"

This pronouncement caused much murmuring of disbelief in the crowd, but the child pointed at the approaching men and said,

"It's true! Look! There's my father!" The child then ran to the still somewhat distant Ruben and was immediately scooped up into the air by his delighted father.

Jacob finally put the breathless, highly embarrassed, but delighted Leah down as the small caravan approached. Then with arms spread wide he shouted, "Ruben, Judah, come to me!"

Ruben wasted no time, and putting down his son, he ran to his father and was hugged fiercely. When he was released from the near bear hug, he said, "My father! We have wonderful news! Joseph lives!" Stunned silence greeted this announcement. Not even the desert insects were bold enough to make a sound for several moments.

Jacob backed away from his eldest son, and the look on his face spoke volumes. In a quiet strangled voice, he said, "You have been in the desert too long!"

Judah, seeing the horror on his father's face pleaded, "No, Father. He speaks the truth! Simeon, you tell him!"

"It is true, Father! He lives, and he is the governor of all Egypt!" Simeon asserted. Pointing to his own garments, he added, "See? He even provided us with Egyptian clothing!"

Jacob stared at them. He held up his hands in a helpless gesture and wailed, "Have my sons all gone mad? Joseph is dead! I have a remnant of his bloodstained coat in my tent! You Simeon and you Levi brought it to me!"

Levi looked acutely uncomfortable at this statement. Then, obviously having to work up the courage to speak, said slowly, "The coat was indeed bloodstained, but Joseph lives! He lives in Egypt." He paused, looking around at the silent crowd that had gathered. "His house is beautiful," he added in a pleading tone.

Asher nodded emphatically and added, "We were there, Father! He eats like the Pharaoh himself!"

This comment seemed to bring Jacob out of the stunned shock he was in. "Do you ever think of anything but your stomach?" he said acerbically.

Benjamin rushed forward, placed his hands on his father's shoulders, and looked him straight in the eye. "It is true, Father! I talked with Joseph myself. He's alive!"

Jacob tore his favorite son's hands from his shoulders and backed away in horror. "Not you as well, Benjamin!" In desperation, he shouted, "All my sons have lost their minds!"

Ruben had turned away for a moment to peer into the distance, but no sooner had Jacob freed himself from Benjamin than Ruben turned back to his father and with an odd smile on his face said very quietly, "Father, if we have lost our minds, then what is that mirage coming over yonder hill?"

Jacob was getting angry now. His son's were all mad! Exasperated, he turned on Ruben and snapped, "What are you blathering about, Ruben?"

Ruben remained calm and said quietly, "Look at the top of that hill and tell us what you see, Father."

Jacob stared in silence at Ruben for a moment, and then said, "Very well, Ruben, I'll humor you." He turned and looked at the top of the hill opposite the camp, at the troops, wagons and supplies Joseph had sent a huge company. Astounded, Jacob blurted, "What are all these wagons and soldiers?" Then, placing the worst possible meaning on the huge armed company, he shouted angrily, "What have you done?"

"We did nothing. Those are from Joseph and the Pharaoh. The Pharaoh commanded Joseph to send wagons for our wives and children and to carry our father. He said we were not to give heed to our possessions for we would have the good of all of Egypt from which to live. Those are the wagons Joseph sent!" Judah explained.

Jacob watched in stunned silence as Simeon ran to meet this mob. At the head of the large armed column stood a stately Egyptian soldier, who was obviously an officer. As Simeon approached, him, the officer bowed as though he were greeting a superior. Then, he and Simeon stood talking quite calmly. An astounded Jacob murmured, "Can this be true?"

"It *is* true Father, and you shall soon see your son once more," Benjamin asserted.

With tears now flowing freely down his face, Jacob said, "It is enough! Joseph, my son, is yet alive! I will see him before I die."

It took several days to adjust to the presence of the Egyptians for they were a fearsome lot, but they seemed friendly and were very protective of the camp. Soon the camp was packed and Jacob took his journey with all that he had and came to Beer-sheba, where he offered sacrifices unto the God of his father, Isaac. Still, Jacob was unsure if he should stay in Egypt.

Mother Leah found him sitting outside his tent one evening in Beer-sheba. Sensing something amiss, she said, "You seem disturbed, my husband."

"I fear to go down into Egypt, my wife. It was in Egypt that Father Abraham nearly lost Sarah, his wife, to Pharaoh. The border guards there are likely to steal from us."

Placing a gentle and reassuring hand on her husband's arm, Leah cut him off by saying gently, "My husband, we have Pharaoh's own troops with us! The border guards would not dare molest us. Joseph is the ruler of all Egypt! They would not dare harm his family!"

Jacob nodded. "I have already sacrificed a lamb and yet I still feel uneasy. I must ponder these things!"

Leah remained seated as her husband rose to go. "I will await your return, my husband," she said quietly

Jacob walked until he was out of earshot of the camp. Then he muttered to himself, "Egypt! The very name fills me with dread! God gave us *this* land! We are not supposed to be in Egypt!"

The words had scarcely left Jacob's mouth when he heard a voice calling his name. It was not a loud voice, but still and small, and yet the sound of it filled him utterly. He felt it in his very bones.

"Jacob. Jacob," the voice called gently.

Jacob knew that voice. It was God. "Here am I," he said humbly.

"I am God, the God of your fathers. Fear not to go down into Egypt, for there I will make of your posterity a great nation. I will go down with you into Egypt and surely bring you up again. Joseph shall put his hand upon your eyes."

Jacob bowed his head and said humbly, "Be it as you command, Lord." Gone were the fear and indecision, and he knew that all would be well because his God was with him.

Jacob then retraced his steps, returning to Leah, who was greatly surprised when Jacob told her what the Lord had said — that they were not only to travel to the land of Egypt but that they were to become a great nation there. Jacob left Beer-sheba with his sons, their little ones and their wives in the wagons, and they took their cattle and their goods from the land of Canaan and came into Egypt. Jacob came with all his seed with him, with his sons, his sons' sons, his daughters, and his sons' daughters into Egypt — seventy in all. Now when Jacob was nigh unto Egypt, he sent Judah to Joseph to direct his face unto Goshen.

All of these things took time. During that time, despite the excitement at the back of his mind concerning the coming of his family, Joseph had a country to run. Thus it came to pass; that sometime later Joseph was sitting in the great room of his home in the middle of the day and the heat outside was uncomfortable. Joseph had retired to the cool of the house with his scribe to study the many reports that he had received earlier that morning. He was quite involved in this when Senbi rushed into the room, and bowing, called out breathlessly, "Master! Your brother Judah has come!"

Joseph was genuinely surprised at the interruption. It took a second or two to register what Senbi had said. "Judah is here?" he asked, slightly confused.

Bowing and smiling at the same time, Senbi said, "He is, my Master. Shall I bring him in to you?"

"Yes, of course!" exclaimed Joseph, delighted. He turned to the scribe at his side. "I think that will be all for now. Why don't you take the rest of the afternoon off with your family. Maybe take that son of yours fishing on the Nile."

The scribe bowed low, and smiling, he said. "I thank you, Master. I shall indeed take him fishing, which he has been begging me to do for some time." The scribe then collected his things, bowed deeply to Joseph, and happily made his way out of the room.

No sooner had the scribe departed than Senbi returned with the tall Judah. "Here is your brother, Master!" Senbi said.

Joseph rushed to his brother and embraced him. "Judah! It is good to see you again! Have you brought our father with you?" he asked

"I have, Joseph! Father sent me on ahead, so that I may direct you to him in the Land of Goshen."

"They are setting up camp there?" Joseph asked.

"They are, and everyone is anxious to see you again!" Judah beamed.

"Then let us not keep them waiting!" Joseph exclaimed. Turning, he called out, "Senbi!"

"Yes Master!"

"Have my chariot prepared. I travel to Goshen to meet my father!"

Senbi was smiling as though his own family had come. "I shall do so at once! I shall also inform Captain Khu so that he and a troop can accompany you!"

Joseph nodded. "Excellent!" Then he shouted, "Asenath!

Asenath!"

Joseph did not normally shout, and thus his cry brought an immediate response from Asenath and several of the serving girls. As they rushed into the room, Asenath asked in alarm, "What is it, my husband?"

"My father has come! He and my brethren are encamped in Goshen! I go to them. Prepare yourself, for I would have you and our sons accompany me."

Asenath's visage changed from alarm to delight in an instant. "I shall do so immediately! Your brethren and your father have come! What a wonderful day!"

Jacob's camp had settled into a semblance of its normal routine. People were lighting fires, fetching water, tending the cattle, grinding flour, and tents were being mended or double checked to insure that the desert winds would not blow them down. Everywhere children ran about, playing games or running errands. Despite the seeming normality, however, there was a current of excitement running through the camp — Joseph was coming!

Every member of the camp was working, but each would stop from time to time to glance at the road that led to the capital, the road up which Joseph would come. Everyone wanted to be the first to sight him.

The excitement was intensified by the fact that very few of the camp could remember Joseph. His was only a sad tale told at the campfire, the tale of the son that had been torn to bits by a wild animal. The result of this tale was that none of the camp ever traveled alone or unarmed. Father Jacob insisted that there were always two or three people when someone had to go a long distance. There were a few close calls, but not one member of the company had been lost to a wild animal or a bandit since that fateful day.

Then came the news that Joseph was alive. It was rumored that Father Jacob wept for two days, but unlike years before, they were tears of joy. All were surprised beyond belief when Pharaoh's wagons and troops had appeared in the camp. Rumors were flying about the camp like insects in a swamp! Some were saying that this Joseph was actually Pharaoh himself. Others simply thought the whole thing was a trick trumped up by the Egyptians to take Father Jacob's wealth. But the brothers put the rumors to rest. Joseph lived, they insisted, and indeed they had seen him with their own eyes.

Even Benjamin, Joseph's only full brother, who was strutting about the camp dressed like an Egyptian noble, swore that his dead brother was alive and was the ruler of all Egypt! It was a confusing and exciting time.

Father Jacob had retired to his tent to avoid the heat of the day, and Judah, along with some of the troops that had accompanied them to their new camp, had left for the capital to fetch Joseph. No one saw much of Father Jacob after that. His wives, Leah, Bilhah, and Zilpah would come and go from the tent but said nothing to the rest of the camp. The remaining brothers also came and went, but they too said nothing, except to their father.

The children of the company had appointed themselves the "official" watchmen of the camp and were often seen standing near the Egyptian soldiers who were doing the actual guarding. This amused the guards greatly, as the children were sure that a poor Egyptian's eyes could not possibly see as acutely as those of a child raised in the desert!

Midday of the fourth day after the camp had been set up, one of the children came running into the camp shouting, "They are coming! They are coming! We can see them on the road from the capital! Joseph is coming!"

Mother Leah, upon hearing the shouting, came to investigate. "What is this that you are shouting in the camp, little one?"

The child, a lad of perhaps five years old, proudly puffing out his chest, repeated, "They are coming! I saw them! It is Joseph and a lot of soldiers!"

Mother Leah looked from the child to the guards on duty. They were all smiles. She then folded her arms and stared down at the child with a knowing look on her face and asked, "You were the first to see them?"

The child seemed to deflate. He stared at the ground digging his toe in the dirt for a few seconds before he answered dejectedly, "No. The guards had to wake me up to come and tell you. I fell asleep in the shade of the tree." This response was greeted by gales of laughter from those that had gathered to hear what he had to say.

Unseen, Father Jacob had joined the company. "What do you say, Mother Leah? How shall we reward our faithful watchman?"

Mother Leah eyed the child with a severe look on her face for a few moments, and then in her kindest voice, she said, "I think he should have his very own portion of the savory meat and bread we are going to have at the celebration!" This pronouncement was greeted with cheers by all.

Father Jacob called to Ruben, who was standing near him. "Ruben, go and look. Tell us how long it will be before they arrive at the camp."

Ruben, with a broad smile upon his face, responded, "Immediately, Father!"

He quickly went to the guard post on the capital road. He spoke with the guards, who were pointing down the road. He then thanked them as he departed and quickly came to his father to report. "They should be here in about twenty minutes or so, Father." Ruben reported.

Those twenty minutes seemed to be an eternity. Everyone stood about staring up the road toward the capital and said nothing. Except for the bleating of the sheep and the goats, the camp was silent. When the little ones tried to ask questions, they were shushed by the tense adults. Finally, the sounds of the troops and the chariots could be heard. When the troops at the road snapped to attention, the camp got their first glimpse of Joseph. Whispers filled the air.

"Look at all those troops!"

"Forget the troops, look at that chariot!"

"That thing must have cost a fortune!"

"Is that Joseph standing in the chariot?"

"He's handsome!"

"Look! See the woman standing with him."

"Could that be Joseph's wife?"

"She's absolutely stunning!"

"Are those his children in the chariot too?"

"She has borne children?"

"Are we sure this man is Joseph?"

"There's Judah beside the man in the chariot!"

"It has to be Joseph!"

Jacob stood unmoving and silent, the tears flowing freely down his cheeks the only indication of his emotions. At long last, the ox-drawn chariot with its gleaming white linen canopy and golden figures on its sides came to a stop directly before Jacob, and a handsome man in a formal Egyptian headdress stepped down and walked rapidly toward Father Jacob. With tears in his eyes and a strangled, "Father," Joseph fell upon his father's neck and began to weep. They stood like that for some time.

Finally, Jacob pushed himself away from Joseph and stood with his hands upon Joseph's shoulders looking him over. At last he spoke. "Now let me die, for I have seen your face and you are yet alive."

Joseph, finally getting control of his voice, spoke with joy. "I shall tell Pharaoh that my brethren and my father's household have come to me from the land of Canaan. Then, I shall tell him that the men are shepherds, and they have brought their flocks and their herds and all that they have. He will then call to have you brought before him. And it shall come to pass that Pharaoh shall call upon you and ask, 'What is your occupation?' That you shall say, 'Your servants' trade has been about cattle, from our youth even until now, as it was for our fathers before us.' This way you may dwell apart in the land of Goshen for every shepherd is an abomination to the Egyptians."

* * *

The Pharaoh Merneptah leaned forward in his throne and smiled as he concluded his story. "Joseph and his brethren did meet with Pharaoh. As promised, he settled them in the Land of Goshen, where they became a great nation inside Egypt. They became teachers, artisans, and even officers in Amenemhet III's army."

A young voice asked, "Are they still in Egypt, Father?" With this query the spell of the master storyteller was once more broken. Salith, the messenger from Pithom, blinked and he was back in the here and now. He had been completely immersed in the wonderful story being told by Pharaoh Merneptah. He glanced about and saw that others too had been under the story's spell.

He then looked up at the dais and saw Merneptah smiling sadly at his son. "No, my son, they are not." He then added, "They stayed with us for 430 years though."

"Why did they leave, Father?"

"Remember what God told Jacob in the dreams of the night?" Pharaoh asked gently.

The child hung his head and said quietly, "I am sorry Father, but I do not."

"He was told, 'I am God, the God of your father. Fear not to go down into Egypt. I will there make of you a great nation. I will go down with you into Egypt. I will also surely bring you up again. Joseph shall put his hand upon your eyes,'" Merneptah said gently.

"Did Jacob die here in Egypt, Father?" the boy asked.

"Indeed he did, my son, but he is not buried in Egypt."

"Then where is his tomb?"

Merneptah looked up from his son and seemed to see another place and scene as he said, "When Joseph's father died, Joseph fell upon his father's face and wept upon him, and he kissed him. Joseph then commanded the physicians to embalm his father. The physicians did embalm Jacob. And forty days were fulfilled for him, for so are fulfilled the days of those who are embalmed. The Egyptians then mourned for him for seventy days."

"All of Egypt mourned for him seventy days? That is the mourning period for a Pharaoh!" said his son, surprised.

Merneptah nodded solemnly. "It is, my son. It is. Joseph was greatly loved both by the people and by Pharaoh."

Awed, the Son asked eagerly, "What happened then, Father?"

"When the days of his mourning were past, Joseph spoke to the Pharaoh, saying, 'If now I have found grace in your eyes, I pray you, let me make a request. My father made me swear. When he was dying he asked that I bury him in the grave he had dug for himself in the land of Canaan. I pray you, let me bury my father in his homeland and I will then return.' Pharaoh then granted him permission to fulfill the oath Joseph swore to his father."

"Pharaoh let him leave Egypt during a time of famine?"

"He did, my son, and he did not go alone but with all the servants of Pharaoh, the elders of his house, and all the elders of the land of Egypt. All the house of Joseph and his brethren and his father's house went also. Only their little ones and their flocks and their herds were left in the land of Goshen."

Pharaoh's son was perplexed. "So, they came back from that journey, so how is it that they left Egypt for good?"

"They were to be a great nation of their own, my son. It was a promise from their God. The children of Jacob were fruitful and increased abundantly, and they waxed exceedingly mighty. The land was filled with them. Then there arose a new king over Egypt who did not know of Joseph."

The boy was astounded. "How could he *not* know of Joseph and all that he had done for Egypt, Father?"

"He was a Hyksos king, my son." Merneptah said simply.

"He was one of the spoilers of Egypt? He was one of the invaders?" the boy said indignantly.

"He was indeed. He said unto his people, 'Behold, the people of the children of Jacob are greater in number and mightier than we. Come, let us deal wisely with them lest they multiply and it comes to pass that, in a time of war, they will join with our enemies and fight against us. We must get them up out of the land.' Therefore they set over them taskmasters to afflict them with burdens, and they built for that Pharaoh the treasure cities of Pithom and Pa Ramses."

The child cried, "I thought that Grandfather had those cities built, not those cursed Hyksos!" His small face showed plainly his distaste for what he perceived to be an insult to his grandfather.

Merneptah laughed heartily at his son's fierce loyalty. "Your loyalty does you much credit, my son! Father did not build those cities. The Hyksos did, but Father *did* repair them and rededicated them to the Gods of Egypt rather than to that cursed god, Baal, the Hyksos worshiped! Thus those cities have his name on them."

"How did the Hebrews escape the Hyksos, Father?"

"Ah! They had a deliverer!"

"A deliverer?" the child asked in eager curiosity.

"Indeed! Joseph was not just a great leader but a prophet. He foresaw their deliverance. He wrote, 'And the Lord has said, I will raise up a Moses. I will give power unto him in a rod. I will give judgment unto him in writing. Yet, I will not loose his tongue that he shall speak much, for I will not make him mighty in speaking. But I will write unto him my law by the finger of mine own hand. I will make a spokesman for him.' Thus Joseph prophesied the lives of Moses and Aaron, the instruments in the hand of their God to deliver Israel, which is what the children of Jacob are called, from bondage."

"Moses! I know that name, Father! Grandfather spoke of him!"

"Indeed he did, and often, but *that* is another story entirely!" Merneptah chuckled.

"Will you tell us that story too, Father?" the child asked. The look on his face was plain. He was pleading for another story today.

"That I will have to think about, my son." He then indicated all the people present with a sweeping gesture of his hand. "There is much work to be done here in the court. I hesitate to waste the time here telling stories."

The child did not give up easily. "Please, Father?" he pleaded.

Pharaoh looked at his son. All could see the love they shared in the great man's eyes. Then, very kindly, Pharaoh said, "I shall think about it, my son." Gesturing to his valet, he signaled for his crowns. After replacing them on his head, he then turned quietly to the scribe at his feet and asked, "Now, Scribe, who is next upon your most noble list."

The scribe scrambled for his writing board and re-assumed his seat at the Pharaoh's feet. As he did so, the assembled company stood, for one really does *not* sit in the presence of Pharaoh, and stretched.

Looking up at the windows set high in the throne room wall, Salith saw that it was now late afternoon. They had been sitting here for hours! Yet the time seemed to Salith only a few minutes. He smiled to himself as he thought, *"That is the true power of a master storyteller: time is meaningless in their presence."* Looking up at the now stolid and solemn king of all Egypt, he would have never guessed those only moments before he had been a highly animated master storyteller and had held everyone in the chamber spellbound with the tale of Joseph.

The session ended rather quickly, and Salith made his way out of the royal palace and to his waiting chariot. The driver was already in his place with the reins in his hands, ready to leave. As Salith mounted the machine, the driver gave him a pitying look and asked, "Long boring session?"

Salith laughed out loud at this, and then, with a wide grin, turned to his driver and said in a mischievous tone, "You are just going to have to wait until we get back to the fortress to find out!" He did not know if he would be as good at telling the story as his Pharaoh, but he was definitely going to try during their evening mess.

As they left the grounds, Salith turned and stared at the diminishing palace. He realized that he had to come back. There was more to the story, and he, like the young prince, was dying to hear it. But as Pharaoh had said, that would be another day.

Author's Biography

William Lyons is descended from the original American colonists of Massachusetts and New Amsterdam. As such, his family has a rich tradition of storytelling. William fondly recalls sitting at his grandmother's feet listening to Bible stories about people like Joseph, Daniel, Jacob, and Moses. During the late 60's he joined the United States Navy; from which, he retired in 1985. Here too, he was immersed in a rich storytelling tradition – "sea stories." He says, "I never tired of listening to the 'old salts' and their wonderful stories."

Having retired from the Navy, William became employed in the public sector and raising his family with his beautiful wife. He also began teaching Sunday School children at his local church. It was here that William discovered his own storytelling skills. Of this experience he says, "I would tell the stories of the Scriptures, and it was wonderful to see the faces of the children as they listened with rapt attention."

After some time, William's family began encouraging him to write out his stories. He began with several short stories; which he shared with family and friends. These were very well received. It wasn't long until William's daughter and his brother urged him to write a book. Then, as William puts it, "The rest is history."